Between the Carries

Jamie Sheffield

2015

"Between the Carries"

Front cover map adapted from U.S. Geological Survey. St. Regis quadrangle, Franklin County New York [map]. N4415-W7415/15. Polyconic projection North American datum. Historical File Washington D.C.: USGS, 1954.

Published by SmartPig through CreateSpace and Amazon.com KDP.
This is a work of fiction. Names, characters, places and incidents are either products of the author's imagination or are used fictitiously. While the descriptions are based on real locations in the Adirondack Park, any resemblance to actual events or persons, living or dead, is entirely coincidental.

ISBN-13: 978-1503081840
ISBN-10: 1503081842

This book is dedicated to Gail;
my wife, my muse, my love, my audience …
without her, there would be no books.

Follensby Clear Pond, Adirondack Park, Northern New York, Monday, 8/25/2014, 8:17 a.m.

I woke up as the first light began to bring an orange glow to the tops of the whispering pines (*and sky*) above me at 5:43 but lay still to avoid waking Hope for another half-hour. She had suffered through a tough and mostly sleepless night, and I wanted to give her every second I could as the next week promised to be very stressful for her (*and me*), and that was if everything went according to plan.

At a few minutes after six, she either sensed the growing light or my wakefulness and shifted to give me a wet kiss. We both moved down towards the slit in the bottom of my Hennessy hammock and dropped out and down onto the pine needles to explore the morning. Both of us went a ways into the woods to take care of early morning elimination, and we met back by the hammock to discuss breakfast. I shook out some Tyler kibble (*a modified GORP recipe*) for me and an equal amount of Hope's kibble for her. As soon as we had scarfed down the basic snack, we picked our way down the sloping shore to the water's edge, jumped down into the warm water (*relative to the cool morning air at any rate*) for a swim as the sun came up, lighting the tips of the tallest pines on the opposite shore.

Hope and I were bandit camping (*a term that I had*

learned soon after arriving in this part of the world, and enjoyed the feel of), avoiding the established campsites that ringed Follensby Clear Pond. We found our home for the last seventeen days (*riding the cooling August nights from the full moon on the ninth to what would be a new moon tonight*) near a sandy swimming spot. From there, we worked our way up (*and inland*) fifty feet back from the water to a flat spot where some long-ago hunter had built/burned a fire pit. We used the pit to cook some of our meals (*despite the illegality of the closeness to the water and the fire pit cooking outside an approved campsite … they call it 'bandit camping' for a reason*). My canoe was far enough up the shore and into the brush to be invisible even if you knew to look for it, and nobody did/would/had.

After we had rung a full measure of enjoyment out of our quiet morning swim, I grabbed the stringer I had anchored to the sandy bottom the previous afternoon after fishing, pulled the two lake trout off, killed them as quickly/painlessly/neatly as I could manage, handed one to Hope, and navigated back up the hill to our campsite. I started one of the burners on my Coleman stove (*not wanting to signal our position too much, as the ranger for this area liked morning paddles, and although we had something of an understanding, I didn't want to put him in an uncomfortable position … we had, after all, been camping far too long in a spot too close to the water*). Once I had gutted/buttered/spiced the fish, I put my foil-wrapped trout over the flame (*flipping and moving it every minute or so, according to the sound/smell of the cooking fish*); Hope ate hers raw, as is her preference.

It was a perfect morning … just me and my dog, seemingly alone in the world, doing exactly what we wanted to be doing.

After we had finished our breakfasts, I buried the bones and skin I had left uneaten (*Hope had left nothing of her trout … and had suggested numerous time while I was eating mine that I had gotten the bigger fish*) in this week's trench privy (*amazed, as I always was, at how easy it was to bury stuff so that woodland animals can't find it … a few inches of dirt, a log or two on top, and it's gone as if it never existed*). Then I set up my solar charging station (*an all-in-one solar-cell and battery setup that was more than up to the task of keeping my Kindle and cell phone topped up*) and hauled my food and other smellies up and out of reach of any beasties that might want to grab them in my absence. After that, Hope and I headed down to pull my canoe out of the woods and into the pond and set out across the still/quiet morning water to Donaldson's Trading Post to get supplies for another week.

Paddling around the peninsula, we passed the island with a lean-to on it (*where Hope and I had snowshoed out to and stayed in for a pair of warmish nights last February after I left her for a few days to keep a promise in what turned out to be a too-nasty affair*), and continued through the narrows into the main body of Follensby Clear. I didn't pass or see or hear a human, but Hope and I were treated to a loon rising up and almost out of the water in a territorial display. We had originally paddled out to the site we'd been living at for nearly three weeks to get out of town and away from people after a bit of work that involved my living with a local artist and her two young children (*but not Hope*) for the better part of a week. The experience had overstimulated/stressed/tired me to the point where I just wanted/needed to get away from the sounds and sights of people for a couple of days. The first few nights had felt so right to both Hope and me that when some key supplies (*tp, butter, Coleman gas, oatmeal, dog kibble, pasta shells, and peanut butter most notably*) showed signs of running out by Monday the 11th, I consulted my mental map of the area, and decided to paddle through Spider Creek and out into the outermost lobe of the Fish Creek Ponds to get to Donaldson's (*instead of simply paddling the shorter/easier route to my car*). Hope and I had stayed on at our hidden (*and illegal*) spot in the woods, and Monday resupply trips seemed to be my new mode of operation.

We passed a flotilla of young kids in bright orange life vests and ginormous/ancient/noisy/loaded Grumman aluminum canoes paddling in the same direction like a zephyr (*speedy and silent … although Hope growled at each boatload of kids … she is an equal opportunity hater of almost every living thing on Earth … I can count the exceptions on one hand, not using my thumb*). Luckily, we were able to get through the huge culvert and into Spider Creek before they did. I paddled through the shallow stream connecting the bodies of water, leaving the relative quiet of Follensby for the early morning motorboat noise of the first tube-rides of the day at Fish Creek Campground. I surfed wake in my small Hornbeck canoe a few times, speaking in low/calming tones to Hope each time (*she had curled up by this time between my legs on the bottom of the boat, shivering and growling whenever a boat came close enough to set her off, roughly 150 yards, depending on their size and velocity*). I paddled under the bridge … making, as always, the hooting/echoing noises my father had made while canoeing these waters when I was a child (*it seems to be an autonomic response to bridges and tunnels when I'm in a canoe, entirely beyond my control … and it annoys Hope*). I pulled my boat up onto the tiny beach across Route 30 from Donaldson's, attached my baleful/grumpy old beagle to a leash for the first time in seven days, crossed the road and parking lot, stuffed the small and pungent bag of garbage I'd brought along into the can outside the main door. We walked in with the few other morning customers who had gotten there right at the opening as if nothing was wrong/unusual about entering a place of business with an obviously non-service dog who tried to snap at the few people foolish enough to try and talk with her (*I'd tied her up outside the door on my first Monday visit, but she instantly began singing a loud/angry/piercing song of resentment and betrayal, at which point the young man behind the register suggested that as long as the store was mostly empty, and I was quick, I could bring Hope in with me*).

I had the Monday morning resupply shopping down to a science, and was swiping my card through the machine in a hair under seven minutes (*not just the fourth prime, but also a Mersenne Prime—a double Mersenne Prime, actually, thinking of this perhaps because my monastic life for the last weeks brought the monk, Marin Mersenne, who spent his life studying these numbers, to mind*), even allowing for the time it took for the guy behind the deli counter to slice and give Hope a piece of bologna (*a fruitless/pointless and nitrate-laden gesture, as Hope still tried to bite him when he attempted to scratch her behind the ears, although only after she happily took his offering*).

"Thanks," a young man behind the register said. "We're gonna be closed next Monday. Ya know, for Labor Day. Summer's winding down."

I wanted to growl or snap at him, like Hope had a moment before, but kept an impassive face, which is easy for me, as I don't emote much. I nodded and left the store, bags in hand. Hope and I crossed Route 30 again and sat at the edge of the water to have a snack and a drink before climbing back into the canoe for the paddle home.

Home … a miniscule clearing in the woods above Follensby Clear had been home for two and a half weeks, but summer was, in fact, winding down. Hope and I had been having a wonderful time, living in the woods like a less-exciting (*thankfully*) Huck Finn, but the gravity and orbit of my life back in town—in the world—was pulling at both of us. I carried an abbreviated shopping load with me today, having made the plan this morning (*while waiting for Hope to wake*) to head back to town Thursday morning. The real world was waiting for us and could not be denied for much longer.

Mickey Schwarz, the person who had known and loved me longest on this planet (*since the death of my parents took them out of the running*), was coming up with his family to visit on Friday for the long weekend. Mickey was important to me. He had made time over the last few years to come up and visit; so I needed to be ready, for him and his family (*Mickey was relatively easy to handle, his wife Anne, and daughters, Mindy and Rebecca, all thought—perhaps rightly—that I was a different species than they were, and had always treated me as such*) to visit. They would be expecting me to talk and emote and care about the things that they cared about … it would be exhausting to pretend to be like other/standard/normal humans for the long weekend.

The other thing that I'd been ignoring all summer, but especially the last few weeks, had been Hope's health. Her last visit to the vet had been filled with bad, if not unexpected, news. She was old and had suffered a life of abuse and neglect before we two had found each other during the course of one of my extreme investigations (*I fill the hours and days when not camping or painting or making camping gear or exploring the woods by diverting myself with interesting research and investigations, some of which involve legal grey—or darker—zones. I had met Hope during a charcoal-grey investigation that had nearly gone very, fatally, wrong for both of us*). Last winter had been long and tough for her … her joints seemed to ache in the cold, and she was scared of ice and snow—of falling/slipping/freezing, despite the booties and fleece jacket that I had ordered for her. We had had a wonderful summer, but I worried that the coming of the cold (*which comes early and hard and for a long, long time to the Adirondacks*) might signal an end of good days for Hope … she wasn't at the end yet, but I could sense/feel it looming, just over the time horizon (*and dreaded it, even/significantly more than I dreaded a long weekend making polite conversation about my unusual life up here, with people who had no space/time/patience for unusual lives or lifestyles*).

Hope nestled in closer to me, looking at the clouds gathering to the southwest, over Tupper Lake like the eye awakening over Mordor (*this was my leap, not hers, although we may have been sharing the same mood/mind after our vacation together*).

"Yes sweet girl, a storm's coming, but it's not here yet," I said. "We've still got some time for fun, and I'll be with you, even when things get ugly."

We hopped in the Hornbeck canoe with our supplies, shoved off, and paddled (*me mostly, Hope just kept spinning between my legs, trying to make a smaller and smaller ball of dog*) back towards our hidden camp in the deep woods … for a few more days of an uncomplicated and happy life before we took the next turn, together.

SmartPig Offices, Saranac Lake, NY,
Thursday, 8/28/2014, 10:38 a.m.

Somehow the fingernail moon of the previous night had signaled that it was time to leave the woods, and both Hope and I decided to break camp early in the morning of the 28th. Hope had been helped in this decision by a nighttime visitation from a pack of coyotes in the woods around our hammock, some close enough to hear not just the eerie calls, but also their nails on the rocky ground and huffs of breath as they ran and leaped. Unlike Buck in *Call of the Wild*, this did not peel away Hope's veneer of civilization, but rather served (*it seemed to me*) to remind her of all of the things she was missing in town, and the safety of walls and doors. I was thrilled by the sounds on all sides of our hammock; but, while spending a large portion of the night holding a shivering/whining/growling/muttering old beagle, was reminded that this was how Mickey and Anne (*and Mindy and Becky, their daughters*) imagined life so far north of *The City* (*as people from New York City tend to think/speak of their hometown*). By morning, I had shifted gears and was ready to move on to the next thing ... a welcoming of what passed for family in my life.

After my parents had died, Mickey tried to take over, to take care of me, but he wasn't really equipped for it (*which is no reflection on him, neither were my parents*). He had been a part of the group of friends my parents helped form to educate all of their children outside the school system, and as such, knew me as well as anyone on the planet. The problem is/was/will be that I was born fundamentally different than other humans, and that difference persists to this day (*although I have learned to ameliorate/mask/modify those differences in ways that ease my passage through the world*). He (*along with legions of others, many of them doctors like Mickey*) had latched/settled on terms like "autistic" or "Asperger's." These are fine terms in and of themselves, but they seem to lack sophistication or specificity when describing someone/anyone/me (*It's always felt to me a bit like calling a duck-billed platypus a 'vertebrate' … technically accurate perhaps, but not adequately descriptive or encompassing nearly any of the things that make the platypodes distinctive or interesting or very helpful in explaining how the beasts make their way through this world*). Mickey had always said that the only reason to put something (*or someone, I had always assumed*) in a box was so that you could put it away with lots of other stuff you could forget about … I liked Mickey's mind and was looking forward to spending some time with him in the coming days.

Anne and the girls (*which is how Mickey often referred to them, and how I always thought of them*) would also be coming up for the long weekend, of course, and they would be, as always, an unspoken cost of having Mickey in my life. Anne had always thought of me (*and sometimes spoken of/to/about me*) as "the odd Cunningham boy" (*in which I was defined first by my oddness, and second by my parents, who had, to be fair, loved, and had been loved by Anne and Mickey long before I was born*), and that described her feelings for/about me perfectly. She resented that I had taken up so much room in my parents' life after being born as I was, and for similarly disrupting Mickey's life over the years (*although to a much lesser degree*). To Becky and Mindy, their daughters, I was just a strange kid who came for holidays and didn't know how to do anything or talk about anything/anybody/anyplace they cared about, including how to have a crush on them (*they were both attractive and intelligent females, as they would almost have to be with Mickey and Anne for parents, but I had no use for their interests or friends or, indeed, for flirting or sexual attraction for that matter*). We had learned to make polite noises and faces and gestures at each other years ago, to avoid upsetting our (*and more recently, just their*) parents. Despite the picture the description above would seem to paint, they were only a trial because they weren't Mickey, and because (*unlike the vast majority of humanity*) I couldn't ignore them entirely.

Hope and I had paddled from our hidden campsite as soon as it was light enough to move around and break camp, gliding through the morning mist on the water to the "new" boat launch just opposite Moss Rock Road (*which was new long before I arrived in the Adirondacks, but nobody except the DEC calls it anything but "the new one" or "not the one at Spider Creek"*). I lifted Hope out of the Hornbeck and onto the sand/water/pebbles at the launch at the same time a truck pulled in with some sleepy looking fishermen. Hope waddled around in the shallows, with the hair of her belly barely touching the water, watching me haul the gear from the canoe up the short hill to my Honda Element, giving short/occasional woofs of disapproval as the fishermen carried their stuff down. When it was time to go, she didn't even try to jump up into/onto the passenger seat ... I was/am more than happy to give her a lift. We turned left out of the parking lot, both of us slightly unaccustomed to the noise and ease of movement of a car after weeks of movement under our own power in the deep woods and waters.

I turned right onto Forest Home Road as we passed

the Fish Hatchery in Lake Clear, telling Hope when she looked up at the blinker noise to go back to sleep. Forest Home Road is shorter (*if not quicker, due to lots of twists and turns*) and both more attractive and less peopled way to drive back to Saranac Lake; the latter two reasons made the decision for me in this case. Putting the Element through its paces on the curves made me think fondly back to a borrowed Porsche the previous summer (*and apparently made Hope think that she might have to bite me*). When we emerged from the woods near the high school, I consulted my co-pilot (*pointlessly*) about breakfast, and overshot my office/home in favor of Dunkin' Donuts (*which is what she always votes for*). With what years of experimentation has proven to be "the perfect dozen" (*three each of plain, glazed, chocolate glazed, and regular jellies*) up on the dashboard (*safely beyond temptation/reach of Hope*), we headed back to SmartPig.

When I first moved to Saranac Lake, I rented both an apartment and an office, having never had/needed either before (*but certain that was what people did*). Six months in to my new life (*having left the literally smoking ruins of my old one behind me in Manhattan*), I decided that I liked having an office, and didn't like having an apartment; I came to an understanding with the owners of the former and let the lease lapse on the latter, and although it had in some notable way rendered me homeless, I've been pleased with my decision ever since. The name SmartPig is a pun based on my last name, Cunningham, which my mother came up with when I was a child. It popped into my head while signing the lease upon my arrival, and the name has stuck through the years.

The business at SmartPig is based on a long-standing Adirondack tradition of dabbling in a variety of fields to make ends meet … I paint (*both houses and landscapes*), stack wood, make camping/fishing/dog gear, and work with various contractors in the building trades as a day laborer. I do endless reading/research in whatever captures my interest, and also undertake/perpetrate investigations as a consulting (*and entirely unlicensed*) detective; it is this last item that has made my life most interesting in the past few years (*as well as also being considerably more dangerous than tying flies or framing houses*).

I managed to get the donuts and Hope and my go-bag (*a small pack I always carry with me that contains the stuff I need to have with me all the time … a bit like a carry-on for life*) up to the office in one trip, leaving the rest of the stuff from my weeks in the woods (*canoe, camping/paddling gear, laundry, trash*) in the Element, to be dealt with later. The office was very stuffy after our long absence, so I opened the windows at both ends of the single long room, dropped my gear on the table by the front window, filled Hope's water bowl, grabbed a trio of Cokes from the Coke-fridge, and plopped down on the couch (*which doubles as my bed on nights when I don't sleep outdoors*) with Hope … and the donuts. I had spent the last nineteen days (*8th prime, layout/dimensions of the board in the game of Go, and Rutherford Hayes, I thought, and was mildly impressed with my recall*) eating and drinking and exercising and sleeping well, but had no trouble shifting gears again, and had finished the box of magical goodness, along with the Cokes … in short order. I decided that it was time to hack some of the growth of hair from the last few weeks off my head.

I gave up on haircuts a year ago. I promise that I didn't think Patty (*the patient woman who cut my hair during my first twelve years in Saranac Lake, despite my fidgeting/flinching*) was going to cut my ears off, or suddenly decide to stab me in the eye, but I always got nervous when I was in her (*or anyone else's*) chair. My epiphany came one morning when I decided that shaving every day was time I didn't want to waste, or commit to, for the rest of my life, so I Amazoned (*yup, I verbed that noun*) an electric shaver, and now shave everything above my shoulders to three-eighths of an inch twice a month. After I had somewhat washed my head and hair and face, run the shaver over all of the bristly parts, applied my un-patented SmartPig Whisker Sauce (*a blend of oils that conditions and smells good*), and coaxed Hope out of the closet where she was busy hiding/growling/whining at the evil and noisy machine trying to eat my head, I sat down and started checking through all of the emails that had accumulated during our absence.

After shuttling emails I was keeping to various folders (*research, work, Mickey, Dot, Saranac Lake, and other*) and trashing the rest, I had planned on heading back out to the Element to bring my clothes over to the laundromat, but Hope and I were overcome with the need to nap. I lay down on the couch, not even bothering to take off my shoes, pulled Hope up and onto my chest, and shut my eyes for a few hours.

I woke to vigorous pounding on my door, and before I could get there to open it, was further rattled by my phone ringing (*I often go weeks without a visitor or a phone call, and to have both, at once, pulling me out of a nap was disorienting after the peace and solitude of the woods*). I recognized the number that was calling my iPhone and accepted the call. While I was waiting for it to connect, I took a peek through the spyhole in my heavy office door (*both the spyhole and the reinforced door were unusual to the point of being noteworthy in tiny Saranac Lake, where many people never lock their homes or cars, but I had been taken unaware a few years ago during a case, and very nearly killed as a result*). I let Dorothy in while I listened to Mickey saying hello into my ear a number of times before speaking to me.

Tri-Lakes Animal Shelter (TLAS), Saranac Lake, NY, Thursday, 8/28/2014, 2:03 p.m.

"Lisa gave me a call on her way to work. Said that she saw an Element with a canoe like yours on it heading back into town from DD," Dorothy said when I waved her into the room. "I detectived the rest like a boss and came over as soon as I got a break in my morning. Are there still donuts?"

Dorothy works at (*runs*) the Tri-Lake Animal Shelter, known as TLAS, and it isn't out of the ordinary for events there to keep her full-tilt busy from the ridiculously early hour that she starts her days until well after dark, events that always make for interesting stories … but I didn't have time for it yet. I shook my head (*in reference to her question about the donuts*), motioned her to the Coke-fridge and couch, and then held up three fingers and waggled my phone by way of explanation. She smiled, mouthed "Say hi" (*I didn't/wouldn't*), and sat down next to Hope on the couch after grabbing a Coke for herself and one for me (*which she kindly opened*).

"Mickey, start over again. I feel as though you had a significant portion of this discussion before you called my phone," I said into the microphone end of my iPhone. Mickey often calls me part way through a conversation, or picks up an old one at the exact point at which we interrupted it days/weeks/months before.

"Tyler. We changed plans. I ended up having to go

to the conference I mentioned earlier (*he hadn't mentioned any conference … at least not to me, but I couldn't see how it mattered, so I didn't interrupt*), the one in Boston. So, I brought Anne and the girls, and we'll be flying out of Logan tomorrow, getting to the airport in Saranac Lake at eleven in the morning, rent a couple of cars, get over to the Whiteface Lodge, settle in to our rooms, and maybe see you for an early supper," Mickey said, all in one breath.

"Sounds good, except instead of all of that, I'll meet you at the airport and help you find your way over to Lake Placid, and then maybe take you out for lunch while everyone else gets settled," I said, by way of counter-proposal. Mickey is an oncologist who, even though he's circling retirement, still gets up to work through files/paperwork before six every morning of his life and is yawning by eight in the evening … if I wanted to have a talk with him, lunch had always been the best time (*and his favorite meal*) to do it.

"That'd be great Ty," he said. "But Anne and the girls are going to insist on a dinner out with you before we all drive back down to *The City*." This was one hundred percent untrue but was also the sort of untruth that Anne and the girls and I fostered, even nourished, for Mickey's sake.

"Also, there's something I need to talk with you about at some point during our visit, maybe lunch tomorrow, something relating to that thing you helped me with a couple of years ago, and those other things you get yourself mixed up in," Mickey said.

"We'll talk when you get here tomorrow. I've got nothing on my calendar until the end of next week, so I'm available whenever. This is supposed to be a vacation for all of you, so don't feel as though you need to do things with me while you're up here … remember, I live here year around," I said.

While our conversation was continuing, Dorothy helped herself to another Coke from the Coke-fridge, pinched Hope's significantly-reduced belly and gave me a thumbs up (*Dorothy had introduced Hope and me originally, and had always felt comfortable judging me for letting Hope put on too much weight since she had come to live with me, but our recent time in the woods got her back down into what some might call her "fighting weight"*), and was now mouthing blah, blah, blah and miming shooting herself in the mouth as the conversation continued.

"It's a vacation, but we're up here to see you, so I want to make sure you don't hide from us, like last time," Mickey said, beginning to sound as though he was ready to wrap up. Mickey loves talking face to face, but dislikes phone calls, and very nearly hates email (*I'm almost exactly the opposite, but make an exception where Mickey is involved*). "I'll look for you in the arrivals area tomorrow morning then."

I produced a reasonable facsimile of a human snort. "The airport out in Lake Clear is smaller than the guesthouse at your place in Litchfield, Mickey. If I stood with my arms out, you couldn't get past me."

"Excellent, Ty, can't wait," he said, obviously moving mentally/physically to get to his next session at whatever conference he was attending. "Love you, boy."

"Love you too, Mickey." We always said this at the end of our conversations, although we both knew that it wasn't exactly true when I said my part of the exchange. It was a ritual, and although I'm horrible at most things human, I'm most (*perhaps only*) comfortable when dealing with ritual.

"Hope looks great. How's she been doing out there with you, wherever you've been for the last couple of months?" Dorothy asked.

"It wasn't even three weeks, Dot," I said. Dorothy's map of the Adirondacks is extensive but is largely limited to the people and the towns and the roads linking them … anything more than fifty yards from a road is wilderness, and you would have thought that I was going to Antarctica every time I went camping.

Dorothy's been a bit closer to me (*and/or more protective of me, or more anxious without me*) since an unpleasant episode last winter exposed her to the sort of things that live under the beds and inside the closets of our world … and more specifically, the world that I choose to move through in my work as a consulting detective.

"Whatever," she said. "She's down maybe five pounds, in a good way, and her coat and eyes and gums all look better than the last time I saw her. What were you feeding her?"

"Fish," I said. "At least one, sometimes a bunch every day, depending on how much fishing we got in … I supplemented them with some dry food every day."

"The whole thing?" she asked, incredulous (*meaning, I assumed, correctly, the whole fish*).

"Trout, bass, perch, sunnies, even a pike once," I said. "They were gone as if they'd never existed … bones, fins, guts, everything. I read some articles on it before we headed out, and they were consistent in their support of it as being healthy for dogs, as long as you didn't cook the fish."

"Hmmm," she said. "Your face changed during the conversation with Mickey, is something the matter?"

"Likely nothing," I replied, surprised that she'd picked up on my shifting mood as I generally don't emote much (*if at all*). "He wants to talk about what I do, a recurring theme in the last few years."

"After last summer getting in the papers, and what he knew about the thing with Cynthia and Barry and all, and that time you helped him out down in Syracuse, he's right, and has got a right to ask," she said. "He loves you, is all."

I went over to the sink and filled a glass with water, not so much because I was thirsty … mainly to avoid eye contact with her when I answered.

"Who knows, maybe it's time to hang up my deerstalker, and just stalk deer or fish, as the case may be, with Hope," I said. "I haven't worked on a case in months, and I don't miss it one bit … we all might be better off if we left that sort of thing to Frank and his ilk."

"Is that what he's calling that new partner of his?" Dorothy joked. This was likely a touchy area for her … she'd helped me with numerous investigations, and had fun doing it (*even when they seemed scary/stupid/dangerous to me*), and then she'd tried going it alone last winter, and had been badly damaged/scared/scarred in the process. We seem to still be working out how she, and our relationship, has been altered by those events; so what she said next surprised me, as I had assumed she would agree with me about putting an end to my dangerous hobby.

"Seriously though, Tyler, you've changed and even saved lives with what you do," she said. "Talk with Mickey, but no matter what, I hope you don't just walk away from it. You're good at what you do, and as far as I can tell, nobody else can do it."

"That seems unlikely," I said. She tilted her head to one side by a touch less than twenty degrees, like dogs sometimes will, and stared at me for a few seconds.

"Let me buy you lunch at the good Chinese place (*the*

bad one had a serious fire last winter, and was still closed, but … old habits die hard), and then we can head back over to the Shelter, and bring this old girl for a walk with some of the new residents," she said, thumping Hope on her side, and effortlessly dodging the old girl's snapping teeth (*perhaps at being called an old girl, more likely due to the thumpings*). "I've got some thoughts about you and SmartPig and my minioning and what it is that you do, and I'd like to talk with you about it all."

"Okay (*I couldn't get past this noncommittal response, as her proposal had the sound/feel of a 'deep' and emotional talk of exactly the sort I am horrible at … I say the wrong things and often miss the point altogether*). Regarding Hope, she'd probably be happier sleeping here while we go out, and I'll take her for a swim after I get back from walking some of the new dogs you've picked up in the last few weeks … any monsters?" I said, referring to the huge dogs that Dorothy and the TLAS often get (*an odd mix of pitbull and lab and boxer and shepherd, which the Tri-Lakes canine gene pool seems to encourage somehow*). Due to their size and appearance, these big dogs spend too much time languishing in cages because they're wild or jumpy or unused to people (*a situation that often develops into a feedback loop*). I originally met Dorothy walking just such a beast twelve and a half years ago. She still gets a kick out of watching me sprinting through the woods at the end of a leash, towed behind one of them.

"Just wait until you get a load of Grendel," she said, giggling a bit and holding a hand most of the way to her armpit. "This tall, I swear."

"Then you're definitely buying lunch."

Lunch was greasy and spicy and enormous, and as she always does, Dorothy made a joke (*that I didn't get … again/still*) in an old lady voice that it wasn't over, "Until you get your cookie."

Grendel lived up to her name ... if I were the sort of person who felt compelled to tell the truth (*which I'm not*), I would not be able to rule out genetic manipulation in her background (*she appeared to have Great Dane, Kodiak bear, mastiff, wolfhound, giant ground sloth, and wolf in her make-up*). Dorothy said she had been turned in by her owner, who had picked her up as a puppy, and was not been able to support the beast she had grown into (*Grendel had been offered up as her name by one of the TLAS volunteers, who thought it more appropriate than Daisy*). After both Grendel (*nee Daisy*) and I had been cleaned up from our walk/run/drag through the woods, I helped Dot pose and take some pictures, before we returned the beast to her cage in the back room.

I have a series of "fake" human smiles that I have learned to mimic over the years, but when I looked over the pictures that Dot and I had taken, I was surprised to see a real (*or at least unintentional*) smile in a number of them (*that's a polite human convention, I was smiling in four out of the twenty-three pictures we took ... experience has taught me, however, that that level of exactitude is unnerving/off-putting to some people*).

"Yup," Dot said, noting my study of the pictures. "You do it for real sometimes these days. I don't think anyone else notices. They all still think you're an alien, but I see it, and Meg's mentioned it to me. If Mickey hasn't already, he will. I wouldn't be surprised if it's part of what he wants to talk with you about."

"I don't know. It could be unconscious, or simply a learned behavior, as a response to certain stimuli. I don't (*feel, I was going to say, and continue in some manner, but didn't, for my own reasons ... private, apparently, even from myself*)."

"I do," she said. "I know. We've both been through

the Mangler (*referring, inexpertly and bizarrely, although I was still able to follow her meaning, to a King short story we'd both read and talked about before*), and it changed us. You can't go through the things your SmartPiggery puts you and I (*I enjoy when she mistakes 'I' for 'me', and never correct her, except in my head, where I always do, but fondly*) through without being a different person on the other side. Neither of us is done changing, but I think I like the Tyler you're becoming. I'm not as sure about the new Dorothy or the new Lisa," she said this last bit under her breath, but loud enough to have a reasonable expectation of my hearing it.

I had no response to this statement or line of reasoning, so I nodded and waved and gave her a #3 smile (*friendly/sincere/helpful*), and headed out the door, certain that there were three different/other things that I should have said/done instead of what I said/did.

SmartPig, Saranac Lake, NY,
Friday, 8/29/2014, 3:43 a.m.

I woke up at exactly 3:00, when Hope bit my hand … it had been resting on her back, as comfortably as the two of us had been resting on the couch in SmartPig *(300 is generally a disappointing/boring number, although I was finally able to dredge out of the back of my head that it is the sum of ten consecutive primes, which counts for something)*. We were both surprised by the bite, and she immediately crawled up my chest to give me kisses, and whine apologetically. She had snapped at me early in our acquaintance, but nothing like this, and certainly not in more than twenty months *(all bets were off with other people, even the few people who she liked would occasionally feel her teeth if they took liberties, or got over-familiar with her)*. We talked it over for a couple of minutes, went out for a walk down by the river to clear our heads, and went back to bed … both of us thinking about the possible import/meaning/portent of the bite while we listened to distant thunder and drifted back to sleep.

Mulflur Road, Saranac Lake, NY,
Friday, 8/29/2014, 2:43 p.m.

Mickey and Anne and Mindy and Becky got off the small Cape Air plane a few minutes before they had been due to arrive; they all looked as though they were glad to have their feet back on the ground (*my experience has been that taking off from SLK is pretty standard, as long as you don't mind small planes, but that landings are significantly more bumpy than is standard, due to the mixed thermals surrounding the little airport caused by so many mountains and lakes*). As they walked the roughly fifty yards from the plane to the building where I was waiting, I noticed that two of the other passengers moved sufficiently differently from standard crowd/flock behavior, relative to Mindy and Becky. It suggested they were coupled with Mickey's daughters in some capacity (*if I were a betting man, which I am not, I would have bet, based on years of watching human courting rituals, that the men were boyfriends, although Becky has been married twice before, and Mindy's been engaged a number of times*). They made it inside the doors, and Mickey saw me.

"Tyler! It's so good to see you," he said.

"Nice to see you, Mickey," I replied, thinking back to speech therapists in my childhood who painstakingly worked to teach me polite conversation. "How was your flight?"

"Oh my God, Tyler," Anne said, swooping in to plant a small/dry/light kiss on my cheek. "It was simply too beautiful flying out of Boston. The harbor and all those white ships, and then the mountains and trees and lakes and no roads once we got up here." She paused, either for breath or dramatic effect (*I'm never sure with Anne*). "But those last five minutes we bumped and dropped and jounced and shot sideways until I was sure we'd crash and be swallowed up by the woods forever."

"A plane went down into the woods a few years ago, but we were able to find it in short order … I actually helped with the search. Everyone on board died, of course … no soft landings up here, unless you're lucky enough to splash down in a lake." I could see by the semi-circle of six sad/scared/angry faces surrounding me now that I hadn't listened/tried hard enough with the speech therapists.

Mickey bailed me out, as he has done for most of my life (*I'm not even sure if he's conscious of it much of the time*). "Show Anne and the kids (*which I took to include the young men arrayed with his daughters*) where the baggage carousel is and help me find the car rental kiosk."

I pointed behind me at a movable (*and now moving*) panel that was in the act of revealing a dozen small bags. "They used to have you carry them in from a spot behind the plane, but the bags sometimes got wet if it was raining, so now they bring them in here for you on a little cart with a covered compartment. The car desk is over here," I said, pointing at a single desk and computer and a man, who wore the hats (*not literally … I thought, remembering Mrs. Portnoy and her lessons on figurative language*) of three different companies.

Mickey and I got the car rentals sorted out in a few short minutes, and walked out into the cool breeze and sunlight to join the others, who were waiting just outside the door.

I pointed in the direction of the sixteen car rental-lot, which I had scoped out as we exited the building, looking for the tag numbers on the key chains the man inside had given us, "Yours are the two on this end. Mine is the black Element at this end of the row closest to the airport. Get your bags in the car, pull out, and you can follow me to your hotel in Lake Placid, okay?"

Everyone nodded, they split up into the two cars (*Mickey and Anne in one, and Mindy and Becky and their boyfriends, Chet and Rob respectively, in the other*), and followed me out and away from the airport. I briefly considered slowing down at the intersection of Route 186 and 86, to suggest an ice cream cone from Donnelly's, a local tradition/hotspot for sixty-one years, but knew that Anne would disdain the idea of a snack so soon before the lunch hour. We drove through Saranac Lake (*I sent a telepathic scratch up through the front window of SmartPig to Hope as we passed my building on Main Street*). I could see Mickey gesturing for Anne up at my office, and then a minute later over to the park where the Ice Castle is built every winter during the Winter Carnival (*Mickey had come to see it once, after an interesting case of mine that also involved him*). We continued to Lake Placid, pulled into the opulent and rustic (*two words I don't generally think of using together, but in this case, it works*) entrance to the Whiteface Lodge, and were fallen upon by a pair of busy bellmen with carts, ready and eager to bring all of their bags up to their suite. The accommodations included three bedrooms with a kitchen and deck and spectacular views of Whiteface Mountain and the actual Lake Placid (*most of the village of Lake Placid is actually on/around Mirror Lake. Similarly, the village of Saranac Lake is on/around Lake Flower … go figure*). The foyer of the suite was bigger than the world headquarters of SmartPig, and the suite likely cost many times more per day than I paid each month in rent, but Mickey could afford it (*and enjoyed spending money on his family more than anything else in the world*). Everyone seemed to know which rooms were which/whose without anything being asked/said (*unspoken human communication mystifies and eludes me, which is an ongoing source of frustration given that everyone else seems to master it without thought or effort*). I waited out on the deck while they all did whatever it is that people do upon arriving at hotels (*I am always ready to leave again as soon as I drop my bag, but everyone else seems to have something urgent to do for 5-7 minutes*). Six minutes and seventeen seconds later (*377 is the 15th number in the Fibonacci sequence*), Mickey found me staring at the castle that sits on top of Whiteface Mountain (*I was thinking about the process of digging out the tunnel that made the elevator from the parking lot near the summit up to the castle possible … 424 feet in, 276 feet up … a lot of stone to move*), and he whacked me on the shoulder.

"How's that barbeque place we passed halfway between Saranac and Lake Placid (*I've noticed that more people, local and tourists alike, leave off the word 'lake' after Saranac in Saranac Lake, than they do before Placid in Lake Placid … I have no idea why, but they do, and it interests/occupies/distracts me*)?" he asked. "It looked good and will save me from tennis with Chet and Bob or shopping with Anne and the girls."

The truth is that Tail O' The Pup is a little touristy, and always slightly more expensive than it is good, but Mickey's neither a local, nor worried about spending twenty dollars versus fifty dollars for a lunch. They serve some good food, have an interesting array of apps, (*including fried pickles, which I enjoy more than seems reasonable/rational/sane*) are quick with soda refills, sometimes have live music (*I don't actually enjoy listening to music, but people are less inclined to talk for noise's sake when there is music in the background, and it's interesting to watch humans listen/appreciate/absorb the different combinations and intensities of tones*). Besides, the seating is ninety-six percent outside, which I liked as it was a nice day.

"It's perfect, Mickey," I said. "You'll love the food, and we'll get a chance to talk."

"Can we take your car, kiddo?" he said. "Anne wants to do a food shop with the girls after they get some lunch. Where should they go?" His eyes (*which I'd spent nearly thirty years watching/studying*) and tone seemed to imply that he didn't want me to suggest barbeque … I didn't (*wouldn't*).

"I think they would like the Brown Dog Cafe. It's tricky and yummy and has a great view of Mirror Lake, or, alternately The Cottage, which is a little more casual and simple and right on the water," I said. Mickey smiled and nodded (*I had a quiet thunderclap of comprehension, as I figured out that both of us were silently betting on Anne choosing The Brown Dog*) and passed my suggestion along on our way out of the suite.

We drove back to Raybrook, me waving at the sign/statue of Smokey the Bear, (*High danger of fire he opined*) as we turned in and I tucked my Element into one of the parking spots back by the cabins, as opposed to the ones out on Route 86 (*which seem to invite/force people to back right out onto the road*). We found a picnic table under some shade that we could have to ourselves. Lunch is Mickey's big meal of the day, and we did it justice … ordering most of the appetizers on the menu, along with a barbeque sampler to share between us. Mickey had a Black and Blue, which is a made by floating Guinness Stout (*the black*) on top of a half glass of Blue Moon Brewing Company's Belgian White Wheat Ale … I had a pitcher of Coke.

We ate, talking about the food and the weather and the new boyfriends (*he disliked them, but less than the last set, which seemed quiet praise for Chet and Rob … and/or Mindy and Becky*). When our attentive waitress had cleared away the last of the food and dropped off another pitcher of Coke (*nasty/sweet/watery stuff from a fountain*) for me and a third Black and Blue for Mickey (*who is still oddly shocked that I don't drink alcohol, and always offers me sips of whatever he's having and enjoying*), he shifted his body and face into a new set of alignments that signaled even to me (*and I'm a poor judge of moods/emotions*) that we were ready to get to the meat of our discussion.

"So, Ty, what have you been doing to keep yourself busy?" he opened. "You look tan as a deep-water sailor, and I love the beard and buzz," he said, ruffling the top of my shaved head briefly.

"I've been camping with Hope for nearly three weeks, and we've had great weather (*if a bit dry, I thought, thinking of Smokey's sign across the road*). I keep busy … helping out at the shelter, designing and building and repairing gear, doing some painting, some construction work, lots of reading and research," I said.

"And the other stuff?" Mickey asked, looking up from his beer and into my eyes with an expression that appeared sad or guilty or worried. "Like that time in Syracuse, or up in Mahoney, or the thing with your shoulder, or that kidnapping business last summer?"

We'd talked extensively, if not fully, about my sideline as a consulting detective after Mickey's troubles in Syracuse two winters ago … the talk included a partial disclosure of some other "cases" I'd been involved in … up in Malone (*not Mahoney*), and how I'd ended up getting shot during the late summer of 2012. He knew that I used my gifts as a researcher and ... out of the box thinker ... to help people (*himself included*) in non-traditional, and not always strictly legal, ways. I'd told him the least I could get away with when he had cornered me and demanded the whole story (*he was clever and knew me better than anyone on the planet, so it was interesting trying to give him enough to satisfy his curiosity, while keeping enough from him to prevent his turning me in or moving in with me ... two things he was probably fully capable of talking himself into ... both for my own good*), and from time to time I shared some of the more boring and/or public aspects of the things I did during my cases. He had inevitably heard a lot (*and likely inferred/extrapolated more*) when a missing persons case I'd been working on the previous summer broke wide open (*it turned out that it involved lots of missing persons*), despite my efforts to avoid, or at least to appear boring or just lucky to the authorities and reporters.

"Honestly, (*which is something that in my experience, people say when they're about to lie, or at least obfuscate, and in this case, I was planning on doing a bit of both*) I think that I'm something of a victim of my own success when it comes to my consulting detective business ... I did much better when nobody knew who I was, but with last summer especially, people talk about and notice me more now than they used to," I said.

"Besides the thing in Syracuse," I continued, "I only ever got involved with these things when the research or the problem interested me. I don't want/need money or acclaim ... I've got too much of both as a matter of fact. I like being/want to be, boring and enjoy spending time in the woods with my dog. I have a few people I care about who are nearly what other people would call friends (*I still don't believe that I have the capacity for friendship or love, although Mickey enjoys arguing the point, and semantics in general, with me*), and I have a new person to help me with my research at the library in Saranac Lake, (*she's no Cynthia … we don't mesh in that way, but Cynthia's dead, at least partly because we meshed too well in some ways, so it may be that I'm okay with not being so close to Mavis*) and more great books and articles than I could read in ten lifetimes. That kind of work doesn't interest me as much as it used to … I've looked under rocks and behind the curtains of human affairs, and for the most part, I don't like the things I've seen … they can get you, or me, killed. My life follows a nice routine here, and you know how much I like routine."

"I know, kiddo, I know," Mickey said, "and it makes me so happy that you've got a life for yourself up here, a life that brings you joy (*I don't know that I would have gone that far, but he was waxing poetic, and maybe sneaking up on some ancillary point that I couldn't see over the horizon as yet*)."

"Yup," I said as he seemed to be waiting for something.

"Crap," he said, taking the last swig of his beer, and making the downward facing circling finger gesture in the air to signal his (*if not my*) need for another round to our hovering waitress (*who looked as though she wanted to bring our check, but smiled/nodded anyway, and went off to get more drinks for us*).

"I've got this friend, Tyler," he began. "He's a professor at Columbia (*Columbia University in Manhattan, I inferred*). He's a brilliant man, but vain and stupid and careless when it comes to personal relationships and sex. Over the years, he's …."

My iPhone rang in my pocket, which was a relief as I was on the verge of interrupting him anyway. I didn't want to take this case, and was glad for an interruption (*which would, hopefully, give me the time I needed to find a way to avoid helping Mickey's friend*). It sounded as though it would require me to work in Manhattan, which I didn't want to do with an Adirondack autumn just around the corner. It had to do with relationships and sex, neither of which I knew/understood/cared much about; it would likely take a lot of time and interviews of lots of angry/hurt/scared people, and me trying to wade through feelings and motivations that I didn't (*probably couldn't*) understand. Pulling in the other direction was my desire not to disappoint or even say no to Mickey … ever … in any way. I had almost never been more glad of a phone call, especially when I saw that it was Meg … I was working with her to organize a fundraiser for the TLAS in a few weeks, and a detail-oriented call would be a soothing break from worrying about Mickey and his friend's problem for a minute or two.

"Hello, Meg," I said. "What can I do for you?"

For a second before she spoke I could hear people shouting, the static of an activated megaphone that nobody has spoken into yet, and slamming doors in the background.

"Tyler?" she said. "Oh my God, Tyler, the blood … it was everywhere!"

"Meg, what blood, whose blood are you talking about? Where are you? What's going on?" I said.

Mickey's head came up at some minute change in the modulation of my voice (*I have always been told that I sound like a computer on the phone, but people who know me for long enough swear that they can tell things from small changes in the tone of my voice*), and he pantomimed paying the check at our waitress.

"Oh, Tyler, it's horrible. He couldn't have …." she began, before being cut off.

"Margaret Gibson, you hang up that fucking phone

this fucking second and go across the street, and wait with Tommy—Officer Morgan—until I know what the fuck ..." shouted Frank Gibson, Meg's husband, and a police officer in the SLPD.

"Frank, it's Tyler," Meg shouted at him, but also (*and accidentally*) into my ear.

"I don't give a rat's ass who it is, nobody, especially that fucking Tyler..." Frank said, and then suddenly became more distinct and clear, even as he quieted down to speak to me instead of Meg. "Tyler, this mess isn't your kind of thing. It's not even my kind of thing. The staties are rolling their S.W.A.T. unit on my location."

"Where are you?" I asked.

"I'm hanging up now, Tyler, read about it in the paper, like everyone else," Frank said, and did, in fact, hang up.

I looked across the road at the DEC headquarters and Smokey and then to the left at their neighbors, the State Police.

"Mickey," I called as I started moving towards the Element, "I have to go. Will you be okay? Can you call Anne to come pick you up?"

"Yes, sure, but Tyler, what's going on?" he asked.

"I don't know, but I have to ..." I didn't finish because I had no idea what I had to do. I walked, as quickly as was possible without running, over to my Element.

I started the Element and drove significantly too fast through/between the cabins in the Tail O' The Pup compound, and towards an alternate exit down closer to the State Police headquarters. As I rolled up to look both ways on Route 86, I heard the wailing of sirens begin across the road, and saw the first of a convoy of state police tactical vehicles with flashing lights, led by a large

UPS-looking truck in S.W.A.T.-black, sway through turns significantly faster than they were designed to be driven, and turned towards Saranac Lake. I pulled out, with not quite enough room for a pair of cars coming, one from each direction (*they both honked and hit their brakes and squealed their tires, but thankfully, there was no crunching of metal and glass*), and stomped on the gas to try and give chase to the receding sirens and lights.

Although I couldn't quite keep up I kept close enough to follow them from Route 86 to Route 3 in Saranac Lake, through the village on Canaras Street to Lake Street, and finally to Mulfur Road, at which point they turned off the sirens and pulled up to a perfectly ordinary looking house with too many people milling around in front.

I pulled in ten seconds behind them, and made my way over to Meg, who was sitting on the curb, crying into her hands … with a splash of blood arcing across her floral print shirt, upward from her left to right side.

Mulflur Road, Saranac Lake, NY,
Friday, 8/29/2014, 3:18 p.m.

I nodded vaguely at Officer Morgan (*whose first name was apparently Tommy*) and pointed at Meg … he shrugged/nodded/waved, and I sat down next to her as he moved a few polite, yet prudent, steps back (*polite he was, giving us a bit of space to talk, but prudent in that he wasn't moving far enough away to actually give us privacy*). We had met the previous year during the wrap-up of the case I had taken on for Kitty Crocker, and as such, he was likely giving me a bit more room/latitude than he would have given other civilians (*that, and he knew Meg and I were friends, and Frank, a more senior officer on the scene as … whatever we were, or were perceived as being*).

She noticed me when I sat down, and looked up briefly, but didn't seem able to find anything to say, and just dropped her head back into her hands again moments later.

"Meg, Frank or someone is going to shoo me away in a minute, so if there's something I should know, or some way I can help, you should tell me now," I said.

Even as I spoke, I could see Frank walking towards us, parting the thin crowd of cops and emergency services people and (*presumably*) neighbors like he had an invisible cattle guard attached to his puffed-out chest and red face. Meg looked up at Frank and reached over to wrap her hand in mine (*something I generally dislike intensely, but let stand in this case, as I assumed that she was communicating something to me, or Frank, or both of us*); Frank looked down at our intertwined fingers/hands/arms, and sighed, nodding.

"Tyler may be able to help, later, if Xander doesn't die … isn't killed," Meg said for both of us.

"Whatever," Frank said. "For now, I need you tell me exactly what you saw. How many people are inside? How is he armed? Why, THE FUCK, you went inside the house if you knew something was wrong?"

"Frank, you know why," she said, seeming to answer his last question first. "She called, I came."

"Who called?" Frank asked, settling into what I had identified years ago as his cop voice … a little flatter overall than his normal, but still friendly and inviting lengthy responses.

"Danica, Danica Kovac. Xander's older sister," Meg answered. "She called me this morning to ask if I would come over sometime after lunch to help her talk with him, with Xander about this fall, about the group home. We've been working on it, on him, all summer … his family and I and some of the involved state agencies. It's a big change for him, and he doesn't react well to changes in his life, in his schedule, in his map of the world as he knows it."

Although I was already tuned in by this point, and needed no special notice, Meg gave my hand a squeeze as she finished her sentence.

"Okay, good so far Meg, but the guys from Raybrook (*I noticed he didn't say S.W.A.T., but looked over at the black panel trucks for a moment*) need to know what's behind that door," Frank said.

"I got here a few minutes late, maybe five after two," Meg said, the talking seeming to calm/steady/focus her a bit. "I could hear him shouting." She saw Frank start to speak and preempted him, "Xander was shouting and knocking stuff over inside the house."

"But you went in anyway?" Frank asked.

"Well, yes. I've known, worked with, Xander for years, since they moved here. He gets upset and a bit wild sometimes, but he's not mean or aggressive or violent … not with me, never with me … at least not on purpose," Meg said, looking down a bit at the end, and subconsciously rubbing a spot up near her shoulder.

"So you went in, and?" I could see/hear/feel Frank straining to keep his voice neutral as he asked, but if Meg did, she gave no sign.

"I knocked, quietly the first time, and then louder. Nobody answered, so I just went in," Meg said. "I could smell blood and bleach and hear Xander crying and talking with someone in the dining room, but just barely over the sound of the sink disposal thing."

Frank was looking past her at a hulking bald man in a dark blue jumpsuit making his way over to us/them. "You're doing great, hon. What else?"

"I went through the kitchen, stopping to find the switch for the disposal," Meg said, answering another of Frank's stares before he could cut in. "Hush now, I didn't know it was a crime scene did I? And anyway, Xander hates that sort of noise, and I thought it would make it easier to deal with him if I smoothed out the environment for him a little."

"That's when I first saw the blood," she said, paling a bit as she remembered. "A bit by the disposal, and then lines and sort of swoops of drops, and a couple of smeary areas leading back into the dining room. It was then that I called out for Danica and Xander, to let them know I was there, and ask if they were all right." I could see Frank cringe when he thought about his wife announcing her presence … he must have already known what she would describe next.

"He was crouched next to her, Xander was … holding a huge knife and a kitchen towel, and everything was covered in blood. His hands, his face, the knife, the towel was black with it, the walls were splashed almost to the ceiling, covered with pretty arcing patterns of it (*both Frank and I looked at her when she said this, but did not cut in*) across that Birdseye maple dining room table of theirs," Meg said, and continued. "Remember when you put a beer right on that gorgeous wood during Xander's graduation celebration in June, dear?" Frank nodded, and subtly reached his hand, which had been on her shoulder, to a pulse-point on her neck, and seemed to look more closely at her face and neck (*her manner was a little distant and spacey, and I wondered if she was sliding into some form/degree of shock*).

The big man was standing next to Frank now, but made a point of not saying anything … he was clearly waiting for Meg to continue.

"I must have made some sort of noise, because he looked up at me, Xander did, and then stood and said in his quiet, flat, voice, and sad face, 'mommy will be sad' and waved the knife in my direction," Meg said, looking down at her shirt front. "That must be when this happened."

"Did he touch you or try to attack you?" Frank asked.

"No, but when he started to come forward, in my direction, I told him to sit down and wait for me, and I ran back out the way I'd come in. I pulled the front door closed behind me and called you," she said. "I'm not even sure he's still in there. They've got nothing but woods behind their house, all the way back to Kiwassa and Oseetah (*a pair of lakes a couple of miles away, to the south*)."

"Ma'am, we've got men around the back of the house, and one of 'em took a peek in through the kitchen a couple of minutes ago, and he's still there. I know Darko, the father, from the summer softball leagues, and I've met Xander a couple of times. It's him," the (*presumably*) S.W.A.T. guy said. "Do you have reason to believe there's anyone else in the house?"

"No," Meg said, "Darko and Izzy, Iskra, are with family in Potsdam for the weekend. I couldn't see anyone else, and nobody else lives in the house with them. You're not going to shoot Xander are you?"

"No Ma'am, my hope is to avoid that today, in this instance," he said. "S.W.A.T. isn't just guns, it stands for Special Weapons *and* Tactics. We've got something in our playbook that should get everyone, Xander included, home alive. Frank?" he pointed back towards the house and he and Frank walked away, leaving Meg and me sitting, still holding hands.

"Tyler, Xander is …." she began.

"I know (*now*). He's the young man you tried to connect me with a couple of times over the last few years. His diagnosis is Autistic Spectrum Disorder, which you thought/think I have also, albeit with a lesser degree of severity," I said, trying to disentangle my fingers/hand/arm from hers.

"He didn't kill Danica, he couldn't have, Tyler. He loves her (*loved her, I corrected, internally*), insofar as he can love people," she said, picking this awkward moment to let go of my hand.

"But he's hurt her before hasn't he?" I asked. "He's hurt you too, on your upper arm and maybe other places … pinching more often than punching or slapping." She picked her chin off her chest and stared at me.

"How do you know that?" she asked.

"The same ways you do … only I've been reading/learning/thinking about ASD since my parents brought me home from the first doctor who tried to stuff me in that box," I said, thinking back to the first time my parents had had "the talk" with Dr. Bernstein … it was a Thursday, October 19, 1989, and everyone else was still talking about a big earthquake earlier that week in California, but my world (*and that of my parents*) seemed to be shaking apart for different reasons. They rented *Rain Man* to watch that night because Bernstein had mentioned it in passing during their consultation about autism, about me. While they sat on the couch talking, they watched Dustin Hoffman and Tom Cruise navigate their relationships/world. I sat on the floor between them, following the directions to build a Lego forestmen castle (*it was the first time they didn't worry about harsh language or sex in a movie that we watched together*).

"Tyler, you could help him … help Xander," she said.

"I doubt it, Meg," I said. "It very much sounds as though the time for anyone to help Xander in any productive way was about an hour ago … and that I couldn't help him in any case."

"What?" she said. "How can you think all of this, everything that's happened, everything that's happening, isn't a problem?

"It's a big problem … it's just not my problem," I said, and then continuing when she flashed a hurt/shocked/angry look at me. "It's not my problem because I'm not in any position to help him, or the sister, or the parents, or you. Right now, he needs to be taken into custody without being killed, which I am, in fact, interested in seeing. Later on, assuming that happens, he'll need doctors and lawyers and psychiatrists and nurses and orderlies and maybe corrections officers … and I'm none of those things. His sister likely needs a coroner and a mortician … again, no help from me. His parents need a counselor and legal advice, which you and Frank can likely help them with … at least to some extent. In this whole process, I'd be useless to anyone, including you." At which point I stopped talking, because Meg was leaking tears without really seeming to be actively crying (*or have any awareness of the leakage*), and I wondered why, in fact, she had originally called me.

"Why, in fact, did you originally call me?" I asked.

She tried to speak three times before she finally got it out, stopping each of the false starts with clacking teeth as she slammed her mouth shut.

"Because, Tyler, you're autistic, like him, like Xander," she said.

"I am not autistic. I'm Tyler!" I said, raising my voice a bit, feeling stupid about my response, and noting an uncharacteristic flush/heat climb my chest/neck/face and up into my hairline. "I'm ten thousand things, and one of them *may* be autistic, but that's a label, a box … designed to help everyone in the world ignore the rest of me."

Meg looked me in the eye, took a breath, and spoke very evenly, "That's a talk for another time, for another place, Tyler. You're not Xander, and he's not you, but he is in trouble, and you have an almost magical ability to help people out of trouble that seems impossible to get out of. When this all happened, your name flew into my head as soon as I came out of the initial shock." I felt that this was only partly true … that she was covering what she'd said before with what she felt I would like to hear.

"It may be that I/you/we can help Xander later, but

right now, the police need to disarm/restrain an armed individual who is notably non compos mentis, and provide medical attention to the sister (*although it occurred to me that the most likely reason they would have had for delaying S.W.A.T. entry was for planning purposes because they had some way of knowing that Danica was, in fact, already dead*). Let's watch … I've read about this, and would love to see a live demonstration," I said, shifting my focus to the team, who appeared to be getting ready for a dynamic entry.

"Jesus fucking Christ, Tyler," Meg shouted, spittle landing on my face and neck. "You really are a bug, what's going on with you? Why did you come? You want to watch?" Frank had drifted back over as the S.W.A.T. team readied themselves, and now glanced back and forth between Meg and me, unsure perhaps, of what exactly was going on (*as was I to some extent*). Meg forced herself to breathe in and out a few times, nodded at me, and then started talking again … this time in a markedly forced and level voice.

"I was thinking," she said, "that you might have a unique perspective on what Xander's going through right now, and be able to relate with what's happening … what he's feeling or experiencing."

"Well, I don't," I replied. "I can't. I have never killed a family member … and I'm not this person." Meg looked sad and angry and scared and was leaking tears and snot, and apparently decided that she couldn't talk with me anymore.

"How can they get Xander out of the house without hurting him, or allowing him to hurt them?" she asked, turning to Frank, who started to speak. I cut in, hoping to start mending whatever fence I had breached/broken with Meg (*it didn't help*).

"Watch this," I said. "It's something between

football and a tsunami."

Since my arrival, I'd been watching a five-man team suiting up in what seemed a lot like the protective gear smart motorcyclists (*if that's not an oxymoron*) wear. They had no skin showing anywhere, helmets and gloves and what I assumed was Kevlar/metal/ceramic armor everywhere, most heavily on their chests and necks and backs. As we turned to watch, they moved towards the front door of the quiet house joined by a sixth man, this one carrying a handheld battering ram, who moved up to the front of the pack. The five man team formed up behind the one with the ram, in a tight knot, the second in line tapped his shoulder three times, and they went through the door in a blur and crash and yelling maelstrom.

One second later, I heard a terrified scream from deeper within the house. Two seconds after that, we could hear the crash of furniture and glass breaking. Two seconds after that, the house was silent again, then some signal must have passed between the team inside and everyone else, because EMTs and other police and crime scene people started pouring into the house from the front and the back.

"It sounds boring and low tech, but those guys were wearing slash and stab-proof armor, and they simply tackled Xander, immobilizing him. He may end up with a broken rib or two, and possibly a break in the arm or wrist that was holding the knife, but it's better than lots of other plans of action they could have come up with to move this along," I said. I didn't point out that by now the EMTs would have likely brought out Danica, if she was still alive … I believe that Meg knew it also/already. Frank turned away from us to go and consult with some of the other police and troopers a short distance away.

"They'll put him on a seventy-two hour psych hold, an involuntary commitment, while they decide what to do next," Meg said. "I need to help Frank get in touch with, and then talk with Darko and Izzy. I'll visit Xander at Whispering Pines tonight, but can you come by tomorrow morning?"

"Because I'm autistic?" I said, still with a bit of heat (*that both Meg and I were unaccustomed to hearing in my voice*). "I can't imagine that I would be much use in that vein because you probably know as much about ASD as I do."

"No, Tyler," Meg said, directing me to look her in the eyes, which I had been avoiding. "I want you to come so you can help me and Frank fix this. Xander didn't kill, couldn't possibly have killed, Danica. A bunch of us have been working very hard for the last fifteen years, so he can have a good life, and this," she said, waving at everything going on around us, "could destroy all of that. The next twenty-four hours could set him on the track to go to an institution, or possibly (*she shuddered*) some sort of prison, for the rest of his life."

"Meg, the knife, the blood, he most likely did it … regardless of your hard work over the years or what you think about him," I said. "It might have been an accident/argument/tantrum, they'll (*I said, pointedly as opposed to "we'll"*) probably never know. A smart cop, your husband in point of fact, once told me that the simple answer is the right answer most of the time in criminal proceedings. The simple answer is that Xander killed his sister and may, in fact, present a significant and ongoing danger to himself or others," I said, quoting a bit of New York's mental health code.

Meg's lips tightened and straightened and her face went from shock to anger briefly, and then I watched her will her features into her patient counselor/parent face.

"Tyler, please do this for me? I'll make blueberry pancakes with berries we picked that day on the Bloomingdale Bog Walk," Meg said. I wondered about Meg's state of shock considering this reference to a hike we'd enjoyed together seemed to be out of character while people she cared about were splayed around us … possibly murderers and murderees.

"Meg, this isn't the sort of thing I want to do, or am good at, and it makes me uncomfortable just thinking/talking about it," I said. "I'll come for the pancakes, but no promises. I'll look at, listen to, whatever you and Frank have, but I want to spend time with Mickey and Anne and the girls, and maybe go camping again with Hope before it gets cold."

Meg's face quickly cycled through an interesting combination of partial expressions … hurt/sad/angry/resigned, and she said, "I guess that I'll take what I can get, Tyler. I'll see you tomorrow morning." I could feel the disappointment coming off her in waves.

"Meg, you seem upset that I'm not emoting/reacting properly to you or Xander or Danica or whoever, but you just got finished trying to label me as being ASD, like him," I said, pointing to the stretcher being wheeled out and down to an ambulance (*he must have either been given drugs to relax/calm him after his apprehension, or knocked unconscious during the S.W.A.T. scrum*). "So why does my response surprise and/or upset you?"

She started to swell up as if to say something, thought better/differently of it, went dramatically and instantly pale, turned slightly and vomited all over the fresh-mown lawn, and then ran off to talk with Frank and the other police milling around the ambulance (*or possibly just ran away from me*).

The Gibson House, Saranac Lake, NY,
Saturday, 8/30/2014, 8:27 a.m.

Without a word, I left the scene and drove back to SmartPig to pick up Hope for a walk. We headed downstairs and took a right out of the front door, walked past the Town Hall, and cut diagonally across the empty intersection to the band shell park on the water. Hope was able to menace a few squirrels and little children, which perversely always seems to improve her mood. She pulled me to the water, which encouraged me to bring her along the side of the road to the boat launch, where there would be better ingress/egress for an old and stiff dog with short legs. Like she does every time, she first cowered, and then growled at the odd concrete teddy bears at the far end of the band shell park on our way towards the boat launch. As tends to be the case during the warm(*ish*) months, the parking lot and ramp itself were crowded with tired and sunburned and cranky tourists and locals and kids and old people and college kids and dogs … all of whom Hope disliked as if she had a personal and well-reasoned grudge against each and every one.

I shortened my grip on her lead and navigated the scene, always aware/conscious of her "bite-bubble" (*the personal space I tried to keep vacant in front of her mouth, so as to avoid her eating strangers*) … it was smaller now than it used to be (*she had less energy to devote to mauling people and things, and also moved more slowly*), but I very much wanted to avoid a hassle of any kind, and some people are convinced that every dog is their friend, and will jam their fingers in harm's way to prove it. We negotiated the minefield without incident, crossed the now empty/green field that I always imagine as belonging to the Ice Castle (*I can see a slideshow of the various castles from every year I've lived here, superimposed on the grass and warm air, every time I walk/drive by*), and found a good spot down by a cluster of birch trees to get down and into the water, without Hope having to jump/climb/fall/fail. She walked out until the ground dropped away enough for her to have to swim, and she did … I stood in the shallows, watching her make small circles at the end of her extendable leash.

The shouts and laughs from the launch, and Hope's obvious enjoyment of the swim, made me feel more an island than ever … 1.3 miles from where I stood, ankle deep in muck, watching my happy dog and listening to happy people was the ongoing wreckage of a number of lives. I knew about it, and other people in the park might be hearing about it soon. For now, the news, the sadness, was contained in a bubble 1.3 miles away … I doubted that even the people living in the houses and streets a few hundred yards away knew what I knew about the death and chaos rolling over and around the Kovac family and friends in the coming days; I wished that I didn't.

Hope poked me with a cold nose, and reached up to give a scab on my knee a kiss, where I must have scratched it sometime, but I fended off her need/want/love for a bit longer while I let the mechanics in the back of my brain knock things around for moment. I knew, or thought I knew, a couple of things that might help Frank and/or Meg and/or Xander (*or his family, I suppose, although they were still a theoretical concept*), and might know more after breakfast tomorrow. But beyond that, I didn't want to get involved with whatever had happened.

Knives and splashing blood aren't interesting to me, they speak of complex (*emotional*) problems with simple solutions, which is exactly the opposite of where my interest in crime lies. More than that, I wanted to spend the rest of the sunny and warm days and weeks with Hope and Mickey and camping and paddling and exploring and growing my mental/internal map of the Adirondacks, and that couldn't happen if I got pulled in to help Meg with her disastrously failed student transition and her ridiculous parallels between him and me.

Hope struggled to get up the bank a bit, and I needed to give her an assist with a pushing hand before she made it … we both looked around to see if any people/dogs/squirrels had seen (*possibly for different reasons, possibly not*), and reasonably satisfied with what we could see, headed back towards SmartPig. I stopped on the way to pick up some boneless spareribs and shrimp lo mein at the good Chinese place, so I could avoid going out again when we got hungry later. They've started giving me astonishingly bland almond cookies with my orders recently, and rather than refuse or throw them out, I give them to Hope, who loves them.

We watched some Netflix, napped, read, ate, napped, and did some thinking, all the while working our/my way through thirteen cans of the perfect Coke from my Coke-fridge (*chilled slightly below the freezing temperature of water, brought down from Canada for its real cane sugar, and always unsullied/undiluted by melting ice*). I arranged the baker's dozen of empties into a third centered square figure, the same configuration I had used for mathematical recreation to explore/envision the grid of city blocks surrounding my house/person at any given time when I was growing up (*sometimes extending the map in my head to 25, to 41, to 61, and beyond as far/long/complex as I could hold the pictures in my head ... it helped to calm me when things with less orderly structures, like my parents or conversations with people, upset me*). At some point in the evening, while I was reading/enjoying an old Lincoln Rhyme mystery, Mickey called and asked me about my hurried departure from our lunch this afternoon. I assured him (*perhaps not convincing him entirely*) that it was nothing of concern, and that after breakfast with "friends" (*a term that I try to use with him, even if/when I don't entirely believe it*), I would come over, and we could take "a nice hike by the water" (*a phrase that he often uses to describe his ideal outdoor experience, not lasting more than one hour, door to door*).

Hope and I were both restless late in the evening, and took three walks during the night, exploring the dark/quiet streets of Saranac Lake, both of us preferring the lack of people and noise and the dangers of interactions poorly handled. We took naps and read for the rest of the night (*neither of us ever sleep more than four hours in a row, and normally, it's more like two or three*). When light started to force its way into the room, at twelve minutes to six, I fed Hope and took her out for a final walk down along the river that runs through town. We moved/crossed to avoid joggers when we could, and got back to SmartPig as the sun peaked over the tall trees in the direction Mickey and Anne and the girls (*and Chet and Rob*) were still likely sleeping (*except for Mickey, who rose at five each morning for quiet reading and strong coffee*) in their suite at the Whiteface Lodge. I left Hope sleeping on the couch, and drove over to the Gibson house on Algonquin Avenue.

I was parked in the driveway, reading and waiting for signs of life from within the house until a few minutes after seven, when I saw Frank's shuffling/shambling form cross in front of the window over the sink in their kitchen, likely starting the coffee machine. I read another chapter in the John Sandford book I'd been enjoying (*I have a lifelong habit of reading multiple books at any one time, switching back and forth among them based on the mood or challenge I'm looking for at any given moment*) before walking up to the door, and letting myself in (*unlike me, Frank and Meg never locked/lock their front door, and their rescue dogs go crazy when people knock, so I'd gotten into the habit of coming in after being invited to do so too many times to simply be polite*), stepping extra heavily and coughing lightly before I walked into the kitchen, so as to avoid scaring Frank.

"G'mornin' Tyler, getcha a cup of coffee?" Frank asked.

"No thanks, Frank, water's fine, and I'll get it," I said, giving the same response that I do every time (*Frank loves/needs coffee the way that I love/need Canadian Coke, and so I take it as a politeness rather than obtuseness that he keeps asking/offering*).

"Meg's a little slow getting moving this morning. She was at the place (*I wondered briefly if he had actually forgotten the name of the psychiatric institution, Whispering Pines, or if he shared the common superstition/fear/hesitancy about such places*) talking with people about the Kovac kid, and then lots of the rest of the night at a mutual friend's house with the parents. What a fucking mess that was yesterday," he said, wincing a moment later, perhaps at his unintended double entendre.

"I was impressed that they/you were able to take him into custody essentially unharmed," I said.

"No shit," Frank said. "I wouldna wanted to be the first guy going in, though. I went to school with Clark, that's the guy who tackled and wrapped Xander's legs so everyone else could grab him. He just had to trust that everyone else would do what they'd been trained to do.

Meg lost her cool with the team leader about them dislocating the kid's left shoulder. She doesn't know how lucky he is. Him not getting shot, not, maybe even, ending up dead, is mostly due to this being a small town, and everyone knowing him and his parents. In big cities like Saratoga or Burlington (*I took real pleasure, which is a rarity for me, from Frank's definition of a big city*), who knows how it would have gone down. She must be coming, now."

The signal that Meg might be up and about was the entrance into the big and bright kitchen of their dogs Toby and Lola, who came over, covered me with kisses, and went over to sit by their bowls, waiting for Frank to feed them. He kept puttering with coffee and breakfast-related condiments (*cream and sugar and butter and maple syrup*), and was either deep in thought or ignoring the dogs intentionally (*my skills at reading/ understanding/ interpreting humans aren't that good, so I couldn't tell*), so I opened the door to their walk-in pantry and filled the dogs' bowls.

"Thanks, hon," he said at the sound of the kibble pouring into the bowls, then coloring when he remembered/turned to see me instead of Meg.

"No problem," I said, ever the straight man (*having no real choice in the matter as my sense of humor is not in line with anyone I've met, to date*).

"She said something about the blueberries, but I was still asleep," he said.

"I've got it, I think," I said, pouring a Ziploc bag of frozen blueberries we'd picked along the bog-trail (*at the Onchiota end*) into a colander to thaw, and getting a box of Bisquick out of the pantry, as Meg walked in, looking tired and sad and pale and a bit angry.

"Sit, Tyler, you don't need to make me breakfast in

my own house."

"Coffee, hon?" Frank asked, barely smiling as he said it (*besides being able to laugh at himself when warranted, Frank has a habit of reading people and doing/saying exactly the right thing to avert, or bring about, some desired effect*).

"What? Yes, please. Thanks," she said, taking the cup and sitting at their round table, to give the dogs a chance to check in with her more easily while taking the first sip.

"You stay there, and let me start the pancakes, Meg," I suggested. "It sounds as though you had a long night, and there is no need for you to be catering to me. I know where everything is." I pre-heated the oven to 375 (*373 actually, tipping the knob so that it was a hair under 375 … 373 is the sum of five primes, as well as being a permutable and palindromic prime … way better than 375*) and got some bacon out of their fridge to accompany the pancakes (*I had a feeling that my thoughts on the crime scene were going to be worth it to Meg, although it would more than balance out in hassle to Frank … but Meg was the bribing party in this case*), and twenty-three minutes later had a wonderful breakfast on the table and a wide-awake audience (*as they'd both had at least two cups of coffee by now*).

I sat in front of a huge plate of blueberry pancakes and bacon, with lots of butter and real maple syrup (*from a nearby sugar bush that Meg and Frank helped at every spring, in exchange for local syrup*). "To avoid wasting time, I have to ask if Xander admitted to killing Danica."

"He has not been interrogated because his mental state and competency have not been fully evaluated and judged as yet," Frank said, in a tone that sounded an unusual mix of bored and angry … maybe officious.

"Well, it certainly must have come up in the eighteen hours since what happened at the house on Mulflur Road," I pushed on, looking at Meg.

She pointed at Frank and said, "You're not in uniform yet, or if you are, go walk the dogs." I looked at Frank's bathrobe for a second, and Meg grunted in frustration at me.

Frank nodded, and Meg continued, "Xander was both confused and confusing while we were talking last night. He said there had been a fight," she looked between both of us sternly, "which is a term that he also uses for argument or disagreement." I nodded.

"He said many times that he hit Danica, but didn't hurt her," Meg said, picking words carefully/slowly/precisely. "He was worried that 'Mom will be sad' and insisted that he had never touched or held the knife."

"That would be the bloody knife he was holding when both you, and then later, the S.W.A.T. team entered the house, and saw him standing over the dead body of his sister," Frank said, sounding as though it was work to keep his tone even/neutral.

"Dammit, Frank," Meg said. "He's scared and knows he's in trouble. When he gets in trouble, his first instinct is to say that sort of thing."

"To lie, you mean," Frank said.

"It may not be lying, exactly," I swallowed my bacon before I had fully chewed it to speak up because it looked as though Meg was going to explode … she was tomato-red. "It's more like he's describing the way it should have gone, or the way he wishes it had gone … as though he's editing the way things happened in his mind/memory."

Meg smiled at me, maybe at the fact that I was speaking/participating.

Frank exploded, "That's fucking great! Couldn't ask for a less reliable or credible witness or suspect, couldya?"

"Franklin Porter Gibson, de-cop-ify yourself right

now, or just leave," Meg said. "Why do you ask, Tyler? I thought you didn't want anything to do with any of this, with Xander or Danica."

"I don't," I said. "But you asked, so I'm going to try and give you something useful this morning. But, if Xander had already confessed or everyone was certain about his guilt, then I didn't want to … muddy the waters (*I grabbed this one out of a dark/dusty corner in the back of my head, thinking again of Mrs. Portnoy*)."

"Muddy them how, Tyler?" Frank said, even before Meg could speak. "If you know something, although I can't for the life of me see how you could, you gotta tell us, tell me. If it screws up the case against the Kovac kid, Xander, then the case oughta be screwed up. I'm ninety-plus percent sure he killed his sister, and should be inside for it, forever. I don't know where, but inside somewhere. Unless, that is, he didn't do it."

"You think he didn't do it," Meg said, looking at me with a few expressions mixed up all over her face. "Isn't that right?"

"I wouldn't say that, exactly," I said. "A couple of things, three in point of fact, got my attention from your description of the events/scene/evidence yesterday … it/they may turn out to be nothing."

"What things, exactly. Wait a sec," Frank said as he tore a to-do list pad with a bear on it off the fridge, and rummaged through a crap-drawer until he found a pencil. "Gimme a list, and then go back through and explain it to me."

"Bleach, the disposal, and lines versus swoops of blood drops," I said, watching Frank write the words down (*spelling bleach incorrectly, not that it mattered/matters*).

"Okay," he said. "Go for bleach."

"If you're sure you smelled bleach," I said, looking at

Meg, who nodded, "then it may be important. Bleach is great for cleaning up or destroying blood evidence, or at least the DNA contained within blood evidence. It doesn't sound as though Xander was cleaning anything with bleach when Meg saw him."

Meg shook her head, somewhat pointlessly (*it was a rhetorical statement/question*).

"I'd be interested in finding out where the bleach was used/splashed/poured, and why," I said. "I would also check the bottle for fingerprints and DNA."

Frank was scribbling.

"Next, the disposal," I continued. "It should be checked for both DNA and bleach. My bet is that you will find bleach and degraded blood down there, along with some chopped up phalanges … finger bones (*I added in the face of their matching clueless expressions*), the tips … where the fingernails, which could scratch and keep someone's DNA, are." I said, wiggling the tips of my fingers at them.

"Why?" Meg asked, looking towards her sink, and at the remains of her breakfast with less enthusiasm than a minute ago. "Why would he, would Xander, cut off her, Danica's, fingers and run them through the—yuck?" she somewhat finished.

"Tyler don't think he did," Frank cut in before I could reply, scratching his scalp with the pencil tip and looking up at the ceiling. "Sure, I follow."

"Well, I don't," Meg said. "Not that I'm entirely sure that I want to."

"Danica scratched her attacker," I said. "Since he/she/they couldn't leave their DNA onsite, he/she/they snipped off the tips of the offending fingers, and dumped them down the disposal, along with a mess of bleach to shred/dispose of the evidence. This would also suggest a missing pair of kitchen shears, possibly," I added.

"Why?" Meg asked. "Why does that point there instead of to Danica turning on the disposal and Xander stabbing her because he hated the sound?"

She looked guilty at her suggestion of an alternative explanation that wouldn't exonerate the young man she'd worked with for years.

"It doesn't necessarily," I replied. "But it's worth checking. The smell of bleach without you mentioning seeing the bottle gave me the idea, as did the fact that Xander hates that type/frequency/modulation of sound (*I did not point out that I also hated that sort of sound and had worked hard for years to control my responses to disposals and vacuum cleaners and other similar noises … I did not, at present, want to strengthen Meg's mental connection between Xander and myself*)."

"Blood in swoops and shit," Frank prompted (*somewhat inaccurately*).

"Meg mentioned blood in lines and sort of swoops of drops, and a couple of smeary areas, leading back into the dining room from the kitchen," I said. Meg nodded as I quoted her verbatim. "The smeary areas made me wonder about bleach and destroying DNA again, and your language describing differing patterns suggests differing patterns/speeds of movement, and made me wonder about two different people possibly leaving blood trails."

"So what?" Frank asked, a little anger creeping clearly (*since I was picking up on it*) onto his face. "We've got lab geeks takin' samples. I hate to break it to you, Tyler, but even though we're living up near the North Pole, we speak science here."

"I get that, Frank, I really do. I know your lab and

crime scene guys are good. I picked their brains last summer pretty exhaustively, but hear me out on this," I said, pausing to see if he was listening, which seemed only to make him madder.

Oddly, Meg smiled, which she covered by sipping her coffee.

"Sometimes," I said, "especially when it seems like a no-brainer, the crime scene guys don't swab everything. Running those tests costs a fortune, especially when the scene was really hosed down, like it sounds as though the Kovac house was."

Meg paled but nodded at this.

"Why run a thousand samples when anyone could tell what happened?" I said. Frank seemed to cool down, and really listen, almost to look ahead to what I was going to say next.

"So how do you know what to sample if you don't want to sample every drop or splash or puddle?" Frank asked.

"I've read up on it, but I'm no expert. There's a Dr. Gruber, down near Albany, and it might be worth it to have him come up before you release the scene for cleanup," I said. "Failing that though, I would have Will Carlisto from your lab look at the smeared spots, and around the edges of bleach-burned areas for samples of blood. Also, look for blood with different directionality vectors." I waited while Frank wrote that down. "He should also look for perfectly round drops in the kitchen. The ones with differing directionality indicators and/or any round drops you can find might be indicative of blood from Danica's attacker. Once you point Will in this direction, he'll have more/better/easier ideas than me … he's pretty smart, and he really understands/loves spatter (*I said this last bit as a compliment, but Meg shuddered a little*)."

Frank nodded.

I reached across and pulled Meg's unfinished plate over to my space, sopping up viscous leftover syrup with now soggy and limp (*but still delicious*) bacon.

"So," Frank said, "look around bleached areas for untouched blood, check the bottle for prints or DNA, take apart the disposal and drain pipes, find the kitchen shears, have Willy look for out of profile spatter, especially round drops in the kitchen, or changes and differences from the norm. Izzat about it?"

"Yup, that should give you more to go on, one way or another. If nothing comes up hinky or missing or different or unexpected, then," I said, looking at Meg with a scripted facial expression that expresses regret reasonably well, "it seems likely that Xander probably killed his sister."

"I feel almost guilty hoping for something to turn up," said Meg. "It'll mean that there's a monster out there among all our friends and neighbors again, and not just a sad accident. Jesus, Tyler, having you in my life is changing my worldview almost as much as marrying a cop has. Sometimes I wish I didn't know all of this stuff about the world, the people, and the scary things at the edges."

"You and me both," I said. " I told you, I'm trying for a more boring life … play with my dog, go camping, read books … I know more about real murders and murderers than I want to. I'm happy to leave this all to Frank, and from here on out, I will."

We were done with breakfast and I was done helping Meg. Frank got up to make some phone calls, still in his robe … so I left to go take my dog for a swim.

Starbucks, Lake Placid, NY,
Saturday, 8/30, /2014, 10:49 a.m.

Hope was still sleeping on the couch as I quietly opened the door to SmartPig, but woke up happy when I wafted the piece of bacon I'd saved her from breakfast in front of her nose. Not knowing what the day would bring, I took a sink-shower (*splashing of face and hair and armpits, while leaning over the large stainless steel sink ... no shampoo or soap, but I did brush my teeth quickly, rubbed in a few drops of Whisker Sauce, and put some Speed Stick on before grabbing a clean shirt from the closet*), and fed Hope a short cup of kibble before heading back down the stairs and out into the warmth of the still-new day.

Deciding that we didn't have time for a swim before meeting Mickey, I drove to the Whiteface Lodge and left Hope in a shady spot in the Element with kisses and open windows. I entered the building, negotiated the lobby and stairs, and made it to the door of the suite without being seen, or talked to, or helped, or questioned. Not that it would have been more than a minor hassle, but it's a game I like to play when entering hotels and businesses and (*yuck!*) hospitals ... I always prefer to enter and exit places without being seen/heard/noted, if possible. When I knocked on the door, gently a first time, and then a bit louder five seconds later, Mickey himself opened it, and waved me in. I could smell toast and coffee and Mickey's aftershave and, faintly, a mix of other male and female masking scents ... these last, and the silence beyond and around Mickey were enough to tell me that we had the space to ourselves.

Mickey sensed my understanding of the empty and quiet and answered my lack of question, "The boys are playing an early game of tennis with the girls (*it wasn't that Mickey was trying to impugn the maturity of either his kids or their current boyfriends … he simply thought of them in the same way he had when they/we had all been four or six or eight years old*). Anne has a spa-morning lined up. I've been drinking coffee and reading on the porch, or deck, or whatever, since the sun came up at 6:30 (*6:18, I mentally corrected, but didn't say*)."

"It's terrific, kiddo," he continued. "A view of the mountains, cool/crisp air, birds and whatnot making morning sounds. In *The City*, it would already be a hundred degrees, and smell like pee and asphalt, and you'd just hear cars honking at each other. You're not gonna believe this, Ty, but I have a machine in my office that only exists to make this static-y noise so it can drown out other, less pleasant noise. Imagine that?" I could.

"You ready for a walk?" I asked, skipping over what I could or could not imagine.

"You bet," he said, enthusiastically. "Do I need to bring anything? Water, first-aid, lunch, raingear?" These last couple of items were mentioned with an air (*and look*) of dread in his voice.

"Nossir," I said. "I'll be bringing a hydropak with some first-aid supplies and other stuff in it because that's what I do, but you don't need anything besides what you're wearing … we'll be back inside of an hour."

Despite my assurances, Mickey disappeared into his room for three minutes to change out of a pair of sneakers into a pair of light-hikers, grab a small Nalgene bottle, and an inexpertly wrapped box the size of one of his bricks of Bustello (*a dark and cheap and burnt smelling espresso that he buys/makes/drinks in endless amounts*) which he handed to me.

"For you to open," he said, beaming (*the slightly clumsy wrapping job told me it was his work … Anne wraps presents so expertly, that they are sometimes difficult to open*), "after our hike."

"It's not a video camera, is it?" I asked, feeling the weight/packaging of electronics and thinking back to the last time we'd shared an interest in a package roughly the size of a brick of Bustello. "My camera takes video as well as stills."

Mickey colored a bit and looked backwards into the suite, despite knowing that it was empty (*and neither of us having said anything incriminating*). "No! No video cameras. It's a … well, you'll see."

We walked out and down, and out and down some more to my Element, and shared an awkward moment when Mickey and Hope surprised, and were surprised, by each other. Hope tried to bite Mickey, and didn't want to relinquish her co-pilot seat in favor of the back, so Mickey climbed into the backseat without a word. Mickey doesn't like dogs and has been living a convenient and harmless lie for decades … he purports to be allergic to them. It apparently started as a way to avoid getting a dog when he moved in with his first girlfriend, and it became institutionalized over time (*he insists that it would be harder to reverse the inertia after all of this time, but I believe that if he didn't perceive a benefit from the misapprehension, it would have ended in the last millennium*). I couldn't care less as we don't live together, and his sin of "lack-of-correction" doesn't hurt anyone or anything so far as I can see. I discovered the lie when doing some research/reading/interviews in the early '90s. I had woken up one morning simply knowing that Mickey was not allergic to dogs (*the minions in the backrooms of my skull had connected the dots while I slept, apparently*). Based on what he insisted be a one-time discussion of him and dogs and allergies and fake allergies and convenience, we don't talk about dogs. We don't talk about his allergies to dogs (*real or fake or imagined*), and we don't mention that we don't talk about it. I'm perfectly willing to be a part of his only ongoing lie (*possibly the only lie, if it counts as one, in his life, as he is, in other ways, a scrupulously, sometimes painfully, even tediously, honest person*), as I live a life filled with lies and omissions and intentional misrepresentations (*one of my concerns is that someday, someone, likely Anne, will ask him exactly what I do, or what I did on some specific date that Mickey is aware of my activities on, and he will feel compelled to hose her down with the truth … I will cross that bridge, and likely burn it behind me to make good my escape, on that horrible day*). That being said (*or in this case, typed*), I don't allow his falsehood to alter my life, when it doesn't hurt him, so when it's just us, I don't bother keeping Hope away from him, or vice versa. They don't like each other, but they don't have to, they both like me (*and the feeling is mutual, insofar as I feel*), and they tolerate each other.

We drove down the hill towards the center of Lake Placid and turned up and past the Comfort Inn on Peninsula Way Road, until we came to the gate and parking lot. I let Hope out, Mickey gently tossed the present for me into the backseat, and we three walked into the woods. The Peninsula Trails loop for miles in and around a small chunk of forest just outside the village proper of Lake Placid. It also connects to the Jackrabbit Trail (*which runs for thirty-five plus miles through the woods, from Paul Smiths to Keene*). We were only going to walk a few miles through the woods and along the shore of Lake

Placid, but it's a pretty place to stroll. Once we had turned off the main trail and onto the Boundary Trail that would take us to the lake and dam, I listened for (*and didn't hear*) any other hikers, or dogs, so I took Hope off her lead to let her run loose awhile. Mickey looked nervously around, as if expecting the police, but after a frenzied thirty seconds of rushing back and forth across the trail in front of us, Hope settled down to walking between us (*with me in the lead, and Hope protecting me from attack from Mickey, who was at the end of our woodland parade*). We reached the dam across the south end of West Lake (*Lake Placid is divided into two parts by a series of almost connecting islands which yields West Lake and East Lake*) after only about thirteen minutes in the woods (*which allowed for plenty of sniffing and peeing and chatting and shoe-tying by Hope and Mickey*). Hope walked straight into the water by the edge of the dam and went for a swim, while Mickey and I sat down on a bench someone had made from a split log and stumps, and we watched her swim slow and small circles in the shallows.

"I have to say, this is pretty great, kiddo," Mickey said. "It seems idyllic up here … for you, I couldn't survive without The New York Times by 5 a.m. (*whenever Mickey visits, I hear a lot about how long it takes for the only paper, as far as he is concerned, to become available*), and for Anne and the girls, this might as well be Siberia. But you've made a life up here, and it seems to work for you."

"It is," I said. "I have. It does." Mickey waited for me to say more, but I had gone back to watching Hope, who was now shaking her coat dry-ish/er by the side of the lake, and eying Mickey suspiciously.

"We … I (*he often included Anne within our circle in discussions, at least to start, but then my lack of need for artifice would convince him to drop it*) worried about you so much in the first year after you left. But I couldn't think of what I could do to help," he said. "I was so scared that you would fall away from me, from yourself, from the person you had become."

I sat still and silent and waiting.

"And of course, you did," Mickey continued. "You moved away from me, and from the person you were in Manhattan (*he only says this as opposed to The City when talking to me*). You grew into the man you have become, are becoming. And he would seem to be a great man, a man your parents would have loved to see, loved to know."

I reached over and patted his knee now, seeing the tears and love and loss, for both me and my parents that neither they nor I could shed, each for our own reasons.

"These things you do, the things that you can do, they are a part of your greatness, and definitely a part of the man you were meant to become. The reason God made you awesome," he said with a smile (*as a child I had asked him, many times, why I had to be different, and he said that God, a concept that I still don't believe/accept/understand, even within Mickey's faith framework, hadn't made me different so much as awesome*).

Hope picked up on something of the emotional import of what was going on between Mickey and me (*even if I wasn't sure myself*), and wedged herself between the two of us, wetting my right leg, and the left leg of Mickey's pants in the process. She growled as menacingly as was possible for the greying/stiffly-moving/short/chubby/elderly beagle. Mickey scooched over a bit farther away and lifted his hands out of snapping range.

"She's a real treasure, that one," he said. "I can see why, out of all the dogs in the world, you picked her."

"Yup," I said, choosing (*as I tend to do*) between the possible interpretations available to me for his statement, the non-facetious meaning of what he said. "Hope is on my side/team in all matters except for those pertaining to squirrels and Irish Setters, in which she is markedly more bloodthirsty than I, or anyone, can imagine (*or stomach, I thought*)."

"The point I was aiming for," he said, "is that the things you can do, with your research and reading and the leaps your brain takes are like magic, or something. At any rate, I think that if you walk away it will not be a profitable use of your gifts. I'm not talking about money here, kiddo. If you choose not to use what you can do to help people, it would be wasteful and selfish and possibly evil."

Mickey believes in evil. Not like some people do, in terms of demons or the Devil, but as choices, and the results or outcomes of choices. To make a choice that did people harm, or even did not do people good, was evil in his worldview. If he thought that I was evil, or could become evil by failing to act to use my intellect and unusual perception/intuition to help people, then he must be right.

"Okay," I said, as we stood and began moving northeast along the shore, watching boats and birds and having hooked Hope up to her leash (*as I could hear, and then eventually see, a group of children and their parents moving towards us from the woods, children that Hope might dream of eating/scarring/scaring if they overtook or passed or came near us*).

"Don't 'okay' me because you think I want you to, or because I think it's the right thing to do," Mickey said. "If you're going to do this well and truly, even when I'm not here any longer (*I took this to mean not in the Adirondacks, because I had trouble manipulating my worldview to include a planet/life/existence without Mickey Schwarz*), then you need to believe it, to feel it, to know it … not in your brain, but in your heart, in your soul."

"I'm pretty sure that my heart is only a muscle for moving blood around my body, and that I don't have a soul (*I didn't want to get into a discussion/debate/argument with him this morning about whether he, or Hope, or anyone else, had a soul*)," I said. "My brain is where all of me that matters lives … input and storage and processing and analysis and output."

"You love. You love her, and here, and me, and who knows who and what else in the midst of all of the data that your ridiculous melon processes all the damn time," he said, pointing down to Hope, and to the woods and waters all around us, and thumping his own chest (*dramatically, I thought*), and then reaching out to tap me, ever so gently, on the temple (*slowing, as he had learned to from my childhood discomfort and fear of unannounced contact, just short of actually touching my skin*).

"Maybe that's how I 'do', or manifest, a soul," I said.

Mickey turned, and looked ready to say something in response to my statement, and then bent to grab a stone and chucked it in the lake. We walked in silence back to the car.

"Coffee," he said, "I need some strong coffee, and a minute to think before I give you your gift."

"Starbucks," I said. He nodded. I aimed the Element for the Starbucks on Main Street of Lake Placid, a place I'd never been inside of before (*since I don't drink coffee, and everything else they have to offer can be had better and more cheaply somewhere else*).

We took Mickey's mysterious box and left poor Hope in the car with all of the windows rolled down … Mickey ordered a quadrupio (*a quadruple shot of espresso, for those not in the know*), and I got an orange/mango smoothie. Our order came up shortly, after more whirring and hissing and grinding and crunching and slurping sounds than would have seemed absolutely necessary. Mickey put four packets of Sugar in the Raw in his cup of caffeinated sludge, and I drank the first half of my smoothie at a pace designed to avoid brain-freeze.

I unwrapped the present as I had learned from my mom and dad, slowly and thoughtfully, having read the card first (*the card said simply, 'To help you find your way and never be lost ... for long. Love, Mickey', with a hand-drawn heart under his name ... we had often spoken of the benefits of occasionally becoming lost in the short term*), and folding the paper neatly before placing it off to one side.

"It's called SPOT, and as I understand it, it's like a GPS, but it can send your location to me and/or the authorities if you get in trouble," he said.

"I read an article about it not long ago. You can send a distress call, with your GPS coordinates, for help, to police and such, and/or send customized messages to family and friends with the coordinates," I said.

I've included a gift certificate to have it activated for a year, and I'll keep it going beyond that if you like it, and use it," Mickey said. "I love the idea of knowing that you're okay when you go out into the woods (*he shuddered a bit when he said, and thought about, this*) by yourself or during the winter, or both."

"I can set it up so you receive an email with my location and notification that I'm all right," I said, "and do a different one for Dot and/or Meg and Frank. What a cool idea (*I said, thinking of another/nested/parallel way to use it to communicate coded messages to my primary minion, Dorothy*)."

"I'm glad you like it," Mickey said. "I know it'll make us ... me, feel safer when you're out in the woods, or when you're doing stuff like last summer or with me that time (*I hadn't told him about all of the other adventures that something like this would have come in handy, and maybe made staying alive much, much easier*). Promise me that you'll use it, and that you'll also think about what I said about using whatever it is that you have, or can do, to help people … to keep helping people."

"I will," I said, purposefully not specifying which/what I was agreeing to. "Thanks, Mickey, really!"

"You're welcome, kiddo," he said. "I am too proud of you, of what you've grown up to become, to lose you. What you do, the way you live, is sometimes dangerous, probably needs to be that way sometimes, but maybe this'll help, and that would make an old man very happy. I love you boy."

"Love you too, Mickey," I answered, and he came around the table to give me an awkward hug/kiss/shoulder-pat.

SmartPig Offices, Saranac Lake, NY,
Monday, 9/1/ 2014, 4:37 p.m.

I dropped Mickey off at his suite, partially fended off an invitation for dinner out with everyone in his party, and drove back to SmartPig to play with, and think about the new toy he had given me … and also what he had said to me during our walk.

I stopped on the way back into Saranac Lake at the Mobil Station to fill my car's gas tank, pick up some supplies, and briefly consider (*for the 1597th time, to the best of my recollection*) getting my Element washed at the semi-attached carwash facility … I discarded the idea, as I always do/have/will, because the car just gets dirty again (*you can't surrender to entropy everywhere, but this has always seemed a ridiculous fight to pick, or line to draw*). Eggs, cheese, donuts, bananas, jerky, and a sub from the Subway sandwich symbiote attached to this convenient stop on the edge of town gave me everything I would need for the next day or so in SmartPig.

Hope and I climbed the stairs and put things away (*I put things away. Hope jumped up on the couch, farting mightily with the effort, spun in three tight circles, and dropped down the well into sleep within seconds of my opening the door*), moving through the single large room automatically, wondering about my nesting impulse. I took three Cokes out of the Coke-fridge, started on the first while dumping a dozen of the eggs into a pot with some water, setting it to hard boil them on my lab-acquired heating element, and planned a day of reading/research and Roku-surfing. After so many years not fully understanding my head, and what goes on inside it, I had learned to trust the machinery and monsters living in the back rooms of my brain, and assumed that they knew what was best for me. I downloaded a couple dozen megabytes of articles and books and studies on autism and involuntary commitment and blood evidence and crime scene science/technique. While some of that was loading, I played at setting up the SPOT GPS toy that Mickey had given me, and bounced through various options available to me via Roku until I landed on episodes of *Star Trek: The Next Generation* (*ST:TNG*) (*pleasant background stimuli while I read and ate and drank and napped and read and ate and napped over the next two days and twenty-three hours … 23 being an interesting number for many reasons, not least because it is part of the first Cunningham chain to have five numbers in it*).

Hope and I seem to have escaped the rest of the world's slavery to circadian rhythms (*or at least the more traditional ones mammals tend to function according to*), and while it's something that I've read extensively on, I don't believe that it is adversely affecting our health. I track/monitor our sleep patterns, along with apparent health/function/productivity over time. We generally function in shorter repeating cycles than others, oscillating between six and eight hours in period length for work and exercise and sleep; this was the pattern we had followed all summer while living in the woods, and was also the cycle we'd been tied to since emerging from the woods days ago. I wouldn't recommend it to anyone else but could see no reason to fight the natural pull/programming of my body and mind.

During one of our waking periods, after having eaten

as much garlic and shrimp and scallops and broccoli and rice as seemed possible (*with slightly more than that for Hope, although she insisted, as always, that she could handle it*) and a quintet of Cokes chilled nearly to the freezing point by my lab-grade fridge (*a.k.a. the Coke-fridge*), I had just started watching an episode of a TV series which reminded me of my adventures the previous summer when I heard the dry and confident scuffing of Maurice, my landlord, on the stairs up to the SmartPig world headquarters. He tried his key, and when it didn't budge the locks (*as it hadn't the thirteen other times he'd tried in the twenty-three months since I'd upgraded my front door security*), he threw his tiny frame against the door and bolts and reinforced frame as well as the bar set into the floor on my side.

"Agch, Tyler," he said, when I opened the door for him. "Why you wann all that crap on you door? You have a fire in here, you gonna burn to death before you can undo all them fancy locks."

"Hello, Maurice," I said. "What can I do for you?"

As a rule, Maurice didn't leave his living room very often and then only with good reason.

"I came by to fix the sink," he said, seemingly completely unembarrassed by the transparency of his lie … he had no tools, and I'd deducted the supplies needed to complete the repair from my last rent check, as we had agreed when we last spoke of the leaky faucet. He pushed past me, mumbled something unintelligible to Hope, who had been growling, but now curled into her tightest possible ball configuration to ignore him, while he pretended to fiddle with the faucet.

"It seems okay, Tyler. No problem here," he said.

"Yes," I answered. "I replaced the faucet assembly five weeks ago. It's working very well now."

"Okay then," he said. "How's everything else going for you? Working on anything? Helping anyone outta they troubles?"

"Nope, nothing too interesting lately," I answered. "I've been camping a lot this summer, most recently out near—"

"Uh-huh, still with the sleeping outside." Maurice had always been dubious of my interest in camping and exploring the outdoors, and only overlooked my using this office space as a place to sleep when I wasn't in the woods because of a favor I'd done him more than a decade ago.

"What about this boy from town?" he asked. Alarm bells started going off in the parts of my brain that apparently had previously been numbed by a perfect balance of spice and grease and caffeine. "The one ever-body says kilt his sister, that sweet girl, Daniella (*we both knew who he was talking about, and correcting Maurice would only slow him down, and he might start tinkering with light switches or the thermostat*)."

I was cautious of falling into one of Maurice's non-logical non-sequitur traps, so I said nothing, taking a page from his book and fiddling with the perfectly functioning faucet for six seconds, even going so far as to pour myself a glass of water that I had no desire for.

"You remember Sophia, Tyler? My granddaughter?" he asked.

"Yes, Maurice, I remember Sophia," I said. I remember everything … every word I read, every photograph I see, and every person that I meet; I particularly remember Sophia because she was a part of my first case as a consulting detective upon arriving in the Adirondacks after the events of 9/11 forced my retreat from Manhattan, and the life/family/everything I'd known before that Tuesday.

"She gave birth to Nathalie, my great-granddaughter," he said, tilting his head back to look at the ceiling, as if some answers or hints were scribbled there, like on the pockets full of post-it notes he always carries around with him, "almost seven years ago … in October."

"That's great, Maurice," I said, for lack of anything better/logical to say … hoping for a light at the end of this conversational tunnel.

"Nathalie … that's her name," he seemed ready to pause, or even begin again, so I nodded, forcefully. "She got the autism, like this boy." He glanced sidelong at me as he said this, and seemed about to say more when Hope, still in ball-mode, growled at him from the couch.

"That dog, she doan like, doan get along with, anyone but you, right?" he asked, pointing at her with his chin.

"She likes Dorothy … who runs the shelter," I said, cutting off my explanation when Maurice nodded vigorously. "But you're right, (*I was extrapolating here, hoping to reach ahead to his point without too much time wasted*) she doesn't like the vast majority of people (*or dogs, I thought, although we weren't speaking of Hope's relations with other members of her own species, and I didn't want to depart from this digression from my afternoon of lounging on the couch*) she meets, or has met, in this world."

"It's tough, to be alone in the world, even for a dog (*especially for a dog, I thought, but remained silent and stone-faced, as is my way ninety-nine percent of the time*)," Maurice said. "But you found a way into her life, and you help her. Maybe she helps you too, I think."

"We get along," I said, starting to feel the direction and destination of this conversation and visit.

"I remember the day," he said, "showing you the office. You all alone. Got nobody. Wouldn't look at me in the eye. Wouldn't shake my hand when we met."

"Now you got that shelter girl, the cop, that woman up to the high school, helps kids with their problems," he continued, giving me the briefest of knowing/guilty/loaded looks. "You got me too, Maurice, who lets you sleep on the couch in his office (*my office, I corrected internally but didn't say*)."

"The world's a tough place if you're alone, Tyler, tougher for some people than others," he said (*as if his point needed bringing home*). "Tougher for my granddaughter Nathalie, this boy Xander, and for … other people with the autism too. I wish I could do more for my Nathalie, and for that boy. I brought a bottle of my homemade wine over to his parents at the hotel they're staying at. Offered them one 'a my empty apartments until they can get back in the home. But they like the pool at the hotel for when, or if, the boy comes home from that place they got him locked up for observation. I hope he comes home to them soon. Must be scary to be so alone, so far from home an' family, not unnerstanding the world like he don't."

"Okay, enough. Maurice," I said. "I talked with the police already about some things that might help Xander, and I'll talk more with Meg (*who I assume was the 'woman up to the high school, helps kids with their problems' that Maurice had referred to moments ago*) once they've taken a look at the scene, but I may not be able to help the boy or his parents at all."

"But you gonna try you best, right Tyler?" he asked.

"That's the only way I know how, Maurice," I said (*except, I thought, when I give something only part of my attention, or quit altogether … but saying that didn't seem likely to get*

Maurice out of my office, and me on the couch with my dog and as many ice-cold Cokes as I could balance on my chest).

He thanked me, rushed over for an awkward, but unapologetic, hug, kissed me on both cheeks (*at which I openly shuddered, and Hope growled again, from the couch*), and rushed out stammering something about checking on the plumbing downstairs while wiping his eyes and sniffing a bit.

I went through the ritual of locking my front door, including the bar in the floor and the bolts that extend into the doorframe on both sides, top and bottom, grabbed a trio of frosty cans from the Coke-fridge and a big bag of Tyler-kibble, and slid down onto the couch next to my grumpy old dog.

During our self-imposed, and unfortunately short and repeatedly interrupted isolation, I spoke with Mickey twice, met him for coffee (*I had a Coke*) once, and suffered through a nearly intolerable/interminable dinner at Maggie's Pub (*which has a more interesting view than menu, but met my needs more adequately than it did Anne's, who was notably/noticeably disappointed by the slightly pedestrian pub menu*).

Hope and I also went on our three favorite walks in downtown Saranac Lake a number of times. The walk from SmartPig to the boat launch on Lake Flower is her favorite morning walk. A loop down to the river out our backdoor and then along Dorsey Street and back up along Broadway was the usual for midday, with the added benefit of taking us by (*and often into*) the Good Chinese place on our way back to SmartPig. The standard afternoon walk for Hope and me to take is back along Broadway to the river, following the Riverwalk down to the edge of town, hoping to see/kill squirrels or ducks or Irish Setters. We enjoy the accustomed patterns of sights and sounds, which give us time to think and relax while walking/sniffing on autopilot.

It was during one of these walks (*the afternoon walk, if you were wondering*), that I felt something tickling one of the clubhouses in the back of my head … the one housing the brain-gnomes in charge of the thought processes that allow/help me to enjoy my consulting detective business. I was interested to note that some part/parts of my brain were hoping that there would be something useful/interesting for me in the murder investigation that Meg had tried to rope me into. I could feel the nascent stirrings of dissatisfaction with the routine of walks and Cokes and reading and Chinese food and Netflix (*I could feel no such stirrings from Hope*), and wondered briefly if detection could be classified as an addiction.

SmartPig Offices, Saranac Lake, NY,
Tuesday, 9/2/2014, 11:53 a.m.

Meg called at three minutes after eight on the morning of the second of September, and asked me if I would be willing to come over to her place and meet with the Kovacs at eleven, to talk (*non-specific, but so heavily weighted with emotional content that even I could pick up on Meg's emphasis, even over the phone … a medium in which I am notoriously/famously weak*). Apparently the minions in the back alleys and office spaces of my mind had been hard at work while the rest of me had been doing some light reading and skimming my way through a Trek-a-thon, because I said yes without pausing, or even giving the matter any conscious thought. Meg seemed as surprised to hear me acquiesce without hassle as I was to give in without/before a fight; she even started to argue the point with me, before realizing that I had entirely reversed my position (*about helping her and Xander*) from our previous meeting. We disconnected awkwardly (*which is nothing new for me, but Meg is brilliant on the phone, with anybody, even making me look/sound/feel good at the end of most calls*), then Hope stepped on my throat, prompting me to get up from the couch, grab a fresh Coke from the Coke-fridge, and take her (*and myself*) for a walk.

I needed to break up our routine, so chose to do our afternoon outing, even though it was, technically, morning. We walked downstairs and turned left on

Broadway to walk down the hill to the river, crossing the street, when no cars were coming, to join the Riverwalk. Following the river and taking the little footbridge, we eventually ended up at Hope's favorite place in town (*besides the couch in SmartPig*) … a wide spot in the Riverwalk with benches and grass and trees and a bank where Hope could easily access the water, which also (*due to its location and traffic flow*) was never crowded with people or dogs. We sat by the water for a few minutes, sharing some jerky, hoping some ducks would swim/float by, and then made our way back up to SmartPig, to hide from the day for another hour and a bit (*and at least one, probably two, more episodes of Trek on Netflix, super-cooled Cokes, and articles from my e-reader's constantly filling/refilling queue*).

When I turned up to the Gibson house a few minutes before eleven, I was a bit surprised to see an unfamiliar car in the driveway, and pulled the Element wheels onto their lawn. I recognized Meg's Kia Soul and Frank's cruiser, but the other vehicle was unknown to me, although I was certain (*after consulting the records room in the back of my head, prompting the grumpy librarian I picture living back there with color/configuration and interesting license plate type/number*) that I had seen it in/around the Tri-Lakes within the period of my working memory (*which is a bit north of twenty-six years in my case, slightly more than twelve of them in Saranac Lake*). Hope was annoyed with me, and my (*stupid, her sad eyes insisted*) plan to get/keep her involved in what I assumed was going to be the next logical step in Meg's consulting me. For this, Hope would have to wait in the car, the alternative was the muzzle, and she hates the muzzle, even as we both acknowledge the need for it at times (*'Yes,' she seems to say, 'I will bite people … I like biting people, so if you want me to be with you and people, I guess we need the muzzle, although a better solution would be if all the people were somewhere else.' ... she's not that different from the writer Charles Bukowski, except that while she feels better when people aren't around, she does hate them*). So, I parked in the shade, opened the windows, and left Hope in the Element for the time being. I walked up to the front door, knocked, and after hearing some noise from inside, opened the door and walked in, knowing full well that the next hour or so would be uncomfortable and challenging for me in any number of ways (*probably for everyone else as well, but I didn't care much about that*) ... at least I had Hope with me (*or, more precisely, near to me*), and she was/is/will always be on my side.

Meg met me in the entryway with an ice-cold glass of Coke. "It's from my yellow-cap collection in the basement, so you can drink it," she said. While taking their son, Austin, on what they called the Victory Lap, a multi-state tour of the colleges where Austin had been accepted to help him make his final decision about where to go (*predictably, at least to me, he had chosen nearby Clarkson in the end*), Meg had come across a display in Ohio of yellow-capped Cokes. During Passover, Coca-Cola produces Coke with real sugar, and the two-liter bottles are easily identified by the yellow-caps and a notation on the label. So, they loaded the back of their trunk with them and kept them cold in their basement refrigerator.

"Thanks," I said, taking it (*appreciating her effort to make me comfortable at least as much as the wonderful Coke, with which she showed her love*). "What's up with the other car, and presumably, people?"

"The Kovacs wanted to get together to talk about what's going on with Xander, and their house hasn't been released as a crime scene yet," she said. "So I volunteered our living room. It's just the Kovacs, now, but a few other people may come by in a bit (*her evasive tone and imprecise language told me that a significant number of people were definitely coming by in the near future*)."

"I bet Frank loves that," I said. "Not awkward at all for/between you and his work."

"Yah, he did have some choice words for me last night (*she knew about this last night, but just invited me this morning … interesting*)," Meg giggled. "His compromise was to take some comp time and change out of his uniform when he came home a couple of minutes ago."

"I guess that means there's been news of some sort about the murder/death/crime scene/evidence," I said. "It must be good, or at least mixed."

"It is," she said, and gave my shoulder an air-pat (*which was one of the conventions she had adopted/adapted over the years to make some middle ground between her need to touch, and my need not to be touched*). "Come on in, and I'll introduce you."

I walked into the living room with Meg, over to the couch, noting with some flutter of nerves the oval arrangement of nearly every available and borrowed sitting surface in the house (*comfy sofa, comfy chairs, all four of the kitchen table chairs from Meg and Frank's breakfast nook set, and three folding chairs which gave off a smell of cold and basement*).

The trio on the couch had to be the Kovacs: Darko at one end, Iskra in the middle, holding hands with a large young man at the other end whose face seemed—different than the others in the room. His eyes did not automatically search out mine for the empathic connection that most people seem eager to initiate with strangers, and the tiny tightening and shifting movements of facial muscles that are the precursors to smiles/frowns/questions weren't there either (*a small voice in the attic of my back-brain whispered that this must be similar to how people perceive a difference in me when we meet for the first time … although I have installed a series of compensatory strategies to make up for the basic software that is missing/ different within me*). They seemed to be sitting calmly, waiting, perhaps (*it occurred to me belatedly, perhaps stupidly, I'll blame nested layers of competing thoughts*) for me.

"Xander Kovac," Meg said, pointedly to the young man at the end of the couch. "This is my friend, Tyler Cunningham. He's a nice man who helped me arrange things so you could be here with Mommy and Daddy (*said in a nominative, not babying, tone*) this morning. He has a funny old dog that you might get to meet later if you want (*his eyes came alive some at this end of her statement, and he looked in my direction briefly*)."

His mother leaned in and in a loud whisper said, "Nice to meet you, Tyler."

"Nice to meet you, Tyler," Xander said in an affectless tone.

"Xander Kovac," I said, mimicking Meg's address, while also remembering similar modes of address from legions of specialists my parents had consulted through the years about me and my *social issues*, "It's good to meet you."

I didn't cross the room to offer my hand for a shake … certain that even if he didn't mind unnecessary human physical contact as much as I did, that he likely wouldn't take offense.

Meg began to talk to the Kovacs about the weather and fall and if they needed something to drink (*they didn't … had, in fact, full glasses of orange juice on the low coffee table in front of all three of them*). She has a gift for filling quiet spaces between and amongst people in a room … while I find it pointless most of the time, it did take the introductory spotlight off me, and allow me to watch/examine the Kovacs. Xander sat calmly next to his mother, not seeming to pay much attention to what was being said in the room, perhaps listening to Frank puttering in the kitchen. Xander's mother, Iskra kept reaching out for Xander's hand, as if to test and re-test the distance; she also cast numerous quick glances at me, my face, my eyes, and her lips moved as if wanting to form a smile or ask a question and then thinking better of it. Darko, Xander's father, was focused solely on Meg, palpably listening hard to every word she was saying (*and if he was listening hard enough for me to palp, then he must have been telegraphing his listening, as Dot would say*). My listening/analysis fell slightly behind the flow of the conversation in the room as I watched the family, trying to pull meaning from their looks and movements and how they held themselves, and Darko had to repeat himself before I forced my internal "tape-delay" to catch up.

"Thank you so much for what you've done for our son, Mr. Cunningham," he said. Meg must have mentioned my thoughts on the crime scene to them.

"You're welcome," I said. "I find crime scene analysis and technology to be fascinating." I could see Meg wince slightly at my (*I assumed*) insensitivity; I struggled to recover/redirect, "I'm sure the police would have gotten around to those ideas on their own." Meg smiled fractionally, which indicated to me that I must have undone some of my mess-take (*a term I'd coined as a boy of five, and hadn't thought about in twenty years … curious*).

"We're very grateful to have Xander out of that *place*," Iskra said. "We know a bit about you from … talk, and from Meg, of course, and hope you'll be able to find the time to help us as we move forward with all of this." She was seemingly comfortable with what I took to be a significant amount of missing conversational connective tissue … I looked at Meg, and caught her looking at her watch, and then smiling to herself, perhaps catching movement/arrivals through the window behind me that faced the driveway.

A number of car doors closed out by the street side of the Gibson house with varying levels of strength/speed/certitude, and I took this as an explanation for Meg's smile and a signal of the imminent arrival of the rest of the "few other people" for our talk (*whatever that meant in this instance/context*).

Frank went to answer the door, and I noted a remarkable (*since I just remarked on it*) change in all three Kovacs: Iskra and Darko both smiled and nodded over my shoulder at people coming in through the front door, and Xander stomped a foot and looked at the carpet between his feet while making fists with sufficient force to whiten all of his knuckles. I could hear Frank offering coffee or juice or soda, and some snacks as he walked the group of new arrivals back through the hallway to the kitchen, and could track the new people also by Iskra's slowly turning smiling face (*her face/smile pointed at the central mass of the noise coming from the group, even though they couldn't possibly see her … the made-up term 'sociotropic' popped into my head unbidden, along with an image of smiling/nodding sunflowers*) … all the while Xander seemed to get less and less comfortable, mumbling to himself, and once reaching out with a pinch-ready finger and thumb for his mother, but stopping himself when she whispered something to him. Meg and Iskra and Darko all noticed but dismissed his behavior/upset, so I assumed that it was a not-unusual social anxiety manifested in Xander's manner.

A minute later, Frank led a group of four people into the room, all with mugs or glasses, one with a thick slab of Meg's coffee cake (*which I would have enjoyed a slice of, but didn't ask for, not wanting to make waves or attract more notice in this setting/situation*). Behind Frank came a tall/bearded/friendly/outdoorsy guy halfway between Xander's age and mine (*he was the one carrying the coffee cake. Meg noted my noting this, and gave a minute negative shake of her head … suggesting that she had an agenda/schedule for this get-together, and didn't want my need for coffee cake to get in the way of things*). Then a stuffy/frumpy man in his late forties who had "social-services-something" written all over him, followed by a fit and fifty-looking Adirondack-suit of a guy (*who I pegged as the family lawyer*). Finally, a woman whose age and status and fit in the group I had no idea about (*having not seen them act/react with/to each other as yet*), but she seemed/felt different to me in her micro-interactions to Frank and Meg and the Kovacs and the living room setting (*lacking most social skills and grace myself, I nonetheless watch/study them closely in others, always hoping to learn/acquire/fake them*). Frank sat in one of the folding chairs by the door leading to the kitchen, and Meg took another of the folding chairs by the couch filled with Kovacs. She indicated the remaining folder to me, and I shook my head slightly, declining the offer in favor of standing/walking/fleeing (*as needed, based on how the next few minutes shaped up*).

"Now that everyone's here, let's get going," Meg said once it was clear that I wasn't going to sit. "Tyler, you know everyone here don't you?" I shook my head, firmly, once.

"Oh, okay then. Tyler Cunningham, meet *Team Xander*," she said, smiling at what must have been an inside joke, and then pointing her way around the room. "Darko and Iskra Kovac, Xander's parents. Xander, whom you have already met. Cameron Renard (*the tall/bearded/friendly/outdoorsy guy*), who is a job coach and community companion for Xander. Phil Macabee (*the social-services-something*) is Xander's service coordinator. Steve Street (*Adirondack suit*) is the Kovac family lawyer and counsel. Barb Gallagher (*the woman I couldn't place*) was Xander's lead teacher in his last few years in the Saranac Lake school system, and we've (*Meg indicated herself and the Kovacs*) asked her to come today because she knows Xander as well as anyone beside his parents, or maybe me. I worked with Xander and his sister and their parents as a counselor for the whole time that they were in the Saranac Lake School system. Iskra and I are also friends."

"Pleased to meet you, Tyler," said Phil, although he didn't sound or look pleased. "But, can I ask why you're here?" Phil took the lead without any hesitation or looks to seek permission from anyone in the group, which signaled to me that he had some form of the lead role in the *Team Xander* group/association.

I didn't speak, being unsure of my role (*or even my desire to have a role*) in *Team Xander*, and having found that a prudent silence trumps a hasty/apologetic/stupid answer any day of the week. Meg looked as though she was preparing to speak, when Darko answered.

"Tyler was able to work with the police to help them find some things which made it seem less like Xander hurt … his sister," Darko said, pausing at the end, possibly unable/unwilling to say Danica's name.

"It's because of Tyler's help that our Xander got out of that Pines place (*this seemed to be wildly stretching the point, but I couldn't see an upside to interrupting or disputing Iskra*) … nobody knew him there. They didn't know or care about his routines, his triggers … just meds and locked doors," Iskra said with a shudder and disgust, clear enough for me to pick up on, for the facility where they must have brought Xander for evaluation/observation after Danica's death. Iskra reached out to pat Xander's knee, and he shied away from her and made a low angry/dangerous/warning sound in his throat with a sly sideways look around the rest of the room … Cameron and Barb both adjusted themselves minutely in their chairs as if readying themselves, and then settled when Xander deflated/relaxed a second later.

"I'd like to be clear on an important point at this time," Frank said. "I'm not here today as a member of the SLPD, but as a friend of the family, and have, in fact, recused myself from any further professional involvement in this matter. Because of that, I will not be able to answer any questions about the inquiry or recent developments in that investigation."

"My understanding is that Mr. Cunningham was able to point the police forensics unit towards some possibly exculpatory evidence, which, while not definitive or positive, certainly suggested, at least to me, the strong possibility of at least one other person in the house at the time of the … incident," said the lawyer, Steve Street. "There was even, I believe some support of Xander's innocence in the form of evidence that could not be found by the police."

"Like the dog that didn't bark," said Cameron Renard.

"From that Holmes story," Phil Macabee said, "*The Hound of the Baskervilles.*"

"The curious incident of the dog that didn't bark was in 'Silver Blaze,' from a collection titled *The Memoirs of Sherlock Holmes*," I said, "not *The Hound of the Baskervilles*, a novel published eight years later, which involves a quite noisy ghostly/demonic hound." I could tell from the faces around the room (*save for Xander's, which didn't change*) that this was a mistake. As the words were leaving my mouth, a number of the heads cocked slightly to one side as the people in the room took another look at the interloping consulting detective, and … wondered.

"Regardless of which story it was in," Phil rode over my correction with a tone that managed to be conciliatory and dismissive and angry, all at once, "we're all very happy that Xander can be back with family and friends in his home community, as opposed to a lengthier stay at the facility attached to Whispering Pines."

My assumption (*which I would check, and have confirmed later by Frank*) was that the disposal and kitchen and dining room had yielded a mixed bag of evidence … Danica's phalanges (*or bits of them*) and bleach degraded blood evidence in the disposal, some atypical spatter in various places (*suggesting someone besides Xander and Danica in the house*), along with missing shears and bottle of bleach (*which the killer/killers must have taken with them*).

"I hate to rain on the parade we seem ready to hold here," said Cameron, "but Xander must have seen something, maybe everything, of what happened that day."

At this point, Xander made a series of low noises, and started to fidget on the couch, pulling a hand free from his mother's, and reaching slowly/deliberately over to pinch her, twice, up above the elbow.

"Now you've hurt Mommy," Iskra said, in a steady and clear tone, although I could see tears shining in her eyes. "Nice touches, Xander." He drew back the offending hand and cocked it as if to slap her, and then started to speak, both unintelligibly and loudly … the people in the room all shifted slightly, as if in preparation for an impending explosion/disaster. I needed to talk with these people in a while (*something that would be impossible if they sprang into physical restraint or retreat/flight modes*), and also to recoup from the Sherlock Holmes silliness (*although I was correct*), as well as to establish my bona fides and utility within this group if I wanted to get anything of use from them in the future … so I jumped in with both feet.

"Xander Kovac," I said in a clear and steady voice (*using his name at the beginning, as my parents and service providers had always done when I was younger, to insure they would help to focus my attention before they spoke to me … and as Meg had done a few minutes ago*), "would you like to meet my dog, Hope?"

Xander looked at a space in the air over my right shoulder as if the words were still there, and then in a voice entirely without affect, "Tyler Cunningham … nice dog."

"Xander, I like her, but she's not really a nice dog. She used to be very sad, and even though she lives with me now, she still remembers being sad," I said. "She's out in my car and would enjoy taking a walk with the two of us."

"Say yes please, Xander," Iskra prompted.

"Say yes please," Xander said, and stood up and walked towards me, taking a parabolic route through the room to maintain the maximum distance from everyone, except me or his parents.

"You folks have things to discuss while we go and meet Hope, but when we get back, I have some thoughts and questions and possibly a suggestion," I said, and then turned and walked out of the house, leading Xander to my Element.

I opened the door, slipped on her muzzle (*hoping that it would only be for a minute*), and lifted Hope down to the ground from the front passenger seat. Xander stood behind me, waiting, and after a moment's thought, I sat down on the grass in the shade under the big maple tree at the end of Frank and Meg's driveway; Xander sat too.

I patted a shirt pocket, pulled out a treat, and showed it to Hope, "Can you be nice for a treat if I take off the muzzle, Hope?"

She said nothing, for a variety of valid reasons, but scowled at me around the nylon muzzle … I had my doubts. I unhooked/unwound the muzzle anyway, switching the treat temporarily to the leash hand, and then had Hope do her one trick.

"Sit. Good girl, now shake," I said in slow and clear and loud tones. She had already been sitting, but it's a part of the routine; when she held up a paw for me to take/shake, Xander drew in a breath as if wildly impressed. I released her paw, grabbed the treat out of the leash hand, and gave it to Hope, who gobbled it down and looked to my hand, and then pocket, for more.

"Xander, do you want to try now?" I asked. He nodded his head solemnly and reached in my pocket for a treat.

"Okay," I said. "Xander, when you're ready to give her the treat, hold the treat in your hand, with your fingers all the way open … good."

He sniffed the treat, looked at Hope, and then nodded at me.

"Xander, tell Hope to sit, and then shake, and if she does, you can give her the treat." I wasn't worried about Hope biting Xander, so much as completely ignoring him.

"Hope to sit," Xander said, in that flat voice of his (*which is probably what mine used to sound like to people … and still does sometimes, especially on the phone, apparently*), "and then shake."

I tried to focus all of my attention on Hope at this

moment, willing her to comply … she didn't. She stood up, walked hesitantly towards Xander, and licked the treat from his outstretched hand. He hooted with what I chose to interpret as delight, at which she growled and ran to hide behind me while Xander reached for my pocket.

"Hope to sit and then shake," he said and reached forward with another treat, most of the way to her. She leaned slowly in and took the treat again, and sat down between my legs while Xander reached into my pocket again.

Three minutes later, I was out of treats, but Xander and Hope were both content and friendly-ish with each other. Xander had streamlined the trick/treat routine such that when he said "Hope to sit and then shake" she would simply take the treat from his hand without biting him (*although also without sitting or shaking*). Both parties were happy with the new arrangement.

"Okay, Xander, now we will take Hope for a walk on the leash," I said.

We all stood and I walked a few feet with Hope trailing at the end of the leash, and Xander walking a few steps behind her, watching the leash. Hope peed and then pooped and then seemed to perk up a bit, and look around, sniffing the air (*perhaps smelling Frank and Meg's dogs, Toby and Lola, both of whom she hated even smelling on my clothes after my visits … it wasn't even worth trying to get her to visit or play with them*). While she was distracted with threats beyond the immediate vicinity, I waved Xander closer.

"Xander, would you like to take Hope for a walk now?" I asked.

"Walk now," Xander said, which I took for agreement.

I slowly/gently took his hand away from the side of his body, put the loop from the leash around his wrist, and then ran the leash through his hand.

"Hold on to this end," I said, shaking the nylon in his hand for emphasis, "and walk slowly with her … she has little legs."

Xander started walking, taking tiny steps of his own and looking back at Hope to see if she was following … I walked a few steps behind Hope who kept craning her neck around to look at me, shocked (*perhaps*) that I was letting her be stolen from our happy home.

Together they walked to the edge of the woods, and when Xander started to push his way through the branches of shrubby maple saplings, I called out quietly.

"Xander, that was great," I said. "Let's take Hope back to my car and then we can go back inside and get a drink … do you like Coke?"

We repeated our slow parade walk back to the Element, at which point I took the leash loop off his wrist, lifted Hope back into the front seat, and unclipped the leash. I was pleasantly surprised that she seemed, at first blush, to dislike Xander less than other people she met … it might have been the treats, but I thought (*possibly I wanted to believe*) it might be something more (*although my mind suggested this thought, it didn't supply the next step to me, and I was content to leave it alone at present*). We went back inside and I could immediately hear that it was not a great time for us to re-enter the room, so I detoured to the kitchen first, making a lengthy production of washing hands, taking down glasses, finding and slowly pouring the yellow-cap Coke (*adding an ice-cube from the freezer to Xander's … I don't like ice, but he seemed to want some*), and then both sliding into/onto the bench part of the Gibsons' breakfast nook (*as all of the chairs were out in the living room*). All the while, I was talking with Xander about Hope and the walk and her wonderful trick, and how good Coke with real sugar is, but was also listening to the conversation fragments making it through to the kitchen from the living room.

The consensus seemed to be that Xander's program had to be drastically altered, at least in the short term, after the murder of his sister, Danica. Not everyone in the community (*or even in Frank and Meg's living room, it would appear*) understood/cared/believed the evidence that suggested another person's presence during Danica's murder; even among those who did, there was concern about how others in Saranac Lake would interpret or react to the murder and to Xander's presence at the scene of the crime, standing over her dead body with a bloody knife in his hand. The argument was made again and again that even given that (*or in some cases, if*) he was innocent, people in the village would deal with, and react to, him differently now. Xander, various people argued, was aware of people's moods/concerns, even if he were unable to express/explain them. Upset or nervous people would lead to an upset or nervous Xander, resulting in outbursts and tantrums. His jobs around the community (*which I inferred from the conversation involved volunteering at a number of stores and the library and a church and the local community college sports complex*) would therefore be put on hold until some degree of closure/certainty was available about Danica's death, and Xander's role in it. No agreement existed among the group in the living room as to what Xander would be doing, and where he would be doing it, until such time as the murder and mystery and cloud of uncertainty was resolved, although Cameron Renard raised an interesting suggestion. It was at this point that I headed Xander back into the room to see if we could come to some arrangement that worked well (*or at least better*) for everyone.

"Xander and I had a nice time with my grumpy old dog, Hope," I said. "We were just in the kitchen washing up and getting a drink … I hope that caffeine's okay (*I wondered belatedly*). He had a glass of Coke."

I looked around as I said this, paused at the living room threshold and noted that most of the others had grabbed drinks of one sort or another, and some had taken snacks from an assortment of bags and bowls that Meg must have set out … Frank looked as though he was content to drink a big mug of (*MY!*) Coke, and munch his way through a large bag of Doritos. The others around the room mostly looked as though they had taken drinks/snacks out of politeness, or to fill their hands (*both alien concepts to me, but my observation of people over the years indicates that they do this all the time*).

Xander's mother patted the couch next to her, and told him to come and sit by her; he made a low and growly noise in his throat/chest, and looked down at the ground. Iskra got up and crossed the room, and then she whispered something in his ear. He nodded while saying "yes" slightly too loudly in her ear.

Xander needs the bathroom," Iskra said, "but probably didn't go or say anything because he's only been here once before and doesn't remember where the bathroom is. Meg?"

"Go back through the kitchen door, turn right, and it's the first door on your right," Meg said.

Xander and his mother went through the door into the kitchen, and a few seconds later I could hear the door to the bathroom open and then close … this seemed like a good time to jump in with my meddling.

"I couldn't help overhearing some of your discussion about the jobs and Xander's program," I said, "and then at the end, Mr. Renard's idea."

"Call me Cam," he said.

"Cam's idea got me thinking," I said. "I have a couple of ideas/thoughts that might seem a bit bizarre at first."

"Tell me something I don't know," Frank muttered too loudly for it to be accurately referred to as being under his breath.

"Human bone dust reportedly smells exactly like those Cool Ranch Doritos," I said, watching Frank look up at me, turning the bag in his hands around to look at it, glaring at me, and then putting the bag in the wastebasket by his seat.

"Now," Frank said, still glaring, "why don't you tell us why Cam's idea got you thinking, and what it got you thinking about that 'might seem bizarre at first.'"

"I heard Cam mention that he had been planning a paddle-trip with Xander for later this month, and that it occurred to him that it might be a good idea to move it up," I said. "It sounds like a good idea to me for a number of reasons."

"I can't really imagine how you're qualified to participate in this meeting," Phil said. "Although I'm sure we're all very grateful to you for helping the police and Xander. How could freezing or getting lost in the woods possibly help Xander or the Kovacs?"

"He's been camping before," Cam spoke up. "He had a good time. Xander can paddle his kayak very well on flat water, and has all the gear and clothes that he needs for a trip at this time of year. It's so nice out in the woods now that most of the tourists are leaving (*I nodded agreement, and irrationally ruled out Cam as a suspect in Danica's murder, knowing nothing about him except that he liked camping in September in the Adirondacks … which was enough for me*)."

"As I said," I jumped in before anyone else could

speak, "I overheard some of the back and forth while Xander and I were in the other room, and think that the trip could be just the break/pause that his jobs and community outreach visits need. A little bit of time to let people get the talk and worry out of their systems, and to let the news about the new police findings filter through the community."

"And?" Frank said, with a knowing, half worried, half amused look on his face. "What's the bizarre idea you have, Tyler?"

"Well," I answered. "There are a couple of nested thoughts and ideas, relating to Cam's plan to move up the paddle/camping trip. First, I'd like to propose that I go along with Cam and Xander."

This caused a few raised eyebrows, not least Meg's, because (*presumably*) I'd told her so forcefully a few days ago, that I wasn't interested in this sort of investigation, and particularly not one that raised the specter of my "difference" so volubly.

"A trip like this would get Xander out of town and away from the fishbowl that we all live in, here in the Tri-Lakes," I said. "I also think it might give Xander and me the chance to get to know each other better, so that I can help him work out how to talk about who it was that killed his sister, so that we can catch the person and fully clear Xander (*if indeed, he should be cleared, I thought, but did not say … I didn't see how it could help the case that I was trying to make*)."

After a momentary silence, everyone started talking at once. I finished my Coke and went back into the kitchen for more while they nattered at each other, nearly bumping into Xander and Iskra, who were pouring themselves still more of my yellow-cap Coke (*I hoped Meg had not been exaggerating when she said that she had filled the trunk of their car with the stuff during their college visits last spring*).

"Hope to sit," Xander said, "and then shake."

"He likes you," Iskra said, "and your dog. What's all the noise about?" She made a point of looking from me to Xander, most likely signaling something (*which I missed/ignored*).

"I like Cam's idea of moving up the dates of the camping trip, and I suggested that I go along on the trip to get to know Xander a little better, and maybe even help him figure out who (*her eyes bugged out at this point in my statement, and I reigned in my word choice a bit*) ... hurt Danica, or maybe just how to talk about what happened."

"I don't know," she said, "getting to know Xander is tricky, and out in the woods, there's so much that can go wrong."

"Camping with Daddy and Dani," Xander said in a loud, flat voice, grabbing his mother's arm firmly, but not pinching.

"I know, dear," she said to Xander, and then turning to me. "He's always loved camping with his father and ... sister. They all look forward to these trips, but this year, Darko, Xander's father, is still recovering from surgery to repair his shoulder, so it was gonna only be Cam and Dani and Xander."

"Camping with Daddy and Markus," Xander said.

"That's right, dear," she said, starting to face him, but turning to include me also. "One year Dani was away with friends, and another friend of the family went along instead, and they had a wonderful time."

Something about this stilted conversation was tickling my back-brain, and I filed it away for re-examination later.

"I'm an experienced paddler and camper, ma'am (*my*

experience has been that ma'am-ing some people will open doors that nothing else will)," I said. "I think that if I could have some time with Xander, to let him get to know me, and vice versa, that I might be able to help the police some more with their investigations."

"We got here before everyone else," Iskra said, "an' talked with Frank and Meg about how you 'thought' our boy out of that place up in Malone, that Whispering Trees place (*Whispering Pines I thought, but kept my silence*). I heard about that evil what happened out on Upper Saranac last summer, but didn't connect it with you until this morning, when Meg told us about you."

"In addition to the camping trip, it would be great if I could get a chance to talk with you and Darko again, as well as the other four members of *Team Xander* that I met this morning," I said.

"Why?" she asked. "What could you hope to find out from talkin' with them that the police couldn't get to in their way?"

"I see things, and think a little differently than most people, and it sometimes helps to have a different perspective," I said, nervously/uncomfortably, feeling that I was exposing too much of me to this woman for reasons I didn't understand.

"Different is good," she said. "The world is filled with people who think the same and do the same as everyone else." She nodded to herself, about something, and went out into the living room, dragging Xander and me behind her.

"Mr. Cunningham will be going camping with Cam and Xander, and they're going to leave on Thursday," she said in a tone that sounded entirely certain, although I didn't see how she could be. "Also, I would consider it a personal favor if everybody in this room would make themselves available to Tyler to talk about Xander and Dani and Darko and I (*me, I silently corrected, wondering why I still did this*) either this afternoon or tomorrow. I'm going to take Xander back to the hotel now, for a swim," she continued. "Xander, does that sound like fun … a swim in the pool?"

She didn't wait for his answer, or an answer, or discussion from the room … she turned, letting go of my hand and holding onto Xander's, and walked right out.

Again, silence filled the room for a few seconds, and then an eruption of talking from every corner. I handed Cam and Phil and Barb and Steve each one of my cards (*with phone and email contact info*), waved/nodded at Darko, and smiled/shrugged at Meg and Frank, and walked out of the house, intent on going for a swim myself (*I didn't have a hotel pool to swim in, but Little Green Pond, out behind the fish hatchery in Lake Clear, was a nice as any pool I'd ever been in, and Hope could come in with me … which most hotels seem to frown upon*). Meg rushed out after me, filled with questions and apologies and questions and busy-ness and questions and worries … I just told her not to worry about anything, that I'd be back at SmartPig later, and she could get in touch with me via phone or email, up until I left on the trip Thursday morning.

"Tyler," she whined as it became clear to her that I was actually leaving. "You can't just drop bombs like that and leave. We've got to talk about what this means to Xander's program, to Xander. I'm not sure you understand what you're getting yourself into. That boy isn't a library that you can just sift through once you get back in the woods."

"With regards to that noise going on in there, there's an old Polish saying, '*Nie mój cyrk, nie moje małpy,*'" I said. "Which translates to, 'not my circus, not my monkeys,' and I have almost never been in a situation where it applied more than that mess in there that Phil seems to think he's running. Cam will call me within two hours, and I'll get a concise 'Xander in a nutshell' tutorial from him … the others I'll connect with later today or tomorrow, and then learn as I go … I'm not exactly unacquainted with autism, you know. On your third point, you couldn't be more wrong … Xander is precisely analogous to a library, only he's a library with an unknown filing system, and in a foreign language. Luckily, I'm the smartest person you know, so I'll be able figure it out as we go."

She shook her head, working to avoid smiling. "Fine, smart guy, make sure you all come back in one piece when this is over."

"I promise we'll all come back just fine," I answered. "We'll have some fun in the woods, I'll figure out how to interface with Xander's system easily and clearly/cleanly, and Danica's killer won't know a thing about what's going on until they're safely behind bars."

The truth is that I often am the smartest guy in the room (*quite often by a disturbing/disheartening margin*), but in this case was substantially overestimating my intelligence/abilities/stealth, as I was wrong on every single point of the promise that I had made to Meg.

St. Regis Canoe Outfitters, Saranac Lake, NY,
Tuesday, 9/2/2014, 2:41 p.m.

Hope and I left, looped out of town and to Little Green for a dive and dash, then Element-ed back into Saranac Lake, stopping by the remaining Chinese place in Saranac Lake (*which was thankfully, the Good Chinese place, assuming you didn't count the Asian Buffet on the way out of town towards Lake Placid, which I didn't, as they didn't do special orders or let me watch them cook or pretend not to see my aging/grumpy beagle when we occasionally both came in, as the Good Chinese place does*) to pick up some spicy/fatty goodness while we planned and waited and thought and watched a variety of shows via Roku. Some thought was begging to climb out of the dark waters of my brain, but kept disappearing as soon as I would try to grab at it … I let it go, assuming/hoping that it would emerge when it was ready (*as they tend to, most likely/often during a nap*).

Cam Renard called eighty-nine minutes after we left Meg's driveway (*well within the predicted timeframe, and more interestingly, eighty-nine is a Fibonacci Prime, a Pythagorean Prime, and the smallest Sophie Germain Prime to start a Cunningham chain of six terms … I have a familial fondness for the Cunningham chains*), just after we'd finished squeegee-ing the last of the food from our plates.

Cam and I talked first about Xander's daily and camping routines, his likes, his dislikes, what sorts of things upset him and/or brought on outbursts, what routines/devices/techniques/props could be used to defuse him when upset or in the middle of an outburst. With Cam in the driver's seat, I had no significant concerns about the camping trip with Xander. When the talk moved on to the trip itself, he suggested that we meet at St. Regis Canoe Outfitters (SRCO) (*a local outfitter, famed for their gear and guides and trip planning help*) for some face to face planning time while standing over the maps. I agreed, left Hope to sleep off her heavy lunch, and walked down the hill and across the river to the SRCO offices in town (*as opposed to the location they maintain out on the Floodwood Road*).

"Tyler," he said, shaking my hand and then clapping me on the back vigorously when I walked in and found him looking at the big map of the Adirondack canoe waters, "thanks."

"For what?" I asked.

"For coming down, but also, and more, for the stuff with Xander, for pushing for this trip. It'll be good for Xander, but it might not be easy the whole time, if you know what I mean."

"I don't," I said. "What do you mean?"

He looked up from the map at me as though I had said something funny, and then quickly adjusted his face to a more neutral position, "I mean that he loved Dani like nobody else on Earth, and she's just gone. Izzy is Mommy and Darko is Daddy, but Dani was special to him, to everyone."

"To someone, she was un-special enough that they were able to gut her and snip off her fingertips afterward with kitchen shears," I said, using my insensitivity in the way that Dot insists can force people to reveal what they're thinking.

He paled, then reddened, then thought about what

I'd said and started to make sounds and motions similar to what Hope does when she's about to throw up … I took a generous step back.

When he recovered slowly, he grabbed my shirt front and said in slow and angry tones, "Tyler Cunningham, if you ever disrespect her, what happened to her, or her memory, within my hearing again, I'll break your nose for you. Do you understand?"

I nodded slowly and mentally pencil-crossed him off the suspects list … his autonomic responses and shock weren't likely faked, nor did his anger seem it (*a part of me wondered if he was aware of how he'd addressed me prior to his threat … I thought not, and filed that way for future ruminations*). Cam seemed to come to a slow awareness of something about himself, or me, or both, and let go of my shirt front, smoothing it briefly before taking a deliberate step back.

"I'll tell you what though, Tyler," Cam said, "whoever did it knew her well enough to get into the house when Dani was alone there with Xander, and also knew that whatever Xander saw, he wouldn't be able to talk about it, or they woulda killed him too. It's someone in the Kovacs' friends and family circle (*I assumed here that he wasn't talking about cell phone plans, and then wondered at myself for digressing enough to bother using brain-bandwidth for that flavor of nonsense*)."

"Yes," I agreed. "But, they were still taking a chance leaving a witness behind … a decision they may regret/reconsider over the next few days. The family should probably be safe at the Best Western (*I imagined the police would keep a car on-hand or make regular drive-bys at the least*), but it's possible the killer might make a run at him/them."

Cam absorbed my words, nodded dully, and then got

there on his own, "So, there may be some danger involved in heading into the woods with Xander, being away from public and crowded places."

"Sure, in theory," I said, trying to inject a gently scoffing, but reassuring, tone into my voice (*which mood I felt, but wouldn't have gone into my words unless I tried to put it there … so I did*), "but most people living in the Adirondacks never get more than a hundred yards away from their car or a paved road, much less into the backcountry via paddle and portage. The odds are that the police will catch whoever did it through their usual methods (*simple/stupid brute-force attack using gazillions of man-hours in place of skill or thought or blind luck, but I didn't say that*), but even if they don't we'll hear the killer (*or killers, I thought, but again didn't say, suspecting that it wouldn't reassure Cam*) coming a mile away, and lose them in the woods."

"Are you certain?" Cam asked.

"Yessir," I answered, "this isn't my first … sensitive case. I've worked, over the years to establish a balance between risk and safety and reward, like you do when camping (*this not-so-subtle re-direct seemed to work, and I could see his eyes drift back down to the table and maps and his mind refocus on the camping trip*)."

We talked about gear and routes and spots to camp and side trips and swimming/fishing spots and generally got enough of a feel for each other as outdoorsmen (*I have no idea what Cam gleaned from our conversation, but by the end of it, I was comfortable with his knowledge of the woods and waters in the area, with his ability and comfort-level with the gear that we'd be using, and confident that he had sufficient experience in the woods … and in the woods with a young man with autism*) to feel assured that the trip would be safe and fun for everyone involved. After looking at various maps and trip options we eventually decided/agreed on a modified version of The Nine Carries route, which would take us back into the St. Regis Canoe Area, into some delightfully wild country.

"You just bring your own gear, minus food and cook set, which Darko takes care of," Cam said. "Meet us at the put-in for Hoel Pond, Thursday morning at eight, already breakfasted, and we'll have a fun time in the woods. Xander's pretty awesome, once you get to know him. Can't promise you'll figure out how to pry shit out of him about what happened with Dani, though. He can close up about bad things in his life like nobody's business. He, what's the term, compartmentalizes, like a son of a bitch. He's like Al Gore's famous 'locked box,' from when I was in college (*the term and pantomimed gestures made Cam older than I had originally guessed*)."

"I'll see you there Thursday morning, ready to be *paddle wet* for eight," I said. "If I can talk with Xander about what happened after he gets to know/trust me, then great, but if not, we'll just spend a couple of days paddling in the backcountry, and then come home and let the cops chew on it until they work it out (*I was certain that Mrs. Portnoy, who had been strangely in my head a lot of late, would be proud of my increased usage of figurative language*)."

SmartPig Offices, Saranac Lake, NY,
Tuesday, 9/2/2014, 3:58 p.m.

I walked home thinking about the trip and started making lists while I took out the still sleepy Hope for a walk. Despite Cam's plan to provide for all of my food needs, I needed to bring kibble for Hope (*yes, we had talked it over, and decided that she would be coming along on this trip, as I had decided not to miss any more warm-weather camping time with her than was absolutely necessary*). I mixed up a new batch of Tyler-Kibble (*almonds, pistachios, blueberries, mangoes, dark chocolate M&Ms, and beef jerky*) and Ziploc-bagged twelve portions for each of the two of us (*three meals a day for four days, more than was needed, but it doesn't weigh much or take up a lot of room, and ending up with extra is way better than running out*). Our planned four-day route would be a difficult traverse of nineteen or twenty ponds and lakes, with a similar number of portages (*depending partly on choices we might make along the way, we could add or subtract both numbers and difficulty to/from our route as needed/desired*). So, my planning and packing and organization tended towards lightweight gear arranged such that I could carry all of it, along with my boat in one crossing at each carry. I had purchased a pack for Hope when she first came to live with me, but she whined and complained so much on our first outing with it, that I had given it to Dorothy to distribute to someone with a less whiny dog. I would be carrying everything for Hope on this trip, and had some concerns that I might end up carrying her if the going got too tough on some of the longer portages.

Messages had arrived from the other three members of *Team Xander* when I got around to checking after my initial burst of trip-related activity: two phone messages (*I must have silenced my phone when plugging it into the charger, and ignored it while kibble-making*) from Barb Gallagher and Phil Macabee, both saying that they could stop in at some point during the afternoon, and an email from Steve Street asking me to come by his office in town sometime in the next day or two. I returned both phone calls, and they each said that they'd be by within the hour … I was willing to take a chance on the timing working out for my talks with both of them, so didn't set specific times with either (*noting, as I did this, that a year ago, I would have anguished over this level of chaos, and wondering what, if anything, it meant*). I figured that I would catch up with Steve Street at some point … if not today, then tomorrow, and then went back to thinking about the trip, happily (*or as close an approximation to happily as I render*).

My one concession to bringing along heavier gear on this trip than was absolutely necessary was for my technology-related gear. My iPhone (*a used iPhone 4s glommed onto a cheap Tracfone account/number … an odd marriage that worked for me*) was loaded with maps and map/compass apps for me … and games and audiobooks and movies and TV shows for Xander (*thanks to some recommendations from Cam during the course of our earlier conversation*). I had recently purchased, and only now placed my iPhone in an armored and waterproof case, that should help it to survive all manner of abuse during the trip. Both solar chargers went into my portage pack (*heavy though they were, with integrated batteries and fold-out solar panels*), so I could alternate and always have at least one of them fully charged (*assuming a reasonable amount of sun during our trip, which looked reasonable to assume, based on my preferred weather app*). My Kindle Paperwhite fully loaded/charged and in a Ziploc bag also went in the pack as insurance (*its ability to hold over a thousand books, and run for weeks at a time between charges would make waiting my way through the delays that were inevitable when traveling with others manageable, or at least less maddening*). I also packed more headlamps/batteries than I could possibly need, as few people ever got to the far side of lengthy backcountry camping trip (*even one without the possibility for complications*) wishing that they had brought along less ability to light the darkness.

A knock and call of hello from Barb Gallagher through my door derailed my thought process, and I opened the door to invite her in. She looked around with more than a simply curious eye, and I intuited that she'd gotten some background on me from Meg.

"Tyler, Meg says this office is as much of a home as you've got (*or need, I thought, but didn't say*)," Barb said. "I don't see a bed."

"Most nights I sleep outside, camping in one of my hammocks," I said in answer. "When I don't, the couch is more than long and comfy enough for me."

"Okay," she said, seeming to cross something off a list in her head. "So what can I do for you?"

"Tell me about your relationship with Xander and Dani and the Kovacs, and why you killed her and chopped off her fingertips," I said.

Barb laughed, then looked shocked at herself, then laughed again. "Ya got me."

When I didn't reply or laugh or say anything (*which Dot has frequently told me is my best strategy as a consulting detective over the years*), she followed up with, "I didn't kill her, Tyler."

"Why not?" I asked.

"I didn't even know her enough to like or dislike her," she said. "She just happened to be the sister of one of my students."

"Okay," I said, moving on (*which seemed to surprise, possibly even disappoint, her*). "Then tell me about Xander." She joined me at my work/kitchen table and pulled out one of the seats to sit in.

"Ordinarily I wouldn't say a word about one of my kids to a stranger," she said, "but a parent asked me to, and Meg seems to think inordinately highly of you (*I assumed that she was using 'inordinately' incorrectly, as most people do, and just nodded, hoping to encourage her to continue*)."

"He's a young man with autism," she said, assuming the mantle/tone/cadence of edu-speak. "He was educated in our district until the end of the school year in his twenty-first year. He has trouble with expressive communication of all sorts, particularly written. His receptive language skills and abilities are unclear, as he's difficult to assess using standard measures. He is physically healthy and robust, having had nearly perfect attendance for the last three years of his high school career (*at this point I was picturing the New York State IEP, Individualized Education Program, which she was following, section for section, in her reportage*). Xander has, as would be expected, a high degree of difficulty with social interactions with adults and peers in his age-cadre due to issues in both verbal and non-verbal communication. Other problems exist with repetitive behaviors and outbursts, most particularly when routines are upset and/or change is introduced into his life (*this was sounding not unlike me, I couldn't help noting*)."

"Tell me about his outbursts," I said, cutting her off before she delivered the entire document orally. "How they compare with, or vary from, what I saw this morning at Meg's house."

"This morning was typical of a minor outburst for Xander," she said. "There were some noticeable precursors, and then he lashed out. In the years that I have worked with him, I have seen a number of similar outbursts, generally with some indications, or warning signs, beforehand, and varying in intensity from less than that, with poking, to much more significant hitting or punching."

"Does he always use his hands?" I asked, "Never a notebook or a pencil or scissors?"

"Good question," she said (*her smile at, and understanding of, where I was going took her most of the way off my list of suspects, if she'd been on there after my initial gambit*). "He has only used his hands since I've known him, but apparently when he was young, he occasionally would bite. To the best of my knowledge, which is pretty extensive when it comes to Xander, he has never used a foreign object during an outburst. I distinctly remember him dropping a pencil one time, and a pair of scissors another time, during an outburst in order to pinch or slap a person. I don't think that using a weapon (*other than his hands, I mentally corrected*) is in Xander's wheelhouse. Do you savvy wheelhouse?"

"Yes," I answered and thought some privacy concerns in Meg's direction. "I understand all sorts of things."

"I'm sure you do," she said, "and if you don't mind (*which almost always precedes something I will/ do mind*), can I ask you …"

I was spared from whatever she was going to ask me by an authoritative sounding knock, followed half a second later by an authoritative looking Phil Macabee.

"Sorry to interrupt, folks," he said, although he didn't look sorry (*and I wasn't at all sorry for the interruption, and didn't care if Barb was sorry, so it didn't matter whether or not he truly was*). "Hello, Barb."

"Hello, Phil," she said in a tone that even I could decipher as unfriendly. "Tyler, nice to talk with you. I hope you got what you needed. If not, please give me a call or send me an email, but it's going to be tricky to connect again as the school year's about to start." As she said this, she picked up her bag, took one more slowly spinning look around the SmartPig office, and left.

"Nice place," Phil said, sitting down on the couch, "just moved in?"

"No," I answered, "I've been here almost twelve years, why?"

"Well, there's not much of you here, is there?" he said. "Besides the crap-pile by the closet (*he waved at my camping gear, in process*), it looks like a hotel room."

"Okay," I said, not knowing where to go with that conversation (*and not caring to explore it further at any rate*). "Tell me about your relationship with Xander and Dani and the Kovacs, and why you killed her and chopped off her fingertips."

He grew red, and started to speak twice before he found the words, "What did that cunt, Gallagher say? I never touched Dani Kovac, never had any improper contact with her, and anyone who says otherwise is a fucking liar!"

"Barb didn't say a thing about you to me, or anyone else, as far as I know," I said, "but I have to say that I'm kind of interested in why you might think that she would."

"She one time got the crazy idea that I was making a pass at her," he said, flipping what looked to be a wedding band like a coin before catching it in his right hand and then slipping it back on his left ring finger, "and I figured she mighta thought the same thing happened with Dani."

"Did it?" I asked.

"Christ no, she's the daughter and sister of clients of mine," he said (*not using, I noticed, the past tense*), "although she was fine."

"Her degree of fineness aside," I continued, "tell me about your relationship with your client (*using his term*) and his parents."

"The state's been involved with Xander's welfare since he was diagnosed a bit after his third birthday," he said. "We provide care and guidance and a variety of forms of assistance (*this sounded like it was evolving into a rehearsed speech*)."

"How much of this assistance has been, or is, financial?"

"Lots of it boils down to money from the state to help Xander, and his family," he said.

"But that was when Xander was considered a minor," I said, "what changed when Xander completed high school, and was Dani involved?"

"Why would you want to know that?" he asked.

"Because if it hasn't and she's not, you're boring and probably not helpful in my investigation (*or a suspect … and also, I thought, thanks to the librarians living in the back of my skull who'd read thousands of mysteries over the year, as well as articles about state agencies and their involvement in the welfare of minors and adults with disabilities, because I wanted to keep jostling you about what seems to be an uncomfortable subject for you*). But, I'm guessing that it has, and she was, so you should just tell me."

I said this last bit without thinking it out overmuch,

and could see him getting red-faced and angry again, so I softened the blow by getting up and walking over to my Coke-fridge to get a double-handful of Canadian Cokes for us to share … I opened two and slid one in front of him.

"Once he got out of high school, he got more money from the state, and his family got more control of it," he said, taking a long swallow of the Coke, starting to talk again, doing a double take, and then speaking, "Holy crap. That's good, but I think it's gonna give me a cold-headache."

"Yes," I said. "They're from Canada, made using real sugar, and I chill them to slightly below the freezing temperature of water in my fridge (*I switched gears, as he already was growing bored with my Coke*) … so tell me why the Kovacs getting more control of the fund from the state affects you, and why it involved Dani?"

"Being the service manager for a kid like Xander involves significant money moving around the board," he said. "Some of those funds are available to whoever controls the purse strings, strictly legitimate ways on my end (*it has been my experience that people who start defending themselves prior to an accusation are normally guilty of something … even if it's just thought crime*). But, I admit that I was concerned that if Dani and her parents took control of the money, it might get tricky with some of their service providers."

"So," I supplied, to move us along past the awkward spot that he had painted himself into, "you're saying that a less scrupulous service provider could find ways to siphon off money that should be spent on services and/or things for Xander, and you were trying to protect Dani and the Kovacs from that happening?"

"Yup," Phil said, "that's it exactly."

"And you never made inappropriate or unwanted advances towards Dani?" I added.

"Wait, what?" he said, and then downed the rest of his Coke (*possibly to delay having to answer*) then he reached for his forehead when the cold got to him. "I told her she looked nice a couple times, and she did, but never … nothing beyond that, I swear. Listen, Tyler, is there anything else? Because I really am quite busy at this time of year, with the school year starting and all."

"Thank you for your help, and I'll get in touch with you by email or phone if I need anything else," I said as I walked him out, locking the door behind him as he went down the stairs.

I got an odd feeling from Phil, about both sex and money (*which my lifetime of reading mysteries would seem to indicate are at the root of most killings*), and his relationship with them both seemed unhealthy (*or at least unseemly, but who was I to judge … I didn't really understand either, having no desire for the former and a superabundance of the latter*). I looked over at Hope, but she was no help … neither did she seem to need a walk, so I decided to head out and try my luck at catching Steve Street in his office. That way I could be done with my interviews and let the minions in my back-brain do their thing (*whatever it was/is*).

Walking down the hill behind the SmartPig offices and across the bridge to Dorsey Street to where the family's lawyer had indicated was his place of business (*a quiet brick building on a quiet street, which seemed apt for an Adirondack lawyer*), I could see Steve Street was in his upstairs office. And I was momentarily surprised by the locked door at the street level entrance to his business … Meg and Dot and most of the other (*few*) people that I know in the Adirondacks never lock their houses, offices, or cars. I made a microsecond judgment/conclusion-leap that he was guilty before I remembered that I assiduously locked all of the doors in my life (*and hadn't killed Dani Kovac*). Everybody, Mickey often reminded me, has secrets, and they all protect and feel about them differently than everyone else. Lawyers are, after all, paid by people to make and guard secrets. I poked the buzzer, and waited for only thirteen seconds before he came down the stairs with a smile and ushered me in and up and into a comfy chair in front of the broad and messy desk he settled down behind (*I trust a messy desk for reasons that escape, but continue to convince, me*).

"Tyler," he said, "what can I do for you?"

"Tell me about your relationship with Xander and Dani and the Kovacs, and why you killed her and chopped off her fingertips," I said, trying for the same words/feeling that I'd put into the other times I'd used it this afternoon.

He looked at me for a few seconds without any expression on his face before responding, "I take it that hasn't garnered you a confession with any of the others, or am I the first you've tried it on?"

"That's not an answer to either of my questions, Mr. Street," I said, "I'm trying to help the Kovacs find some answers, and maybe get some closure (*I have no idea what that means, but I'd heard Meg say it in numerous similar situations … it's possible nobody knows what it means, but it seems to placate, or at least quiet, them*)."

"Is that how you do it then?" he asked. "Detecting? Is it just a series of outrageous questions, and then waiting for answers? Seems a bit like chucking darts at a board while blindfolded, no offense (*something people seem to say adjacent to something offensive, in my experience*)."

"The blacktailed red sheetweaver is a tiny spider in the family Linyphiidae," I said, speaking more to observe his reaction to my hosing him down with seemingly pointless science than to explain myself or my existence (*which seemed like a waste of time, regardless of whether or not he was a murderer*). "Sheetweavers make a horizontal sheet-web upon which they wait for their prey, which fall down onto the web after running into the tangle of stopping threads up above."

He sat across from me, looking slightly bored, but willing for me to continue (*my ability to read human emotions has been improving in recent years, although I still don't trust my interpretations enough to utter them outside my brain*), so I did.

"I have found through the years," I said, " that if I put stopping threads out there, people will eventually trip over them and fall into my web … that's a metaphor."

"Yah," he said. "I got that. Let me start with your second question first. I didn't kill young Dani, nor did I chop off her fingertips. I assume the killer did so based on worries that their DNA was under her fingernails. The answer to your first question is less titillating and more complex; let me give you a précis, and then you can redirect as needed. Does that sound acceptable?"

"Perfectly," I said.

"I first became acquainted with the Kovacs when Darko and Iskra wanted to open a restaurant twenty-five years ago. They came to me for legal advice and services. I have been their lawyer for all matters of business and family since then," he said, took a deep breath, and continued. "I have helped them through various business and family matters in the intervening years, most recently some trust and estate matters revolving around their children's future with regards to the non-insubstantial assets that the Kovacs have built through the years."

"Complex issues nested within all of that, given Xander's lifelong need for some level of support," I said, hoping to keep him talking and get more of a feel for him.

"Quite," he said. "There are significant holdings in trust for both him and Danica, and with her death, the structures of support and maintenance become even more byzantine."

"Byzantine structures of support and maintenance are the waters that lawyers swim in," I countered. "It sounds as though Dani's death might help you keep busy, and generate more billable hours."

"Watched *The Firm*, have you?" he said. "Yes, it will keep me busy … busier than I want to be. I'm a small town lawyer. I do lots of taxes and wills and probates and real estate closings. I take off mornings and afternoons in the appropriate seasons to go hunting and fishing. That's not a Lexus parked outside, (*he waved out the window towards Dorsey Street where I remembered a green Subaru, sporting a roof rack with canoe brackets, which seemed more sensible than a Lexus for the Tri-Lakes*) Tyler. I make good, but reasonably small, money. It is appropriate and adequate for my chosen lifestyle, and I like things simple. The simple and boring truth is that there would have been no reason for me to kill Danica Kovac because I didn't, and don't, stand to gain anything I want or need from her death. Exactly the opposite, as a matter of fact. Danica's death messes things up for me. Because of my longstanding affiliation with the Kovacs, I need to help them work through this crisis, my help will all be related to paperwork, and all of it ten times more busywork than the rest of my practice combined. Fixing this is going to occupy almost all my time for at least the next month."

This made some sense to me, and I paused momentarily, played the mental tape back and forth over the last couple of minutes for a look or hesitation or word out of place, and could find none; it was annoying. I had eliminated my four top suspects, and would likely have to broaden the scope of my investigations (*and sheet-web*). I told Steve that I had a paper to look at and other people to talk with (*not really sure if I did/wanted to, but also being predisposed to not giving up*). He nodded and grunted and settled back into working on some papers so he didn't look up as I let myself out of his offices.

The Whiteface Lodge, Saranac Lake, NY,
Tuesday, 9/2/2014, 7:18 p.m.

At twenty-three minutes past four, after noodling with piles of gear and packing/re-packing for a while, Mickey called and invited me to join everyone for a swim in the pool at the Whiteface Lodge, and an early supper (*Mickey has worked early/long days for so long that he has adjusted his body to always wake before dawn, and is ready for bed by nine … so early suppers are a way of life in/with his family*). I dashed outside with Hope for another quick walk, changed into my swimsuit, grabbed a set of mostly clean clothes to change into for supper (*laundry in my world is mostly somewhere along a continuum, lots of shades of grey, and very little of it that is absolutely clean or filthy dirty … like most things in life*), bid Hope a good nap, and pointed my Element in the direction of the fancy pool at the Whiteface Lodge.

Midway to Lake Placid, my phone rang, and certain that it would be Mickey, I reached over to the passenger seat and flipped the switch to accept the call … I know it's illegal, but those (*and most other*) rules only apply to me when/if I get caught breaking them, and in this case I didn't.

"Mr. Cunningham. You need to stop what you are doing for the Kovac family," a computer generated voice said. "Sticking your nose where it does not belong will result in people getting hurt. There has been too much violence already, nobody wants more. Tell the Kovacs 'no,' and find someplace else to be for the next week. You have a cute dog, but it seemed to be limping this afternoon when you were walking it down by the river."

My mind was racing, chewing over the data the caller had given me in the initial seconds of the call, but not returning any answers or plans of action. I passed a mountainously huge hitchhiker at the railroad tracks which I mark as the outer edge of Saranac Lake (*on my internal/personal map*) when driving out of town towards Lake Placid, and it didn't occur to me until after the call terminated that it was Barry, my personal ghost, whose hauntings had been absent for nearly six months.

"Who are you, why keep your identity confidential?" I asked, "Why were you watching me and my dog this afternoon?"

I was interested as much in the manner and time delay of the response as I was in the response itself. While listening closer, I could hear a dull click of the call being muted, and a twenty-three second delay before the same computer-generated voice came back again.

"I obviously wish to remain anonymous (*he/she used the correct term, despite my suggesting 'confidential'*) for my own reasons," the voice said. "I was watching you to get a feel for the kind of person you are, never having met you before (*which seemed possibly to be trying to jam our never having met down my throat a bit too hard*)." The muting came on again, another pause, and then, before I could speak, the voice continued, "I hope you will be smart enough to heed my warning and leave this whole affair with the Kovacs alone, for everyone's sake." The connection broke before I could ask anything else.

My first thought was bringing my phone over to Frank Gibson's house, to let the police see what they could find about the number that had called me, but I almost immediately dismissed the idea. There had been nothing directly threatening about the call (*although it was a bit creepy and menacing*), and given the fast turnaround time on their surveillance/call/responses, I was willing to bet that this person was smart enough to use a burner phone for the call. I also rejected the idea of involving (*or trying to involve*) Frank and/or other police because it would draw attention to myself, and possibly anger the caller, which I did not need … yet.

I dropped the phone into the passenger seat again, and noticed/noted that I had apparently driven on autopilot through most of Raybrook (*which my internal mapping system indicates ends and turns into Lake Placid at the top of the hill with big stones blocking off what Frank has assured me was once a drive-in movie theater*) without noticing much of the drive. The rest of the way I spent looking forward equally to a swim in what was reported to be a very nice pool, and to the opportunity to talk over the phone call with the smartest person I knew in the world (*besides myself*) … Mickey.

"How you doing, boy?" Mickey asked when he answered my knock at the door of their suite (*having found yet another way into the heart of the hotel without passing the front desk, I hadn't even started with disguises and props yet … you should see me with a clipboard and a dark blue, slightly grimy, jumpsuit*).

"Great (*my standard answer to Mickey, it's often true*)," I said. "Lead the way to this pool I've heard so much about … if I go first, they'd probably dart and net me."

"You're developing a sense of humor, kiddo," he said. "And people said that you couldn't, or wouldn't."

"Thanks, Mickey, but I wasn't joking," I said, "I've heard stories."

"It'll be a couple of minutes while everyone gets ready," Mickey said, smiling, "you know."

"I don't think I am early," I said … a polite

convention, I was exactly on time.

"Nope, as per usual, you are on time, and everyone else … isn't," he said. "It's a perplexing hallmark of standard human behavior." Mickey and I share a disdain for lateness (*and those who choose it as a lifestyle*) unless brought about by emergencies.

"I put a Coke in the freezer about half an hour ago, in anticipation of your arrival," he said. "You better get it before we forget (*I seldom forget anything, but Mickey likes to paint me with all of his human frailties … it's sweet in a way, if you think about it*) and it explodes."

I nodded and walked back into the heart of the suite to get/defuse the Coke-bomb, shielding my eyes from movement I caught through one of the open bedroom doors … it was more human skin, along with a thatch/patch/covering of pubic hair seen out of the corner of my eye before I could avert them fully. Mindy was significantly less body-conscious than I was comfortable with, and I had spent too many awkward moments during my life trying not to see a body that most human males would almost certainly enjoy looking at. It had happened with enough frequency that I had often suspected she was experimenting/messing with me, although Mickey had assured me that it was simply her way. Chet passed the open doorway, saw or heard me futzing in the kitchen, and shut the door slightly too firmly (*public nakedness was apparently not his way*). I wandered back away from the core of the suite to find Mickey sitting on the deck with a brightly colored beach towel slung over one shoulder, rolling a short and fat cigar between his fingers thoughtfully (*he smokes about twenty of these each year, and only when he is in the woods, which sometimes includes semi-rural Connecticut, but I still judge him for it … he's my national treasure, and I worry about cancers or his heart, unsure of what would fill the space he takes up in my life*).

"Thanks," I said, holding up the can and shaking it slightly, feeling the sluggishness inside that suggested the partial formation of ice-crystals, "very thoughtful of you." I opened the can very carefully/slowly, and drank a first, slightly crunchy, mouthful.

"We've got a few minutes at least," Mickey said, turning his chair to look at me as I leaned against the railing (*I see the mountains and lakes all the time, I wanted to spend my time while we were together looking at, and talking with, Mickey*). "Something has changed since the last time we talked. There's something in your eyes and face and the way you sit (*lean really, but I didn't see any point in correcting him while he was on a roll*), something has moved or shifted."

I hadn't wanted to start this, or any significant, discussion yet, so I tried to deflect with biology, "I had a spectacular poop this morning. I think improving my diet while camping has helped things in that department (*this line of talk always worked when I was eight, distracting him from whatever he tried to pin me down with serious talk*)."

"Nonsense, boy," he said, "that hasn't worked with me since you were eight. If you want to see the inside of that pool without a full-on family discussion (*Mickey could/had/would call in the whole family to discuss one member's issues until resolution/consensus was reached, and knew that I knew/remembered it*) first, then you need to spill right now … although I'm always happy to hear about great poops, Ty."

"Okay," I said. "I left you at lunch on your first day to visit the site of a murder at the behest of a friend (*Mickey's the only person I can use words like behest in front of without having them throw things at me, so I do*). She, Meg (*Mickey met Meg, and Frank, before, during an earlier visit to the*

Tri-Lakes), wanted me to 'use my gift,' or whatever, to help this young man … at least partly because she thinks we share a bond owing to the fact that he's autistic, and I'm … whatever I am, or whatever she thinks I am."

Mickey nodded and didn't say anything in that way that clearly says continue.

"I gave her husband, Frank …" I said.

"The cop," Mickey interrupted, checking to make sure his memory was intact/correct/accurate.

"Yes," I continued, "the cop. I gave him some ideas that I had, based on her description of the crime scene that might exonerate, or at least cast some reasonable doubt on the young man's guilt. It did. Then I made the mistake of accepting an invitation over to their house to meet the young man, Xander, and his parents, and a team of people who care about, and help him/them. I think I'm now committed to helping."

"No big deal if your tips or ideas, helped Frank to shift the focus of blame and/or the investigation a little," Mickey said. "That should be all the help this Xander needs. Who was killed?"

"His older sister, Danica," I said, watching Mickey wince (*which I didn't understand … who would have been a good/acceptable murder victim?*). "At any rate, his mother rode over the whole crew of people there, and invited me along on a camping trip with Xander and an aid, in the hopes that I'll get to know Xander better, and that I can help the royal *them* figure out what happened to Danica … what Xander saw or knows or thinks about that afternoon."

"This all sounds well within your wheelhouse," Mickey said, "and considerably less dangerous than that thing with Cynthia that ended up with you getting shot, or the creepy stuff from last summer."

"Well, Danica's murder was … messy," I said, stopping there, choosing not to mention blood spatter on walls and the ceilings. "And, I might have gotten a phone call from the killer on my way over here this afternoon."

"Okay," Anne said, choosing this moment to stick her head out and onto the deck, "I think we're all finally ready. Sorry to keep you waiting (*she obviously was not sorry, or she wouldn't always do this, but it was nice of her to say, as Mickey always reminded me*)."

Mickey whirled in his seat, unintentionally flinging his cigar ash at her, "Ty and I need three minutes, dear (*he said, holding up three fingers, thumb and pinky locked, in her direction*). Can you wait in the living room while we talk?"

Anne glared at us both, but mostly me (*not likely for this particular event/moment/delay, but for a thousand like them during my lifetime, a thousand hiccups in her life caused by a son they didn't share, that she hadn't wanted, didn't want*). "Certainly, love, we'll just head down to the pool, and you can catch up when you're ready."

After she had sighed pointedly (*the point of which was slightly lost on me*), and pulled her head back inside, the five of them left the suite in a flurry of compliments and deprecating comments about swimwear and towels and sandals and sunhats, Mickey turned his chair to fully face me (*which seemed stagecraft to me, as he could obviously see/hear/understand me before*).

"Tell me about this phone call," he said. "Everything about it: what the person said, how they said it, what you said, how it was left between you, your thoughts, what the police said when you told them, and what's going to happen next/differently because of the call."

I love Mickey's mind; it has helped to shape my mental processes and interface with the world of humans over the years in ways that I can't even measure.

I related the content of the call, word for word: the fact that the caller had used a text-to-speech program to hide their voice/identity and likely a burner phone as well, what conclusions I had drawn about the caller and call, that I had opted for a swim with Mickey over a fruitless hour or three spent with the police, and that I planned not to do anything differently as a result of the call (*which wasn't strictly true because I had the beginnings of a plan under construction in one of the backrooms in my skull … it just didn't seem to be shaping up as a plan that Mickey would like*).

"That's just stupid, kiddo," he said.

"What part?"

"All of it," he said. "Well, nearly all of it. This is what WE (*I definitely heard a royal 'we' in the way that he said it*) pay the police for. You need to loop Frank in, and cancel the camping trip and come with us when we head back down to *The City.*"

"That's sweet, Mickey," I said, "but unless I'm wrong, which I'm not, the police/FBI/DHS couldn't help tracing/dealing with the phone call."

"Yeah, but …" he said.

"Also, this is exactly the sort of thing I'm good at," I said. "Exactly the sort of thing that you, and everyone in my life seemingly, wants me to do. So let's work this out. Think about all of the mysteries we bookclubbed (*yes, I verbified that noun, and I'd do it again*) over the years, and tell me why I need/have to push forward at this juncture?"

He closed his eyes, shaking his head slightly in what I know from years of Mickey-watching is a gesture of frustration with a world that makes no sense.

"Take me out of it," I said. "Imagine it's Travis McGee or Spenser … what's the phone call mean?"

He kept his eyes closed, but stopped shaking his

head in that way, and after seven seconds, responded, "It's a mistake. The killer is giving you a handhold or foothold … a place to get some traction. If he, or she, just ignored you, you wouldn't have anything to go on, but the call gives you stuff to work with."

"Go on," I said, pushing him into the Socratic type of back and forth we had enjoyed over the years when discussing all manner of books and writing. "What else did I get from the call, the caller, and reacting the way that I have?"

"The caller is educated and knowledgeable … how did they know about the trip?" he asked.

"Exactly," I said. "They must almost certainly be within the group of people that I met with this morning, or possibly one generation/circle/ripple out from it."

"And your refusal to comply," Mickey continued, getting into it now, "will likely force them to make further, possibly more revealing mistakes."

"Correct," I said. "I can use a timed/limited/differentiated release of information to winnow down the list of possibles, and as Thufir Hawat says, 'Remember, the first step in avoiding a trap is knowing of its existence.' (*One of the movies I'd loaded into my iPhone for Xander after talking with Cam Renard was 'Dune,' so it was on my mind … and now occurred to me that it was Paul's father, Duke Leto, who shared this advice in the book, albeit saying it in a slightly different manner/context.*) I already knew that this person was out there, but now I know that they're inside the team's communication circle and willing/likely to take stupid chances to try and end an investigation by me decisively, rather than simply letting it fizzle. That tells me/us, or at least suggests, something else … what?"

Mickey leaned his head back and looked at a spider web in the corner above the deck railing for a few moments before answering, "It means that Xander knows, or could be presumed to know the identity of his sister's killer. The killer could be, should be, by the logic of mysteries we've read, considering cleaning house by eliminating Xander."

"And finally?" I prompted. "Given the givens that I've been given, and have given to you." Mickey and I both smiled at my forced and horrific construction, but it was gallows humor, if it was humorous at all (*which it probably wasn't*).

"So you think Xander will be secure as long as he's with his parents and in town," Mickey said, "but he'll be exposed and highly vulnerable once he embarks on this camping trip … but less so with you along, than if he was just with this guy, Whatshisname?"

"Cam Renard," I said. "Yes, and that's the other reason why I can't/won't be driving down to *The City* with you to hide out. If I were to roll over and show this person my belly, then their attention would quickly be drawn to Xander, who is a markedly softer target, especially since with the proper manipulation of events, he could be made to look like a primary suspect again … as my, whatever he is, Frank, likes to say, 'cops like easy answers because they're almost always the right answers' … chancy, but possible."

"This is addictive, boy," Mickey said. "No wonder you keep getting mixed up in this sort of thing. Now quickly, before they come back up from the pool and Anne leaves me forever, taking the girls with her (*this could/would/will never happen for literally hundreds of reasons, but I took his point as stated*), how can you adjust the variables in such a way that will keep you and Xander and Whatshisname safe out in the woods, while still allowing you to poke the killer enough to keep their attention and eventually end them up in the clink?"

"Some misinformation," I said, "coupled with a controlled release of our location, such that Frank or similar (*I looked over, and he gave me a nod to indicate that he understood*) will know where and when and—once it happens—who to scoop up. My goal is to wring a confession out of the guilty party in an inspiring 'I suppose you're all wondering why I've brought you here today' speech in the woods, surrounded by dozens of members of the law enforcement community and one shame-faced, and handcuffed, and maybe leg-ironed, killer."

"Sounds super." Mickey said, "What's the downside?

"Well…" I said, "to date, the conclusions of my plans have never worked out in exactly the way I imagined, with anything. I don't know why. They should … my plans are great, but humans often seem to make a left-hand turn when I think they'll go straight or turn right or just sit down."

"Stupid humans," Mickey agreed, with a smile on his face that I didn't understand.

"Exactly," I said. "Let's go. I want to check out this pool, I understand it starts inside and continues outside and they keep it heated through the winter … even the outside part."

We went, we swam, and the pool was spectacular! Mickey arranged through some complicated hand signals and/or pre-arrangements with the cabana boys to have drinks brought out for everyone when we two finally arrived … champagne for everyone else and iced Coke for me. Anne was mad at me, but then she often is (*and my relations with her aren't noticeably better when she isn't angry, so I didn't/don't worry about it*). The girls seemed to be having fun with their beaus (*Anne's term, which she used more than made sense in conversations I kept hearing through the course of the afternoon, as more bottles—and cans—kept arriving*). After a few attempts by Chet and Rob to draw me into their conversations failed, they left me alone with my thoughts and swimming and smiling at Mickey (*one of my fake ones, but one of the good ones that he likes, a #2 … friendly/gentle/clueless*) who kept winking at me and touching a finger to the side of his nose (*like we were in some heist movie*). It was a good day, one to keep for the vault, for the rainy/sad/crappy days, possibly because I knew that I was on the edge of something … something bigger and badder (*worse, really, but badder goes better with bigger in this instance*) and less certain than I had lead Mickey to believe.

I was heading out to fight dragons again, knowing in advance that my vision was faulty, and my armor and lance and sword were prone to failure, but instead of feeling apprehensive or fearful (*I don't really do fear in the general course of events*), I was excited to be doing it again. Despite the months of downtime, and thinking that I wanted a safe and boring life, I could feel my world and vision and brain and body/limbs all coming into focus in a way that they hadn't since the last (*and every*) time that I gambled against the "bad guys" … my unusual melon against their guns and knives and proven willingness to hurt and kill. I liked the feeling of being on the edge of the contest, and relished the cushy life and soft hours with Mickey and his family all the more because of how rough/ugly it might get in the coming days.

When the sky started darkening (*I pulled up the table in my head, sunset would be at 7:29 today*), the girls made noises about going back to the suite to change and get ready for dinner.

"Ready to join us for supper, boy?" he asked. "We're

going to Desperadoes tonight, for as much Tex-Mex as you can eat."

"And Margos," Mindy and Becky chimed in, as if they'd been waiting.

"Thanks, but I'm afraid that I'll have to back out of dinner tonight," I said. I saw a flicker of upset/sadness/panic race across Mickey's face. "I need to head back to SmartPig and release the hound, and continue with preparations for the camping trip." We hadn't spoken more about the trip and its import … to me, to Xander, to my mysterious phone caller, but I could see Mickey remember and extrapolate through to scary contingencies.

"Are you sure?" he asked, his voice edging upwards into the tonal range I recognize as desperation/panic. Anne looked up from a brief hunt for her sandals when she registered his tone.

"Yup," I said, "but I'll stop by in the morning with some donuts before you guys head back down … I'll make sure to bring some of those maple-frosted ones that you like (*Mickey insists that he can't get them anywhere else, which is untrue, but it costs me nothing to humor him*)."

I could tell from the way his face was scrunched up, especially around the eyes, that Mickey wanted to talk about it more, anything to stall my departure (*that he now/recently remembered heralded his eventual departure, and the coming of my camping trip and murder investigation, which meant an exposure to the possibility of actual, as opposed to theoretical, danger*). Anne sensed something because she walked over and put a hand on his shoulder and murmured something in his ear, to which he shook his head slightly, in annoyance. The until-recently-fun afternoon was slipping away, unexpectedly derailed, and the girls and Chet and Rob now picked up on the static/interference, and looked at the (*obtuse and obfuscate*) triangle that Mickey and Anne and I formed … I took the initiative in an attempt to rescue the tattered remnants of the festive mood everyone (*else*) had been enjoying for the last few hours.

"When you get there, tell your waiter or waitress that you want to order a round of Anniversary Cadillacs," I said. "My friend Meg says they're the best margaritas available on the planet."

This served to distract Mindy and Becky from the dip in the happiness quotient at our end of the pool area, and got Chet and Rob talking about the merits of various Mexican beers; I don't drink alcohol as a rule, but having looked at the list once, could remember/recite all of the beers that Despos had on tap and in bottles. When I managed to back away from the conversation a few minutes later, Mickey had a brave smile on his face, and only someone who had spent decades studying his face would have detected the sadness in his eyes. Anne busied herself with sandal straps until I left the pool area.

Best Western Mountain Lake Inn, Saranac Lake, NY, Tuesday, 9/2/2014, 8:57 p.m.

Leaving Lake Placid, and Mickey, and the wonderful pool, felt an odd combination of necessary and wrong to me. I was thoughtfully analyzing everything that had happened in the last few days, and only came back to full awareness once I passed Turtle Pond (*which feels like the outer edge of habitable Saranac Lake to me when driving in from Lake Placid*). It was at this point that I wondered/worried about Xander and his family at their hotel.

I slowed down as I passed Casa Del Sol, the second-best Mexican restaurant in the Tri-Lakes, on my right, and made the next turn into the Best Western Mountain Lake Inn. I drove a loop around the circumference of the building and parking lot to see if I could tag anyone following me, and also to try and spot the police presence, if any. An empty SLPD cruiser sat parked out front of the entrance/office with an empty spot next to it, so I pulled in and turned off the Element. I decided to take a walk around the perimeter of the building counterclockwise from my car (*which was, obviously, twelve o'clock*). As I walked, I pulled on the non-front-door exit handles that occurred at semi-regular intervals around the building and was pleased to find that none of them pulled open (*this didn't make the place Fort Knox, but I was glad that a prospective killer would not find access so easy*). When I got most of the way around (*roughly 3:30, if you're still holding onto the clock idea*), the lights of, and movement inside, the pool enclosure grabbed my eye. I could see Iskra and Darko Kovac sitting at one of the tables in their swimsuits, talking with a policeman in uniform (*which I imagined must seem quite formal, and certainly warm, in a hotel pool area*) while Xander floated face down in the pool, arms and legs starfished out in all directions.

While I finished my circumnavigation of the hotel, I searched for occupied and/or new cars in the lot. Seeing none, I grabbed my still damp suit, and walked in through the main entrance.

"Hi," I said to the young guy behind the desk, "I need to go in and see the cop and the Kovacs by the pool."

He might have said something if I had allowed my tone to contain any uncertainty or the slightest hint of questioning rise in the final sounds, but I did not, so he did not. I walked into the pool area with my hands well out from my body, my bathing suit plainly visible.

The policeman launched himself out of the flimsy plastic deck chair, making it skitter back a few inches before it caught on a tile edge and flipped backwards with more noise/commotion than seemed probable. It was clear that he didn't know me any more than I knew him, and while one hand rose in a classic "STOP" gesture, the other dropped towards the handgun on a right side drop-leg holster (*which, in my admittedly limited, but arguably intensely considered experience, often indicates someone more shooter than desk jockey, which seemed a good thing, so long as he didn't shoot me*).

"Tyler," Iskra said, in a slightly louder than normal voice, especially given the bouncy acoustics in the pool room, "how nice to see you."

"Mr. Cunningham," Darko said, "thanks for coming

(*which seemed odd, as we hadn't made plans to get together, but I was glad to have the policeman's concerns allayed, which they were … he picked up his seat and sat down again*)."

"I was passing through town, saw you enjoying the pool, and thought that I would stop in for a minute to chat," I said.

Xander had not looked up or appeared to notice my entry into the room, but his starfishiness (*starfish-osity?*) had streamlined a bit, and his head was now oriented in my direction. He was still face down in the water, and now I could see that his flotation was facilitated/supported by a mask and snorkel.

"We went on a cruise a few years ago, and one day we all tried snorkeling," Iskra said, seeing my eyes flit to Xander in the pool. "I ended up staying with Xander in the shallows by the beach all day while he floated there. He'd stay here all day and night if we let him. The manager is a friend, and we often visit when Xander's having a tough day."

"I imagine the weightlessness and feeling of pressure from all sides is comforting," I said, thinking about how I had enjoyed swimming all of my life.

"Sit down and let's talk for a bit," she said. "We'll need to get him out of the pool before nine if he's going to get a good night's sleep. You are still planning on going on the trip, aren't you?"

"Yes," I said, following her and Darko over to the table they had claimed with various bags and towels and drinks and snacks and books.

"We heard about you," Darko said, "you know, around town, and some from Meg an' Frank. We've talked about it, and we want to pay you, for helping Xander with the police investigation, and for goin' on the camping trip, and for whatever you can do to help find out what happened with, to, our …" he didn't finish his sentence, but stared down and into the pool. Xander was still floating, seemingly unaware, but again oriented his head towards us.

"I don't know if I can do anything more at this point (*although I was reasonably sure that I could, and possibly already had, and probably would do more in the next day or so … possibly everything*), and even if I could, I'm not sure that I could, or would, take money for it … especially not for going camping at the best time of year with two interesting people. Maybe a meal at your restaurant sometime."

"Anytime you wan'," Darko said and started to push forward along this vein when Iskra cut in.

"So you talked more with Cam about the trip and about Dani," Iskra asked. "He's a nice guy. He didn't hurt my baby. He threw up and then fainted the one time my Xander gave me a bloody nose during an upset." She paled after saying this, thinking about her reason for exempting Cam, and why it made sense.

Xander made some splashing noises from in the pool, and we all turned to look at him for a moment before I began my report.

"I was able to meet and talk with Cam and Phil and Barb and Steve since we got together yesterday at Meg and Frank's house," I said. "I feel like I agree with you about Cam, and the rest of them too, so I was hoping to get another perspective … of them and your feelings about them all, and how or why they interfaced with … your daughter."

"We'll have to talk careful about it," Iskra said. "He don' look like it, but he hears everything, and something we say now could come back to the surface later tonight, or two days from now while you're in the woods, and cause a major meltdown."

"Cam's been with Xander for years," Darko jumped in first. "He's family. Loves Xander, loved Dani, like they were brother and sister."

Iskra nodded, "Yup, he and Dani talked alla time about their plans for Xander's future. They had a house picked out for him and Cam to live in, with a coupla other guys. Cam insisted that they wrote the legal stuff up so that it was easy for her or us to have control over who worked and lived with him. Cam din wanna be named in the document so that it would be easier for Dani or for us to shift legal custodian status if we wanted to. Dani wouldna done that without Cam's insistence, neither would we knowing Cam like we all do. But, Cam always looks past himself in Xander's future. He loves him."

"Barb, we know from the school and annual review meetings, but not that well outside of that stuff," Iskra said. "She was a little clinical for Dani, a little cold, but I think that's the job. We had a time a few years back when Xander bit a TA hard enough to draw blood, and Barb wanted him educated outside the building for a while. Dani didn't like that much, I can tell you. Xander was fine going to the Town Hall for a coupla weeks, but Dani never much liked Barb after that. She felt she should've pushed harder for Xander to stay in the school building with his friends." Iskra looked at the pool briefly.

"Macabee looked at Dani wrong when he thought nobody was watching," Darko said. I thought he had said all he wanted to on that subject, but after a moment he continued, "Dani was a good looking girl, anybody woulda looked at her, Cam looked at her, you ... (*he trailed off here, and I felt him jamming that thought into reverse and through a three-point turn*). She was attractive. Macabee looked at her, thought about her, like a fat man does fried chicken (*this made me just a touch queasy, which I imagine was the effect that Darko was looking for, although probably not for the reasons I was feeling a bit sick*). She felt it too. She'd ask me or her mother to come along when she started talkin' with him last year about Xander's state and federal money. She din't feel comfortable with him. He din't like her messing around with the funding, the money, taking more control of the money from him to us, to her, to Xander."

"Daddy will come swimming?" Xander asked his father. He may have picked up on the tone, or sheer quantity of his father's speaking, or he may have simply gotten lonely in the pool. Darko shook himself like a dog, stretched, peeled off his shirt, and dove into the pool to swim around with Xander, leaving me with Iskra, and what would, to people besides me, be an awkward silence.

"Steve Street," I said eventually, to re-establish prime in the conversational pump (*to needlessly labor a metaphor from a police procedural mystery I'd recently read*). "He gave me the impression that he has been working with you and Mr. Kovac since before Dani and Xander were born."

"He's a good man, Steve," she said. "Without his assistance and advice over the years, we'd still be scraping along with our first restaurant. He's been a help setting things up for Xander, now that he's out of school … and with what happened, he's had to fix lots of stuff, rewriting and adjusting and who knows what … lawyers, ya know?" She smiled in an "us against them," that people seem to adopt when talking about the law and lawyers … I nodded and served up a #7 (*slyly agreeing and gently subversive*).

"Dani sometimes got frustrated with the layers of paper Steve had to make to surround everything for Xander. She din't understand," Iskra said. "She thought her classes up at North Country Community College gave her the right to grill him about his work for us, and Xander and her."

"Hmmm," I said when she didn't continue, and the silence felt labored.

"Why did you agree to go on this trip, Tyler?" she asked. "We appreciate you steering Frank and the police to the stuff that shows Xander din't do it, din't hurt Dani, but why go camping, go in the woods with Xander and Cam?"

"Why did Dani spend so much of her time/life/energy helping Xander?" I offered as an answer, although it wasn't.

She straightened and thought a moment before answering, pausing long enough that I thought I had angered her. "They made each other better, Mr. Cunningham, from the day we brought Xander home from the hospital, and put the two of them down on the grass in that tiny yard in back of our old house, not the one you musta seen the other day, the one up on Olive Street. She loved him and it changed them both. I slept easy the last few years, knowing that he'd be fine after we're gone, 'cause she'd take care of him. She'd'a walked across broken glass for that boy. He knew her too, loved her in his way. I don't know what life'll be like now for him, without her, I have trouble seeing his future. Sounds wrong to say, but I can't. I guess Cam'll help, and other people, but they're not his family."

"My parents wanted a sister for me," I said, struggling to put my thoughts together in a way that would make sense to her, as well as me, in answering her question from a minute ago. "They tried for years before, and especially after, I was born. I think they thought she (*they always talked about the missing sibling as 'she', as if they could see, and already knew, her*) would do for me what Dani did for Xander. She never came along, and they're gone, and I had a hard time after they died. What I do is in part related to what/who I am, my difference, but I'm good at it, and it helps people, and I'd like to help Xander and you, and maybe even Dani." It seemed as though this last piece of our conversation came out of some recent input on the parts of Meg and Mickey and Dot … it made me uncomfortable and confused as I was saying it, but it also felt true.

She smiled at me, looked down at my hands and noticed my swimsuit, and asked if I wanted to go for a swim before they headed out. I did, so I did.

I didn't want to interfere with Xander and Darko, who seemed to be involved in some game or routine that they both knew, but appeared as random splashing and diving to me, so I swam awhile to unkink my muscles after sitting in the uncomfortable plastic lawn furniture. After a few laps, I wished them a good night and headed out into the dark and cold of the almost-autumn night.

Dorothy and Lisa's Apartment, Saranac Lake, NY, Wednesday, 9/3/2014, 12:54 a.m.

I pointed the Element towards downtown Saranac Lake and home, but re-thought my decision to re-occupy the couch with Chinese food and TV for the night, and gave Dot a call to see if I could stop in for a few minutes to talk. Lisa answered, and said that they'd just finished dinner, and that she'd put a plate aside for me, along with some Cokes on ice (*it seemed awfully late for dinner to just be ending, but they both keep odd/variable schedules, and who was I to judge anyway, as long as I was going to get fed*). Lisa (*Dorothy's wife*) and I had had a much warmer relationship since I'd gotten involved in some trouble they'd made for themselves the previous winter. Everything that Lisa resented about me had been useful in the resolution of this issue. As a result, the two of us had been much closer ever since (*sometimes/often much closer than I wanted to be, with her, or anyone … sometimes there was hugging*).

I stopped momentarily at SmartPig to pick up Hope and some food for her, she was excited about the food, but somewhat disappointed minutes later when we arrived at Dorothy and Lisa's place and a very brief walk was brought up short so we could head upstairs to their apartment.

"Tyler and Miss Jackson (*a pop-culture reference that I had looked up, but found a reach, that Lisa used to refer to Hope, because she was/is 'nasty'*)." Lisa welcomed us into the entryway as we topped the stairs, as though she'd been waiting. Perhaps she had. "C'mon in, supper's still warm, and I've got a bone for Hope."

I went through the long/narrow apartment, back towards the kitchen, through their living room, scaring/scattering cats as I went (*most dogs like me, cats never do … I think that cats are smarter or more perceptive or something about some piece of me that is missing, and they steer clear, while dogs fall prey to my ear-scratches and cookies and belly-rubs*). Settling down at the kitchen table, where a place had been set for me, I moved the setting to the other side of the table, so I could have my back to the wall and not the hallway (*I find I am more relaxed eating in this way, given some past surprises*). If Lisa was surprised/confused/offended by this shift, she hid it well. I sat and looked at the huge cast-iron frying pan hanging on the wall over the table as Dorothy shuffled in, wearing fluffy slippers designed to look like twin Pomeranians … Dorothy glanced from me to the frying pan and smiled back down at me (*near the conclusion of the nasty business last winter, I had pulverized a man's hand with that very piece of cast-iron in the service of Dot's and Lisa's safety and well-being … Dot knew the details, Lisa did not*).

"Lisa's chicken curry is awesome this time around," Dorothy said, which would seem to imply that sometimes it's not … not so. I have always enjoyed it, although it varies considerably in spice and heat and even ingredients from batch to batch.

After Hope had whizzed through the too-small (*she insisted, with long suffering eyes and a tiny moan)* dinner, Lisa handed her an uncooked soup bone to gnaw on. Hope took the bone without a wag and went to hide between Dot's Pomeranian slippers, making contented grunts and sighs as she set to work on the bone.

"So, what's up?" Dorothy asked. "Did Meg drag you into the thing at the place with the kid?" Dot and I have watched *Ocean's 11* a dozen times, and she loves the way the hoods talk, and tries to affect their manner of speech when we talk about the work that I do … it often falls flat or is simply confusing.

"Xander … yes," I answered. "I'm going to try and help clear up the question of who killed Danica." I cast my eye pointedly towards Lisa, who was doing something at the fridge, with her back turned.

"Lisa knows the family, the Kovacs, and was in school with Danica," Dorothy said. "I already told her that given Meg's connection to the family, I thought it was likely that you'd end up with a finger in the pie (*I had no idea what this figurative language meant, but nodded sagely, my #2 nod, the result of years of study/practice*)."

"Dani was a few years behind me in the high school," Lisa said, turning around finally to give me a Coke in a frosted mug with what appeared to be rocks in the bottom. "But everyone knew her and, you know, small town. The stones are to keep the drink cool without watering it down (*I'd read about them, but had not seen them before … clever idea, assuming that they were non-reactive to the acid in the Coke*)."

"Why would someone kill her?" I asked, tact and subtlety never having been a strong point of mine. I could see this reflected in the eyes of both women as they heard/processed my question.

"They wouldn't," Lisa answered. "She was sweet and pretty and kind and smart, devoted to her brother and popular all through school, but not in the mean-popular cliques, if you know what I mean. (*I didn't, not exactly. I didn't go to school and was never sweet or pretty or kind or devoted to anyone in particular or popular … but I had seen public school in TV and movies and read books and listened to people talk about it.*) She finished high school tied with two other kids for top of the class, and she could have gone anywhere, but she stayed in town, went to North Country for Business Administration, so she could be here for her parents … and more, for Xander. She didn't give up having a life for Xander, like some people said. It's more like she built her life around being there for him."

Lisa stood and walked over to the wall to adjust the heavy frying pan hanging there, a symbol of the life that she had built here with Dorothy (*and also of the both entirely reprehensible and necessary illegal actions I'd taken last winter to help secure and protect that life*).

"She came with him, Xander, to the shelter," Dorothy said. "Once a month or so, she and Xander would help with stuff like shuttling laundry from washer to dryer and sweeping the halls and playing with cats. Seemed nice, I can't imagine why anyone would kill her, but bad people do bad things for reasons that good people don't understand (*it sounded like a memorized phrase, even to me, and I'm weak at tonal variations and analysis*)."

"Sessions with Meg are helping, aren't they, sweet potato pie," Lisa asked/stated, perhaps picking up on my noting the tone of that particular phrase. "We're not having nightmares near as much, and go out to The Waterhole and a couple of other places from time to time now."

"We weren't talking about me, we were talking about Danica Kovac," Dorothy said, but smiled and reached her hand out to cover Lisa's. "Meg's a sweetie to talk with me once a week or so, won't take a penny, but we pay her in pies anyway." I assumed Meg and Dot were talking about the violation/assault that Dorothy barely survived this winter (*at the hands, literally, of an evil man who could/would no longer be able to hurt her, or Lisa, or the shelter, which he had threatened to burn it to the ground, dogs and cats included*).

"I'm more interested in you," I said. "I care about you, and you're not dead, not beyond help." Lisa looked a bit shocked when I said this, but Dot just smiled.

"Of course you are, Tyler," she said. "We all are, but generally don't say it out loud, but you'll help this girl's family, especially her brother, all the same, right?"

"I sort of have to now," I said, and explained about Xander playing with Hope and talking with Iskra, and being volunteered for the camping trip, and my interviews with the inner circle of *Team Xander* and the ominous phone call.

"Do you think he followed you here, that he's watching us now," Dorothy asked, her eyes a little wide, and a panicky tone in her voice. "Tyler, he (*I found it interesting that she assumed a male, noting that I did also, although I tried/try to keep an open mind*) …."

"Dot, I drove a couple of loops through town on my way here," I said. "And with almost nobody on the road, I can tell you definitively that I was not followed."

Lisa slid her hand from beneath Dorothy's, protectively placed it on top, and glared out the windows. "So you're here for help," she said, "not because you missed us."

I was fascinated watching her face as different emotions were dancing across it in quick succession … fear, anger, gratitude, resignation, compassion (*all familiar to me from flashcards shown to me a thousand times by various therapists in my childhood, all strange to me because they were concepts that had no grounding anywhere inside me but in memories*).

"You're right," I said. "I came here tonight to ask for some help, but this is my thing, not yours, and I can find someone else—Meg, I think—to help if you can't."

"Tyler," Lisa spoke in an angry and flat and loud

voice, "take Hope for a quick walk, and give us a couple of minutes." Dorothy looked as though she was going to say something, but Lisa squeezed her hand, hard, and made a shushing motion with her lips.

I got up and convinced Hope to leave the bone so we could go out for a walk in the grass and trees behind the house Dot and Lisa live in. Hope found some interesting things to sniff, peed in a couple of spots, growled bravely at some loons flying west from Lake Flower to Lower Saranac Lake for the night, and then dragged me back up the stairs to Dot and Lisa's apartment.

Clomping extra loudly up the stairs to give the ladies time to finish up or compose themselves, or whatever people do when I give them extra time in this manner, I rattled the doorknob more than was strictly necessary before entering. Hope ran into the kitchen growling at the ladies (*she suspected them of stealing, or at least chewing on, the bone they had given her … she's a suspicious soul, and the scars she bears speak of it being well-deserved*), then passed me on her way out of the room, taking her bone out and away, to an undisclosed/secure location.

"Dot wants to help," Lisa said, in a tone that I tentatively pegged as angry and disappointed. "I'm less sure, although, of course, we're both very grateful for what you did for us in January. We, I don't want to leave you hanging, but …"

"I completely understand, Lisa," I said. "You've got Dorothy back from the monsters living under the bed, monsters you didn't really believe in, and now you think I want to put her back in their way … where she could get hurt, again." Both ladies nodded slightly.

"I don't want that any more than you do, really," I said. "Let me tell you what I'm thinking." I changed my earlier plan, on the fly as I spoke. "If you're comfortable with it, great … if not, I'll talk with Meg or John (*although I knew for a fact that John, another person who has helped me with less-than-legal solutions in the past, was visiting friends and family in Ireland for the next few weeks*)."

"Sounds fair," said Dorothy, in a scared/brave voice (*and if you don't think humans can be both at once, you don't have a fully-developed understanding of the concept of bravery*). "Lay it out and let us poke holes in your Tyler-logic (*Dot was alluding to the fact that my logical/methodical plans often forgot to take into account the human element, which, in the past, had led to all sorts of trouble*)."

"Okay," I said. "I'm going to head into the woods for a four-day camping trip with Xander and Cam Renard. Through a clever/skillful combination of misinformation and the controlled release of real information, I plan to fool the killer into revealing him or herself at a time and place that can be overseen by Frank or fellow members of the law enforcement community."

"Sounds good, nearly perfect," said Dot. "So where do we, or I (*Lisa muttered 'we' under her breath, which brought a smile to Dot's still scared face*) come in?"

"If—when—something goes all pear-shaped (*an expression that Dorothy loves using, means nothing to me, and worse, she can't/won't adequately explain/define it*)," I said, "I want to be able to reach out to you ladies as my Plan B."

They both nodded, showing a noticeably growing skepticism.

"Mickey's in town with his family," I said, with them nodding through this apparent non-sequitur. "He gave me a gift that I think can come in handy."

"The place Xander and Cam and I are going to be camping," I said, "the Saint Regis Canoe Wilderness, is serious back-of-beyond, even for the Adirondacks. Cell phones won't work in most of it, and where/when they do, it will be spotty and intermittent. I think that I can make this work to my advantage, but this GPS Spot device that Mickey gave me can provide me another edge in the woods."

"I heard about some tourist using one to get pulled off Marcy because he was unprepared," Dorothy said, and Lisa nodded to herself. "I don't see how we can help with something like that."

"It does more than just call EMT and forest rangers," I said. "It can also send you one of three emails with my coordinates and different messages preset and embedded."

"I think that I see where you're going with this, Tyler," Lisa said, "and it sounds tricky."

"It is," I admitted, "a little, but if you've got a pad and pen, I can draw it out, and it should be easy from your end." She rummaged through a significantly overloaded crap-drawer next to the fridge, and eventually came up with a scuffed steno pad and a nearly empty Bic pen (*I always somehow lose them before they get that far down in ink*).

Short of calling EMTs and forest rangers for help, there are three buttons," I said. "Each of which sends the current GPS coordinates and a different message to anyone on your email list. The first one is 'OK,' which can be a daily check-in to tell people that I'm all right. The second has a picture of helping hands, and I'll use it to communicate that I need to be picked up at the indicated location, with some medical reason, but not an emergency. The third button allows for a custom message, which I will use to ask for a re-supply of food at the given coordinates. Each of those will be explained in the email message that I can preset the machine to send

… does that make sense so far?"

"Yeah," Dorothy said, "but you haven't gotten to the tricky part."

"True, but it doesn't get too much trickier," I said, "at least not from your point of view. Call the 'OK' button A, the helping hands button B, and the custom message button C. Okay, now … actually give me that for a minute." I said, reaching across to grab the pad and pen from Lisa and worked out the following table:

Button/Combination	**Message**
A (OK button)	OK, fine, just checking in
B (Helping hands button)	Delayed and need a pickup at the location given for a non-emergency medical reason
C (Custom message button)	A re-supply of food is requested at the given coordinates
A and **B**	Send Frank to the given coordinates ASAP
A and **C**	Bring my money, and your cousin's big truck (with towing gear) to the given coordinates
B and **C**	Call Kitty and her lawyers, and get them up here ASAP
A and **B** and **C**	Meet me at the given coordinates in 24 hours with all of my money

I slid the paper over to them, gave them a minute to look it over, and then asked, "Does that make sense?

Don't count group messages you get more than an hour apart, in case I send an 'OK,' and then change my mind a couple of hours later … Sound good?"

"Yeah," said Lisa. "But there are (*she paused to math it out, which made me like her a little more*) fifteen possible combinations given those three buttons. Why use just seven?"

"I thought of using more," I said, "but worried that the order in which they were sent could be confusing to me or to you. Assuming that I am able to transmit, there should be no possibility of confusion as A and C means the same thing as C and A, and so on."

"Clever girl," Dorothy leaned over and gave Lisa a kiss on the top of her head (*which confused me a bit, since I'd come up with the idiot-proof system … not that I wanted a kiss, on the top of my head or otherwise*). Dot saw my expression and whispered, "Jurassic Park (*I knew that, but didn't want to explain my look, so just moved ahead*)."

"So," I said, "just to be clear … none of these should expose you to any risk, as I'd only enact them after something has gone down the drain in my planning, and any of these directives would only be given as a part of the cleanup (*Dorothy paled a bit at my word choice, and Lisa gave her a knowing look/stare/scowl, which had me wondering how much Dot had shared about our adventures with Lisa*)." I didn't talk about hiding bodies, or fleeing to Belize, but those options were certainly in my mind (*and thankfully, owing to my inability to emote as per standard human norms, not on my face*) … and might be flitting through Dorothy's brain (*as she knew the full extent of some of my 'cleanup' activities in the last few years, when things went wrong in some stage of the execution of one of my plans*). Neither of them had mentioned/questioned the options that involved bringing the bricks of cash I had kept stored above the acoustic tile in their bathroom for the last several years, which was just as well … any scenario stemming from this camping trip that required the judicious (*or even the injudicious*) application of fifteen thousand dollars to remedy would mean that I was deep in the weeds (*or woods, as the case might be*).

"Sounds reasonable," Lisa said, in a tone that left some room for doubt about that (*even for me*). "I sure hope you don't need any of that kind of help, except maybe for A or B or C, singly." She was joking, a little, but it made me feel better to see that she understood the device and plan and its implementation.

"I shouldn't need any of those this time out, but I'd love to keep you on the email notification list beyond this trip … if you're okay with that, it could actually help with normal, non-bad-guy camping trips as well (*which of course, is the device's original purpose … not to help me with crime-fighting*).

"Yah," Dorothy said, visibly shifting gears. "Now, how about a movie?"

We *agreed* upon a ridiculous rom-com that Lisa was excited about, and she and Dot spent the next two hours snuggling on the couch, while Hope kept wiggling/wriggling trying to find the perfect spot on my lap from which to watch the movie (*which she also seemed to enjoy*). Occasionally, either Lisa or Dot would shift enough to make their ancient couch groan, and Hope would raise her rheumy eyes in their direction and growl, as if to remind them that they could be quiet or leave (*their own home*) … Dorothy knew better than to giggle at Hope (*it just made matters worse*), but Lisa couldn't always stifle hers. We had a pleasant evening, talking about the long-term residents at the TLAS, new dogs and cats, and upcoming fundraisers. Dorothy and Lisa's cats were notable in their absence, either due to Hope's presence or my own, but neither of us minded, and if Dot and Lisa did, they kept it to themselves. I spent a few hours not thinking about murder and murderers and being caught in the deep woods between Xander and someone who might want to kill him/me/us in the next few days ... it was a nice break. I was rested as well as sorry to go when the movie ended and Lisa and Dot began making exaggerated yawning and watch-checking motions; Hope and I left.

As we were about to climb into the car, Dot burst out of the bottom of the stairs leading up to their apartment and ran over to catch me/us.

"Tyler," she said, "promise me you'll get in touch with that stupid thing if you need my help. Although she doesn't show it, Lisa's more grateful than scared as a result of the crap last winter, and I promise you, I'm fine."

"I promise," I said (*being fully comfortable and versed in lying to people's faces as I was, this was not a huge commitment on my part*). "I don't want you injured/incapacitated/dead and also have concerns now that Lisa is somewhat inside the minion circle." She nodded with understanding and started to speak, before I interrupted her.

"Significant portions of a plan are now set, and I would only need your help if things go all wobbly (*another phrase she liked, that I didn't fully understand*). If I do get in touch through the GPS-Spot, I will likely be asking you to help by doing something illegal. Think about that, and then possibly consider sending Lisa to Watertown to visit with her family for a few days if you hear from me."

"That's not a bad idea, but the main point is that even damaged and a little scared of the monsters in the closet, I'm your minion." She gave me a quick pat on the shoulder, and reached down to ruffle Hope's ears before running back inside (*at which time, I noticed her bare feet, and the wincing/mincing steps she took running across the gravel in the parking area*).

SmartPig, Saranac Lake, NY,
Wednesday, 9/3/2014, 6:25 a.m.

I drove a few looping runs around the approach to the building that housed SmartPig, slowing down to check parked cars, and trying to peer into shadows, but saw nobody, suspicious looking or otherwise, except for Tuesday night drinkers at the Waterhole (*who always look a little suspicious to me, and especially to Hope*). We pulled around the back to our assigned parking spot behind and between Main Street and the river, got out, gave Hope a chance to pee, and then walked cautiously up to SmartPig for the night. Once inside, I put all of the upgraded locks and bolts, including the floor-mounted bar, in place, and breathed out some tension I had been unaware of holding.

First order of business was booting up my computer, checking email and a few websites I monitor daily for news and new posts, and going to the GPS Spot website to set up the messaging options as I had discussed with Dot and Lisa (*which was a bit different than what I had originally planned*). Hope was snoring on the couch long before I had finished setting up, and then testing, the GPS Spot device (*having first substituted my email address for Dorothy's and Lisa's and Mickey's*). Once the testing proved effective, I switched the addresses back to the original plan, with Mickey just getting the 'OK' message, and Dot and Lisa getting all three. I spent much of the rest of the night reading various books and articles on all manner of topics, not sticking with any subject for long … restless reading.

I caught a couple of short naps, the last of which while light began to creep into my east-facing window at 6:24 a.m. (*624 is the sum of twin primes 311 and 313, and a Zuckerman number to boot.*) I roused Hope, grabbed my in-town go-bag (*which carries an iPad, snacks, various tools, headlamp, water, money, hat, fleece, extra leash for Hope, and spare keys for everything for which I have a key*), and headed down and out to the Element with Dunkin' Donuts and Mickey on my mind (*I won't specify which had primacy in the growing light. Nobody needs to know*).

The Whiteface Lodge, Lake Placid, NY,
Wednesday, 9/3/2014, 9:08 a.m.

I picked up two boxes of a dozen donuts, and one half-dozen box at DD on my way through town to see Mickey and crew off on their trip home. The first box was for Hope and me: three each of regular glazed, chocolate glazed, regular jelly, and regular dunkers (*Hope's favorite, after years of testing, although she occasionally strays to other sectors of the box*). The second box was for Mindy and Becky and Chet and Rob: four each of regular glazed, regular jelly, regular dunkers (*boring, perhaps, but a dependable and classic mix*). For Mickey and Anne, I got a half-dozen box to avoid stress for/to/by either of them: two of the maple frosted, a chocolate glazed, a regular glazed, a regular jelly, and one of the manager's specials (*which Anne secretly loves, always some monstrosity of cream-filling and pink frosting and rainbow sprinkles … Dorothy also loves these, calling them unicorn poops*). Hope and I snuck up to their room through an emergency exit that some smoker on the staff must have wedged open when sneaking out during the night to steal a few minutes of nicotine poisoning, and was quietly ushered in by an already wide-awake (*and significantly caffeinated*) Mickey at one minute of seven (*659 being a prime that is also the sum of seven consecutive primes, all of which felt lucky/good*).

"How you doing this morning, boy?" he asked.

"I'm well," I said. "How was dinner last night?"

"Desperadoes is always super, and great fun," he said. "Those anniversary margaritas were a big hit with Anne and the kids."

"Not you?" I asked.

"Nah, I stick with Dos Equis," he said, as we moved into the kitchen, where he refilled his coffee, and pulled a Coke out of the fridge for me, sliding it across the counter. "It's a nice place with fun food and fast service.

"Yup," I said cracking open my box, and sliding his across to him. "I've never had/heard complaints."

"Oh my God!" he said as he inhaled most of the first maple frosted. "That and a strong cup of Bustello is the breakfast that God must have had when he finished making the world."

"I can't speak to that," I said, tossing Hope a half of one of her dunkers, "but it is how Hope and I start most days, when we're not camping, and it's working out so far."

Mindy shuffled out in a long t-shirt and as I far as I could see (*which was considerably more than I wanted*) nothing else, gave her dad a peck on the cheek, whispered a sleepy hello to me, grabbed a jelly from my box, and kept shuffling her way back into her room and closed the door behind her (*while Mickey was fiddling with something in his briefcase that lay open on the kitchen counter, I stealthily opened the other dozen box, and stole a donut out of it to replace my missing jelly*).

"I like this Chet fellow, but I still sometimes wonder about you and Mindy, kiddo," Mickey said, looking at the closed door behind which lay his youngest. "The two of you could be good for each other."

"I love that you think I'm worthy of your daughter, Mickey," I said, only half-heartedly fending off this old discussion/matchmaking, "but we'd drive each other crazy in minutes (*I only care about half of that equation, but mentioned both for Mickey's sake*). We have nothing in common except loving you, and I couldn't give her any of the things she needs from a partner."

This had come up at various points in the past, but we'd all managed to avoid major discomfort/embarrassment over Mickey's plans for us. Although one time, at age seventeen, I did have to flee *The City* for nearly a month (*a prolonged sailing trip with a friend of my father's, if you were wondering*), when it got too real/invasive for me after a nasty breakup for Mindy seemed to actually have her thinking about it for a day or two.

Mickey poured himself a fresh cup of coffee and grabbed me another Coke from the fridge (*it wasn't one of the real sugar ones, or nearly cold enough, but we all have crosses to bear, and in exchange for time with Mickey, I would have endured a warm mug of Tab*). We headed out to the deck with our donuts in hand to watch the sun cook the steam/fog off the lake, and melt the frost off the top 500 feet of Whiteface.

"There's nothing I can say to talk you out of the camping trip, and all the other stuff," he asked, "is there?"

"Nope," I said, "the way it's played out, I'd be leaving this young man who lives down the road from me, in the lurch … in harm's way."

"Funny, you saying it in that way," Mickey said. "You two do live in the same neighborhood, maybe in more ways than one."

"Ugh," I said. "Spare me the psycho-babble, Mickey. Xander's not at all like me."

"Yuh-huh. On reflection, I might counter that an argument could be made that you have more in common with him than you do with Mindy in there," he said, pointing a thumb towards the closed bedroom door through which she had disappeared a minute earlier.

I started to speak and then shut up, breathed deep and looked out at the mountain with the castle on top of it, shining in the morning light.

"My whole life," I started, slowly, and then picked up speed until the words were spilling out of my mouth almost faster than my tongue and lips could form the sounds. "I lived with being 'different' by knowing/believing/insisting, internally at least, that I was unique. If I can be categorized/ labeled/ put in that box, then I'm not unique, not Tyler, not anything special … just … 'that autistic Cunningham kid.' I'm the weird man-child with no home, no family, no friends … just a 'neurodevelopmental disorder characterized by social deficits and communication difficulties, and restricted or repetitive behaviors and interests, and in some cases, cognitive delays.' All things being equal, I'd rather be Tyler."

"Oh, you colossal dumb fuck," Mickey said (*Mickey rarely curses, so it took me aback*). "Of course you're Tyler: first, last, and always. The word autism (*Mickey's old school, he came up before everyone in my 'neighborhood' of difference was on the Autistic Spectrum … he still talks about autism and Asperger's and PDD*) doesn't define you any more than hypertensive (*Mickey's old-fashioned and has high blood-pressure, what can I say, besides that it worries me … the hypertension I mean*) defines me. Labels can provide useful information sometimes, but mostly I ignore them, be they on the neck of my polo shirt (*he reached back to flip the collar of his shirt, showing me that it was from Lands' End, was size large, and was one hundred percent cotton*), or my son (*at which point he reached over and pulled me in for a combination hug/ kiss/ hair-muss*).

And despite your pouty and whining monologue, you've got a home, got a family, got friends … even if you are a slightly weird man-child."

We sat there for a bit, thinking and breathing (*more loudly than a minute earlier, both of us being a bit worked up over opposite sides of the same issue*), taking sips of our drinks in the cool morning air, and eating another donut each.

"That was very kind of you to say, Mickey," I said. "But at the end of the day you're guilty of attempting to suborn your 'son' to hook up with your daughter a couple of minutes ago."

Mickey sat for three seconds, and then barked out a sharp laugh. "Did that hurt, Tyler?" he said. "You made a joke. Anyway, it sounds better to say 'son' during a dramatic speech than godson or adopted son, or whatever you are … you're my son, boy, and it's a moot point anyway, because you're never gonna be with Mindy. God knows I never believed it. I just wanted two people I love to be happy, and have something in their lives that's brought me so much joy."

We could hear sounds beginning from multiple sectors of the suite behind us, so at this point we got up and Mickey said, "Somebody tell a joke." (*This was a tagline signaling the desire to transition out of an awkward moment from 'Moonstruck', a movie we'd watched dozens of times in the old days.*) We went inside to help the rest of his family get their days started and to organize things for the drive back down to *The City*. Anne protested gratuitously about how she couldn't possibly eat that carnival-ride of a donut that I got her, but on my next pass through the kitchen (*to get Hope and I each another donut*), it was gone, and Anne was washing her hands and face at the kitchen sink with guilty vigor. Everyone was up and showered and packed a while after eight, and then they all slumped around the kitchen table with more coffee and donuts for nearly an hour, until porters came, whisked all of the bags away, and we followed downstairs to cars that the valet-squad had fetched.

Mickey and Anne gave me hugs (*his close/fierce/urgent, whispering in my ear that he wanted to take me with him, but that he understood why he couldn't, and why I wouldn't go … Anne's was loose and quick and casual*), the girls waved (*having learned years ago of our mutual dislike for Tyler-hugging*), and Chet and Rob swooped in for bro-hugs that they swapped at the last minute for stiff shakes (*with barely wrapped/engaged thumbs*). They all piled into the rental cars, started them up, and drove off and away and south.

I wanted to do nothing but hide inside of SmartPig for the next twenty-three hours, until it was time to leave for the camping trip with Xander and Cam, so that's exactly what I did (*although, as too often happens, things didn't work exactly as planned*).

Hoel Pond Boat Launch, Saranac Lake, NY, Thursday, 9/4/2014, 8:18 a.m.

Hope and I drove back to SmartPig, stopping on the way at Hannaford's (*the layout of which is much more appealing to me, both mathematically and from an avenues of escape point of view, than the Price Chopper located in the same general area*), to pick up some last minute supplies for the camping trip (*despite what Cam had said, I would not be counting on anyone to feed Hope and me while out in the woods*). Hope waited in the car for me, filled with donuts and relieved (*perhaps*) that the people I had been spending too much time with (*from her point of view, if not mine*) had left … finally. We drove back from Lake Placid to Saranac Lake, turning right as we passed through Raybrook onto McKenzie Pond Road, the road less traveled (*it may have made all the difference, I'll never know … but it did increase my confidence that we weren't being followed by the forces of evil, which made some difference, at least to me*), and then swinging wide on our route back to SmartPig to stop at Stewart's to fill my gas tank (*so that I wouldn't have to think about it the next morning*). While there we got gratuitous morning black raspberry ice cream cones for Hope and me before looping through the more arcane neighborhoods and streets of Saranac Lake on my way to the parking spot.

Hope deigned to pee on a low bush next to the parking lot, on our way up towards Main Street, which saved me having to detour with my bags for a fully implemented walk, and we squeaked our way up the elderly stairs to the SmartPig door, got inside, and secured all possible locks once we were in (*even before putting the stuff away, or organizing it*). I know my SmartPig security system earns me no end of ridicule by my landlord, Maurice (*who nevertheless approved my upgrades*), and Frank; but neither of these people knew, or would ever find out, how close I had come to dying that September afternoon nearly two years ago. After that invasion of SmartPig, I had upgraded the door and locks (*this despite the fact that I had opened the door and essentially invited my would-be killed inside … it made sense to me at the time*), and installed a peephole in the door. Dorothy knew what had happened, and still mocked me for my Fort Knoxian security measures … this in a town when most people didn't lock their front doors, and many left car keys over the visor so they wouldn't get misplaced.

Be that as it may, I felt better once Hope and I were on the other side of my solid oak door, and it had been locked and braced (*with bars going both into the frame and back/down into the floor … measures that had to be special ordered and installed by craftsmen who were generous with their raised/skeptical eyes*). Once we were secure, I unpacked and repacked my food and gear and clothes, making some adjustments in the inclusion/exclusion of various items, based on some worst-case scenario planning. I charged my iPhone and solar systems (*there seemed no point I could imagine for going into the woods with their batteries at anything less than full charge*), and packed everything that could conceivably suffer from getting wet in freezer-weight Ziploc bags. Once happy with packed packs and checked checklists, I pushed the portage pack and paddling/camping go-bag (*which was a tiny bag like airplane carry-on that would be at hand, always, while paddling*) and

Hope's camping leash and collar all by the door (*there was no chance that I would forget them, but that's just how I do things*), and shoved the tiny sleeping/snoring/farting dog who had sprawled impossibly across most of the couch to one end while I occupied the space I had cleared.

We watched episodes of *Firefly* and *ST:TNG* and *Battlestar Galactica* that we'd seen many times before … it was like comfort food to me, and possibly to Hope as well, as the patterns of action and actors and outcomes seemed familiar to her even as they were to me. Many of the scenes acted out on the small screen had been a part of my programming and memory and background and makeup for years, weaving themselves into my coding, moral and behavioral, as much as (*sometimes more*) than the flesh and blood people I knew and had known in my life … the same was true of books that I'd read and re-read over the years. Again, I felt on the brink of some epiphany that kept skipping barely ahead of, and beyond, my reach … as per usual, I ignored it, assuming that the minions in the back of my skull would announce the outcome of their toils when they were good and ready.

Sometime in the early afternoon, while making another trip to the Coke-fridge for icy refreshment/sustenance, I was bothered for the fourth time by a noise on the edge of conscious hearing in the stairwell leading up to the SmartPig landing. The old building that we occupy shifts and expands and settles during every part of every day of every season, and the heat and cold and input and output systems make odd gurgling noises in odd places, but these noises were different than the background creaks and squeaks that Hope and I have grown used to during our tenure in the ancient/weathered/tired building. Although I was ready/willing/happy to ignore them, when Hope growled and focused on the door, I crept over as quietly as I could manage to take a look.

Having seen someone in a movie get shot through the peephole, I held my hand over the viewport to block the light for a pair of anxious seconds before replacing my hand with my left eye (*my eyes see, or at least communicate information to my brain, in slightly different color schemes, and for fine detail in dim light, I trust the left eye, which is more Ectochrome than the right eye, which I perceive as being slightly more Kodachrome in color palette*). I could see nothing but black through the peephole, which initially I thought might be a thumb or (*worse*) another eye looking back at me, but after a slow seven count with no change, I decided that someone had put duct-tape (*or similar*) over the viewport. This left me in an uncomfortable position, in that a part of me wanted to open the door and clear the obstruction, while another (*significantly more sizeable/rational and perhaps fearful*) part just wanted to call Frank Gibson to come and slay the beast outside my door while I curled up on the couch with my doggie. I took a middle route, on the assumption that the former option was stupid and the latter might be useless (*the response time of the police could be upwards of an hour absent bloodshed or actual wrongdoing, more than ample time for whoever/whatever was on the far side of my door to make good their escape … I also disliked the idea of calling in the cavalry when there was a possibility that I could make this all turn out right in the end*). I called out through the door, although standing off to one side of it (*the image of an oaken-door penetrating shotgun blast rendering Hope an orphan held negative appeal for me, on a number of levels*).

"Hello," I said. "Who's out there? Surely we can talk about this like rational people."

"Whoever's out there isn't too fuckin' rational, and doesn't want you to call them Shirley," said a familiar voice behind me, which nonetheless made me jump and drop my newly opened Coke, resulting in a noisy/fizzy/drippy/sticky mess.

"Barry," I hissed at my own personal ghost, "you made me drop my Coke … and be quiet!"

"Moron," Barry said. "Whoever it is out there can't hear me; couldn't hear me if I shouted," which he did with the last part to prove his statement, which was, of course, true.

Barry was a figment of some part of my brain (*I don't have much imagination, so I cannot blame him on that part of me, as he's too large to fit in my imagination, both physically and metaphysically*); he had started appearing to me during times of stress shortly after I killed the actual/living Barry, leaving his corpse at the bottom of a deep and hidden mineshaft in a ghost town (*fitting*) in the central Adirondacks. I had been seeing less and less of him in recent months, but as this was a stressful moment, it was a fitting (*if not welcome*) time for him to make an appearance.

Hope was fully awake now, and barking at me and the space that Barry's large frame appeared to occupy. I didn't believe in ghosts, much less ghosts that my dog could see, despite Barry's continued and bothersome presence, (*which I took to be some flavor of PTSD*) but Hope was obviously bothered by my talking to thin air, and whenever I did so, would bark at me and the considerable amount of empty space I perceived Barry to take up (*in life, Barry had been well over six feet tall, broader than a doorframe and likely tipped the scales at four hundred or more pounds*). I turned and bent down to comfort and quiet my dog, ignoring both Barry and whoever/whatever was outside my door for a moment while I rubbed her ears and scratched her chin to help her re-acquire her calm; it was at this moment that I heard the distinctive sound of a pry bar tearing into the wood of my door and doorframe.

"Um," Barry said, smiling and pointing over his shoulder at the door, "how solid is that door and frame that you put in after Justin and I talked our way in that time?"

"Plenty solid," I said, in a loud/projecting stage voice, now aimed at whoever was hacking at my door/doorframe. "I told Chris that I wanted it able to withstand a charging rhino. Unless they brought demolition charges, they won't be getting in through the door."

That was a slight exaggeration, but only a slight one … the door and frame were significantly solid and had been installed with an eye to keeping people out with little/no concern for cost.

I went over and knocked on the door, "Hello," I said, "I called the cops when I first heard you, and even if they stop for donuts and coffee (*I hate to perpetuate a stereotype, but that's what came to mind … I was nervous/jittery/frightened … to the extent that I do those emotions, or states of being*), they'll arrive before you get in here. Even if you were able to defeat my door and locks, you'd walk into me unloading both barrels of my shotgun into your chest and face from back behind my couch. These home-defense loads I've got in here (*snapping the heavy-duty hole puncher at my desk up and down with an authoritative metallic 'snick-click' sound*) will deliver a cloud of twenty-eight lead balls, each a third of an inch across, into your body at a hair under nine hundred miles per hour (*nobody, not even me, understands feet per second, so I took the extra microsecond to translate into miles per hour*). If you force me to do this, I'll probably have a bruise the size of a pancake on my shoulder by dinnertime, but all of your favorite internal organs will have become external puddles on the cute runner at your feet that my landlord just replaced last winter."

"Jesus, Tyler," Barry said, "laying it on a bit thick, arncha?"

I (*pointlessly*) held up a finger in front of my mouth … Barry could only be heard by me, and Hope was ignoring me, barking at the door, either because she could hear the pry bar noises, or because she sensed the direction/intent of my address/outpouring.

The scraping and scratching intensified for another thirty seconds, and then tailed off. I heard the creaking of old steps as the person walked down the steps, and could sense them at the downstairs landing, see it in my mind. They wouldn't go out the front door, onto Main Street, so I went to the window overlooking the back of the building and parking area. Unfortunately the awning Maurice had installed to keep the snow falling off the roof from landing on his tenants also shielded people (*and this person, at this instant, most particularly*) from view from my window. The person must have worked out sight lines from my rear window, and was able to hug the side of the building to stay out of my vision until they got around the corner, and away from the scene. I waited a minute more, looking out through the tiny gap at the bottom of the door for movement/shadows/shoes, but seeing nothing I opened the door and inspected the damage.

The havoc that had been wrought on my door was more impressive than it looked at first glance. The peephole had been covered with nail polish, or something similar, in a disturbingly evocative shade of crimson (*I assumed that I could remove it later with acetone, which I keep under the sink, along with all manner of other nasty chemicals*). Scratches in the door by the main visible lock (*there were other locks on the inside that my visitor hadn't been able to get at … would have needed a Sawzall with special blades or a cutting torch to get past*) and some small chunks of the door and adjacent frame had been taken off by the person in a possible attempt to expose the lock enough to slip it with another piece of metal or credit card (*although not as easy as it has been made to appear in movies and books, this is possible with more primitive or aged locks and doors … not mine, however*). I went back in and locked everything back up again, and reflected for a moment on how the expensive/extensive upgrade had all been money well spent.

"No shit," Barry said, in a continuation of his annoying habit of commenting on my thoughts as though I had spoken them aloud. "Yah, it may be annoying, but since I live in that rat-hole, it's only fair that I can hear everything you think, right?"

"I don't know, Barry," I said aloud, "have you tried living in someone else's brain?"

"Have I?" Barry answered, loud enough to rattle the windows, if his voice had actually been traveling via sound waves, instead of simply bouncing around the inside of my addled brain. "Every person I ever met, and some I just saw on TV or movies. Not for nothing, Tyler, but yours is the last melon on Earth I'd have chosen to spend the rest of time inside of … all those stupid fuckin' numbers, you never get laid, read all the damn time, and haven't had a drink since I got locked up in here."

"Things are tough all over, Barry," I commiserated. "I hadn't seen you in a long time before today … maybe yesterday, if that was you on the way to Raybrook (*he nodded*). What, if anything, do you do when I'm not seeing you?"

"Mostly play solitaire," he said, "up in the lil' house I had along Arnold Drive. Solitaire and working out with some free weights I got—had—up there."

I marveled that my brain used up bandwidth/space in some corner of my head keeping him on-hold, instead of simply blinking him out of existence … then it occurred to me that maybe it did, and the story about endless games of solitaire and weightlifting was a way to try and squeeze a bit more guilt out of me over having killed Barry nearly two years previously. Barry started to speak up, to say something about his existence and the contest which he had lost to me, but I tuned him out, lay down on the couch, patted it to invite Hope up, and went to sleep with her reassuring warmth and weight on my chest, while Barry muttered to himself and pulled a deck of cards out of a jacket pocket.

When I woke up it was dark outside, but the air had the latent warmth and ambient noise of early evening … when I looked at my watch, it was only 8:17; still a reasonable hour to call Frank and Meg.

"Hi Meg," I said, when she picked up the phone. "How's Austin liking Clarkson so far?"

"He'll be done with his second week of classes day after tomorrow, and he's just loving it, Tyler," she said. "How sweet of you, I'll tell him you asked after him. Are you still planning on going on the camping trip with Xander and Cam? Nothing happened did it?"

I don't know if Meg is psychic or sensitive (*I lean towards sensitive, largely because I don't want to make space for psychic phenomena in my worldview*), but this was the perfect opportunity to abandon the pretense of normalcy, to drop the lone-wolf detective routine, to ask for help in finding out who had been knocking at my door this afternoon, to pass the buck to other people … people who were paid salaries to do this kind of work, to expose themselves to danger (*which sounded dirty to me … I felt/heard Barry chuckle in the back of my head*). I could say the right combination of words (*I had three alternatives worked out and on-deck in my mind at this instant*), and be talking to Frank in five seconds, and a busload of cops within an hour of that, and they might very well be able to work outwards from the scratches on my doors and frame to find out who had killed Danica and threatened me and my dog on the phone, and, most recently, tried to get into my offices and at me (*and Hope*) … it would be so simple/easy/smart to do.

"Nope, nothing happened. Say Meg," I said, "I've got a big favor to ask. Do you think that you and Frank could come by to pick me up tomorrow? It would save me having to leave the Element out at Hoel Pond for four days, and figuring out a way to pick it up at the end of the trip."

"Sure," she said, "no problem, but how will you get back into town at the end of the trip?"

"I suppose that I can hitch a ride back in with Xander and his parents," I said, and thinking ahead to a next possible question, "I could probably do that at this end of the trip also, but I wanted you especially, and also Frank, there tomorrow, in case they get cold feet about bringing me along on the camping trip … to talk them back into it."

"Oh," she said. "I shouldn't think that would be necessary, or a cause for concern. Apparently you impressed Iskra and Xander as well. She said that he's been talking about you and Hope ever since you met. Are you bringing Hope along on the trip?"

"For sure," I said. "She loves camping, seems able to tolerate Xander, and has finally gotten used to riding in the Hornbeck (*my canoe*)."

"Okay, then," she said, "Frank and I will meet you

out front of SmartPig at 7:40 tomorrow morning. Sound good?"

"Yes," I said, "but make it 7:30, and meet me around the back of the building so I can load my boat onto your roof rack."

She thought for a few seconds, seemed about to say something, and then just answered, "Yes, of course, Tyler, we'll see you then," and hung up.

With a police escort (*unintentional on Frank's part though it may be*) to get me from my front door to the boat launch at Hoel Pond, I was confident that we could get into the water and on our way without mishap tomorrow. I had drafted an email to be sent on a time-delay to Frank once we were on the water, outlining the facts as I knew them, my suspicions, and my plan to force the hand of Danica's killer; he would be angry with me, but if things worked out as I hoped/planned/anticipated they would, everything would be fine (*if they didn't work out as I hoped/planned/anticipated, then there was a better than even chance that Xander and I would be dead, in which case I didn't care much whether or not Frank was angry with me*).

Hope looked up at me from the couch as though she wanted to go out for a walk, but it seemed like a poor risk to take at this juncture; we were too exposed here in town ... starting tomorrow, we'd be in the back of beyond, and I'd be able to see and hear anyone coming near to us from a mile away. I lay down some newspaper, in case she really had to go, got another of my favorite sci-fi series/episodes running, and settled in for the evening and night ahead of us.

Frank and Meg were knocking on my door (*and calling my name, which let me know that it was them and not murderers/zombies/aliens*) before I knew it. I let them in with an apology, stopping only to splash my face before scooping up my bags and Hope's leash and following them downstairs. Frank asked about the obvious damage to my door and doorframe as we left the apartment, but I played it down as stupid/drunk college kids probably wanting to get in and take my laptop … he seemed reasonably convinced (*or at least put off enough not to push any further*). I didn't see anyone/anything suspicious in the parking lot behind the SmartPig building, the transfer of my boat and paddle and PFD and throw-bag to their car took only a minute longer than it took Frank to put my bags inside, and allowed time for Meg to take Hope down to the river for a much needed walk and pee and poop (*Hope doesn't like Meg, but she does hate her less than she does most people, and will walk for her on a leash without snapping/growling at her constantly*). I asked Frank to take Forest Home Road, instead of Route 86 to Route 186 … it would have lots less traffic, and be much easier to tell if someone was following us (*as far as I could tell, nobody was*).

We pulled out of Forest Home Road across from the Fish Hatchery in Lake Clear, and turned left onto Route 30 for the last few miles (*just a shade under five miles, actually*) until the turnoff just past the Saranac Inn Golf Course which lead us to the rutted dirt road which we bounced along (*bottoming out in one particularly deep mud puddle*) along the edge of one fairway until the road turned right and into the woods by Hoel Pond. I could see a number of cars parked near the steep log steps leading down to the water, two of them must have been there overnight, but two had people leaning against them … as we got closer, I could see that Xander and Darko and Iskra were leaning against one car (*which had an Old Town Loon, a nice and stable recreational kayak on its roof*) and Cam Renard was fiddling with a sleek looking Wenonah canoe on the roof of his Toyota wagon. We pulled up at the far end of the line of cars, got out, and had an awkward moment of nobody speaking (*which I didn't mind, although I could feel Meg and Frank shuffling their feet*) until Xander looked past me into the backseat.

"Hope to sit and then shake," he said, and people chuckled briefly. I let Hope out, and we started moving stuff down to the water.

My dark grey carbon fiber Hornbeck canoe weighs a small handful of paperclips under thirteen pounds (*yes, I know this for a fact … and it's twenty-nine paperclips*). It can fit me, Hope, and all the gear I need for an extended paddle/camping trip in the Adirondacks during any season in which I care to get my feet wet. Xander's boat, on the other hand, looked (*based on the grunting and heaving that Xander and his father were doing to get it off the roof of their car and down to the water*) to be crowding seventy pounds. They were only able to stuff a few dry bags in the front and back of the kayak before they started piling the remaining bags on the shore. Cam's boat was a long and narrow Kevlar canoe, which looked designed more for speed than cruising, but he seemed comfortable loading a number of his, and then Xander's leftover bags into the space all around the single seat. As he started to slow down loading bags, I picked up the last few, and found space for them in the front and back of the Hornbeck, eyeballing the boat as it floated to insure that the load was generally balanced front/back/left/right (*I don't do port and starboard … that's for bigger boats or fancier captains than mine and me*).

Xander and his parents went up by their car to hug and talk, and I was able to overhear some of it … it ran from "listen to Cam and Mr. Cunningham" and "make Mommy happy and proud of her big boy" and "always wear your vest in the boat." (*The last request seemed pointless as he'd been wearing it since Meg and Frank and I drove up.*) Cam grabbed a few last minute items out of the trunk of his car, and then got into his boat and waited, floating ten yards offshore (*a bit east of north of the launch, in line with St. Regis Mountain, as opposed to northwest, which was to be our initial direction of travel to the culvert, and beyond Turtle Pond*). I scooped up Hope and dropped her onto the floor of my boat, and then sat down too, allowing her to spin a few times before settling between my legs with a sigh and a groan and a fart that made me glad she'd be eating better food for the next four days (*no Chinese, good or otherwise, back in the St. Regis Canoe Area*). I paddled my boat backwards, away from the launch with my stern pointed at the culvert we'd be passing through in about eighteen minutes. I took a few pictures of Frank and Meg and Xander and Darko and Iskra and Cam, and wondered if I should say something to Frank or Meg (*Spenser never wonders that about Hawk when he's heading out … neither does Travis McGee about Meyer … I waved and pretended to catch the kiss that Meg blew me, and told Frank to look for an email from me this afternoon, which only earned me a confused look from everyone on shore*).

At 8:18 a.m., Xander climbed nimbly into his Loon 138 and shoved off with the strong confidence of an experienced paddler.

Quite an interesting number, 818 … it's both pallindromic and strobogrammatic, as well as having only two factors besides 1 and itself … 2 and 409, both primes; 2 is the only prime that is directly followed by another prime, and 409 is the seventeenth centered triangular number. I chose to take all of these as good omens for our journey (*completely ignoring Barry smiling/waving at me from next to Meg, and the fact that 409 is also the http code status code for 'conflict' … both of which might be somewhat nervous-making to someone who lets themselves be swayed by that sort of nonsense*).

Slang Pond to Long Pond Carry, St. Regis Canoe Wilderness, NY, Thursday, 9/4/2014, 10:13 a.m.

Paddling across Hoel Pond is the gateway to a number of trips, both long and short, in what is known as the St. Regis Canoe Wilderness (SRCW). It always primes the pump of my memory, pulling up a variety of maps and routes across the woods and waters. Passing the rocky point opposite the boat launch, I could see/hear Mickey and Anne and Becky (*no Mindy on that trip, I can't remember why, which must mean it wasn't specified*) and my mother and father and myself twenty-two years ago in clunky Grumman aluminum canoes (*alternately noisy and gritty and scalding or freezing to the skin*) pulling in at a dock that's no longer there at the base of the big rock face across the pond from the launch … Mickey complaining about his canoe being broken (*he was half-joking. Anne was entirely serious in her follow-up complaints as their boat kept moving in large and looping parabolas instead of the straight course my parents were able to maintain in their 'non-broken' canoe*). The taste of Tootsie Pops at nine in the morning, and folding the waxy wrapper into a smaller and smaller square, the sound of paddles dipping and dripping, and the smell of wind moving over water. I have photo and video and audio albums in my head of it all, especially the culvert.

At the northwest end of the pond, there's a big culvert where Hoel Pond dumps into adjoining Turtle Pond. I have been through the culvert fifty-seven times (*sometimes once per trip, sometimes twice on a no-shuttle trip*). You could go up and over the railroad tracks (*it's only twenty feet in elevation and less than a hundred feet of walking*), but we/I never did … we always slid/slide our boats through the tunnel, bent nearly in half, like crabs, and yodeling. My father was big on yodeling in tunnels, and it has stuck with me through the years (*except when driving through them … that would be silly*). Cam got to the beach at the Hoel Pond end of the culvert first and stretched for a moment in the knee-deep water before heading into the culvert in front of his boat (*to avoid scraping his nice boat at the end when there's a drop of roughly fourteen inches down to the water level of Turtle Pond*). I watched his boat and bulk eclipse the light from the other end as he approached the tunnel midpoint, and then began to see the light again as he got to the end and stepped down into the pool, waiting under the end of the culvert in Turtle Pond. I waited, floating, for Xander to beach and choose; he followed Cam down the tunnel, only from behind his boat … I could hear the Tupperware boat scraping as he let it slowly down into Turtle Pond. I semi-crawled down the culvert in front of my boat, yodeling and hooting like an owl (*Hope stayed curled up in her tiniest ball on the floor of my canoe, waiting for the nightmare to end*), and was rewarded by both Xander and Cam looking back into the tunnel to see if I was injured or just crazy (*I hoped some third option might present itself, but didn't offer any explanation*).

We all stood around for a minute, enjoying the nicer sand on this side, the small fish swimming around our legs, and drinking and grabbing a quick snack (*each out of his own boat/bag*). Xander was first back into his boat, and hugged the left-hand shore, weaving around, and sometimes under, the fallen trees that formed all manners of triangles with the woods and the water. Cam and I followed shortly, paddling gently in the still cool morning, more in the middle of the narrow pond that slanted to the northwest, taking us farther and farther from the cars and into the motorless/roadless wilderness. When a pair of loons put on a display for us at the narrowing of the hourglass shaped pond, Hope raised her chin above the gunwale of my canoe and gave them a lazy growl before dropping her head back into my lap and falling asleep again.

At the far end of Turtle Pond there is an extreme narrowing/shallowing (*which I know isn't a word, but should be*) of the water into a creek that connects it with Slang Pond. I have paddled through this connector in times of high water or light loads, but this was neither, so I climbed up and out of my Hornbeck and walked it, and Hope, through the narrows, climbing back in once the water was deep enough to guarantee that I wouldn't drag/scratch/snag on the bottom. Xander followed me through the creek, dragging his kayak, nose up a bit (*as he didn't have a bow-line long enough*), which made the stern end grind through the gravel and sticks a bit. Cam seemed to debate for a few seconds before climbing out (*likely his longer boat and lighter overall load could have made it through, but he did have a nicer/newer/shinier boat*) and walking ahead of it down to Slang.

"Dani and the leech at Little Clear Pond," Xander said as we were floating on the still water. It was the same water as before, but now a part of Slang Pond, waiting for Cam to get back in his boat, watching him wipe leaves and mud off his ankles.

"No, buddy," Cam said, "Dani's not here this time, and we're on Slang Pond."

My mixed bag of memories from the last few days flitted through my head, and something slipped into place with an almost audible clunk … Darmok. There's an *ST:TNG* episode that should be on any rational person's top ten list, that involves Captain Picard and Dathon, the captain of a Tamarian ship and their attempt to communicate. The challenge being that despite the universal translator (*a 'deus ex machina' that's always bothered me, although that's not important now*), the United Federation of Planets has not been able to establish communications with the Tamarian people because they seem to be stringing words together in a random/repetitive/ confusing manner. It turns out that the Tamarian language is formed exclusively of metaphors … this radically different mode of communication made for a very interesting and mind-expanding episode. I felt as though I might have the end of a loose thread indicating something interesting about Xander, but I wanted more time to think about it.

We paddled across Slang Pond and chose not to stop at either the small campsite midway across the short pond or the rocky picnic bluff at the far end. The picnic spot is beyond the carry to Long Pond, so I almost never get there, plus it is more difficult to land and get out in the Hornbeck (*funny how my choice of boats affects my choice of stops*). We pulled into the marshy and mucky put-in at the end of Slang Pond, under the white DEC sign signaling the carry to Long Pond, and I got out first, sinking in about halfway up my calves (*and worrying a bit about losing my water shoes in the muck when I stepped out*). I pulled my boat most of the way out, put on my portage pack, and then lifted Hope to dry land … this was the start of the first real carry of our trip.

"Dani and the leech at Little Clear Pond," Xander said again as he pulled into the slip I had just cleared.

"Xander Kovac, I can check you for leeches once we

get to the Long Pond end of the carry, okay?" I asked. "The light is better on that end, and there's a nice beach and sand and place to sit … okay?"

"Okay," Xander repeated, possibly just parroting my sound, and/but I believed that I heard (*or read*) something on his largely immobile/inscrutable face that seemed to understand and agree with what I had said.

"Found an Easter egg, did you?" said Cam as he pulled his boat up and into the leaves and muck. "It's a cool feeling, but don't get frustrated when it doesn't always seem to work."

"What do you mean?" I asked, knowing that the term Easter eggs, as Cam was talking about them, refers to surprises that programmers leave in software or games or websites, but I wasn't sure how that applied to this situation.

"Our friend sometimes talks as if he is showing you a picture or snapshot from his past … a memory," Cam said. "Sometimes you can tell, or figure out what it means. Other times it's impossible to tell what it means, or it just doesn't mean anything … a scrambled signal."

It occurred to me that Xander might well be bilingual (*in a sense*), speaking English and Xander, and while his ability to express himself in English was often limited by the way that his input/output worked/works, it was similarly likely that he was often more able to communicate in Xander, and that we, the vast bulk of humanity, weren't fluent/conversant/passable in his memory or metaphor or snapshot mode of communication. We were like Picard and Dathon (*the Tamarian captain, in this metaphor, played by Xander, while I was Picard, although my head is less shiny*), both parties frustrated at not being able to express themselves or be adequately understood.

In any event, we all got to the far side of the roughly 2,000 foot forested and mostly level portage. The environment appeared odd to me for some reasons until I noted that the trees were composed almost entirely of beech and birch (*not the maple and spruce and balsam more common along this pond route*). Xander and I and Hope made it in one trip: him dragging his essentially indestructible kayak (*still loaded with dry bags and paddle*) through the woods; me with my pack on my back and canoe over one shoulder; and Hope staying within ten yards of me at all times, but never under the shadow/reach of my canoe (*as she was/is scared that I'll drop it on her, or maybe that it will jump off my shoulder to smash her flat*). Cam took two trips, which meant that he would be walking three times the distance Xander and I would on these portages … no big deal on the short portages, like this one, but he'd feel it, and we'd end up waiting/wasting significant amounts of time on the longer carries (*there were some that were over a mile ahead of us in the coming days*). Xander and I walked down the log-reinforced steps into the water with our boats, and he stood still to let me inspect him for leeches while Hope swam in small circles a few feet out into Long Pond for her own reasons. Once I had certified Xander leech-free, I waded out into the clear water to enjoy the feel of clean white sand under my feet (*even with Tevas on, you can tell the difference*), and dove into Long Pond to clear my legs and my hair and my mind of the mud and bugs and mental baggage that had accumulated during the carry and before that, floating on my back and looking into the cooling bluish autumn sun as Hope swam out to hug/hold me in the water.

Cam made it back with his second load about ten minutes later, and none of us could think of a good reason not to have at least part of our lunch at such a nice spot, so we broke it out … Cam and Xander had brought sandwiches for me, and I shared mine with Hope, which got Xander wanting to show Cam her trick using part of his own sandwiches as treats. Hope ate well; we all did.

Campsite on Long Pond, SRCW, NY,
Thursday, 9/4/2014, 1:33 p.m.

We headed out to the south through Long Pond, Cam and I discussing favorite campsites on the route (*which varied greatly depending on group size and weather and season*). Eventually we agreed on a site that sits out on a peninsula about halfway down the final westward turn/leg of the pond towards the long portage out to the parking lot near the gated end of Floodwood Road. We wouldn't be using that carry on this trip, but it's always good to have an escape hatch in case the weather turns or someone gets injured or sick.

It was a gorgeous day, and all three of us were paddling at a good rate of speed when Cam called out, "Xander, race to the beach," pointing ahead to the wide sandy opening where we'd pull out our boats to explore our campsite for the first night.

Xander and Cam dug in, moving their paddles through the water forcefully … this must be a tradition for them because they were up to top speeds before I could pour on the extra effort for my boat. After a hundred yards, it was clear that Cam was holding back … his boat was longer and narrower and designed for crossing lakes at speed while Xander's kayak was too wide and short to attain nearly the same top speed. My Hornbeck canoe was light and narrow, but lacked the length to reach the speeds that Cam's was capable of, but he kept adjusting his pace and course to make it appear as though it was a close and hard-fought race to the very end … and he let Xander's boat touch the sand first.

All of us got out of the boats huffing and sweating (*except for Hope, who seemed a bit angry with me for splashing her occasionally while I had been paddling hard*). We walked around stretching and panting for a minute before all of us dove in to cool off … the day had warmed up from around forty degrees when we pushed off from the Hoel Pond put-in, to around seventy-five degrees now, and it was very sunny. The water felt wonderful, cool, clean, and clear. I opened my eyes and mouth, and could taste the pond's goodness and see fish fleeing before the three children of man that had invaded their peaceful world. After my dive and long pull/strokes underwater, I stood quickly (*knowing from past experience that if I didn't, Hope would catch up to me, and scratch me while trying to climb my back or front*).

"Daddy at the fair," Xander said when he got to his feet and slogged his way back through the water to shore.

"See," Cam said, "means nothing to me, and I've been with him for years. Sometimes it's just sounds that we hear as words."

Maybe, but, it occurred to me, they might well mean something to Xander (*probably did*), something for which we simply lacked the contextual clues necessary to decipher it/them.

"Xander," Cam said, "Let's get these boats on shore, and unpacked, and we can set up camp, okay?"

"Set up camp," Xander said. "Okay."

I lifted the portage pack, and my go-bag from the canoe, and walked a short distance from the central clearing (*as hammock-campers and tent-dwellers have differing needs regarding campsites, I gave them plenty of room*), and found a nice spot between two perfect trees quite close to the water about forty feet farther out the peninsula. Dropping my packs, I went back to lift my canoe up and onto the shore, out of the way and off to the side, among some blueberry bushes that had long since been picked clean of the summer's fruit. Dark grey as the Hornbeck canoe was, and smaller than the other boats, it would probably be invisible to anyone paddling by. My hammock was at the top of my portage pack, along with a tiny spare … just in case (*Hope had put her nails through one night, and we'd both taken a surprising three foot drop in the pitch black … she bit me in surprise/fear/dismay, despite the fact that she'd engineered the gear failure*). I hung the primary in less than three minutes and didn't bother with the tarp, which I'd brought, but left in the pack, as the weather sites I consulted before heading out this morning promised no rain for at least the next two nights.

After setting up my hammock, hanging my filter bag (*I decided long ago that pumping a filter to purify water is for muttonheads when the Earth's gravitational pull wants to do it for me*), and grabbing snacks for Hope and me, I wandered back towards the site where Cam and Xander had dragged all of their gear. My backbrain had worked out a complex formula for rating the relative importance of an item/bag, and balancing that against the weight and awkwardness of them, factoring in the ground space needed for a tent, which allowed me to map out the exact location of where they would be sleeping, possibly even before they knew it themselves (*pointless, but 'fun' for me*). Based on these calculations, I offered to help set up their tent, but Cam waved me off. He suggested that I could gather some wood for a campfire tonight. So, I wandered down the length of the peninsula, grabbing branches and logs from the woods on either side of me and throwing them into the path behind me as I walked farther from the campsite. When the imagined bean-counters in my head tapped their ledgers and nodded "enough," I turned around and headed back along the trail, at first just loading my arms, but eventually making a travois of sorts from downed pine branches to carry all of the wood behind me in a dragged litter.

I pulled my load of wood back into camp as Cam and Xander finished throwing the majority of their gear into their tent, a four-person (*assuming two of them were tiny, as I always thought when gauging tent capacity claims*) Eureka Timberline, a tough and dependable tent that I see lots of in the Adirondacks (*although since I've tried sleeping/camping in hammocks, I can't imagine why I ever bothered with a tent*). I walked past them and to my hammock spot, to refill both my in-hand Nalgene and the hydration bladder in my go-bag, drinking my fill straight from the filter when I had finished topping up. I looked around for Hope, as she generally stays on my heels when we first get into the woods (*her comfort, and distance from me increasing on a gentle curve hourly until she reaches a wander-radius of roughly fifty yards once we've been in the woods for three days*). I spotted her near Xander, hoping for more treats in exchange for sitting and, if need absolutely be, shaking.

Before heading back to the tent, I grabbed a small bag of each of our kibbles and flopped down with my back against a tree. I patted the ground next to me and spilled out a quarter cup of Hope's food on the ground. She ran over and started pecking it out of the mixed needles and twigs while I pawed through my own bag of trail mix, high-grading some M&Ms and mango and the occasional nubbin of jerky … letting my fingers make their own choices.

"So," Cam said, "what are you thinkin' for the

afternoon, Tyler? Some fishing or a paddle back to Pink Pond, and maybe explore a bit, see if we can bushwhack our way back to Ledge Pond. We've got a couple of hours until it starts getting dark."

"Just under six hours until actual sunset," I said, "and probably more like four and a half until it gets too dark to move through the woods easily. If it's cool with you and Xander, I'd like to climb Long Pond Mountain. It's been a couple of years since I've been up there, and it should be nice today."

"Hot though," Cam said, shaking his head slightly. "It's closely wooded in there, and we'd be hot going up and down."

"I sort of told Frank Gibson that I'd give him a call this afternoon," I said, lowering my voice and watching Cam intently, "to let him know how things are going."

Cam had been rooting around in a daypack for something, and now he stopped, and looked at me for a few seconds before speaking, "What's all this then *(which he did in a passable John Cleese from 'Silverado' … Cam was much better at impressions than was Dorothy)*? You're not just a tourist along for the ride on this trip, are you?"

"Xander," I said, holding up Hope's leash and jiggling it enough to make the metal parts clink, "could you take Hope to the water for a drink, and then maybe for a short walk up to the point and back?" I pointed beyond my hammock when he came by to grab the leash, to make sure that he knew which direction I was talking about … he went (*Hope did too, although her sighs led me to believe that she would have preferred to stay sleeping next to me*).

"I think that I have a way to work out who killed Danica Kovac," I said, once Xander was out of earshot, "with your help. All of this is based on my assumption, and sincere hope, that you're not the guy."

"What? Me?" Cam asked, "I could never …."

"I didn't think so either," I said, cutting off what I could guess would be a long and boring defense/defensive argument. "You don't seem organized or cold enough to do it the way it had to be done, and then be able to come to a team meeting for Xander so soon afterwards. If you'd been sleeping with her (*he started to say something, but I held up a hand and kept going*) … If you'd been sleeping with her, I could see you killing her with a knife like that … it's a passionate act, you seem a passionate person (*he took this with a nod, not knowing that I saw it as a weakness/flaw/shortcoming in his, or any human's makeup*), but you couldn't/wouldn't have done all of that other stuff to confuse the crime scene and police. That's why I took a chance on you, and this trip (*not a big chance … I guestimated it at about eight percent*), so we could smoke out the killer."

"And to do that, you need us to climb Long Pond Mountain this afternoon?" Cam asked.

"Yup, that's the first step," I said, "It's a tricky plan, that …."

"Unless you need me to know it, I don't want to," he said. "It'd just make me nervous around Xander, which can screw him up. I need you to promise me, though, that your plan involves all three of us coming home safe at the end, and whoever did that horrible shit to Dani, and exposed Xander to it, going inside forever."

"Don't worry," I said. "The worst thing that might happen is that our camping trip might end a couple of day's early, once the police catch the person."

"So," he said, "should we head out now, so you can make your call sooner rather than later?

"Nope," I said. "It'll actually work better if we time it so that we make the call around five."

That way Frank could call *Team Xander* together with only a minimal delay around sundown (*after it was too late for our killer to get out into the woods for the night*), and he could monitor phones and movement to see who took off, eager to expose his/her own guilt (*but more on that later*).

"Okay, then," he said. "I'll hang a bear bag with our food and take a small swim, and then we can head out. There's a fair bit of paddling and walking and climbing between us and the top of Long Pond Mountain."

Long Pond Mountain Summit, SRCW, NY,
Thursday, 9/4/2014, 5:04 p.m.

The three of us spent an hour eating a real lunch (*or another lunch, depending on your view of things*) and gathering more firewood and swimming. Xander mostly spent time floating in the water facedown breathing through a snorkel, with no mask … or spent time with Hope making her sit and not shake for treats. Then we headed out in our mini-flotilla back east and then north and then west again along the surface of Long Pond to get to the end of a long bay. We took the path that lead up first to tiny Mountain Pond, and then from there up an ever steepening and narrowing path to the summit. Despite Cam hinting around it a fair amount, Xander did not complain (*although he did say, "Daddy in Henry's Woods" a number of times, but neither Cam nor I could guess what that meant*).

Hope was the one who was not up to the hike. She'd made numerous hikes and climbs with me in the past. At the beginning of the summer, she and I had a long day of paddling and portaging and climbing when we had set out one morning at first light from our bandit camp on Follensby Clear Pond, paddled across Upper Saranac Lake and into Saginaw Bay, climbed Weller Pond Mountain and then paddled across Weller Pond and Middle Saranac Lake to meet Meg and Frank and Austin on their pontoon boat moored at the beach on the far side of Middle Saranac. It was a long day, and she had done it all. Today though, she began to slow and limp and complain before we got too far past Mountain Pond, and I ended up carrying her the last few hundred yards of the mountain on my shoulders, which was undignified and sweaty for both of us.

We got to the top at 4:48 and all lay down to breathe and drink and eat some of my special GORP mix for a few minutes. Once we had stopped sweating and panting and groaning like old men (*and one old lady*), I dug my GPS out of my backpack and handed Cam the listing for a geocache that was hidden near the summit, asking him to go and hunt for it with Hope and Xander. The explanation took a minute, but the concept of hidden treasure with the GPS pointing the way and clues to help were enough to get Xander going (*as they headed in that direction, I passed Cam a matchbox car as a potential trade item, in case Xander found something in the cache that he liked*). I was shocked to see two dots on my iPhone, signaling decent reception when I turned it on, and oriented myself and the phone towards the nearest tower (*in Paul Smiths, with a not insignificant amount of tree and topography between me and it*).

"Frank," I said. "Can you hear me okay?"

"Tyler," Frank said, "I got your email, and this is exactly the sort of tricky shit that I hate, and that you agreed not to do anymore."

"True," I said. "But, Meg asked and Hope didn't hate Xander and he was being railroaded and he had his family taken away from him, (*or at least part of it, but I wasn't going to quibble with Frank about details like that from the top of a mountain whilst trying to catch a killer, and yes, I used the word 'whilst' … how do you like them apples?*) and … well, I might be just grown up enough to admit that Xander and I are not as different as I may have yelled at your wife not too long ago."

"Jesus Christ," he said, "don't go all mushy on me, kid. I need you to be the sociopath I've always thought you were, at least until you help me pull this off, and get the three of you out of the woods with skins and fingertips attached."

"I like the sound of that too, Frank," I said. "So here it is … you already got some of this in the email I sent, but it probably bears repeating. The response time for the bad guy getting in touch with me to warn me off helping Xander was too quick for it to be someone outside *Team Xander*, or at most, one circle/layer/generation of gossip out from the core group. You need to have Meg get them together right after this phone call, and make sure that she knows, and shares, that I've been able to hack Xander like a computer and that I am ninety-eight percent sure that I know who the killer is. Make sure they know that we're going to finish the trip while I keep working on getting the whole story out of him. Tell them we called from Long Pond Mountain, and that we'll be finishing the loop through Bessie and Nellie and Fish Pond and so on, finishing up at Paul Smiths College on Lower St. Regis sometime on the seventh."

"Meg's gonna be pissed if I don't tell her everything," Frank said, "She won't like being used like this."

"I agree," I said, "and if you think her poker face is up to fooling a roomful of people, including a cold-blooded killer who snipped off a young girl's fingertips to hide incriminating evidence, than you go ahead and tell her, Frank. You make the call."

"Well, shit," he said, "when you put it like that, I guess I can tell her tomorrow or the next day, once things start moving."

"I think it would be better," I agreed, "but you do what you think is best … safest."

"Now tell me again," Frank said, "why you're so certain this person will come after you instead of leaving well enough alone. And why you think they'll make their move on St. Regis Pond instead'a any of the dozens of other ones you're gonna be paddling over the next few days?"

"As I laid out in detail in my email, St. Regis Pond is a chokepoint," I said, consulting the detailed maps in my head. "It is a location that we'll have to pass through on our way out that they could control pretty easily. There's a lean-to on one point near the center of the pond, and a campsite on another peninsula similarly situated. From either spot you can see and control the entire pond, and nobody is going to be able to sneak up on, or past you from either spot, because of how thick the woods are there."

"Yah, so we don't want to let this person, the killer, get out there, right?" Frank said. "But, we need to let them think about it, right, and start to act on it?"

"Right, this person is aggressive and pro-active, so they'll come out to where they feel they can get at us (*I didn't want to get into exactly how aggressive and pro-active the person was, didn't want to mention the phone call, or the attempt to break into SmartPig while Hope and I were inside*), at Xander and Cam and me," I said. "If you and yours (*meaning him and other members of the local police force*) monitor the major access points to St. Regis Pond, those being the boat ramp at Little Clear Pond, and the launch on Upper St. Regis Lake, then I bet in the next day or two, you'll see one of the members of *Team Xander*, or someone close to the inner circle show up with a boat and a weapon of some sort … likely a hunting rifle. I bet that if you can get a warrant based on that, you'll find scratches on their arms or neck from their attack on Danica Kovac."

"Sure, it all sounds good, but mebbe a little sketchy, Tyler," Frank said. "What if we scoop them up and they plead the fifth, or don't even say that much?"

"That would be the smartest thing to do," I said. "But if they think that they're still exposed somehow, or that Xander can hang his sister's murder on them, then they won't take the chance to leave well enough alone. The truth is, though, at that point, I've done my bit, and the rest is boring detail work and checking bank records and gas purchases and alibis and so on. That's not really my thing … you and other cops, you're much better at that sort of thing than I am, Frank."

Okay, I hear you," said Frank, in his winding down or fed up voice (*I have some trouble telling them apart*). "All of this oughta work, but I want you to consider, just consider, that the best thing for you to do might be to come out tomorrow morning, cut the trip short. Failing that, if anything feels the slightest bit hinky, you can pull the plug on the trip out at Fish Pond, and walk back on the old forest ranger jeep track. You know where that is, right?"

"Yup," I said, "the southeast corner of Fish Pond (*I could picture the whole area in my mental map, but I wanted to do the nineteen carries, with Xander and Cam, and get the bad guy … I wanted all of it, for all of us*). I skied out on the old track last winter with Hope … yup, we could just leave the boats and walk out if we had to, but I'd prefer not to, if everything goes okay at your end."

Xander and Cam were coming back. Xander was waving something over his head, and Hope trailed along behind, walking better now (*if I thought she had the capacity for it, I would have suspected a hustle on her part, to get me to carry her up the mountain*), so I ran back over the conversation to see if we'd/I'd forgotten anything … I didn't think I had.

"Frank," I said, "I have to go now. Be sure to let it all slip to the group: the location and timing of this call, that I believe I've miraculously figured out how to get the useful information out of Xander's head, what our route is going to be over the next few days, and make sure to cover those access points so that you can scoop up the bad guy (*or gal, I thought, trying to be an equal opportunity crime-fighter*) before they can get out into the boonies to get at us. Sound good?"

"I got it, Tyler," Frank said. "See you in a day or so. Remember there's no downside I can see to bailing out on this trip early if your Spidey sense, or whatever, starts tingling."

"Okay," I said. "Talk to you later, Frank. Bye." I hung up and turned off the iPhone to conserve the battery for Xander's use later, once we got back down to camp.

Xander and Cam and Hope told me all about the geocache, and we all agreed that Xander got the best prizes in the whole ammo-can (*a book of Sudoku, and tiny compass that could be pinned to a sleeve*). We were cutting it close, but if we hustled down the hill and back across the pond, we should be back at camp close to dark, so I picked up Hope in my arms, swung her around my neck, and started back down the hill as fast as I could manage.

Campsite on Long Pond, SRCW, NY,
Friday, 9/5/2014, 6:28 a.m.

We made much better time going down Long Pond Mountain than on our way up as gravity was helping this time. The only tough part was my having to bend forward so much to keep balanced with Hope draped around my neck (*I noted that I would need plenty of Advil later, but that I had plenty of Advil*). We didn't pause at Mountain Pond for more than a few seconds to admire the fading light pouring through the trees on the far side of the little pond, coloring the top halves of the evergreens above/behind us. I let/asked/made Hope walk the rest of the way down to our boats from Mountain Pond, and she did fine, moving with almost no limp, and keeping ahead of the three of us. Cam was talking with Xander about dinner, and about the prizes he'd found when he "won" the geocache. If they were at all nervous about the coming darkness, they were both doing a good job of hiding it. The sky was still blue and yellow (*depending on where you looked*) when we slid our boats into the water. It was difficult to see the surface with all the overhanging trees and no direct sunlight left anywhere (*except much farther west, of course*), until we got out on the main body of Long Pond.

Paddling east, roughly two-thirds of a mile down a long arm of the pond, away from the sun, we watched the last remaining sunlight climb up the pines on the opposite shore (*I could see in my mind's eye those last rays reaching out unstoppably to Montpelier, Vermont and Lewiston, Maine and Yarmouth, Nova Scotia and eventually Lyon, France and beyond*). The dark was increasing as we rounded the turn and headed into the narrows. Xander spoke loudly, pulling my attention back from a multitasking consideration of maps and positions and lumens and speed and distances.

"Dani in the big storm, when the house was dark," he said.

Cam and I slowed our paddling to talk with him, I didn't know the context of the event he was referencing, but given all the givens, I could take a reasonable guess.

"Xander Kovac, I know it's getting dark," I said, "but soon we'll be back in camp, and we'll have dessert before dinner, and then I've got a surprise for you. Does that sound good?"

"Dessert and surprise," Xander said, "Good."

"I thought that one of us might sprint ahead and get the fire started and hang a flashlight at the landing beach for our site," Cam suggested.

"That's a good idea," I said. "Since you know Xander, and he knows you, how about I do the sprinting, even though my canoe isn't quite as sprinty as yours?"

"Mr. Cunningham, go?" Xander said, with some tension/excitement leaking into his normally flat voice.

I pulled the headlamp out of my go-bag, temporarily discomfiting Hope, and turned it on to one of the flashing settings (*it was, in fact, the first time I had set it to flash on purpose … although it ends up in that mode by accident more than would seem likely in day-to-day use*). I put the lamp on my head facing backwards, and said, "Follow the light. I'll guide you back to camp, guys, and then there's a movie for Xander to watch."

Before we could get into a discussion of which

movie, or the concept of movies while ensconced in wilderness in general, I paddled at as fast a pace as I knew I could maintain for the twenty minutes (*or so*) it would take me to get back to camp. I could hear their voices receding behind me as I settled into the rhythm of paddling at speed, noting (*as I do*) that sustained high-speed paddling involves an almost entirely different set of motions/muscles/stresses than does regular paddling. Regular paddling seems to involve (*for me*) mostly my arms and shoulders, with back and torso remaining mostly fixed in space. When paddling for speed, I find that my arms are much more rigid and fixed, while my back and shoulders and torso rotate more with each stroke. My assumption is that it's an artifact of being self-taught, and the former is more comfortable and stable for the long haul, while the latter makes better use of the stronger muscle groups in my body.

At any rate, I rounded the right hand/westward turn and continued down the last stretch of pond. I was barely able to see their tent in the fading glow of daylight bouncing down from the few clouds in the sky over Long Pond (*my hammock, being dark earthy tones, like my canoe, was completely invisible*). As I scraped up onto the beach and helped Hope out of the boat, I waved my light over my head a few times, and then hung it on a tree at head-height, making sure it faced outwards, towards the oncoming boats that I could no longer see in the growing grey of evening. I quickly made a messy pile of dry pine branches and scraps of birch bark and topped it with layers of progressively larger twigs and sticks up to a top layer of a few wrist-thick ones stacked log-cabin style. I pulled a fire-cheater (*a cotton ball soaked in Vaseline*) from my go-bag, pulled a few tufts/strands loose, and lit it with a Bic lighter before dropping it down into a central vent/hole I had left in the messy fire-pile. Then I added another small handful of birch bark strips … the cheater would burn for at least five minutes, which was longer than the dry wood in the fire pit needed.

It started in smoke, but grew to fire and light in under two minutes, and once I could tell nothing surprising was going to happen in the fire pit, I jogged back to drag my canoe up and out of their way, and to see what I could do to help with dinner before they arrived. I remembered where Cam had hung his bear bag, and went to retrieve it at the same time I started to hear faint rhythmic splashing that grew in intensity, as Xander and Cam glided into the landing. I dropped Cam's bear bag near the fire and went down to help them get out of/up/away from the water.

While Cam started fussing with pots and pans and grills and food prep, Xander came over to remind me of the promised surprise (*which, since I had revealed it as being a movie, was not much of a surprise … but I had never liked surprises, and given the givens, perhaps Xander didn't either, so maybe it was for the best*).

"Xander Kovac," I said, "will you help me make supper for my dog, Hope?"

"Yes," he said, "supper for Hope," and he reached for the nylon bowl I had held out for him.

"Thanks," I said. "She's been snacking all day, and unless I'm wrong (*which I wasn't*), she'll likely beg some bites of our suppers, so she just needs two little scoops of the dog food, okay?"

"Okay," he said, taking the proffered bag of dog kibble, and pulling out two mounded scoops into the bowl while she danced around at his feet like the puppy she hadn't been since the previous millennium. Xander laughed at my usually grumpy old dog and put the bowl down for her. While she ate, I took out the GPS Spot device and sent out the 'OK' signal (*which seemed to go through in under a minute*). Xander watched over my shoulder, and spoke only when I shut the device off.

"Surprise," he said, "Movie?"

"Yeah, well I talked with Cam the other day," I said, "and I downloaded a couple of movies and TV shows on my iPhone that he said you like watching. *Dune* and *The Maltese Falcon*, and a few TV shows."

"Movies on Mr. Cunningham's iPhone," Xander said. "Watch now … please," with the last word added in awkwardly and as an afterthought, perhaps to appease one of his therapists, his version of Mrs. Portnoy.

"We've got dessert ready to go now," said Cam from behind us, "and the rest of the food will be ready by the time we're done with our s'mores, so let's save the movies until after dinner. Okay, Xander and Tyler?"

"Okay," we both said, neither of us entirely happy about it, but we followed him over for s'mores.

Cam had cut and peeled a trio of striped maple branches for the marshmallows, and he offered a stick to each of us, along with a handful of marshmallows.

"Be careful you guys," he said, winking at me from the side Xander could not see. "You don't want to stab anyone, or burn your marshmallow. Just a little brown is the best way."

"A beginning is the time for taking the most delicate care that the balances are correct," Xander said, and it rang a bell, both clearly and oddly.

"That's from the beginning of *Dune*," I said.

"Yup," Cam said, "Xander loves that movie. He used to watch it all the time with Dani. Plus what's true for interplanetary feudal society with economies based on a single hyper-valuable commodity is also true for building the perfect s'more. You need to balance everything perfectly."

"True," I said. "That's why I only use one graham cracker when I make mine (*having a cracker on top and on the bottom is too much dry and crunchy for the campfire treat, not enough sweet and melty*). I don't mean the David Lynch movie, *Dune* (*or even the Sci-Fi Channel's mini-series*), I mean that those are the words … the exact words … that begin the book written by Frank Herbert in 1965. Xander's had the book read to him or he read it … and he understands/remembers it well enough to apply it to this situation."

"That's cool," Cam said, "but no real biggie, and not a surprise. Xander can read a little, and he often brings books around with him in his backpack to places he goes, especially books that were made into movies he likes. He just grabs them. The thing that most people don't get about Xander is that because his input/output is different, and he don't talk like the rest of us (*I wasn't sure if the poor grammar was to make a point, or because Cam was distracted or thinking hard*), it doesn't mean he's dumb. He's not, he's really quite smart … just different."

"I know that expressive and receptive language and communication is radically different …." I had said, before Cam cut me off.

"No, it's not only the stuff that everyone knows about autism, or ASD as they refer to it now," he said. "His experience of the world is fundamentally different than the way you and I experience it. For us, it's like we're in the movie, but for him it's as if he's watching the movie, or reading the book, but the book's always changing, and sometimes it talks to him about something that happened way back at the beginning, or hasn't happened yet. It's stressful for him in ways that we don't, can't, understand."

"That's why he (*and I, maybe*) likes patterns and repetition and routine," I said/asked. "They're like a bookmark to help him keep his place, keep track of where he is and what's going on."

"You saw him this afternoon," he said, "doing the floating thing?

I nodded.

"That's all part of the same thing," Cam said, handing Xander another five marshmallows, and sliding over the cooler, on top of which were the squares of chocolate and the graham crackers. "We, he, discovered that on a trip to Bermuda that the Kovacs brought me along on a bunch of years (*how many, I wanted to break in and ask, but didn't*) ago. We all went snorkeling and it was okay, but mostly he just loved the feeling of floating and breathing in the water. I tried to talk with him about it one time and got the feeling that he liked the pressing, the pressure, pushing on him from all sides. You might have seen him reaching out to touch the walls or other people or jumping and stomping his feet into the ground? He likes the physical feedback, it places him … helps him place himself in the world, in his world. It stops him drifting. When he's drifting, unsure of his place, his routine, it's when he's least happy, least comfortable or able to communicate effectively with us, with the rest of the world. That's when he's unsure of his place and what's going on."

I turned to look at Cam, disappointed with myself for seeing so little beyond the beard and tan and outdoorsy friendly act; this was someone worth knowing, worth picking apart like a library or an online archive … he could help me get to know me, more. He noticed the expression on my face and smiled.

"You're not him," he said, "not even close, but you're about as close to him as you are to me. It must suck, in a way."

"Why," I asked, "would you say it 'must suck'? I do what I like to do, camp all year, know people, people who care about me. I'm smart, I read, and I help people."

"Oh yeah," he said. "I get all of that, and that's all good, but you know there's a gap, a void between you and everyone else. I can feel it in you, see it in your eyes. Xander doesn't know. Sure he gets stressed when routines break down or when he has to do things he doesn't want to with people he doesn't like or know, but I'm pretty sure he thinks that's how everyone lives, what everyone's movie or book or whatever is like."

Hope limped over and nuzzled me, and I reached absently over to the cooler and picked up one of the outrageously-sized graham crackers (*honestly, no decent or right-thinking person needs a graham cracker that is four sections across ... your mouth would just dry out entirely, and the flavor's too boring anyway*) and broke it into singles, giving her one every fifteen seconds or so while both of us thought our thoughts (*me about the nature, and possible curse, of self-awareness, and Hope likely about how she'd rather be eating some forbidden chocolate more than another section of a wildly large graham cracker*). Xander tried to extinguish a flaming marshmallow by waving his stick around.

"Xander," Cam began, be carefu ..."

The flaming marshmallow went flying off into the darkness (*thankfully not in the direction of their tent*), and I unconsciously reached down to grab Hope's collar before she could give chase in an attempt to upgrade her evening snack. Watching, and then replaying the event in my mind, I was reminded of a trebuchet that I once built and used in Central Park with disastrous results.

Cam had, in the meantime, bounded off, and stomped the firebomb out before it could ignite the dry and highly flammable forest floor. When he came back, he had obviously shifted gears and started gathering dessert supplies up and putting them away, in favor of tin plates with smoking and blackened foil packets on them.

"Smells good," I said as I gingerly picked the foil open, managing to only slightly scald my fingers on the steam as I succeeded.

"Hobo stew for dinner from Mommy," Xander announced. "Daddy venison, little carrots, blue potatoes, mushrooms ... which I don't eat ... butter, salt, pepper, rosemary, and a pinch of oregano."

"Xander, I guess you've had this before," I said. "It all sounds like stuff that I like."

"No new foods on this trip," Cam said. "New foods are something that take a long time for Xander to get used to. Every snack and drink and food item and even the way it's presented is the same as it's been for years. The dessert first plan only worked because he likes s'mores, and from now on we might have to keep doing it, or we'll get a meltdown."

"Sorry," I said, "I didn't know."

"How could you," he said, "and anyway it worked and got us back to camp before full dark, which is the important thing. He doesn't like the dark. Do you Xander?"

"No," Xander said, quickly and forcefully and with no small amount of fear in his voice, which reminded me that he hears everything, even if he doesn't/didn't specifically listen to everything.

Dinner was good, although too much food for me (*luckily, Hope was willing to help me finish my hobo stew*). While we ate, Xander and Cam talked about, more nearly recited, the itinerary for the rest of our trip, in terms of both food and travel, as well as most of the things we'd be seeing and doing. I enjoyed watching the two of them interact, particularly in light of my earlier discussion with Cam. We all threw the used foils into the fire to cook off the fat and leftover food, (*I made a mental note to retrieve them from the ashes in the morning before any fire was started*) and Cam gathered the plates and bowls and utensils. He was starting down towards the water when I held up a hand.

"Let me do the dishes," I said, "and you can help Xander get going on whichever movie he wants to watch."

"Watch *Dune*," Xander said, taking the iPhone from me as soon as I pulled it from my shirt pocket. I barely had a chance to switch it to airplane mode (*to save batteries while it looked for signals it could not possibly find down here among the trees and in the shadow of so many hills*).

"He'll have no trouble finding and playing the movie," Cam said. "Dani always let him play with her phone. Every once in a while, he'd figure out her code, and fill the thing with those eye-candy games and weird apps he'd find somehow."

Xander found his way into *Dune*, turned to Cam and said, "Xander in the tent, goodnight."

"Are you cool if he takes your phone with him?" Cam asked. "The battery'll be run flat by morning, but he'll have a better night if he can watch the movie and play with your stuff until he gets sleepy. I hope you've got everything backed up, back in the world, so you can repair it once we get home (*the thought of someone, anyone messing around with my phone and the information and resources I had in there made me decidedly uncomfortable, but I am adept at keeping my face neutral, and did so, nodding rather than putting words to the lie*)."

I walked down to the shore with my headlamp on, followed by Hope. We waded into the pond, and I pot-walloped everything. It's a hijacked term that my father used to mean scrubbing with sand and pebbles until reasonably clean (*forest rangers that I know would frown upon the practice, but my father always said, "people have been doing it for a long time, and the lakes and ponds and fish and bears are all still here")*. I made sure to chuck the first "scrub and rinse" of each batch as far out into the pond as I could. Hope played the role of pre-wash, licking each plate and cup and bowl and piece of silverware clean before I got to it. We made/make a great team.

By the time I got back up to the fire pit, the fabric of their tent had that particular glow to it that only modern electronics seem to bring. Xander was talking along quietly with bits of the movie, and Cam was making a ceremony of ripping open a foil-pack of Backwoods cigars.

"Do you mind?" he asked, waggling the pack in the air between us as I settled down on the lid of one of the coolers.

"Not so long as I don't have to smoke one of them," I said. "I actually somewhat like the smell of the smoke outside and in low concentrations, plus there's an argument to be made for it keeping away the bugs (*not that there are many bugs at this end of the summer*)."

"Cool," he said. "You answered my next question as well." He leaned towards the fire pit to grab a stick with one lit end to allow him to light his cigar like a cowboy (*or maybe like an Adirondack Guide*) of yesteryear.

"So are you done for the night?" I asked, gesturing at the tent and Xander within. "Does he settle down and sleep through the night? That sounds odd, like I'm talking about a baby. I don't mean any disrespect. I'm curious."

"No," he said. "I get it. When I'm tired, I'll get him up to pee once more. Otherwise, there's a fair chance he could pee in the sleeping bag. Not because he can't control it, but it's just not a big deal to him. Remember, like watching a movie or reading a book, he can't always be bothered with paying attention to the little stuff. After that, he'll sleep for a while, most of the night maybe, and then wake up. He'll stay in the tent until I'm up though, because it's the rule, but also because he's more than a little scared of the dark. He's got a flashlight and your phone and some toys and books and stuff, and on these things we generally get up when it gets light, which should be around …"

"Exactly 6:23," I said. "I'll be up by then also. You guys might also hear Hope and I get up and move around a couple of times during the night. I don't ever sleep eight straight hours, and in a hammock on cool nights, I tend to get up to pee a couple of times." It seemed as though I was oversharing, and wasn't fully certain why.

We stayed up and talked about life in a small town, people we knew in common, the kidnapping case I'd been involved in the previous summer (*yes, I admitted, I did use crazy-glue on their skin as an alternative, field-expedient, restraint*), his boat, my boat, what it's like camping out in a hammock when the temperature drops below zero, and a painfully circuitous discussion of his current/past/hopeful girlfriends to determine (*I think*) my dating/sexuality status (*I didn't/don't/won't date, and could best be described as asexual*).

"Nobody ever?" he asked, in an incredulous tone, while lighting another cigar. "Not even out of curiosity?"

"Never," I said, feeling a freedom to speak honestly that I hadn't had before. His questions and interest didn't make it sound/feel as if I'd done anything wrong (*beyond being me/different*), perhaps because we were out in the woods, or (*and this one made me momentarily guilty, an emotion/feeling I generally don't do*) because he'd worked with Xander for years and seemed to enjoy time with him despite his obvious differences.

"Can't," he pressed, "or don't want to?"

"Both," I said, poking the fire and reaching out with a toe to rub the sleeping belly of Hope, "or neither. I'm not attracted to other people, of either sex, in the ways that most people seem to be."

That seemed to kill that line of conversation, as it has in the past, but without the negative feelings/looks/comments I ordinarily associated with "the talk." We compared/shared stories of portages with our boats, rough water we'd paddled, mountain climbs with/without great views, the local Amish bacon versus all other bacons, Canadian and Mexican Coke versus the ordinary stuff, and shelter/rescue dogs versus purebreds.

"Father! The Sleeper has awakened," said both Xander and Paul Muad'Dib from within the tent and the Arrakeen desert of *Dune*.

"How long has he been watching that?" Cam said, at least partly to himself. "It's about time I shuffled him outside and then off to bed."

"Paul takes *The Water of Life* about five minutes short of the two hour mark," I said, "and there's only about eighteen minutes left of the movie, unless Xander likes watching the credits."

"Outstanding!" Cam said. "Xander Kovac, twenty more minutes and the movie's over and it'll be time for bed for all of us." Digging out a small flask from his pack, taking a sip and then wiggling it in my direction, he said, "Can I offer you some cocoa additive? Peppermint Schnapps."

"No, thanks," I said. "I don't drink ... alcohol."

"I thought as much," he said, "but didn't figure it would hurt to offer."

He asked about how Hope and I found each other, and I heard myself telling him more than I usually do (*although none of the stuff/ details without a statute of limitations*) about how my dog and I put a dent/slowdown in Adirondack meth production, and then Cam and I made plans to meet over at the TLAS next week to get Xander back into the shelter (*without Dani, who had been his previous partner in those visits*). At this point, I could hear Sting (*as Feyd-Rautha*) talking trash inside the tent, and then getting stabbed through the chin and up into his brain for his troubles, and started gathering my stuff and preparing to put out the fire. Cam started to ask something, and then smiled as he heard the closing credit music.

"That must come in handy," he said, "keeping shit like that in your head."

"It's a blessing and a curse," I answered because, of course, it was/is/will be for me, as well as for Adrian Monk, who coined the phrase in this meaning/incarnation.

Hope and I left the area around the fire and headed into the dark to take care of our nighttime stuff, mostly organizing, repacking, and hanging my portage pack, with the go-bag stuffed into the top of it. I sleep better if my gear is stowed neatly, and rather than hang just my food, I hang the entire bag (*ever since I had a squirrel chew a bag up where a tube of toothpaste had opened earlier in the day and had not been one hundred percent cleaned up, I hang everything*). I shut my light off, climbed up into the hammock with my Kindle (*for when, not if, I woke up during the night ... hoping I could avoid waking Xander and/ or Cam*), invited Hope up inside with me, and went to sleep.

I woke up twice during the night, once a few minutes before one o'clock to pee (*Hope was doing some form of dance on my kidneys that I was powerless to resist*), and once about a quarter past four, when I heard some fishermen put a boat down by the water's edge at the end of the long carry in from the Floodwood Road. I read and had a drink and ate a small handful of human kibble and went back to sleep both times. I never heard either Xander or Cam until 6:27, four minutes after the chart in my head for September said the sun would rise in this area, on this day, and then it was only when Hope shifted to growl at the form next to our hammock.

"I thought you said you'd be up," Cam said, in a tone designed to signal that he was kidding. "I'm gonna start the fire for breakfast in a minute (*pancakes and butter and bacon and maple syrup, as Xander had told me last night*)," and he started to walk back down the point towards the fire pit and tent and Xander.

"Wait," I said, "don't forget to grab the foil from last night's dinner out of the pit before you start the fire." I had planned on getting it, but Cam had beaten me out of bed.

He turned back towards Hope and me, looked over and beyond us by a bit, and said, "Huh? There's no trail or portage there, I wonder … that fisherman must have pulled to shore to take a …"

I assume from both context and speech patterns that Cam was going to say "dump," but he didn't finish his thought because at that instant his head snapped back in a pink mist (*adulterated with drops and clumps and chunks*), and as he started to crumple, I heard the loud/flat/clapping sound of a high-powered rifle, that shouldn't fill these woods until (*I thought for the tiniest bit of a second, reaching for two Saturdays after Columbus Day*) October 25th.

I put it all together before Cam finished falling to the ground, but quick thinking couldn't undo my hubris and underestimation of an adversary … at least not for Cam, who was irretrievably dead.

Campsite on Long Pond, SRCW,
Friday, 9/5/2014, 6:34 a.m.

I slid/dropped out of the slit in the bottom of my hammock, landing on Hope as we half-turned in our descent. She squealed and bit me. I spent the next few seconds waiting for a bullet to open up my head as well. The shot and attendant oblivion didn't come, and I noticed that, not surprisingly, I had company.

"Hello Barry," I said to the ghost who haunts only me, and only when I'm stressed or in danger. "Whoever it is can't see us clearly enough through the brush to take a shot, right?"

"Yah," Barry answered. "Whatshisname was standing tall and when he got clear of any obstructions, the shooter popped him. You know what that means?"

"It means all kinds of things, Barry," I said. "It means the shooter recognized Cam, was the noisemaker that I took for a fisherman at four this morning, has been waiting since before first light for a decent shot, is set up (*I used Cam's direction of gaze in his last moments and my knowledge of the shape of Long Pond to make a guess*) approximately 270 yards to the west of us on the bump of land east of the portage, is confident/competent enough to go for a headshot at that range, so is probably a hunter, and is now waiting for me to panic and expose some vital portion of myself for him to shoot off."

"I was just gonna say it means you're fucked," Barry

said. "But you're prolly right about all that other stuff too."

"Maybe not," I said, "he's got us pinned down, but he's over there, and as long as we don't forget about the high-powered rifle and walk around, he can't shoot us. Beyond that, I've got a game changer in my bag that can break the stalemate in our favor."

I low-crawled over to the tree I'd hung my bags from, and risked a hand by reaching up high enough to undo the knot, allowing the stuff to drop with a loud crash to the ground next to us. I reached over and pulled out the GPS Spot and turned it on, preparing to send the A & B signal (*send Frank to the given coordinates ASAP*). I felt, for a moment, as though things might work out (*except for Cam, of course … things weren't going to work out for Cam at all*), when I heard the unmistakable sound of the tiny tent zippers being unzippered. I grabbed the straps of my pack tightly and turned to look at their tent.

"Cam will make pancakes and butter and bacon and maple syrup," Xander said as he started to climb out of the tent.

"Don't even think about it," Barry said (*somewhat facetiously. Living in my skull as he did/does, he knew that I had not only thought about it, but I'd made a decision*). As I scrabbled/turned around to face the tent and started crab-walking in the direction of the voice, Barry complained, "If that mook in the woods pops you, I'm all the way dead, and bad as this is … gone is gone."

I wasn't getting there quick enough because I could see that Xander had finished with the bottom zipper and was now standing crouched in the tent's doorway pulling the vertical-ish zipper up to let him out, and into the line of fire. At the moment the tent's door was fortuitously facing the sunrise and away from the shooter, but the geometry of the scene would change in an instant, when Xander exited the tent and was standing in the clear … exposed. I shifted, from crabbing along below the level of the blueberry bushes and other scrub lining the shore, to running stooped over. I was shockingly aware of a cold line starting at my waist and growing colder as it rose up my spine to my head … all of it now exposed to what I knew, from firsthand experience, to be an expert shot who wanted to kill us.

"Duck and weave," Barry shouted, but I didn't have time or the inclination to listen, and simply ran straight at Xander, utterly surprising the bigger man when I tackled him as he came out of the tent (*stretching and scratching as everyone does when leaving a tent first thing in the morning*).

"Xander Kovac, the person who hurt Dani is here and wants to hurt us," I said, wincing a bit at my insensitivity, but needing to get my point across. "You need to stay on the ground and not stand up. Can you say that back to me?"

"Person who hurt Dani is here," he said, looking scared and sad. "Stay on ground, not stand up. Hide and seek?" A small, hopeful smile made me wish momentarily that I was a hugger (*and that Xander was a huggee*), but neither was the case.

"Yes, hide and seek," I said. "Go back in the tent, low, like a bug, and wait for me to call 'Olly Olly Oxen Free,' okay?"

"Okay, wait in tent," he replied, and back in he crawled.

I low-ran back to my gear, with Hope at my heels, and activated the second button in the A & B combination, which should alert Dot to call Frank and have him race to my/our rescue. That done, I took a second to breathe, and only then noticed the stink coming from Cam's corpse … blood and shit and something else (*maybe brain and skull*) with only a hint of urine. It bothered me to think of the pile of meat and bones sitting nine feet away from me as the person who I had a pleasant evening with a few hours ago … it bothered me more to think that if I thought/acted more cleverly/defensively, he might be alive this morning.

"Coulda, shoulda, woulda," said Barry. "What you gotta do is keep the kid under cover and stay cool until the Gibson cavalry arrives, and hope that the shooter isn't smart enough to figure … aw fuck!"

We both heard the sounds of stuff being thrown into a Royalex canoe (*I can't explain the differences here and now, but once you've heard stuff thrown into a variety of canoes, you can tell them apart*) at the same instant, and drew the same conclusion (*logically, since we both occupy the same brain*) … the shooter had gotten tired of waiting for one or both of us to show ourselves, and was moving closer to get/take/make an easier shot. There was no stay and fight option, so running away was the order of the day, but I had no idea how we (*meaning the three of us still living*) could outrun a bullet from a person able to make a headshot at nearly 300 yards. I threw a map of the area onto a projection screen in my head and tried to come up with something that would yield a positive outcome. The clunk/scrape of the shooter stepping into their boat and pushing away from shore helped me decide … it wasn't much of a plan, but ….

"Too fucking right," Barry murmured from beside me. "The big difference between staying here and trying your plan, is that your way you'll die out of breath, or maybe drown before you get a chance to bleed out from multiple gunshot wounds."

"Thanks for the vote of confidence, Barry," I said,

turning around and running back to the tent, scooping up my bag on the way. "I'm going with my idea, but if you've got a better one, I'm all ears."

Barry smirked and tilted his head, mocking me.

"Xander Kovac," I bellowed, feeling guilty for my loudness, but the excess adrenalin was spilling all over my calm at this point. "We're leaving right now, a race in the boats. Come out now."

He came out of the tent without his shoes on (*I was also missing mine, having just woken up a few minutes ago, when all of this started*) but with his snorkel uselessly poking out of a pants pocket, and I grabbed his arm and pulled him to the beach and boats, and perhaps our only chance. I could hear my iPhone in his hand, playing the scene from *The Maltese Falcon* when Joel Cairo holds Spade hostage in his own office to search for the Falcon … that was roughly a half hour into the movie, so he must have been watching for a while this morning … I was glad he hadn't gotten up/out with Cam, or I might be leaving two dead bodies behind, instead of just one.

I dragged our boats into the water, and threw my pack and Hope into mine, scrambling back to the bushes for my paddle, and only then catching sight of my would-be (*probably be?*) killer just clearing the shore and getting into a routine of paddling. Thankfully, I could see that he had a short fat Old Town fisherman's canoe, and a single-bladed paddle … if we could only get launched, we might have a chance to pull away from him once on the water … there was a chance (*and I could work to improve on that if we lived beyond the next three or four minutes*). I got back to the water's edge with my paddle and checked to see that Xander had his; he did but no PFD (*I almost giggled at the thought of getting a ticket from a forest ranger at this point, and took a breath to try and control the panic that was growing inside me, feeling as though it was going to burst my skin all over*). I shoved his boat into the water and away from the campsite.

We were on the far side of the peninsula from our attacker, sitting low in the water, with bushes and such between us. It was just possible that he (*I knew his sex now*) didn't know exactly what we were up to yet (*that would change very soon*). Hope tried to climb up and out of my Hornbeck, swept up in the upset/panic of the morning, but I couldn't allow that, so I grabbed her by the collar and jammed her back into the bottom of the boat and thundered at her, "STAY."

Long Pond end of the Bessie Pond portage, SRCW, NY, Friday, 9/5/2014, 7:17 a.m.

Pushing my boat out and away from shore, one foot in and one foot shoving, I did a crazy balancing act (*that nearly ended the escape right then and there because I came very close to tipping into the pond*) for two long seconds before regaining my balance, grabbing both gunwales, and sitting down, only partially on my dog, who had the good sense not to say anything. I twirled my paddle into position and starting digging desperately at the water in front of my boat, willing my little boat to go faster and faster from the horrible man and weapon behind us.

"Xander Kovac," I called as my boat passed his, struggling to keep my tone even and quiet-ish, "remember we're racing … first one to that rock sticking out of the water gets a prize."

"Effie and Sam in the office," Xander said, and then continuing in his imitation of Effie Perine's voice from *The Maltese Falcon* (*which was, by the way, better than all of Dorothy's imitations … ever … put together*), "Look at me, Sam. You worry me. You always think you know what you're doing, but you're too slick for your own good. Some day you're going to find it out."

I was chilled by his pick and prescience and seeming understanding of the situation, and decided in an instant that I owed him some small measure of the truth of our situation. "Xander, the man behind us hurt Dani and hurt Cam, and wants to hurt us. If we can paddle faster than him, and hide in the dips and bends of this pond, I think we might be able to get away, but it will be hard and scary."

Xander didn't say anything but began to paddle a bit faster/harder and soon caught up and started to edge past me. Hope whined up at me from the bottom of the boat, and I took a half-second that I didn't have to give her a belly rub, and tell her that I loved her (*which might even have been true. I don't know exactly what the words mean, but it seemed as though she did, and she quieted down for a while*).

"Hey Steve," I shouted over my shoulder, at Steve Street, the Kovac family lawyer, "too bad you brought a bathtub to a canoe race … you'll never catch us in that thing."

"Are you fuckin' crazy, Tyler?" Barry asked, suddenly appearing beside me in a much longer, much bigger, and entirely imaginary Hornbeck canoe, that was keeping pace with me. "Rule number one of fuckin' canoe chases is never, ever, taunt the only guy who's armed with a rifle."

"I need him to keep chasing us for a bit," I replied to Barry, keeping my voice low, so Street wouldn't hear me. "If he lands on our campsite point, instead of paddling after us, he can shoot us both before we make that bend in the pond just ahead."

"Steve, I thought it was you, even at the beginning," I shouted, lying (*but forgivably I assumed*). "But I didn't want to perpetuate a cultural bias/stereotype against lawyers without real evidence … which I guess I've got now."

I looked back and it appeared that he was not stopping at our campsite, not getting out to steady his aim on a branch and take two easy shots … he was continuing his chase, enabling us to make it around the next bend in the pond. Once past this initial hurdle, we had a chance (*not a big one, but a chance nonetheless*) as long as Xander and

I made good use of the terrain (*by which I meant effectively hiding in the bends and coves and peninsulas of this pond*). I kept an occasional eye and ear on Street to make sure he didn't land and line up a shot on either/both of us. By now he would have figured out that he should have landed and shot us from there, but he might not have a map of this pond (*as well as the ones beyond it in every direction for miles*) in hand or head, and might be hoping/planning for a longer straight shot (*literally*), in which he could take the time to land and line up his rifle with one or both of us (*I wasn't counting Hope in this case, because I assumed that he wouldn't bother shooting her … and I didn't want to think more about her being left out in these woods alone, thank you very much*).

The truth was, assuming the map in my head was accurate (*and it was*), once we rounded this bend and turned north up Long Pond, he'd be unable to line up a shot (*because of convenient landforms getting between us*) until the pond branched off into a number of cloverleaf-like bays at the north end … at that point, he could land and shoot us if we hadn't opened up the gap enough to make the shot too difficult for him. To be sure, this would be a challenge for Xander and Hope and me because the technicians in the operations-center of my brain were telling/ordering me to head to the northernmost bay and take the carry up to Bessie Pond. This required balancing the risk of a longer exposure to risk of gunfire on Long Pond with the increased chance of safety and escape if we could make it to woods and water deeper in the SRCW (*as opposed to re-tracing our steps of yesterday, and heading back to Slang Pond, along which route he could follow us, and have a straight and easy shot at us in the water from the Slang end of the carry*). I followed and even agreed with the logic behind the decision my back-brain had made, but with some trepidation about going even deeper into the wilderness with my old and grumpy beagle and a young man who might decide to melt down or freeze at any moment, while being chased by an accomplished killer, armed with a rifle that he knew how to use at range.

A bullet buzz-thwapped by my head (*honestly, that's the sound it made while zooming by*), a few feet off to the right, followed almost instantly by the sharp and thundering report. I turned partway to glance over my shoulder and saw Street sliding the rifle back into the bottom of his boat, and picking up his paddle to continue giving chase.

"No way that out of breath, and in a moving canoe, he's gonna hit someone else in a moving canoe from a few hundred yards," Barry said. "No fuckin' way. Plus, if this chase lasts long enough, his rifle's bound to rust sooner or later, laying it in the bottom of his boat like that." Barry said this last bit with a smile that I could feel, I didn't take the time for visual verification.

"Thanks, Barry," I said. "Do you have any helpful thoughts or ideas?"

"Yup," he said. "Paddle faster than the guy with the rifle."

Hope growled in his direction (*likely because my having conversations with my imaginary friend, who had once tried to kill me, made her nervous and angry, but in this case I chose to interpret it as annoyance with his inappropriate sense/timing of humor*), and I paddled and paddled and paddled … beginning to feel the first edge of a cramp, and fully cognizant of the fact that I'd had nothing to eat or drink so far this morning, and neither had Xander. We might well have a long and stressful day in front of us (*unless it ended abruptly/early/soon with a little help from the Kovac family lawyer … a cheery thought*).

We were hundreds of yards ahead of Street now, and widening the gap each second. The narrows were straight ahead of us, and beyond that would be the open expanse of the pond between us and Street. If he was smart enough to land and shoot from the point that jutted out into the cloverleaf juncture of Long Pond, he might have a shot (*in both senses of the word*) … probably not a head shot, but who needs artistry, in the backwoods, a bullet in the trunk would kill either/both of us … just as surely.

"Xander Kovac," I puffed, feeling the end of my strength somewhere out in front of me, not too far, angry that I might not have enough to get Hope and this young man home safely. "Let's have one more race. If you can get to that white sign over there (*I pointed with my paddle to a white spot barely visible more than a thousand yards ahead … possibly imagined and/or supplied by my brain because I knew it was there and wanted to be able to see it*), I'll give you my iPhone, to keep."

"For true, Mr. Cunningham?" Xander asked. "Yueh's gift to Paul."

"Maybe a bit," I said, "but yes, for true, you can have the iPhone if you make it over to the white sign first."

I was startled again because he was referring to a piece in the book *Dune* where Dr. Yueh gives Paul Atreides a small and nearly magical gift (*a tiny electronic bible*) to assuage Yueh's guilt about a secret he was hiding from the youth … again Xander managed to pull a relevant reference/metaphor that he shouldn't have been able to (*I would very much like to get to know him and his brain better, if we survived this day*) … he'd obviously read *Dune* at some point in his life, or at least chunks of it.

We paddled and paddled. Hope was shivering and crying between my legs on the bottom of the boat, having reached some doggie conclusion about the general shape of our day from the hurried departure and the gunshots this morning (*she hated that sort of noise, even on a good day … I kept her in and watched loud movies on the 4th of July, and during the fireworks of Saranac Lake's Annual Winter Carnival*). Xander was talking to himself (*or me possibly, but I could make nothing of the isolated words and phrases that I picked up as we panted and grunted our way across the open water*). Barry and I were silent except for the increasingly noisy breath sounds I was making (*Barry seemed unfazed by the chase*). A cold spot grew on my back, below where my neck joined my shoulders, and I could feel/hear the shot, and imagine how I would tumble forward and out of my boat, leaving Hope in the middle of deep water, and Xander paddling for the far shore, to win a race, and then the nothingness beyond … for both of them.

Chancing a peek over my right shoulder, I saw Street's boat nosing into shore, and him stepping out and reaching for his rifle … stumbling a bit and then recovering, disappearing up and into the undergrowth for a moment, then reappearing, his head only (*with a yellow ball cap … funny how your, or at least my, brain grabs for details at the oddest moments*), from behind a waist-high boulder (*glacial erratic, I corrected myself*), steadying his rifle. I imagined for a second, that I could see my death in the black mouth at the end of the barrel (*although, of course, it was much too far for me to see anything other than the general shape*). Turning back around and yelling for Xander to paddle, I sensed the cold spot at the top of my back more than ever, and was waiting, almost hoping for the terrible impact that would end this horrible cat and mouse game/chase.

Street fired, and I heard him racking the bolt, pausing, and then firing again. He did this eight times before he stopped (*presumably to reload, which might have told me more about his rifle, if I knew more about firearms, which I don't*). I didn't have any holes in me/my boat. Xander was still paddling, and I started to believe that we might make it. That's when the next shot hit me.

It didn't, of course, thankfully, hit me … it hit my boat, a couple of feet behind me, making a hole in the Hornbeck, thankfully not in me, and thankfully (*also*) above the waterline. But the noise and sensation of it hitting the boat, passing through the carbon-fiber hull and into my portage pack so close behind me was enough to allow/force me to auto-hypnotize myself into believing Street had shot me. I slumped forward and felt the pain where I had been imagining it would hit, and Hope stretched her long nose up and kissed the tip of my (*substantially shorter*) nose, which brought me back from my un-fun daydream.

"Paddle, fucknuts, or he really will hit you," screamed Barry, in my ear, like a hundred drill sergeants from a hundred movies, and I did … I paddled.

Street kept firing, and reloading, and firing, and reloading … even after we finally reached the opposite shore and dragged our boats into the dense brush and thick trees that made up the shoreline at the north end of Long Pond.

I could see the rock location where Street had been firing from, but could no longer see his yellow cap; neither could I see his boat on the water … yet. He would be thinking about what came next, and while he did, Xander and I needed to eat and drink, if we wanted to be able to continue running from him, even in the short term. I snuck down to the water's edge and filled my Nalgene and hydration pack with pond water, barely reaching my arm out of the brush enough to dunk the bottle and pack under the surface of the water (*Giardia was a long term worry/issue/luxury that I forced out of my mind, since my gravity filter was still hanging on the tree by my hammock back at last night's campsite*). I kept an eye on the pond where Street's boat would have to appear if he was planning to make the crossing, while I got out some kibble for both humans and dog. As soon as I poured a few cups of Hope's food onto the ground for her, she began to nibble at it while I pushed a few handfuls of my version of GORP into my mouth, and then held the bag out to Xander.

"No," he said, "pancakes and butter and bacon and maple syrup."

"For fuck's sake," Barry said, thankfully neither Xander nor Hope nor Street could hear him bellowing. "Now is not the time for him to be a finicky eater, Tyler."

"Xander, I know we were going to have pancakes this morning, but we're going to have them later," I said, feeling not the least bit guilty about this needful lie, "once we get to Fish Pond. But for now, we need to fuel up with some of my special treat food. Do you like M&Ms?"

He nodded, and I handed over a bag for him to look at.

"If you want, you can just eat the M&Ms out of it, but I think you'll like the other things too … there are blueberries and yummy nuts," I said, holding up a finger in Barry's direction to head off his inevitable "yummy nuts" comment as Xander reached into the bag and took out a few M&Ms. "Good, huh? That's better than nothing."

I kept an eye on, not the horizon, but what seemed like it, the peninsula from behind which Street would come sooner or later, intent on killing all of us *("Except Hope and me," Barry offered with a smile)*. While the seconds ticked by, and we ate and drank (*I traded GORP bags with Xander when he had cleaned out all of the M&Ms from his, I think he got some fruit and nuts in his mouth by mistake, which I chose to count as a victory*). I watched and listened, waiting and hoping for Frank (*or someone … anyone*) to swoop in with a helicopter and get us up and out and away before the next phase of this chase started.

It was over a mile's carry up to Bessie Pond, and then a series of tiny ponds and carries beyond that … we could probably be safe-ish if we could reach Bessie, but it all depended on how much Street knew about this particular trip. The maps didn't show an extra pond between us and Bessie because it had only been made in the last few years by beavers damming up a stream. If he tried to run us down on the carry without his boat before we (*with boats and no shoes*) could reach Bessie (*which would be the book/map smart thing to do*), then he'd have to turn around and go back for it, wasting time. If he knew about the beaver pond (*which was only about a hundred yards in from Long Pond*), then he'd be on us before we could make it to Bessie in our bare feet. We could leave the boats and head into the woods, but that seemed penny wise and pound foolish, given that we had faster boats and no shoes for hiking in deep forest. All of these thoughts, and a thousand more, ran through my head while we spent a few minutes snacking and drinking, and then refilling the bottles and hydration pack. I dug out a pair of aqua socks I had shoved in my portage pack; Xander was willing to wear them when I offered the option of them or bare feet (*I felt that I could manage the hardships of scrapes and punctures better than he could*). He'd slipped them on when Hope gave a low growl and I turned to see Street's boat nose around the edge of the peninsula … we had to go, plan or not, we did.

Bessie Pond, SRCW, NY,
Friday, 9/5/2014, 8:53 a.m.

"Time to go, Xander," I said. "We've just got a short walk through the woods, and then another short paddle."

He muttered something under his breath, but since he started dragging his kayak, I didn't inquire or ask him to repeat it (*not wanting to interrupt the flow of useful activity*). Hope stayed between Xander and me on the short walk between Long Pond and the beaver dammed marsh/pond. As we started getting back into our boats a few short minutes later, I reached out with my brain and mental-map and math to try and figure how close Street was to the shore from us … not far enough. I pushed Xander's kayak free of the muck and followed him across the short neck of water (*not more than fifty yards, but enough, maybe, to slow Street down and allow us the time we needed to hustle across the longer carry up to Bessie Pond*). We got across and a short distance up the portage, and then I believed I could hear sounds behind us.

"God damnit!" Street yelled. "Can't I catch even one break?"

Presumably he was referring to the beaver pond in his way (*which he evidently hadn't known about*) as he'd run up the trail with his rifle to try and shoot both Xander and I before we reached the far end of the portage. I had trouble feeling sorry for him, all things considered and kept walking as fast as I could barefooted. The need for speed and the extra weight from my canoe and pack was pressing my soft feet harder and harder with each step into the rocky/pokey/ouchy ground (*mind over matter can only take you, or in this case me, so far*). I was more than ready, but less than happy, when Xander dropped his kayak in the middle of the path a few minutes later, and turned to me while sitting down on a fallen log.

"Movie now, then pancakes," he said, getting my iPhone out of his pocket.

"Xander," I said, trying to manufacture a gentle and relaxed tone that was very much not in keeping with my mood/feeling/outlook. "The bad man is coming, and he could hurt us, shoot us, like Miles Archer at Bush and Stockton, in the movie, *The Maltese Falcon* (*I was hoping that was in his metaphorical wheelhouse of similes*). If we can get to the end of this carry, and on the water again, we should be okay (*I was probably lying, to myself and him, but it might save us, at least in the short term*)."

He got up and started walking down the path talking to Hope and grumbling at me. The kayak was still in the middle of the trail, and I almost called him back, but then reconsidered. We could make better time without him having to drag the thing across every portage, and if I dumped most of my gear (*and just threw a couple of things into my go-bag*) my canoe should have the freeboard to take all three of us … just. I took Xander's paddle apart, and threw the two halves as far as I could manage, one on each side of the trail, propped the kayak up on a big rock and in the crotch of a tree so that it would block, or at least slow, Street's passage through the woods, and took off after Hope and Xander … as fast as I could hobble/limp at any rate. I had the barest outlines of a plan knocking around in my head and caught up to the two of them a few hundred yards farther down the trail.

They were walking at an ever-slowing pace, but fear and adrenalin and the barely-gripped edge of an idea had me pumped up and I was nearly jogging by the time I caught up to them.

"Xander," I said, throwing down the portage pack and canoe and grabbing a few necessities out of the bigger pack and stuffing them into the smaller go-bag, "I have two chocolate bars here (*Hershey's Special Dark was one of the meltdown interrupters mentioned by Cam during our pre-trip talk, but I figured they might also be useful to head off and/or avoid one*), you can have one now, and one at the end of the portage if you'll drag my canoe the rest of the way to Bessie Pond, and then stay there with Hope until I catch up ... sound good? Can you say it back to me?"

"Drag boat to pond, wait with Hope, good," he said (*I felt horrible about asking him to do so much, but I couldn't think of anything else at this point*).

"Great," I said, thrusting both chocolate bars into his hand, turning to make sure that my paddle was clipped into my boat, giving Hope a pat/rub/scratch, and then turning around and running back down the trail towards Street. I felt guilty about the bribe for a number of reasons: it was a little degrading/demeaning, it would establish a pattern for our relationship which I was not happy about, I could/would run out of suitably motivating bribes before we got out of this mess (*and if our relationship was built solely on exchange, then once I was out of goods he might not 'do business' with me any longer*) ... I tried not to let any of this worry me, or enter my voice, as I only really cared about making it through the next ten minutes (*if I/we didn't, then nothing else mattered*).

A few winters ago, I was snowshoeing up Scarface Mountain from the trailhead in Raybrook on a gorgeous February morning after a cold night in which six inches of new snow had fallen on top of what snow we already had. I had hit the trail by first light in the morning and had not seen a soul since leaving the parking lot, when I came across fresh mountain lion tracks and still-steaming scat in front of me. It crossed and then followed the trail heading up towards (*eventually*) the summit of Scarface. I started jogging, hopefully to see my first mountain lion, and was disappointed a few minutes later when its tracks veered off the trail and doubled back in the direction I'd come from. Not knowing any better (*which seems to be how the best stuff happens, or is discovered/ learned*), I left the trail and followed the mountain lion tracks for a few minutes, up a gentle rise. They seemed to loop back and to the left, and I eventually ended up on top of a ridge overlooking the trail I'd been walking eight minutes prior. The area was obvious/visible where the cougar had stopped to watch me, and perhaps thought about taking me in ambush while I foolishly followed it hoping for a picture (*it hadn't eaten me, obviously, but it could have, and the trick stuck with me, apparently to this very day*).

When I stopped, about halfway back to where I had left Xander's kayak, I listened for a frustrating twenty-three seconds (*I had silently promised myself and Xander and Hope a full thirty seconds, but I couldn't handle waiting the final seven seconds*) … nothing. After wedging the kayak between the rock and tree limbs, I had peeled off the trail and climbed up a short hill through the woods, picking my way along a ridge I'd seen off to the right as I originally had made my way down the trail. I came to a spot three noisy/sweaty/scratchy/foot-stabby minutes later, and was roughly fifteen feet to the right of, and twenty-five feet above, Xander's kayak, still blocking the trail. I looked around to find what I needed, grabbed them, and sat down to slow/even/quiet my breathing and wait for

Steve Street to catch up on the trail.

"About fucking time," Barry said from beside me (*in a shocking lack of solidarity, Barry was not missing shoes as I was, was not all scratched up and bleeding as I was ... he looked rested and ready for whatever the afterlife had to throw at him*). "If there was ever a guy needed killin', it's this one."

"Barry," I wheezed quietly, half-listening for Street's approach, "I appreciate the moral support, even if it's amoral, but I don't want to kill Steve Street ... or anyone ... I wish, fervently/daily/resolutely, that I hadn't killed you. I simply want to hurt and/or scare him enough to make him realize that his best bet is to make a getaway, rather than waste his time chasing Xander and Hope and me through the woods."

"Yah," Barry said, chuckling a bit, "good luck with that. This guy's a couple slices short of a loaf, and he's got a hard-on for the kid, along with anyone standing between them. I'll give you mad props for your respect for life, even if it comes a bit too late for some of us, but Jesus Christ, Tyler, Ghandi would have killed this motherfucker ... twice."

I was about to explain myself to ... myself (*essentially*), and to congratulate Barry on his use of hyperbole in debate, when I heard a low cursing and hollow thunking noise down the trail that anyone used to backcountry portaging recognizes as not taking a turn tightly enough with the canoe on your head, and bashing it into a tree or some such. I settled even lower and quietly waited for Street to get to my deep woods roadblock. Two minutes later the canoe came into sight, with what I assumed were Street's legs underneath it; a minute after that, he came to a full stop in front of Xander's kayak. I had debated when to take action, and so it was at this moment that I lofted a huge and solid log down at the spot where I imagined his head would be, under the shell of the canoe.

The log fell perfectly, spinning lazily towards the top/center of the canoe as he stood there, thinking (*probably*) of what to do about the unexpected kayak in his way, not knowing, not even suspecting that I was dropping a safe (*well, a log anyway*) on his head like Wile E. Coyote on the roadrunner, only much more successfully. The log hit the top of the canoe, and Street dropped under it instantly, as if the ground had opened up beneath him.

After a slow thirteen count, the canoe started to lift on one side, and I threw another big log down smooshing his arm and likely rattling his brain in the process. Ten seconds later it started to lift on the other side, and this time I lofted a fair-sized rock, which made a fantastic noise when it slammed down onto the front end of the canoe (*I couldn't tell you if it was, in fact, the bow or just the end that faces front when he's portaging … it varies from canoe to canoe*). I waited a few seconds, making sure that my next few missiles were in place, and then yelled down to him.

"Steve," I said, "It's Tyler … from the other day. If you're still conscious under there, knock twice on the skin of the canoe."

A second later there came a slow pair of knocks from under the canoe.

"Good," I said, "I'm glad. Now stay under there until I say differently, or I'll put all of the logs and rocks that are up here down there, on top of you and your canoe … if you understand, give me another two knocks."

He knocked again.

"You've got a bolt-action rifle with you, yes?" I asked. "Don't bother knocking, I heard it earlier. Moving the canoe as little as possible, and keeping in mind that I've literally taken the high ground and so far have only been throwing smaller logs and rocks, take the bolt assembly out of your rifle, and throw it a few feet up the trail, away from Long Pond."

A bit of rustling and some metallic sounds, which although necessary/expected, made me a bit nervous, and came from beneath the canoe. Then a thin arm snaked out and threw the mostly L shaped piece of steel a few feet in front of his boat ... it clattered off the front, which must have scared him as he yanked his arm back in very quickly.

"Thanks," I said, "I know that I feel better now, knowing that I won't have to kill you. I imagine it's a frustration to you that you can't kill Xander and Hope and me ... Hope's my dog, by the way, but that's not important right now. What is paramount to the situation is that minutes after you shot Cam Renard this morning, I was in touch with Frank Gibson, and by now they're on their way out to recover the body. You're as good as caught. It's not a secret anymore, or at least it won't be in a few hours, so you should use this time to go away. There's no longer any point in killing Xander. If you understand that and would like for me to let you go, give me two more knocks on your canoe. If not, then do nothing, or try and escape, and I'll pile the rest of the forest on your head from the top of this cliff and then call it a day. Your choice."

Barry was sitting on the edge of the cliff, swinging his legs forward and back, smiling as we both heard the expected two knocks.

"This worked nice, Tyler," he said. "But you're being Tyler-smart and real-world stupid again, making the same Tyler-mistake you always do, countin' on nutjobs and scumbags to act rationally, or at least your version of it … lettin' him go for Christ's sake," and he snorted with laughter.

I faltered here for a moment, unsure because I had defeated and disarmed the bad guy, and now it made sense to me to send him on his way. I didn't want to make some sort of half-assed citizen's arrest. Surely, Frank (*and all the other Franks*) would be able to pick up Steve Street before he got too far down the road, but I'd been here before, and made similar assumptions and had been proved wrong time and again for either overestimating or underestimating humans. I thought about it for another second, and then addressed the canoe.

"Steve," I said, "Can you hear me okay? You can talk now, for this part, but stay under the canoe if you don't want to bring on all manner of blunt force trauma."

"Yes," he said, "I can hear you."

"Good," I said, "I'm having something of a debate with my inner demons (*waving at Barry, who smiled and waved back*), and a part of me thinks that I should make a day of it and kill you so I don't have to keep looking over my shoulder. Can you think of a compelling reason, moral and sanctity of life arguments aside, that I shouldn't kill you here and now?"

"The fact that you're asking is proof that at some level you don't want to kill me," he said, getting to the crux of it (*'fuckin' smart people,' whispered Barry from inside my head*).

"Also," he said, "you managed to beat me when I had the drop on you and had my rifle, and now I don't have either. I'd have to be pretty stupid to come after you again."

"Point taken," I said. "So say I'm convinced … how

do I let you go, and how do I know you're gone?"

He had thought, down there under his canoe, for thirty-seven seconds before answering.

"I've got it," he said. "I walk back down to the beaver pond leaving my now useless rifle right here, you follow close, or at a distance, whichever suits your fancy, and watch me paddle away. I portage back to Long Pond and get in my boat and whack the side of it so you can get a feel for where I am before I paddle away. You never see me again, and vice versa."

"What's to stop you waiting an hour and coming back down the trail," I said, "after Xander and me … and Hope, my dog (*I felt as awkward leaving her out as including her, and I'm certain he couldn't have cared less*), to kill us during our afternoon naps?"

"Common sense," he answered quickly. "You beat me to a standstill when I had all the advantages. If I came after you later, you'd likely get the drop on me again, and only then you wouldn't have this debate before killing me."

"True," I said. "You convinced me. Leave the rifle and go back down to the beaver pond. I'll follow from a distance, and watch. I'll be waiting to hear you set out on Long Pond ten minutes later. If I see you again, I'll kill you … twice." I nodded to my old friend, Barry, who stood up to dust himself off for our walk back down the trail.

It seemed like a good plan, and I didn't have to kill anyone, which made it a borderline great plan. Street did his part, and headed back towards Long Pond. After a decent interval, I returned to the trail, retrieved Xander's boat and paddle pieces (*and threw the bolt and rifle onto opposite sides of the trail in their place*), grabbed the gear and portage pack I'd dumped when we'd split up, and dragged everything the rest of the way down the portage to the shore, finally, of Bessie Pond.

Walking down the last fifty yards of the carry, and squelching my bruised and cut feet into the cool/soothing mud and sphagnum moss, I dropped the kayak and portage pack, said hi to Hope and Xander, and continued into the mucky/twiggy/leechy water at the launch. Once I was out over my head (*where Barry might argue I'd spent the last hour and a half, or longer*) I took a deep breath and dove, swimming down and out as far as I could before surfacing. I looked back shorewards and saw two anxious faces watching me.

"I'll be back in a minute, and explain what's next," I said.

"Pancakes and butter and bacon and maple syrup?" said Xander, with a hopeful and slightly desperate tone in his usually flat voice.

Fish Pond, SRCW, NY,
Friday, 9/5/2014, 2:07 p.m.

After my swim in Bessie Pond, I waded ashore, discreetly peeled a pair of leeches off my left leg (*I/we didn't need Xander melting after all we'd been through this morning*), pulled a bag of human kibble out of the go-bag, and shared it back and forth between Xander and myself. He was muttering about pancakes, every minute or so, raising his voice a bit, and once reached over and gave me a sharp pinch on my arm, but I felt that he was, perhaps, resigned to disappointment, as he never escalated to a full-blown meltdown as Cam had described them. I passed a few chunks of jerky and some pistachios to Hope, who happily gobbled them down while I tried to think my way ahead, listening (*and trying not to look as though I was listening*) to the woods behind me. Between Hope and Xander, I was travelling with some perceptive beings who had had a rough start to their day, and I didn't want them to pick up on my worry.

The map in my head was likely more accurate and detailed than the one in my go-bag, but I hauled out the printed one anyway, just to make sure. Bessie was only the first pond that we got to on this carry, but not the one we needed. We would have to backtrack a hundred feet or so, and take the left hand fork (*as opposed to the right hand one, which had taken us to Bessie*) and portage another hundred and fifty yards to Nellie Pond. We would need to paddle across Nellie to get to another portage (*this one much shorter than the last*), which would take us to Kit Fox Pond. From the far side of Kit Fox (*which a strong boy could have thrown a small rock across*), we had another short (*albeit slightly longer)* portage to Fish Pond. Fish Pond was our goal, at which point I fully expected to be rescued by Frank and/or the forest rangers and/or the state police. After all, my GPS message would have led them to come across the peninsula on Long Pond, where they would find Cam and the abandoned campsite. They'd be anxious to find us. I showed the map to Xander, explaining my thoughts, although it didn't appear that he was paying much attention.

"iPhone broken," he said, which would have been easy enough to believe, given the morning we'd all had, but I wanted to check … it started and then died again, signaling a dead battery which was easy enough to fix with my charging setup.

"Xander," I said. "Your iPhone isn't broken. The battery is dead. I can charge it once we get up to Fish Pond (*a lie, as I could have charged it right here. It was a lie I was happy to tell in the service of our forward progress to one of the nice campsites, perhaps even one with lean-tos, on Fish Pond to await the cavalry*), okay?"

"Okay," he said. "Lunch now?" I could understand his hunger pangs, despite all of the snacking he'd been doing, he hadn't had any real food (*or even any great quantity of my human kibble)* since dinner last night.

"Xander," I said, "I have another chocolate bar for you now, for fuel to get you to Fish Pond, and once we get there, we'll catch a bunch of fish (*Cam had told me that Xander liked fish and fishing, so long as he didn't need to touch/clean/gut/cook them*) for you and me and even Hope to eat. Sound good?"

"Good," he said, looking at Hope, perhaps thinking of her fishing with us.

We set out on foot, then paddling, then on foot, then paddling, then on foot, and finally paddling on the shockingly big water (*after all of those tiny ponds*) of Fish Pond. I kept listening to the woods and water behind us, scared/hopeful/anxious about what or who I might hear, but I heard nothing but the expected woodland sounds, and allowed myself finally to picture Steve Street hopping in his car and driving away from us/this/here. The midday sun was hot and bright and clear and served to burn off some of my fear and apprehension as we paddled out into the middle of the southern bay of Fish Pond. But, it also reminded/reinforced how tired I was and I assumed Xander was as well (*Hope had been riding during the paddle portions of our day, but walking the portages, and highly stressed earlier in the day, and an old lady to boot, so I could assume that she was tired, too*). This, in combination with a nagging concern for Barry's words about me being Tyler-smart in a (*mostly*) non-Tyler world convinced me to aim for the campsite directly across from the end of the carry from Kit Fox Pond, and set up shop there.

We pulled our boats ashore and Xander and Hope went up to the clearing and fire pit immediately, while I carried/ferried stuff up from the boats. My portage pack and go-bag had a number of useful items in them. Xander's boat seemed to have nothing in it that we needed up in the campsite, but I heard something rattle around when I flipped his boat (*not expecting rain, but it's a habit once acquired not easily ignored*). I pulled out his snorkel and hooked it over/through a loop in my shorts to allow me to carry other stuff up also … thinking that he might want the snorkel so he could do some of his floating/meditation this afternoon.

"Xander Kovac," I said. "We're safe now, but just in case, if anything happens, if anyone comes, you take Hope up into the woods and stay there until I call 'Olly Olly Oxen Free', okay?"

"Okay," Xander said, walking up the hill, munching on some people kibble, not appearing to listen to me, but not openly/actively rebelling either.

After setting up my spare hammock (*this one lacked bug-netting, but is still way more comfy than the ground*), I gathered a bit of firewood from close by, not bothering to ask Xander or Hope for their help. They were both asleep in the hammock almost as soon as I set it up.

I kept an eye/ear on the far shore for signs of movement (*which would most likely signal a bull-headed stick-to-it-tiveness on Steve Street's part that would bewilder/surprise, but not truly shock me*). By the time I had set up camp, gathered firewood, set up the charging station and iPhone, and refilled the water containers that we still had, I was reasonably sure/comfortable that Steve wouldn't be coming. I headed down to the water to catch some fish for a late lunch for the three of us.

The area in front of where we had landed, and subsequently pulled up our boats, was a wonderful mixed environment for pulling in a variety of lake fish, if you didn't care what you got (*and I didn't, although I hoped for no pike, as they are tough/nasty/muscled beasts that I often end up hurting by accident before I get the chance to kill them humanely … this may sound like sophistry to non-fisher-people, but it's not*). There were shallows with weeds and lily pads, a narrow stream pouring off the hillside into the pond, downed trees providing shade and shelter, and I sensed from the cold and current, that it dropped off quickly and possibly even had cold springs bubbling up through the sandy bottom nearby. I rotated through the somewhat limited supply of lures in my backcountry fishing kit (*a variety of Mepps Aglias and Comets*) and soon had my low-rent stringer (*a long piece of paracord with two bowlines and a carabineer*) filled with perch and sunnies and a couple of bass.

I was looking forward to cooking a nice big lunch for Xander and myself (*and giving Hope as many of the pan fish as she wanted*), when I heard the tiniest possible metal-versus-wood noise from the opposite side of the bay (*a scant seventy yards away*). I started to bend down to look into the tree line across the way when I heard a loud popping noise, and it was as though the top of my head came off. I stumbled back a pair of awkward/nerveless steps while other shots from the handgun plowed into the shore/water around me, before my legs gave out. It hadn't occurred to me that Steve Street might be carrying another weapon. I fell into the water, crashing into one of the downed trees that was giving shade to the fish, on my way down (*curious, now recalling something that Barry had said earlier in the day about drowning while bleeding to death, and already getting the first inklings of what could possibly be a useful idea*).

Fish Pond, SRCW, NY,
Friday, 9/5/2014, 2:13 p.m.

As soon as I hit the water, I knew I wasn't dead … fatal gunshot wounds to the head don't sting. I had the presence of mind not to spring right back up and out of the water after my knees collapsed, I stayed limp and floating in the water to think for a few seconds.

Steve Street had obviously reconsidered his options, and decided that having another firearm (*this one apparently a handgun of some sort, based on the noise it had made … along with the fact that I wasn't dead, since he was shooting at the outer-edge of its effective range*) tilted the balance enough in his favor to make another encounter between us seem like a good/smart idea. Based on the last ten seconds, I had to agree with his assessment.

It was a reasonable assumption that he would be paddling over in my direction to finish off (*or make certain of*) the job on me, and then find Xander up in the woods (*where I hoped he was hiding with my dog at this moment*). I was face down in water two feet deep, and bleeding from a significant, but not life-threatening, head wound (*when either my head or the pond water moved, I couldn't exactly be sure which, I felt a not-insignificant tear/flap of skin opening and closing along with the motion*). I had no weapon besides the small blade on the multi-tool that I have/use for fishing, which luckily was still hanging off me thanks to the leash I attach to it (*having learned from experience that a jump/wiggly/slippery fish can make you drop and lose any tool that isn't attached*). My fishing pole was not within sight of my eyes, which were open and looking mostly at the water and weeds and sandy bottom and a dead tree which I had smacked into during my fall. I could only pray that the tree was providing me some measure of cover. I felt the sensation of something buoyant snagged in a belt-loop, and I was deliriously happy when a fumbling left hand (*I was floating in the water with my right side facing out, and towards Steve, and my left side to the shore, and presumably not visible to him*) found Xander's snorkel. Slowly, moving as little as possible, I brought the snorkel up to my mouth, bit down on the mouthpiece, and breathed in, hoping that the exposed end wasn't too exposed.

I nearly choked and coughed (*and likely would have given everything away in the process*), when I breathed in a mouthful of water but managed—just—to restrain the cough and simply swallow the water that had been partly filling the tube. My next inhale was ninety-nine percent air, and it felt wonderful going in, which made me realize I'd been holding my breath and hiding as a pretend corpse in the water for most of a minute. Now I was able to focus on other things, like Steve, and how a three-inch blade and a borrowed snorkel could be used to defeat a handgun in close-quarters combat.

The sounds of him shifting around in the canoe, along with the rhythmic splash of the paddle in the water, were off to my right (*and slightly behind me*), and getting closer with each passing second. I starfished my arms and legs infinitesimally, and managed to rotate my body, floating in the water, in what I hoped would be/appear a natural dead-body-in-water movement. I caught Barry's hand motions out deeper in the water and looked his way. He was, bizarrely (*if there was any bizarre left in a world where I talked and traveled with my own personal ghost*) using a SCUBA setup, and giving me a complex set of hand directions … not unlike what you see in movies and TV between members of tactical units before beginning an operation. Thanks to the miracle of modern PTSD (*and the fact that we shared one brain*), I had no need to follow/understand the hand signals. I tilted my head towards Steve in an painfully slow manner (*the glacial speed with which I rotated my head on my neck was particularly agonizing in light of the lack of time that I had, and the fact that he might, at any moment, decide to put a couple of 'safety' rounds into my lifeless body*). My intent was to watch for an agreed upon confluence of things: his proximity to me, a continued paddling motion/rhythm (*that would indicate his not being about to shoot me … again*), and my readiness for the admittedly foolhardy action I was about to take. All three lined up nicely about sixty-one seconds later (*61 is the 18th prime number, the 9th Mersenne Prime, a centered square and hexagonal and decagonal number, which occurs three times in the list of Fortunate Primes and are so named because of their discoverer, Reo Fortune, not because they're lucky … which is too bad, because I was hoping for luck*). During those sixty-one seconds, I (*slowly*) opened the (*admittedly tiny and not very deadly-seeming, particularly when compared with a handgun*) blade on my multi-tool, undoing the catch on the carabineer/paracord stringer I'd been using. I made sure that I kept the former attached to my belt loop while releasing the latter to drift away (*hopefully not to go too far, for the seemingly contradictory reasons that the fish would surely drown horribly tied together as they were, and that/then I would not be able to eat them*).

Hearing/feeling the paddle hit the side (*inside*) of his canoe less than ten yards from me, I took an especially deep breath, spit out the snorkel, pulled myself quickly/fully down and into the water by the tree I'd been resting/sheltering against for the last few minutes, swam along the bottom of the pond … intentionally stirring up as much muck and crap as I possibly could, since I had/have no idea how far/fast/effectively bullets can penetrate the water, or how significantly parallax distortion in water can affect aim (*I made mental note to study both of those things when/if I returned to my office*). When I got out and under Steve's canoe, I pushed hard off the mucky bottom and rocketed (*somewhat … I wanted to rocket anyway)* upwards, trying to stay as close to directly under the boat until the last split second, when I diverted my momentum to the left side of his canoe (*in the hopes that he was right handed, so his gun would be farther away when I broke the surface*). I reached one hand out of the water to grab his gunwale at the apex of my upward motion, and then with my other hand starting from my hip, pushed up against the water, propelling myself, and the left side of Steve's boat, downwards in a fast/sharp/hard movement that defeated both his balance and his boat's stability, and tipped the whole package ignominiously into the pond … and on top of me.

My plan (*Barry's plan, really*) was to take full advantage of the first second or two of Steve's (*everyone's, but most specifically Steve's*) atavistic fear of capsizing/submersion. He was going from fully clothed/dry and armed and travelling across the surface of the water, totally in control and in charge of the situation, to the exact opposite in an instant. His fear and shock and surprise would cause him/anyone to freeze for a couple of moments. I needed to strike while he was off-balance, afraid, caught up in the chaos of the whirlwind as he tipped and spilled into the pond water, with me.

His first instinct was to swim up from the water to the air, so I pulled him downwards. If he even had the gun anymore, he had forgotten it (*possibly forgotten what a gun was)*, and spent a split-second trying to scramble back into the flooded canoe (*which would float, forever, even if sawn in half, thanks to the brilliant formula that makes up* Royalex). During this time, I grabbed the knee of his jeans with one hand (*in the frenzy of the moment, I wasn't immediately sure which one ... playing back my internal tape of the event later, I grabbed his left pants-leg with my right hand*), ran my left hand out along the leash of my multi-tool until I got the end with the open knife blade, grabbed it firmly, and stroked the sharp blade across the inside of his leg roughly halfway between knee and crotch, cutting deeply and firmly. The effect was instant.

Steve howled from the surface of the pond and lashed out at me with both legs, flailing crazily. He connected with my nose and some key component of it crunched very loudly, perhaps because I was underwater, perhaps because he broke it. In either case, I swam back and down and away from his legs, noting a spreading cloud of darkening water from the area below his waist. He brought both hands down instantly to his thigh, and I saw the bright silver L of his dropped handgun spinning/drifting slowly down to plug/sink in the muck and twigs at the bottom of Fish Pond. As Steve started to descend below the surface of the pond, he let go of his leg with his right hand and pulled himself back up into the air, and onto the floating/swamped canoe. It was only then that I broke the surface to take a much-needed breath (*secure in the knowledge that the danger to me and Xander and Hope had passed ... Steve Street was dead and simply hadn't stopped breathing, or, more to the point, bleeding, yet*).

"Wait for it," Barry said, from his position dog-paddling on the other side of Steve's swamped canoe. "Now he'll want to talk, want your help."

"Tyler," Steve gasped, looking around crazily, and finally finding me treading water safely out of range, "You have to help me. I'm bleeding, pretty badly (*a serious contender for obvious statement of the year as the water around him continued to redden, as his face and hands continued to whiten, the one in direct proportion to the other*)."

"Yes," I said. "I know. I cut you. I'm bleeding too, I'm pretty sure that you broke my nose, Steve."

"To hell with your nose, Cunningham," he said. "We need to get to shore and apply pressure to the cut."

"I don't think so, Steve," I said. "I begged you. This morning I begged you to leave, and we discussed in detail what would happen if you tried again."

Steve groaned and shifted hands, perhaps trying to stem the flow of blood from the wound in his leg, his mouth going underwater for a second and then coming back up spitting out water, his eyes bright and wide and scared and more than a little crazy/crazed.

"Besides," I said, "I don't think it would do any good at this point, even if I wanted to help, to save you. I sliced your femoral artery with a very sharp, if embarrassingly tiny, blade, and I'd bet (*based on my research, as well as movies and TV I've seen, I'd likely win*) that the business end of the artery has retracted back up towards your hip/groin. Judging by the water around you, and your pallor, you've lost a couple of pints already."

I wondered where the stringer with the fish I'd caught earlier was, and hoped it wasn't currently being bathed in the cloud of blood that Steve had disgorged, and was continuing to pump, into Fish Pond. I was already hungry when I had finished fishing, I'd need sustenance even more after I was done dealing with the aftermath of all of this, and I didn't much fancy the idea of fish marinated in Steve.

"This is important, Steve. Dot will want to know details," I said, but he seemed to already have trouble keeping his eyes and attention on me. "Steve, stay with me here. Can you tell me why you killed Danica Kovac … I think we all know that Cam and your attempts at me and Xander and Hope (*he was having a harder and harder time focusing by the minute, but he looked especially confused for a moment*) … my dog, we've covered this, Steve … everything after Dani seems a classic bad-guy blunder-spiral, not being able to avoid scratching the itch, but I'd like to know about Dani, so I can tell Dot. She's a curious one."

"I think you better speed things up here, Tyler," said Barry, swimming over and looking closely at Steve, shaking his head. "Simpler questions, maybe. Might I suggest something in a yes or no?"

"She wanted to buy him a house," Steve said, "a house and some roommates and a trust, funded to keep him comfortable in perpetuity. What's he need with a house? He's not even a person, not really, just a noisy, messy, expensive pet."

I started to speak, to redirect, but Steve interrupted (*perhaps didn't hear me*).

"But that 'thing' is gonna live virtually forever. I've talked with his docs. He's healthy as a horse, and all their grandparents lived way past ninety, even back in the old country of Whoknowswheristan."

"But why kill Dani," I asked, hoping to get a better answer before Steve went the way of the Dodo, "and how did it happen that afternoon?"

"She called me up," Steve said, "and ordered me to come immediately, like I was a servant she could summon. She'd found a referral document and some financial powers paperwork I'd slipped into a pile of stuff for Darko and Izzy to sign. They never looked at that stuff, only signed where I left the stickees."

He slipped away again and was underwater for a few seconds this time before he spluttered his way back up and onto the side of the boat. "It was a tiny account, forty, maybe fifty thousand … out of nearly two million … a payment for the off-the-book stuff I'd been doing for Darko for years. He wouldna minded … had joked about it before, it's where I got the idea."

"She found it there," Steve said, "buried in with all the other stuff, that and the referral, just exploring the idea of an institution for Xander after they're gone … it was enough to set her off. Once she got rolling, she was yelling about how she'd get me disbarred, put me in prison … I lost my head."

"Fuckin' lawyers," Barry said to me, "am I right?"

Steve Street closed his eyes, started shaking/seizing, then stilled momentarily and opened his eyes to look straight at me.

"I would have …." he said, and then sank beneath the water, gulping like a goldfish, unable to finish his old man Smithers routine … on this side of Fish Pond at any rate.

Barry ducked underwater, presumably to watch (*I didn't want to get gallons of 'Steve' up my nose and in my hair and eyes, so I just waited*).

"Damned if you didn't kill him twice," Barry said, upon surfacing thirty-two seconds later, "it was a photo finish … maybe Quincy or some other CSI-guy could tell for sure, but I think he died from drowning *and* blood loss."

I swam in towards shore, wanting to get away from the blood for a minute until it dissipated, and nearly tripped over my stringer of fish … I dragged them most of the way to shore and looped the stringer over a log in the water.

Twice, I thought, and smiled to myself … slightly.

Fish Pond, SRCW, NY,
Friday, 9/5/2014, 3:24 p.m.

I wanted to stop, cook up some fish, take a nap in my/the hammock, explore the backcountry of the SRCW with Xander and Hope and Cam, but none of that was going to happen … things had to be taken care of, and with likely little or no time in which to do it. I kept expecting to hear a helicopter or floatplane or ranger and cops who had driven in along the old jeep trail from the fish hatchery. I needed to sit and carefully think things through, but I couldn't indulge myself in that luxury … yet. Climbing out of the water, I walked up the bank to the clearing where I had set up the hammock and our rudimentary camp, and last seen Xander and Hope.

"Olly, Olly, Oxen Free," I called out, hoping that neither of the ones I was calling in had just kept running once they hit the tree line (*or, worse, caught one of Steve's wild shots in a squishy part*). "Xander Kovac, I've got a couple of episodes of *Alias* on your iPhone that you can watch while I (*must—not—say—hide evidence of murder*) finish catching us all some late lunch."

I could hear them before I could see them. They must have gone all the way up the hill behind the campsite. Xander and Hope eventually (*it seemed like forever to me, but was, according to the internal chronometer, only thirty-seven seconds*) came out of the woods; Hope's leash was wrapped six or seven times around Xander's wrist (*she hates the sound of gunfire, and would have tried to get away, with extreme prejudice*). I held out the iPhone (*still tethered to the charger, so it would keep filling with power*) and one of my dwindling supply of chocolate bars, and traded them to Xander for Hope. Everyone appeared happy with the exchange. Xander climbed/fell into the hammock and I heard the theme music from J.J. Abrams' nearly perfectly executed serial before Hope and I started back down the hill to the water.

My tiny backcountry fishing pole was resting on the sandy bottom a few feet out from the notch that years of campers had cut into the hillside. I picked it up, put one of the hooks from the lure I'd been using through a guide halfway down the rod and drew in a bit of line to tighten it with the tiniest bend before chucking it up on land. Xander's snorkel was vertical off the bottom of the pond, a bit of trapped air in the tube provided nearly enough buoyancy for it to float a bit. I snagged it for Xander, in case we got a chance to let him float later (*and hopefully in another pond, one with less Steve in it*), and hooked it, once again, through a belt loop. I had almost certainly lost some of the stuff from my pockets, but didn't worry about it as it wouldn't be traceable, and was also likely nothing I couldn't replace. Finally, I noticed something thumping against my knee, and looked down to see the multi-tool on its lanyard/leash, shiny blade still open … I closed it and dropped the tool into my shorts pocket.

As I waded out, deeper and deeper into the pond, my feet left the ground. I had to swim out to grab Steve's swamped canoe, shooting briefly past it to grab the wooden paddle that thankfully had stayed relatively close on this wind-free afternoon (*I wouldn't have liked either leaving it or hunting for it*). I pushed the paddle under the seat and thwarts of the flooded canoe, so it was all one piece. When I pulled it in, was amazed, as always, at how difficult it was/is to move a canoe with a few hundred pounds of water sloshing around in it, when the same canoe will skim across the water with a couple of hundred pounds of paddler inside it … the difference must be the inertia. Once we got close to shore, I flipped the canoe to get a lingering higher concentration of Steve's blood out of the water, sloshed it around with clean water awhile, and then emptied it completely and pushed it up on shore.

Turning back to the pond and looking for Steve, I panicked briefly when he was not where he should have been, where he had sunk/drowned/bled-out/died. I remembered reading a couple of articles that recently-drowned human bodies are nearly of neutral buoyancy in fresh water (*which makes some sense, given how much of our bodies is water to begin with*), and thus subject to moving/floating around in the smallest of underwater currents. I had a nervous/crazy moment when I scanned the far shoreline, certain to see him standing there, with yet another gun (*this one perhaps a derringer hidden in his boxers*). From my vantage point, up at the campsite, I could see into the water. I scanned left and right for his white/pale skin and found him skimming slowly along the bottom of the bay, facedown and headed in a northerly direction, out towards the main body of Fish Pond. I swam out to a point above and slightly in front of him, dove down the twenty or so feet to the bottom, where he was, grabbed him by the back of his jeans, and hauled him up to the surface … slow going with all that dead weight, even if it was essentially neutrally buoyant. Lost in thought, as I was swimming to the surface of Fish Pond with Steve in tow, I was thinking about mass versus weight, the apparent/relative weights of objects when contained in liquids of similar densities, and how in this case, it was actually Steve's hydraulic resistance as opposed to either his mass or weight that made bringing him up to the surface so difficult. When I broke out of the water and into the air, I took a good look around for Frank or any of his minions (*or superiors … or employment-pyramid, laterally-equivalent colleagues*), and, seeing none, dragged Steve back to shore, and maneuvered him onto the floor of his canoe.

Choosing to wade through the shallows of our bay, I pushed his canoe with Hope at my heels, heading to the southern end, only about fifty yards from our campsite, to the cut in the bank marked by the portage sign for Clamshell Pond (*another of the little ponds hidden in the beautiful backcountry of the SRCW*). I dragged Steve and boat ashore. Steve had a length of quarter inch nylon rope attached to the bow of his boat, and although it would hurt and leave a bruise/mark, I made a big loop in the rope, put it around my shoulder, and started dragging the boat up the slope and away from Fish Pond, tearing up my feet more with the weight and resistance of Steve and his canoe. About 150 yards along the trail, I stopped to breathe and sweat and groan and rub my shoulder, and decided that I was far enough in to head cross-country with my load.

It's been my experience in the world of geocaching that the great mass of people won't go more than twenty feet into the woods, off-trail, unless there's ancient pirate gold (*or matchbox cars and refrigerator magnets*) involved. I was roughly 400 feet from Fish Pond and maybe double that from Clamshell Pond. Besides, there were no geocaches closer than the one on Long Pond Mountain (*which was over two miles away*), and no reason to leave the portage unless you had to pee. I turned right/west off the carry/trail and broke through the wall of saplings as gently as one could when dragging a canoe with a dead body in it. We went fifty yards (*much farther than anyone would venture off-trail to pee*) and then another seventy-five yards before I found what I was looking for … a hole in the ground where a big tree had tipped over, taking its root ball with it.

The hole was deeper than I needed, and not quite as long (*Steve's canoe was likely twelve feet, and the hole was a couple of feet short of that in length*). I pulled his paddle out of the boat and used the blade end to hack both ends of the hole a bit, caving the dirt and sand into the bottom of the hole until it was long enough to accommodate the canoe's length without any of it sticking up above the prevailing ground level. I maneuvered the canoe into the hole like a (*not particularly challenging, but satisfying, nonetheless*) puzzle piece and started filling the boat with sand/dirt that I was able to chop off the root ball hanging above/behind the boat. All the while, Hope sat a few feet away, staring at me with confused patience (*which is as warm and loving as she gets*). When the boat was filled nearly to the gunwales (*at least in the middle portion, where Steve's body was*), I started making quick trips to grab fallen/downed branches and trees to fill in the ends, and lay over the top, starting with smaller ones, and gradually finding heavier and heavier ones (*until the last layer of four to six inch diameter logs was mounded on top of where the canoe had been*). I scrambled through the woods, with Hope's help (*she liked this game*), grabbing balsam and maple branches and draping them across the burial/hiding mound. Eventually, the mound would settle, and the leaves/needles would brown, but the logs should keep out the largest predators for long enough to let the autumn rains and freezing cycles of winter and raccoons and various mustelids and worms and bugs and such do their job of breaking Steve down into his constituent elements.

Finished, Hope and I went back down (*up?*) the portage back to Fish Pond and swam briefly to wash off the sweat and bugs and dirt and thoughts of Steve, before heading north through the shallows up the small bay to our campsite, grabbing the stringer of fish on my way, and starting a fire as soon as I got back to the camp.

Fish Pond, SRCW, NY,
Friday, 9/5/2014, 4:44 p.m.

I gave Hope a pair of small, dead sunfish to begin with, and started cleaning the others. Hope got the heads and guts of four good-sized perch and a pair of hefty (*but not award-winning, or even 'call home about' worthy*) bass while I hollowed them out, oiled them up, sprinkled them inside and out with my proprietary SmartPig mix of herbs and spices (*cracked pepper, sea salt, dried garlic, rosemary, oregano, orange peel, and brown sugar*), and wrapped them all in sheets of heavy-duty aluminum foil. Despite being assured that I'd be fed during the trip, I was glad to have brought the kibble for Hope and me, along with some of my backcountry cooking staples. I knocked the fire down, moved the coals around with a poking stick, and put the foil-wrapped fish on top of the coals, flipping them regularly while being careful to look/listen for the difference between steam and smoke, sizzling and burning.

When I pulled the packets out of the coals nine minutes later (*having shuttled them around the fire to cook on hotter or cooler spots, each according to its thickness*), I dug through my pack for a pair of mostly clean long-handled spoons (*with gear and clothes, I find that binary distinctions of clean and dirty are too limiting, so I think of all of these things in terms of shade of grey*), with which to pick apart the fish. Hope was still working on her fish, and by the sound of

Sidney and Michael arguing about the size/reach of SD-6 on *Alias*, Xander was only partway through the second episode of the series.

"Xander Kovac," I said, "if you would like some fish, it's ready."

I heard the dialogue stop, Xander awkwardly rolling out of the hammock (*it does take some getting used to*), and jogging over for our very late lunch. A rough-hewn log bench worked for a table, and I set the packets of fish on that, along with a Nalgene and the hydration pack, both of which had been filled with fresh pond water and a Gatorade analog. We needed to fuel up for the last push of the day (*I wanted to make sure that we had vitamins and minerals, as well as fats and protein from this meal … we'd had a good flow of carbs all day from the SmartPig GORP*), to get off Fish Pond and down to Clamshell Pond.

I'd decided this while cooking the fish; we needed to get away from this pond before Frank came looking for us. I had some business to take care of back in the world, before we got rescued. Taking the pair of long carries to Clamshell, and from Clamshell down to Turtle made the most sense: it was quick and easy (*one pond and two portages, not a half dozen of each like we had faced on our way up from Long Pond*). It would be quiet/lonely/empty (*we'd been lucky avoiding people so far, but that couldn't last unless we headed away from the popular routes, and almost nobody took the portage/trip to Clamshell, as it was/is a long/wet/avoidable walk*), and it would facilitate our exit from the SRCW in an unexpected manner/place. Xander and Hope and I could stash our boats in the woods at the southeast end of Turtle Pond and walk out along the train tracks at the top of Hoel Pond where nobody would be looking for us.

"Arvin Sloane and Danny, in *Alias*," said Xander, "Arvin betrayed Sydney."

I didn't want to read too much into what Xander was saying. He had just watched the first couple of episodes of the series (*a show which Cam had said Xander had enjoyed watching with Dani*), but I sensed myself wanting to infer things, and wondering how much Xander had seen and/or understood of what happened this morning and afternoon (*and the day that Dani was killed*).

"Yes, he did," I said, "but he can't hurt you or your family anymore."

Xander stared at me for a long moment, and then bent back down to his food. A few minutes later, we finished.

"Xander," I said, "I know that we've had a long day, and you must be tired, but to clean up from what that man did, I need another day of your help. Another day of paddling with me and Hope before we go home, and then, I'll take you to the Blue Moon for breakfast (*Cam had mentioned that this spot, in downtown Saranac Lake, was a longtime favorite of Xander's*)."

"Sydney helps Vaughn," he said, "then pancakes at Blue Moon."

In the series *Alias*, Sydney Bristow agrees to help Agent Vaughn of the CIA topple SD-6, a secret/corrupt/evil organization that had hurt and lied to Sydney … it did not seem as though I was reading too much into this exchange to take this statement as tacit agreement from Xander.

"Okay," I said, "Why don't you go pee and swim with Hope, and I'll pack up camp and get ready to go."

The two of them went into the trees above the campsite to do whatever they did, and then went down into the water to splash and fetch for a minute. Xander found his snorkel (*which I had laid on the deck of his kayak*), and went for a swim/float. In the meantime, I put out the fire and packed up the hammock and policed my gear and topped up the water supply (*thinking/repeating to myself all the while that 'dilution is the solution to pollution'*). I debated worrying about Xander seeing the gun, or some other sign of Steve Street, on the bottom of the pond, but decided that I couldn't much control what he saw without running an even greater risk of a meltdown, and that he might need some time to de-stress after the day we'd had.

I did a final lap around the campsite, headed down to the water's edge to rally the troops for our last big move, and then had a thought while I grabbed the GPS Spot unit and dropped it into my boat, climbed in, and thumped the bottom to get Xander's attention.

"Xander Kovac," I said, "I need to go around the corner up there (*pointing north and then east*) and tell my … daddy (*I had no way to explain Mickey on the tip of my tongue/brain. The character, Dixon, from Alias would occur to me three minutes later, but by then it wasn't worth turning around to explain it to Xander*) where I am, and that I'm okay."

Sending a message would placate Mickey and Dot, and probably filter down to Frank and the other Franks, letting them know that Xander and I were okay (*they would likely assume that we were okay, and that because I'm odd that we were continuing the paddle trip*). I could race around to the far end of Fish Pond, near the carries for Mud and Ochre Ponds, hopefully fooling them into looking for us over there, and possibly along that route.

Xander nodded and dunked his head back in the water and Hope continued to gnaw on a fish head on the tiny beach at the base of the hill leading to our temporary campsite. I paddled as fast as I was able around the point and down to the eastern end of the pond, the work of a little less than fifteen minutes. I sent the 'OK' signal from under the sign for the carry to Ochre Pond, waited for the confirmation light, and then hopped back into my Hornbeck and raced back down to join Xander and Hope. I was mildly surprised not to have seen other campers on the water (*although I did see smoke from one of the campsites on the northern shore, but never any people. So ostrich-like, I assumed they didn't see me*). It was late for the summer season by at least a week, which, back this far in the woods, was probably enough to thin the crowds to nearly zero. I pulled back into our bay and was mildly creeped out by the floating body in the water until Xander raised his head and spoke to me, snorkel still in place.

"Phraum nups," he said, "thwumper dub popey sigil."

"Sounds good," I answered (*entirely unsure of what he had said to me, but assuming that it had to do with candy or a movie that I likely owed him*). I nosed my boat into the shore to pick up Hope and take the world's quickest pee. I also drank and ate some, all the while negotiating with Xander for him to come in and dry off and get ready to go. It took the promise of another chocolate bar to get him out of the water, along with additional promises for a few episodes once we got to the next pond, and a bag of gummy bears for dinner (*I had some behavioral/ nutritional damage to undo when I finally got Xander out of these woods, but that would be tomorrow's problem, and for someone else to worry about*).

Clamshell Pond, SRCW, NY,
Friday, 9/5/2014, 5:33 p.m.

The portage was easy and uneventful, Xander and Hope went in front of me, and neither of them even looked at the broken/bent/crushed foliage and undergrowth on the right hand side of the trail where I had left the portage to go and hide/bury Steve. Even accounting for increasingly heavy boats as the day wore on and on and on, we made it to the shore of Clamshell Pond only twenty-seven minutes after stepping out of the waters of Fish Pond. Due to a mix of my desire to maintain a low profile, and my proclivity for bandit camping, we eschewed the legal campsite on the eastern shore of the pond, in favor of a wonderful peninsula on the western side. We pulled the boats perhaps unnecessarily far up into the woods and set up the hammock well back from the open rock … if a ranger came racing through the pond in search of people, there was a reasonable chance that he would miss us (*which was the way that I wanted it for another eighteen or so hours*).

"Gummy Bears for dinner," Xander said as if I might have forgotten my ridiculous promise/offer/bribe, "iPhone *Dune* in tent."

"Here are your gummy bears, sir," I said, handing him the bag. I had another socked away in case of an emergency, along with four more chocolate bars, a couple of bags each of human and doggie kibble, and enough supplies for another fish meal or two … beyond that, I would need to come up with less tangible rewards/incentives.

"Xander Kovac," I said, once he started eating his supper (*thinking, 'good news first'*), "the iPhone is fully charged, so you should be able to watch a movie or two before we need to recharge. The bad news is that we don't have a tent."

"No tent," his voice was characteristically flat, but he stopped eating, and looked at me with genuine fear *(the first I'd seen on this trip)* in his eyes. "Go back, bring Cam's tent!"

"Nope," I said, only now feeling the storm that had snuck up on us, "but you and Hope can have a sleepover in the hammock. I'll sleep underneath you, on the ground, and I've got a nightlight for you, if you want."

Xander started eating gummy bears again, and turned on *Dune*, starting from when the Atreides land on Arrakis this time (*which to my way of thinking is the real beginning of the movie*), but he kept looking at the diminishing light filtering down through the trees, and I got the feeling that we were all of us in for a rough night.

Clamshell Pond, SRCW, NY,
Saturday, 9/5/2014, 6:29 a.m.

Sleeping out in a hammock can be an unnerving experience, especially the first time. You can feel the trees moving at either end of your bed, and when you turn (*even slightly*) you rock for a while (*unless you've rigged stabilizers, which I didn't for Xander … more stuff to get in the way, and my backup is a simple Grand Trunk single, a very basic design*). The forest/night/beasty sounds are right there, loud and easily direction-identifiable, not kept at bay by a tent-wall (*despite the fact that tents are made of very sheer nylon, people feel as though they're 'inside' when sleeping in a tent, while it's easy to feel like a meaty piñata when hanging in the woods overnight*). The sensory input that surprised me the most when I started hammock-camping was the olfactory (*whenever I use the word in her presence, Dot makes a joke about how it smells mustier than the 'new-factory,' and then she giggles on and off for the next ten minutes … I missed Dot and Good Chinese Food and my couch at SmartPig, a lot, and very possibly in that order*). When in a tent, you smell sleeping bags and feet and farts and whatever everyone had for dinner; in a hammock, you smell whatever the air-current du moment serves up … the bog off to your right, smoke from across the lake, the slow rot of needles on the floor of a spruce forest, and sometimes the musky scent of animals passing by in the darkness.

Xander watched his way through *Dune* and a few

more episodes of *Alias*, skipping back and forth to parts that he liked, or were meaningful to him for some reason (*either at the moment, or in general … he was happy and quiet, so my plan was to leave him alone and question nothing*). Darkness fell gently in the woods around us, the wildlife's shift-change chatter was the biggest hint of the move from day to night. When the first *Alias* episode with Quentin Tarentino in it ended, I turned on my headlamp, grabbed my spare (*'two is one, and one is none', useful backcountry wisdom that also makes your bag heavier*). I rolled out from under the hammock before struggling to my feet (*I have crossed some age/fitness threshold whereby lying on the ground for hours at a time makes me feel as though I'm much older than I am and as if I had been beaten with a stick until the person doing the hitting got bored*). Looking above him into the trees, so as not to blind him, I spoke to Xander for the first time in hours.

"Xander," I said, "we should go find a good tree to pee on, and then get to bed. I'd like to get an early start in the morning. Would you like to borrow my headlamp so you can find your way in the woods?"

"Yes," he said, "borrow headlamp. Cam will make pancakes and butter and bacon and maple syrup?"

"No," I said as he started to swing up and out of the hammock, pausing only to gently help Hope down off his lap. "I'm sorry, Xander. No Cam and no pancakes. I can try and catch more fish first thing, and cook those up if you're tired of GORP and gummy bears."

"Yes," he said, swinging his headlamp around and making lightsaber noises (*as every rational human does when they wear a headlamp for the first time*), another backcountry Jedi. "Mr. Cunningham will catch more fish."

"Okay," I said, "how about that big white pine over there? Or maybe that paper birch, they normally don't get that big around, you know. Sloths generally only poop once a month or so, and they climb all the way down out of their tree to deposit it at the base, scientists believe it's done that way to return the nutrients to a favored tree. I feel the same way when I'm camping; some people say I talk/think too much about pee and poop, but it's an important part of nutrient cycling and seed dispersal in the forest."

Xander was, by this time, done peeing (*at the base of the white pine, if you were interested*), and gave no response, or even any indication that he had heard/listened to me … most people are like that when I talk about nutrient cycling and seed dispersal. He was no longer swinging the headlamp's beam and making the noises, but he was looking around at the extent of the woods and their darkness, with big, scared, eyes.

"Xander Kovac," I said, "would you do me a favor and let Hope sleep with you in the hammock tonight? She sometimes gets scared sleeping on the ground in the woods, and will sleep better if you could hold her and pet her and tell her that she's good, and safe, if she hears something during the night."

"Let Hope sleep with you in the hammock tonight," he said, "yes."

"Okay," I said. "Time for all of us to go to bed."

I have a nightlight of sorts that I always hang from the foot-end of my hammock; it's a keychain with a small vial of encapsulated tritium, which should glow for the next ten years or so, before I need to replace it. One night, when I woke up with a full bladder, I wandered away without my headlamp, and not surprisingly, couldn't see in the dark to find my way back to the hammock after I was done peeing. Generally, I use/have a flashlight, but don't want to count on having it, the gentle green glow easily/faultlessly guides me back to bed and has no batteries to run down. For Xander, it could also do double duty as a nightlight, to keep the darkness at bay. He seemed to like it, and once he and Hope had layered up in the long underwear and socks and hat and glove liners and lightweight fleece blanket I'd brought along in case of unexpected cold (*which I guess this counted as*), they seemed to settle down nicely.

Well, I thought so. Until, that is, we heard a flight of loons passing overhead (*from generally north to approximately south, by my reckoning, from Fish Pond towards Hoel Pond … the direction of travel that we would hopefully be following in a few hours*), talking to each other about whatever loons talk about … fish and fishing, possibly. The wing sounds and gabbling de-calmified Xander, and he snapped on his headlamp again, to scan the dark for attacking Gaviiformes … none were forthcoming/apparent in his hurried looks into the treetops and the ground all around the hammock. He stood, dumping Hope to the ground, and started talking very loudly, flailing his arms, shining his lamp directly in my eyes, and scaring Hope enough that she ran behind me and growled at him from between my knees.

"Xander Kovac," I said. "There's nothing in these woods that wasn't there all day. We're safe here, I promise you."

Because of this, or coincidentally, I have no idea, he moved in very close to me very quickly, and reached out with both hands, slapping me in the ear with his right hand, and pinching me very hard just above my elbow with his left.

"Ouch," I said. "Xander, that hurts, and while I know you're upset, this isn't going to help, I'm not the one who made it dark … or scary."

Even as I was saying it, I could feel it being useless

nonsense, could almost see the pointlessness of the words, as they clattered, unnoticed by Xander, to the ground around him like snow or leaves. He moved in close to me, slapping and grabbing, and I became aware of how much bigger he was than me. Xander simultaneously swatted my damaged nose and yanked my hair, which dislodged the torn section of scalp from its preliminary/rudimentary healing, and the resulting yells from me surprised and quieted him momentarily.

"Daddy with a story," Xander shouted in my face when our quiet moment was done, his mouth an inch from my nose (*I could see Barry looming behind him, summoned by my fear/surprise/stress, and wondered briefly if Xander might bite my nose ... it suddenly seemed very exposed, with his proximity to my face*). "The lights and a story and cocoa, after the storm."

I worked very hard not to jerk back from him, or to heed my instincts and punch him in the throat (*my nose was throbbing from Steve's kick this afternoon, and I really didn't want to see if it could get 'more' broken*). While trying to ignore Hope barking and snapping from around my feet, I also remembered that he was completely out of his element at the end of the worst week in his short/confusing/scary life. I believed that I could translate his issue and suggestion, within an acceptable margin of error.

"Xander," I said, "I have a lot of stories that I can read to you. We'll rig a light using your headlamp (*which would also save me from the intermittent/painful night blindness I got from his shining the lamp in my eyes every few seconds*). I don't have any cocoa, though ... how about some cocoa pills ... M&Ms?"

"Yes," he said in a huff, with tired stress in his voice that I understood (*even if the events leading up to it were something of a mystery to me*), "cocoa pills."

I rooted around in my portage pack for one of the remaining bags of people-kibble, passed it to him, and gestured for him to get back in the hammock, which he did. Grabbing the Nalgene bottle, which I'd filled before sundown, along with the hydration pack, I drank half of the water and dumped the rest. Through some pantomime and simple directions, I indicated to Xander that he should drop his headlamp into the bottle, and when he did, the opaque whitish plastic reflected the light from his lamp nicely, making a softer and bigger glow that he held, smiling, in his lap (*the opaque Nalgenes had been less common since the general public found out a few years ago that plastic bottles were made from chemicals … shocking … and people seemed to feel that the clear bottles were 'cleaner' somehow, or had fewer chemicals in them … I liked the slightly squishier opaque bottles and was especially thankful for them tonight*).

"All the wet, red and hot, all over me," Xander said, "like the Baron and his slave. The tall man said he would eat my Mommy and Daddy if I told." He said all of this in a quiet, secret, sad voice.

"I know, Xander," I said, although I didn't/couldn't know it in the way that he did, "but he can't hurt you or your Mommy and Daddy now … he's gone."

"Dani and Gutman and shouting and the fake falcon," he said, and I was able to see his mind making a mashup of his sister and Street and that scene from *The Maltese Falcon* when Kaspar Gutman finds out that the falcon they have finally gotten ahold of is a fake … his disappointment and anger and shock and rage, and what that translated to in that house that Xander was forced to witness. For a moment, I wanted to kill Steve Street again, for what he had done to Dani and Xander and Iskra and Darko … and Cam (*who could possibly have been another 'friend' insofar as I have friends*).

"Xander, let me read you one of my favorite stories," I said. "Okay, Xander?"

"Okay, Mr. Cunningham," he said in a quiet and tired and sad and sleepy voice.

The final ingredient in my recipe/plan for not getting hit/pinched more was my Kindle … I got it out of the Ziploc freezer bag I use for a travel case and picked a story at random from the first page of possible selections. It was a Tony Hillerman book I'd downloaded because I was thinking about driving out west and exploring the Four-Corners Region with Hope, once the first serious snow came (*to ease her transition into that most hated season of cold and snow and aching and freezing bones/joints/paws*). I started reading, entirely unaware if Xander was listening or interested or awake, although once I got into the rhythm of reading aloud (*something I have almost never done),* I was able to let some portion of my brain work with my mouth and throat to continue making the correct sounds while I explored the scene with my ears.

Hope had calmed down nearly as soon as Xander climbed back into the hammock, and I could hear her breathing enter the slow/steady/deep pattern that indicates she is nearly asleep. Xander was rustling the bag of GORP, sifting through the bits he didn't want for the dark chocolate M&Ms, and every few minutes shaking and unscrewing the Nalgene bottle to look inside at the headlamp doing its thing. I could hear a tiny and periodic grinding noise far up in the trees around us that experience told me was various grubs/beetles/borers turning tiny bits of huge trees into sawdust, one bite at a time. Out on Clamshell Pond, across from us on the eastern shore, the splash of a beaver's tail echoed as something spooked it while it worked on the dam I'd seen on our way in, at the little outlet stream that flowed down eventually to Ochre Pond. A few fish splashes added to the nighttime symphony at various points around the pond, although I could detect no pattern suggestive of predators hunting. The whole time I was engaged in listening, a gentle breeze sustained a low whistling sound from the wind in the pine needles sixty or more feet over our heads. All of these noises went unheard by Xander, now that he was focused on the words of the story I was reading (*it occurred to me that a similar distraction was going on with his olfactory input … having the bag of almonds and M&Ms and jerky and mango so close to his nose must surely be drowning out the other, less accustomed smells of the backcountry night*).

I read until my throat began to hurt, and then stopped, unsure if Xander had fallen asleep, or if he was just mellow and swinging in the hammock. Not wanting to upset the welcome calm that had crept into our camp, I carefully grabbed the iPhone, and set the music player to loop randomly through a quiet and peaceful collection of Mozart, so I could get some rest myself. I use it when trying to push back the in-town sounds that upset Hope and me when we're holed up in SmartPig. Then I (*gently*) dropped the iPhone into Xander's lap, next to the bottle of light that he was holding in both of his hands, fully asleep. Thankfully, the pain and fear I'd seen on his face, and even heard in his voice, earlier was completely gone.

I walked a short distance into the woods to pee, but mostly to stretch and try to get blood moving and to regain my circulation. Xander had most of my warm clothes, but I slid into the final pair of wooly socks, a fleece that wouldn't have fit him (*too small*), some wind-pants, and a polypro skullcap. I went back to my space under the tree, under the hammock, under Xander, and moved the portage pack into place for use as a (*crappy/lumpy/scratchy*) pillow, and tried to get a few hours' sleep before the machinery of tomorrow got cranking loudly enough to wake us all. Hope poked my ear with a shockingly cold and wet nose a minute after I lay down, and followed that up with some face-kisses. Thirty seconds later, she crawled and circled and went to sleep on my fleece-covered chest, having apparently jumped down from the hammock and Xander without waking him when she noticed me leaving her side.

Awake and shivering now, I watched the thin grey band of light on the eastern rim of the sky/trees/world. Barry was standing out on the rocky peninsula, down by the water, visible mostly because his vast bulk blocked out enough light to draw my attention (*and because the devious men, and his sometimes jailors, in my brain wanted me to see him. I'd learned, mostly, to stop questioning his presence*). I gently shifted Hope and the fleece to the ground before slowly rolling to my feet. The music was still looping, the Nalgene was still glowing, and the bag of human-kibble was mostly empty on Xander's chest … I was happy/eager to let him sleep a bit longer. So crept to the water's edge where Barry was waiting.

"Barry," I said, "what's up?"

"Besides us," he answered, "nothing. Gee-whiz, Tyler, you sure take me to some swell places. This must be where people from the middle of nowhere go when they want to get away from it all. If Tupper's the asshole of the Adirondacks, then this must be that place on your back that you can never reach if you got a bug bite. Why are we here, Tyler?"

"Well," I said, "this is the best way to get …."

"No. What I mean," he said, riding over me with more volume than I was comfortable with (*I was on the verge of shushing him, when I remembered that I was the only one who could hear him*), "is why come this way at all? If we stayed on Fish Pond, or used your GPS-toy, Frank and the rest of the Adirondack '5-0' would have come running, or you could have walked out the six miles on the Jeep trail from the end of Fish Pond back to the Fish Hatchery. This whole side trip seems like needless and pointless difficulty, with some risk and no real upside."

"We need to do it this way if we're going to keep both me and Xander free from hassle and questions," I said, "and tie this up neatly (*the idea of which I liked almost, but not quite, as much as hassle/question avoidance*), but it should be pretty easy and clean from here on out."

"If you say so," Barry said, sounding entirely unconvinced (*which should have, but didn't, signal to me that some part of my brain didn't think it would be smooth sailing from here on out ... I had an easier time if I thought of Barry as an entirely separate entity living inside of me, an endosymbiotic relationship*). "But honestly Cunningham, what kind of questions are you worried about? I never even heard of anyone killed in a case of self-defense that was more justified, or who needed it more."

"Barry," I said in a whisper, since he could hear me at any volume, "I'm handling this, have my own reasons, and am pretty sure that you know what they are, since you live inside my brain, so if you wouldn't mind too much, could you just leave me the hell alone?"

Barry popped out of existence and I circled back into the woods as quietly as possible for the fishing gear, and spent the next hour casting from various points on the rocky peninsula into the dark and still pond. I caught a trio of perch and a few sunnies, and when I heard Xander climbing out of the hammock and talking to Hope, I decided to call it a morning. Leaving the stringer of fish in the water, I went back into the woods to find enough branches and birch bark to suffice for a short-term fire. Once I got the fire going, in short order, I cleaned the perch for Xander, gave the sunnies and perch-detritus to Hope, assembled foil packets for the three perch, and threw them onto the coals, flipping them around with poking-sticks periodically until they were done. I made my breakfast of half of the last bag of GORP and about a liter of water. Everyone seemed happy, and we were packed and ready to go a few minutes after the official sunrise.

Turtle/Hoel Pond Culvert/RR-tracks, SRCW, NY, Saturday, 9/6/2014, 7:46 a.m.

We had a three minute paddle down to the end of Clamshell Pond, and then all three of us piled out of the boats for the portage from Clamshell to Turtle. It's a bit more than a mile with some small rises and valleys and streams, along with one significant hill in the middle. In the damper/muddier parts of the carry, some boardwalks span waterlogged stretches and can be tricky to negotiate, especially in/for bare (*and tender*) feet, like mine. Xander's kayak kept sliding off the boardwalk, and after the sixth time, he stomped away, leaving it in the sphagnum moss.

"Xander Kovac," I said, "we're almost done with the boats, but we need them for a little while longer. We've gotten past the hardest part of the portage, and are probably only ten minutes from the water at Turtle Pond (*it was more like fifteen to twenty, but I was okay with lying to Xander, unsure as I was of his grasp on the passage of time*). Then we just have to paddle about a thousand yards to the southern end of the pond … if you can do that, I'll give you the rest of these chocolate bars (*I dug them out of the portage pack to show him, as a visual aid*) then and there. Deal?"

"Deal," he said, although in an even flatter tone than usual, and swinging close to me with his pinching fingers out and ready … he was tired and sore and ready to crash in front of the TV for a day or two. I couldn't blame him.

Hope and I wouldn't mind that either (*but if things went as planned, the two of us should be munching our way through an embarrassingly large pile of Chinese food from the good/only place in time for the lunch special pricing, which ends at 3 p.m.)*.

We made it through the woods and down to the water's edge by a quarter after seven, and all three of us piled into the water to wash the trail muck and squashed bugs and morning sweat from our bodies. Xander screamed and ran from the water as we were finishing up, and it took a few minutes before he was able to calm down enough to point to the leech on the back of my leg, which I flipped off and back into the pond with the tip of a stick. He refused to set foot in the water again, and for a moment I thought the whole plan/day/(*world?*) was ruined because he climbed into his kayak six feet from the water's edge. I was barely able to drag him and the boat into Turtle Pond. He paddled slowly/awkwardly, not dipping anything except the blades of his paddle into the water, apparently for fear of leeches scrambling up the shaft to devour his hands (*the thought/image of which was enough to creep me out momentarily, so I decided to cut him some slack*).

When we pulled into the shallow and sandy water by the culvert at 7:42 … it was still too early to run into most paddlers, and a bit late for early-morning fishermen. The pond/culvert/trip hadn't changed since we had paddled through this set of ponds less than two days ago, but Xander and I arguably had, and Cam certainly had. I didn't even try to reason with Xander about leeches, and dragged his boat all the way up onto the beach to the left of the culvert. He climbed out of the kayak and held out his hand.

"Chocolate bars for Xander, Mr. Cunningham," he said, "now. Yes."

I fanned them out and pressed the bars into his hand.

"Xander," I said, "we need to drag these boats east (*I said this pointing to the left*) along the train tracks about fifty yards, and then hide them in the woods, so nobody steals them (*that wasn't exactly the reason, but it would do*). Once we do that, we'll walk on the tracks for a mile, for twenty minutes (*it was actually more like a mile and a half, which in the awkward gait that railroad track forced, and given our/my footwear shortcomings, it would take more like forty minutes, but again, I thought I could fudge it a bit with Xander in the final lap*)."

I put on a couple of pairs of socks, for cushioning, not warmth, got the pack and canoe on my back, and headed up the short incline to the tracks. Xander followed behind me, and Hope was walking slowly by my side, so I didn't stop at the top. I turned left/east instead and walked for sixty yards before finding what appeared to be a good spot to dump the boats (*and most of the gear … I grabbed a couple of things for the go-bag, and went*), throwing a mix of fresh and old tree branches across and on top of the stuff, for later retrieval.

Long Pond Portage, Floodwood Road, SRCW, NY, Saturday, 9/6/2014, 10:26 a.m.

Xander and Hope and I walked, slowly, along the railroad tracks by Hoel Pond until we reached the far end of Hoel Pond Road, a gravel road servicing a number of camps along the northeast end of Hoel Pond. As soon as we reached the road, I found a shady spot to drop my gear, got out the GPS-Spot, sent the A & C combination. (*which would only send Mickey an A or OK signal, but would send both A and C to Dot, which would tell her to: 'bring my money, and your cousin's big truck with towing gear to the given coordinates.'*) Dot's cousin, Rory, runs his own garage and towing business in Tupper Lake, and had become overextended in the last year (*according to some conversations with Dorothy that I had mostly ignored … nodding and making pseudo-sympathetic noises where necessary*) due to an unfortunate/debilitating addiction to shiny things with engines in them. Now, all we had to do was wait for them to come.

I set up the hammock and the iPhone and charger for Xander and poured a mound of kibble out to fill the travel bowl for Hope, and I was content to lie in a shady spot and listen to *The Maltese Falcon* and most of the second Quentin Tarentino episode of *Alias* before I heard the deep rumbling of Rory's truck rolling down the gravel road to us.

"Hello," said Dorothy, once she had swung /climbed

down from the cab of the truck, "D'you guys need a lift?"

It seemed a little forced, and her shining eyes, plus the way she scooped up Hope to cover her with kisses, gave it away a little, but I knew better than to say anything yet. She gave me the look I've seen a dozen times that says I have lots of explaining to do … but later. I nodded, acknowledging both the look and the message.

"Thanks for coming, Dot," I said. "Rory," I nodded in his direction. It had been plain to see during our single meeting (*even to me, and I don't tend to see much of what people are thinking/emoting*) that he thought I was a weirdo. I couldn't come up with any compelling reason or evidence to dispute him, so I didn't, and we had nodded our goodbyes/goodnights at the end of the Christmas party, both of us likely certain that we wouldn't see the other again.

"So," Dot said, "what's the plan, Stan … Tyler."

I often miss this trick, which both amuses and annoys Dorothy to no end, and is likely why she keeps doing it.

"We're going to pick up a car from the Long Pond Boat Launch, out on the far end of Floodwood Road," I said, "and tow it to the parking lot next to the McDonald's in Tupper, and leave it there. That's it."

"And for this," Rory said, "you're going to pay me...?"

"Five thousand dollars," I said, "except I figure the tow's only about two hundred, so the rest … the forty-eight hundred, is to forget about me and the car and Floodwood Road and everything. Does that make sense?"

"Yup," he said, "thing is though, Mr. Cunningham, it seems like the money is either too much or not enough, if you know what I mean."

"Rory—" Dorothy interjected, before I could answer

(*and better than I would have*) "The money is like the little bear's porridge … not too much, not too little, just fucking right (*which is not exactly how I remember the story*). Don't stupid yourself out of a gift from God. This could pull your fat out of the fire, and keep you and your business going for a while. This won't come back on you, ever, will it Tyler?"

"Nope," I said, using tones that should serve to indicate more certainty than I actually/currently felt. "Nobody's going to be looking at how the car got there, they'll supply their own answers, and assume that he switched cars, or got picked up by someone."

"Okay," Rory said, "good enough for me. Let's get going."

Rory's Big Truck (*which was how Dot spoke of the thing, with capitals implied*) had a crew cab, which was where Xander and Hope and I sat. We drove back out Hoel Pond Road, made the right hand turn onto Floodwood Road, and followed it for more than four miles to the turnoff for the Long Pond boat launch. Three cars were parked at the end of the parking lot closest to Long Pond, a state police cruiser, a forest ranger's truck, and a fire/rescue vehicle, and the boulder usually blocking the road down to the pond from vehicles had been dragged to one side, implying that there were more vehicles down at the water.

Luckily, all of the people who had driven these vehicles here (*and all of the other ones, implicit down by Long Pond*) must be down at the water, or out at the campsite, doing whatever people do twenty-eight hours after a murder takes place. I had a plan to help Rory escape much notice if there had been any law enforcement types up here, but it was even easier this way. I spotted Street's car and pointed it out.

"The dark green Outback," I said, pointing, "down at the end, trying to hide behind the van."

"Got it," said Rory, "You're sure?"

I was, but I've been sure about lots of things in my life, and double-checking almost never hurts. I jumped out and down from the crew-cab, leaving Hope with Xander, and walked around the car. The license plate positively ID'd it as the one I'd seen at Steve's office, and a sticker on the driver's side rear window identifying the owner as a member of the New York State Bar Association (NYSBA) closed the deal, as far as I was concerned … I gave Rory a thumbs up.

Rory's Garage, Tupper Lake, NY,
Saturday, 9/6/2014, 11:37 a.m.

He whirled his truck around in reverse, backing up to within a foot of the front bumper, hit some button on his way out of the truck that lowered a tow-bar, and hooked Steve's car to his truck as quick as I've ever seen it done. By the time I was starting to feel exposed in the parking lot, we were on our way out of it. We passed a few cars, but nobody in law enforcement, until we had gotten back onto Route 30, and were about to make the turn onto Route 3, near Wawbeek and the remarkably tiny/fun Panther Mountain … by that time, we were just another vehicle on the road, a tow truck hauling a vehicle with undisclosed issues, and as long as Rory kept his speed under control (*he did*) and didn't get in an accident (*he didn't*), I felt that we were well within the acceptable risk zone.

Rory pulled into the parking lot adjoining the McDonald's lot, and parked on the far side of a big rig that had either just unloaded, or was about to unload, a couple of cubic yards of cheap stuff at the dollar store. He dropped the tow bar (*and by proxy, Steve's car*) to the lot before he got out of the truck. Unhooking the Subaru was even quicker than hooking it up had been, and he was back in under a minute to pull the truck up and over to McDonald's, where he actually parked (*now nearly seventy-five yards from Steve Street's Subaru, without anyone seeming to have noticed anything*).

"I could eat," Rory said. "Who else? My treat (*I guess that Rory was feeling his newfound wealth*)."

"Thanks, Rory," I said. "I'd love two Bacon Habanero Ranch Quarter Pounders, a Sweet Tea with light ice (*at this point, Rory began writing on the back of a greasy purchase order slip*), and a nine piece McNuggets, no sauce."

"What," he asked, "no Coke. I thought you were all about the Coke."

"No," I answered, "I can't handle their fountain soda and the mix is almost always off at this place. Xander (*I said turning to him*), would you like something from McDonald's?"

"McDonald's, yes," he said. "Two Filet-O-Fish please and Oreo McFlurry with napkins to wipe my mouth."

"Large fries and a small Coke for me," said Dorothy. "Thanks, Cuz."

He checked the order and headed inside for the food, leaving us alone in the truck for a few minutes. Dorothy reached into her backpack, pulled out, and then passed back a small waterproof box. I grabbed an intact and still-strapped stack of fifty-dollar bills (*which are always wrapped in a brown strap if you were wondering … twenties are wrapped in violet straps, hundreds in mustard colored ones, for reasons known only to the Federal Reserve, since the bills are essentially self-identifying*) and an envelope from the OtterBox. I did a quick finger-count of the bills to make sure, and sealed the cash in the envelope as Rory came back with two big bags of food and a drinks tray.

Rory handed out the drinks first, asking us to use the cup holders if we didn't mind (*to all appearances, we didn't*), and then passed out the food. We all ate in silence, except for Hope, who generally sings/hums happily to herself when she eats McNuggets (*not other food, only McNuggets*) … this time was no different.

When everyone had finished, we all took a not-so-stealthy glance over at Steve's car while Rory brought the garbage to the overflowing can back towards the McDonald's, as if expecting to see crime scene guys climbing all over it, or dusting it for prints … nobody was. Rory returned, cleared his throat, as if about to start a discussion that he was uncomfortable with, and I headed him off by handing him the envelope. He squeezed and bent it, as if he could count the money through the paper, thought about opening it briefly, thought better of that idea, stuck the envelope into an inside pocket instead, and drove us back to his garage.

Rory and I nodded at each other while he and Dot hugged it out. I held my go-bag with one arm and my dog's leash with the other … Xander stayed very close to me. I spotted Dorothy's van, walked over with Xander and Hope, and got in … content to wait if Dot had stuff to say or talk about with Rory. She didn't, and forty-nine seconds after pulling into his garage's parking lot in his big truck, we drove away in Dorothy's slightly less big van, and headed back to Saranac Lake.

The Gibson House, Saranac Lake, NY,
Saturday, 9/6/2014, 1:04 p.m.

"Where am I taking you guys?" Dorothy asked. "And how much can you tell me about what really happened out there in the woods?"

As soon as we had pulled away from Rory's Garage, I had handed Xander the iPhone (*I still had trouble thinking of it as his, but I assumed that I'd get there sooner or later*) along with a set of ear buds from Dot's glove compartment. Once he had started noodling around with one of the games I'd downloaded for him, I reached down into the front cup holder of Dot's van to grab her phone and waggled it in her field of vision. She nodded.

"Meg and Frank and Darko and Iskra," I said, anticipating her question who I was going to call, "I'd like to get them all together to give them a kinder/gentler version of what happened, so it can become accepted and rote before the audience for our story gets larger and/or more police-y. If you can avoid laughing or smiling, you're welcome to stay for it."

"I'd rather hear a short version of the juicy stuff," Dot said, "and then skip the boring version, and go home to take Lisa out for a hike and dinner date in Lake Placid and not be associated with the mess, or its cleanup."

"Fair enough," I said, "hang on a second."

I called Meg, who was frantic the second she heard my voice, even after I told her that Xander and I were fine, and on our way over. She screamed for Frank to call Darko and Izzy on her phone, and tell them to come over.

"Meg," I said, "It was Steve Street. Steve shot and killed Cam Renard, he's the one who killed Danica, and he's still out there, somewhere … so the Kovacs, especially Xander, will need security until they find him. That being said, I don't want police, besides Frank, in the house while Xander and I are talking with you and his parents, for obvious reasons (*I couldn't think of any, but Meg was very smart, thought I was very smart, and I assumed that she could come up with some obvious reasons that made sense*) … there'll be time enough for that after they've found new legal counsel."

"The Kovacs are on their way," Meg said, "We'll see you as soon as you can get here. Where are you calling from?"

I hadn't figured out the optimal answer to that as yet, so I just hung up, turned off the phone, and put it back in the cup holder.

"So it was the lawyer, huh?" Dorothy asked, shaking her head. "I thought as much when you told me about the whole thing. And the story is that you let him get away? Fat chance! Tell me why we just moved his car, instead of him being behind the wheel, pointing it towards Mexico or Reykjavik? (*I didn't point out that nobody could drive to Reykjavik*)"

"You always think it's the lawyer," I said, "always. And no," I paused again, before continuing with some relief (*I was happy to be able to share the full story with someone, even if they might not understand/condone/forgive what I had done … to Street, to Cam, to Xander*), "I didn't let him get away, although I wanted to, tried to … he's dead as a doornail, which interestingly enough, is a turn of phrase that has been in common usage to describe dead things since William Langland used it in a poem in the mid-fourteenth century …"

"Tyler, shut up," she said. "We don't have much time, certainly not enough for fourteenth century poetry. Tell me what happened: to Cam, to your nose, to Steve-the-dirty-murdering-lawyer-Street, why we had to move the car, what's gonna happen, what you're gonna tell everyone else … everything!"

"I will," I said, "Although I'm pretty sure he just went by Steve (*I've been working on developing jokes to share with Dorothy, based on my study of the form, and I've been getting better in the last year*)."

"Now's not the time or the place to practice humor," said Dorothy, eventually smiling just a bit through her grumpy face, "but not bad. Now give."

So I did … everything that I could fit into the time it took to drive to Meg and Frank's place, which meant a basic description of events, with a bit of detail added in a couple of places.

When I finished, Dot was quiet for a while as she worked through everything that happened and then she said, "Wow, Tyler, you're a fucking hero. You rescued yourself, your dog and most importantly that boy, with just a few new scars on you to show for it. But I don't understand. Street is the bad guy here, this was all self-defense. Why did you cover it up?"

"I'm not the hero in this story, Dot," I said, "not any more than Street. We both manipulated events, moved people around like chess pieces, and got a couple of people killed in the process. All of it, on my end, because I gamed it out, and screwed up … again. I structured the scenario so Street had to come after us. That's not self-defense or heroism … it's pride and stupidity and everyone but me paid for it (*thinking now of Cam yesterday morning and Xander last night, and even Street, who all things being equal, would probably prefer being in a warm jail cell to the cold ground between the carries*). I couldn't live with praise and smiles, like what happened last year after the Reineger/Edelman thing, so I did my best to … make it all go away."

She would want more later, but that was enough for now, and it let her know what parts of the story to play dumb, or just plain lie about, with Lisa and other people. I promised to give her a call around 10 p.m. to debrief her further just as she pulled over to let the three of us out at the head of Frank and Meg's driveway. She sped away just before Meg ran out the front door to hug and kiss all of us … giving a big cry and fuss when she saw my nose (*which to be fair, was spectacular … no more blood as I'd washed it away, but it was leaning off to the right side of my face by a substantial amount, and I had a split/swollen lip and a pair of black eyes, based on what I'd seen in the vanity mirror of Dot's car*) and scalp laceration (*which had bled a lot, and then stuck back down in place like a puzzle piece … it was itchy/puffy, and would need someone to look at it … maybe Dot, after all of this was done tonight*), before leading us all inside (*Hope got a bone and hid in the downstairs bathroom to avoid a scene with Toby and Lola*).

"Jesus, Tyler," Frank said when he saw me. "What happened to your head?"

"Honestly (*I wanted to kick myself for starting this way, since I have a theory that this always precedes lies, but I was committed, so I charged ahead*), it's the most embarrassing and least impressive part of the whole story, but since my face is right out there in the open, let me start with how it happened, and then I'll loop back around to the beginning."

The Kovacs weren't really listening much, they were

hugging and kissing their son … touching him as if to make sure that he was truly there, really safe.

"Last night Xander had to sleep out in my hammock, and he's, well, a bit scared of the dark. Some loons overflew our campsite, and he got upset. I tried to calm him down and he hit me, a little by mistake and a little on purpose. He was lashing out in fear, and anger and frustration. I understand that and don't blame him at all. That's what broke my nose, and I cut open my scalp falling down and hitting a jagged rock."

I made a point of not looking at Frank while saying this last piece because I felt that if anyone would doubt, or see through this portion of the story, it would be Frank.

"Okay," Frank said. "We can come back to that later. Start with what happened after the phone call from the top of Long Pond Mountain, which in hindsight … well, screw hindsight. What happened?"

"We had a fun night out," I said. "Camp-cooking at its finest, with dessert first, right Xander (*Xander didn't respond, or even appear to hear my prompt, which was okay with me … much of, most of this story would go better if he didn't say a thing until I had laid the tracks for 'the official story'*)? He watched a movie in the tent while Cam and I talked into the night. We all went to bed around ten or ten thirty."

"I woke up the next morning because Cam came over to talk with me about breakfast plans (*I could see no upside to mentioning that I thought I heard, might have heard, Steve Street getting into position around four in the morning, so I didn't*), when all of sudden I heard a loud bang and Cam dropped like a stone."

"What'd you do then?" Frank prompted, and it occurred to me for the first time, that he might be feeding me directions and trying to help me shape the story.

"After Cam was shot, what'd you two do?"

"I ran as fast as I could, staying low, like in the movies," I continued. "I told Xander to get in his boat, threw Hope in mine, and we took off paddling."

"Thank goodness, he was on the far side of that peninsula from you," Frank said, nodding at me.

"Yes, we were lucky that he couldn't see us to shoot us too," I said, "and by the time he came around the corner in his boat, we were leaving him behind. He shot in our direction again at the end of Long Pond, but I think we were too far away, or he wasn't a good enough shot."

"And then you got away?" Frank asked/stated.

"Yes, once we headed up farther into the wilderness, and he didn't follow, although we didn't know it, so we kept pushing hard all day long. When afternoon rolled around with no sign or sound of him, I started thinking clearly again, and tried to decide on the fastest way back out again, so we headed down to Clamshell and spent the night there, which is where this all happened (*pointing at my face and scalp*)."

"And then," Frank asked, "this morning?"

"Right," I said, trying to see ahead through the story for possible pitfalls, "we slept in a bit, as it was a late and bad night's sleep for both of us, then we made the portage, paddled out, and got in touch with Dorothy to give us a ride here."

"And the gear and boats?" Frank asked, looking relieved and trying to help me bring it the rest of the way home, "what about them?"

"Well," I said, "most of the gear is still out on Long Pond, luckily I had enough stuff in my go-bag to keep us going until this morning, although Xander didn't get his pancakes and butter and bacon and maple syrup either morning."

"Fish and Kibble and McDonald's this morning," Xander said loudly, smiling over at me, "Hope ate nine McNuggets."

"Yeah," I cut in quickly, "Dot brought us to McDonald's for some food on our way here … we were starving. And I promise that I didn't feed your son kibble, Mr. and Mrs. Kovac, that's just what I call the trail mix I make (*I also call it a timely deflection*)."

"You saved our boy's life," Iskra said, "and just look at what he did to you. I'm so sorry about your nose, and so grateful to you, Mr. Cunningham. I can't get over the idea that Steve, a man who visited me in the hospital when Dani was born, ate dinner in our house, could do those horrible things. I hope they catch him soon, so he can be made to answer for what he's done."

"Me too, Mrs. Kovac," I said. "Me too. And once I leave here, I'll go over to Hoel Pond and get our boats from where we hid them this morning, and I can bring Xander's here for you to pick up whenever."

"No hurry on that, Tyler," she said. "Can I call you Tyler (*I nodded*)? I feel closer to you than we are because of all that's happened. We'll have you over soon and thank you properly with a big meal in our home, but for now, I think we'll take Xander to our hotel for a swim. How's that sound, big guy?"

"You should know," I said, and something about my tone brought Frank's head up quickly, and with some form of warning in his eyes, "Xander was very brave and very good throughout a frightening ordeal with too many changes for him to be expected to deal with, but he did. I also have to warn you that I had to bribe him with candy and treats, and may have ruined his eating routine for the short term. When he, and you, and all of this, has settled down, I owe him a breakfast at The Blue Moon, and I'd like to pay up."

"Well, in the meantime," Meg spoke up, "I'm taking you out for a meal and a thank you and a chat session. We are going out for some tricky food and drinks."

"I assume that you mean Liquids & Solids," I said, referring to Meg's favorite restaurant in Lake Placid, "but I'm pretty sure they don't open until four p.m."

"For today," she said, "I'm taking a page from the book of Tyler. One of the owners owes me a favor, and I'm calling it in with this. We'll have the place to ourselves while they set up for the afternoon and evening."

"Sounds good," I said.

"It will be, but first though, you look, and smell like you could use a shower (*and shoes, I thought*), so head upstairs, shower up, and Frank can grab some of Austin's clothes for you that'll fit well enough. Frank bring him upstairs and make sure that he knows where everything is."

"C'mon up, Tyler," Frank said, although I hadn't known/thought I was going anywhere until a second ago, Frank was already eagerly moving. "I'll get you some of Austin's stuff and a towel and such."

"Thanks, Frank," I said.

The Kovacs looked surprised at the shift in the group but were already adjusting and gathering their things to head out to the hotel for a swim.

As we started upstairs, Frank said, "I'll write up all that stuff you just said as a statement, and have it ready for you when you get back from lunch with Meg, okay?" Frank continued without waiting for my answer, "We should get that all into the system ASAP, so you and the kid don't get bothered too much. I'll boring it up a little, and polish some of the edges before getting it back to you, okay?"

He seemed to be saying all of this more to himself than to me, as he rooted around in a hall closet for a towel, and in the bureau and closet in Austin's room for clothes that would fit me (*luckily, Austin and I are about the same size, because Frank is big enough for two of me to fit into his clothes*). While I may not be very good at picking up subtleties in conversation, it felt a bit (*through my haze of exhaustion and throbbing and guilt*) as though he was saying something important to me.

"Sure, Frank, what's up?" I said drawing his attention away from the stack of towels and clothes he was putting on the table outside the bathroom.

"We fucked up, Tyler," Frank said. "You and me, trying all manner of slick shit, got that dumb hippie kid killed, dead as last night's supper. I'm sure I don't wanna know any more about the chase and getaway in the SRCW than what you said, but it sounds too easy, which with you, prolly means something much trickier. Whatever! We'll get Steve Street before he gets too far, and until we do, we'll have people on the Kovacs to keep them safe, like you said, although I can't imagine why he'd bother to go after the kid or the parents now. Our forensic accountants, no shit, that's what they're called, will find what there is to find, and he'll be cooked," he said and handed me a pair of old sneakers that would likely be a bit big, but would fit well enough to get me through the next few hours and then home.

"I'm sorry, Frank," I said. "Sorry, if I forced you into something dumb or dangerous for Cam and Xander. I thought I had it figured out, but I just didn't look at it from the proper angle or something. I'll always feel bad about Cam … we could have been friends. He was a nice guy."

"You can always feel bad, maybe will," Frank said, "but Cam's always gonna be dead. I've said it before, and I still stand by it, Tyler, you definitely do more good than harm in your strange ways of helping people, but people get hurt. Seems like every time people get hurt."

Frank picked up the stack of clothes and towels he had collected and pointed me toward the shower. "You go get cleaned up and let Meg take you out. She feels a need to, maybe, take you out for a talk and an apology and some quiet time, and a meal at that kooky place she likes over in Lake Placid (*Meg is a big believer in the healing power of food/drink*). I'm going back down to say goodbye to my friends and start making some calls. I'll get to work on that statement for you."

Liquids and Solids, Lake Placid, NY,
Saturday, 9/6/2014, 3:22 p.m.

We drove in Meg's little Kia Soul, which she often joked was like a baby Element (*it's not … not even close*). Hope initially wanted to sit in my lap up front, but this didn't work easily/comfortably, and seemed to make Meg nervous, so I lifted Hope into the back seat, where she spun four times in a small circle, and curled into her tightest ball configuration and immediately began snoring.

"Do we need to stop off at the urgent care or hospital?" Meg asked as soon as we had pulled out of their driveway, "your nose looks painful, and the scalp wound probably needs cleaning."

"I'll take care of it later," I said, thinking that I might either deal with the issues myself, or ask Dot to help me yank and straighten and set and clean and stitch and unguentify as/if needed. "Tell me why you're taking me out for a tricky, and favor-calling-in, late lunch, instead of spending the afternoon with people you've been friends with forever, who need more counseling than I do, and have suffered greater and more recent losses than I have."

She pretended to concentrate on her driving through the four-way intersection at Town Hall in Saranac Lake while ignoring my question … this wasn't convincing. Meg doesn't, seemingly can't concentrate on her driving, which is why she keeps running into things (*but never people … yet*). I gave her a few seconds, and then gently coughed into my hand (*which hurt my nose more than seemed fair*).

"Let me answer that briefly and in a couple of parts, and then shut the hell up until I have a drink in front of me," she said.

I nodded.

"Today, the Kovacs are deliriously happy to have their son back," she said, "and to know, thanks to you, who killed their daughter. Today is a good day, and they don't need to look at, or under, the bruise, or scab, of their life this afternoon. The hurt will re-emerge tomorrow, or the next day, and that's when I'll be up in their grill. Today, I'm gonna be all up in your business. I'll take the sting out of my intrusiveness with tasty beverages and interesting food."

"Sounds good," I said.

"So let me map out our session and drive in silence until we get there (*as if I would miss the small talk that she likes to fill quiet with*)."

She took McKenzie Pond Road to avoid an interminable construction project that had been threatening for months, but not actually happening (*so far as I could see*) … it didn't matter, the car was comfy, Meg was quiet, Hope was sleeping, the back road was pretty. Meg almost missed the turn for Old Military Road, which would allow us to skip most of Lake Placid, only veering into the right hand turn at the last second. Again it allowed us to skip the crowded parts of the always mostly empty Adirondacks. I could feel the houses and businesses up ahead of us, but also remembered the wonderful glacial erratics in the small and wild triangle of land bounded by Routes 86 and 35 and 35A. It was a miniature treasure at the edge of the busiest tourist town in the Adirondacks, and knowing about it seemed like money in the bank to me (*or better*).

Meg grabbed a parking spot in front of the restaurant/bar door at the far end of Station Street (*it was shady and cool, so I didn't worry about Hope, who didn't even wake when we opened and closed the car doors*), and we walked right in (*a small part of me, perhaps in the neighborhood of my brain where Barry hangs out, was disappointed that there was no secret knock or gorilla-like bouncer barring our way into the off-hours and empty-feeling eatery*).

Liquids and Solids is a spacious and dark and comfortable space with a long bar by the door. The bottles and jars of unusual ingredients stored along and behind the bar tell the observant person that it's a bit out of the ordinary as soon as they walk in, as does even the most cursory glance at their menu. Local produce and cuts of meat and methods of preparation that many people may not have seen before are an everyday occurrence at L&S. The staff were sitting around a large table midway down the long rectangular room, and a couple of people looked up, and then at their watches, with some confusion, until (*I assumed*) the owner who owed Meg a favor, waved us to pick whatever table we wanted. Meg led me down to the far end of the room and sat at a table for four, as far from the L&S staff as was possible while remaining in the room.

A red-headed, frizzy-haired, curvy, and slightly flighty bartender I recognized/remembered from coming in once before with Dot and Lisa last spring (*who had distracted both Dot and Lisa, although each for different reasons, that Dot tried/failed to explain to me later, but apparently had something to do with the complicated structure of their relationship*) after Dot had mostly recovered from her assault of last winter, detached herself from the group, picked up a pair of clipboards with a sheaf of paper on each, and wandered our way.

"Hiya, Meg," she said, "and you must be Tyler."

"Hey Randy," Meg answered. I said nothing.

"Let me start you guys off with something to drink, if you'd like," Randy said, handing Meg and I each a clipboard. The front sheet had a fascinating array of cocktails, their only downside being the alcohol in each (*which was probably hard to avoid in a bar*), "and then you can figure out what sounds good on the menu, or Chris said the guys could just whip something up for you if you've got an idea of what you'd like."

Meg looked up and down the top sheet, and made her decision quickly, "I'll have a Balsamic Fizz. Tyler's choice is gonna be trickier, though. He doesn't drink."

Randy looked at me with that fleeting double-edged judgment that most people have for those of us who don't drink … is he weird for not drinking, or just a recovering alcoholic (*there tends not to be an option C*) before pushing ahead. "Well then, what looks good? What do you like?"

"Maybe something with tropical flavors, but not too sweet," I said.

Randy tilted her chin back, as if looking at charts and ingredient lists above my head, and then smiled. "Got it. How about pineapple juice and coconut milk (*she saw me start to shake my head*), no wait, to cut the sweetness, I'll mix in some ginger-infused apple cider vinegar, and start things off by muddling some mint in the bottom of the glass. Sound good?"

It did, so I nodded.

"I don't know what else we're going to want," Meg said, "but we'll definitely want to start things off with some fried brussels and those steamed buns."

"Great," Randy said. "I'll get all that started, and we can figure out the rest when I come back with your drinks. You guys are in for a treat. It'll all be yummy."

It was … the drinks were great (*I even let Meg talk me into a sip of the three different cocktails that she flitted through during our meal/talk*), and the food was fun and fabulous and funky and fresh. I felt bad that I couldn't share with Hope, but I'm sure that she slept well out in Meg's car. We kept trying things, some we ordered, and some the owner or Randy the bartender or the chefs must have sent out … but it was all wonderful (*especially after a couple of days of panic and GORP*).

I think the sensory spectacle of the restaurant was a part of Meg's plan to get me to lower my defenses … it worked.

"I'm sorry, Tyler," she said, out of nowhere, seemingly referring to nothing, as I popped a niblet of fried duck heart into my mouth.

"For what," I asked.

"Everything," she answered, "dragging you into this mess with Xander, manipulating you, pushing your buttons about autism, trading on our friendship, taking up your time while Mickey was here with his family, forcing the issue about who and what you are … everything."

"That's a lot to apologize for," I said, "I guess you did owe me this awesome lunch, and while the iron is still hot (*that one was for you Mrs. Portnoy*), I'll grab the last of that rabbit terrine."

"I'm serious," she said, and as if to prove her point, she rearranged her face from what Dot calls Meg's *food-gasm* face to what I think of as her counselor expression. "I stepped over the line, and it could have ended up getting you and/or Xander killed. Beyond that, I had no business pushing you towards a definition of your difference or even your, how do we refer to it, your 'calling' in life. I wanted something, and tried to take it, or make it happen, without regard for you as a person, as a friend."

I ran one of the few remaining brussel sprouts from our second order around the bowl to sop up the butter and mustard and garlic, and then tossed it into my mouth with a sigh, "Meg, you're being stupid."

She goggled and gaped and gasped and gawked at me.

"You're one of the few people I care about on the planet," I said. "You probably know and understand me more than most people do, including myself. You've seen and experienced what and how I do what I do for more than ten years. When people you know well, both socially and professionally faced a crisis that was outside your wheelhouse, you reached out for the person you thought could best help them, and got a tiny bit frustrated when he/I was in a transient existential crisis of his/my own."

"Transient?" she asked, getting to the heart of a couple of matters with one word, like pinning the thought to a board.

"Yes," I answered. "Transient. I'm not Xander (*she started to say something, but I waved her off, while finishing up my fifth 'Tyler', as Randy had taken to calling the drink she'd built for me, and moving it to the edge of the table to signal for another refill*) … I know that's not what you meant. I'm not Xander, but I'm not-not him entirely. I think that I learned a lot talking with him and Cam back in the woods, between the carries … about me and my place in the world."

Counselor Meg nodded a therapist nod and indicated that I should continue … and moved her glass to the edge and looked around for Randy.

"I'm a consulting detective," I said. She nodded sagely (*and not a little drunkenly*), "I'm a lot of other things as well, but one of the things I am when I'm at my best is a consulting detective. I can do and see things other people can't see and do. Sometimes I make mistakes, and because what I do occasionally involves bad people willing to hurt others, every now and then people get hurt (*I had a momentary impulse towards truthiness, about how sometimes I hurt people in the line of my duty, as I saw it, but just as quickly talked myself out of it*). I feel bad when this happens, but what bad and hurtful people do isn't … can't be my fault."

Meg nodded, which I initially took to be agreement with my statement, but then she picked up and handed both of our glasses to Randy who swooped in (*and had likely been the actual/intended recipient of the nod*), grabbing the glasses, along with some of the empty plates. I decided that I was okay with the ambivalence/uncertainty left hanging in the air, and ordered the chocolate pot de crème with bacon in it … it was all good.

The meal was apparently on the house, but I left a big tip for Randy and the chefs, and thanked everyone. Then I took Meg's keys and walked her out to drive her home. Before I had finished adjusting the mirrors of her car (*which seemed, curiously, to be set for someone a few feet shorter than Meg*), she and Hope were snoring a duet.

SmartPig, Saranac Lake, NY,
Saturday, 9/6/2014, 5:37 p.m.

After dropping off Meg, and signing the statement Frank had prepared (*and boring-ed up a bit*), I begged a ride home from Frank. I briefly considered heading out to Hoel Pond for the boats and gear, but was easily able to talk myself out of it by making plans for the afternoon that didn't involve anything more strenuous than lying on my couch with my dog and watching TV. First, though, I needed to get a new phone. I climbed into the Element, and debated where to pick up a new cell phone (*since I didn't take the iPhone from Xander before Frank and Meg hustled me out of the house, and I didn't like my odds of getting it away from him the next time I saw him*). In the end (*which came after 2.31 seconds of gentle and one-sided debate*) I decided in favor of Radio Shack out in the Saranac Lake Plaza (*which I still think of as the Grand Union plaza),* entirely because, of the places in town where I can easily/cheaply/quickly buy a cell phone for near-immediate use, that's the only place located less than one hundred yards from a Dunkin' Donuts.

Hope and I made it back to the parking lot and up the back stairs to SmartPig in thirteen minutes with a dozen of DD's finest, and a new ultra-cheap Tracfone clamshell phone. I locked and barricaded the door (*not that I was expecting trouble or anyone, but it was an attitudinal as much as physical fortification of the SmartPig premises*).

I got out a trio of ice-cold Cokes from the Coke-fridge, blew through the donuts (*with some help from Hope*) cranked up my laptop, and raced through my emails, ignoring even the important ones … they'd keep for a few hours. I had a batch of my bacon Velveeta fudge in the food fridge and thought the adventures of the last week justified a little chocolate decadence. I opened up a tin of Vienna sausages so Hope could join in on the celebration and got to work on the fudge and a few more Cokes for myself while we watched episodes of *Alias*, skipping back and forth through the series to our favorite episodes.

While the TV was serving up some fun and espionage, I let my fingers do the walking on the keyboard of my laptop, setting up what must be my fiftieth Tracfone over the last ten years (*47 is the number the bean-counters in back chimed in with a few seconds later, and who was I to doubt myself*). I have tended to drop/switch/replace phones and phone numbers after a few months for various reasons, real and imagined, good and bad. Although I have an essentially perfect memory, I still program in a handful of numbers every time, and these numbers, as much as anything else I can think of, form the boundaries, the borders, of my world. Those few people whose numbers I have to have entered in the phone (*despite knowing them cold*), and who would be getting an email from me in the next hour or so, informing them of my new number, and to expect a call from me in the next week or so to update them on my expected travel and camping and activities/plans for the coming months, now that summer was essentially done.

My first call was going to be to Mickey, and it would be in a few minutes. I had shown him more of myself, or my truth, than ever before, and he still loved me. Mickey, more than anything or anyone else, had convinced me to gird myself in the armor and head into the woods to fight another dragon. It hadn't worked out as I had hoped or planned or wanted, but it had worked out better with my help/interference/manipulations than it would have otherwise, especially for Xander, a boy at once like and shockingly different from me. A part of me wanted to tell Mickey everything, another part (*I pictured this part as a green-visored accountant*) urged a repetition of the story I'd spun for Meg and the Kovacs (*Frank had heard that one too, but I had no idea what he believed*). When the time came, I would likely give Mickey something in the middle.

Hope interrupted my deep thoughts by patting my face, hoping for a bite of fudge, now that she'd worked her way through the Vienna sausages. My nose hurt like crazy and reminded me to get my first-aid kit out, and to check online about setting my own broken nose. I was part way through that when my laptop booped, announcing an email from one of the few people I had gmail-designated as important. It was from Mickey, wondering why some stranger kept answering my phone. He wanted me to know that he had gotten some weird sets of coordinates from the GPS-Spot, and for me to call at my earliest convenience. I finished scanning/averaging all of the webpages I'd accessed with medical advice, dabbed at the flap of angry skin trying to reattach to, reacquaint with, my skull, and tried to convince my grumpy dog that she'd had enough bacon Velveeta fudge. Then I dialed Mickey on my new Tracfone.

"Hey Mickey," I said, when he answered the phone. "Yes, I'm back early. The trip was really something … let me tell you all about it. Got a few minutes?"

The End

Tyler's Bacon/Velveeta Fudge

8 ounces Velveeta cheese
2 sticks butter
1 teaspoon vanilla extract
1 cup chopped walnuts
1 cup bacon bits (or crumbled bacon)
32 ounces confectioners' sugar
1/2 cup cocoa powder

Grease the bottom of an 8-inch square pan with a nonstick spray.

Over medium heat, melt the cheese and butter together in a saucepan, stirring constantly until smooth. Remove from heat and add the vanilla and walnuts and bacon.

Sift the sugar and cocoa into a large mixing bowl. Using a spatula, pour the cheese/butter/but/bacon mixture into the sugar and cocoa and stir until completely mixed.

Transfer the fudge from the mixing bowl and into the greased pan, pressing it down firmly. Given the amount of oils in this fudge, you may want to pat the top of the fudge with a paper towel to remove the excess oil after you've patted it into the pan.

Place pan in refrigerator until candy is firm. Cut the fudge into small squares with a sharp knife, adjusting the number of cuts to insure you end up with a prime number.

ACKNOWLEDGMENTS

Writing Between the Carries was both journey and exploration for me. I wanted to take a look at what Tyler is, and is not, within the context of his life in the Adirondacks and also within the confines of one of his adventures. I wanted him to be challenged in new ways, both during the mystery portion of the book, but also by his supporting cast during the parts of the book that occur along the edges of the story. I am happy with the final product, feeling as though I told a fun story and let everyone, myself included, take a look under the hood of Tyler Cunningham.

Trying to write a third book is an interesting process. People doubt you can write a first book, wonder if you have a second one in you, but in many ways take a third book for granted. By the time you've gotten this far into the writing, you can manage the word count and the daily routine and the pre-planning and slow grind of editing and polishing, but you may, like Ben Franklin suggested about fish and houseguests, doubt how fresh the protagonist (and novelist) is after three books (although BF was talking about days). With the love and support and help of better friends and family than I likely deserve, I worked through both the doubts and the third novel.

As with my first two book, the folks at National Novel Writing Month (NaNoWriMo) provided me with an organizational framework that allowed me to write the first draft in a fabulous and hectic month (July 2014). Amazon's self-publishing services, through CreateSpace and Kindle Desktop Publishing (KDP) provided me with not only the means to publish this book, but also an abundance of useful information and resources that made it much easier to do so.

The Adirondack Park continues to be both an inspiration for, and a character in, this book. The natural beauty and empty space and peace that the Park, and especially the Tri-Lakes Region, provide a perfect setting for my life, and for Tyler's.

The people in my life, both private and professional, played a bigger role in this novel than in the previous ones, and for that I'm very grateful. Although I'm often asked about who the characters in my books are based on, there's no easy (one person) answer. The people living in my books and head are amalgams of many people I know and have known (and sometimes people I imagine). Xander and Tyler are more than a little me (or vice versa, I'm not sure which), and also glommed together from hundreds of adults and children I've known and worked with over the years. Dot and Frank and Mickey and Meg, and their families are made up piecemeal of family and friends and acquaintances of mine. Hope is a frankenhound, with bits of dogs I've known and loved throughout my life. I have no idea where Barry comes from (or where he goes when he isn't talking through me).

The Tri-Lakes Humane Society (TLHS) is a massive force for good in the Adirondack Park, and an inspiration to me as a writer and a human being. The Tri-Lakes Animal Shelter (TLAS) in my books is loosely based on the TLHS … everything good about it is true, the illegal activities were, of course, entirely made up. We've brought four dogs home from the TLHS to live with us, and all of them were instrumental in helping me write the book in one way or another.

The students that I have had the opportunity to work with, and learn from, over the years at Lake Placid Middle/High School have helped me to celebrate our differences, and explore some of the various ways that there are to see, and experience, the world.

Friends and family have inspired and supported me throughout the writing and editing process, and I can't thank them enough. My parents (Jim and Jill Sheffield), sister (Sarah Sheffield), wonderful son (Ben), and wife (Gail Gibson Sheffield) all gave me the time and space and loving support that I needed to follow this dream, and their love gave me the courage to try, again. Rick Schott, Bryce Fortran, Derek Murawsky, Kevin Curdgel, and Stephen Carvalho have helped me expand my map of the world through their friendship while camping in all seasons. Countless other friends have also offered encouragement, especially Jonathan Webber and Gail Bennett Schott who have given me unending support and positive vibes during the writing and editing process.

Over the past three years I have enjoyed an incredible outpouring of support from readers of *Here Be Monsters*, and *Caretakers*, as well as *Mickey Slips* and *Bound for Home* and *Fair Play* and *Promises to Keep* (the short novellas in the Tyler Cunningham series, collectively published under the title *The Weaving*). It is one thing to put creative ideas on paper, a completely different thing to know those ideas are being read and accepted by people all over the world. It is that acceptance and encouragement that moved me from being someone who writes, to being a writer. That is what made *Between the*

Carries possible, thank you all for that.

A big shout out to the entire staff at SmartPig Publishing for their tireless efforts throughout the process … thanks to my wife, Gail!

We were joined by Superstar Editor, Kathy LaPeyre this time around (although she didn't read this, so please excuse any errors in the front and back matter). Kathy has done a fantastic job helping to polish my third novel in a thoroughly amazing way, and I'm tremendously grateful to her for all of her help.

While I couldn't have done it without any of you, any errors or omissions are all mine.

ABOUT THE AUTHOR

Jamie Sheffield lives in the Adirondack Park with his wife, Gail Gibson Sheffield, and son, Benjamin, and two dogs, Miles and Puck. When he's not writing mysteries, he's probably camping or exploring the last great wilderness in the Northeast. He has been a Special Education Teacher in the Lake Placid Central School District for the last 15 years. Besides writing, Jamie loves cooking and reading and dogs and all manner of outdoor pursuits.

"Between the Carries" is his third novel.

Follow the ongoing adventures of Tyler Cunningham:

"Here Be Monsters"
"Caretakers"
"The Weaving"

and read other works by the author.

Visit Jamie Sheffield's website:

www.jamiesheffield.com